Where Heroes Were Born

Pillars of Peace: Book III

By Tom Dumbrell

Copyright © 2022 Tom Dumbrell

All rights reserved.

ISBN: 9798834555520

"A hero is someone who has given his or her life to something bigger than oneself."

—Joseph Campbell

Characters of the Quadripartite

Cornesse

Francine – The adoptive sister of King Cyrus of Peacehaven, and Chosen Shield to Queen Mathilde of Cornesse. Fran grew up in the Low Country in Easthaven before her parents were killed. After Cyrus saw her to safety, they grew up with their adoptive father, Osbert, and brother, Edgar, until Cyrus's journey toward finding his true identity saw them join the royal family in Highcastle. She has performed her duty to Mathilde with professionalism that has grown into friendship in the five years they have spent together in the Cornessian capital, Nivelle.

Queen Mathilde – Mathilde is fearsome with a blade and clever. Her army's intervention helped spare Easthaven from defeat during the Battle of Highcastle. She had a brief notion of pursuing a romantic relationship with Cyrus, who did not share her feelings. She has since remained unmarried, much to the consternation of her council, instead pursuing a life of service to her country.

Lucien – Lucien was chosen shield to Queen Mathilde before retiring to spend time with his family, enabling Fran to assume the role. He and Cyrus once went sword-to-sword to prove Cyrus's worth to Mathilde. Against all odds, Cyrus won the contest, and an alliance was born.

Peacehaven (Formerly Easthaven)

Locke – The youngest son of Lord Ramsey, whose father served during the Battle of Highcastle. Locke does not share his father's warrior instinct, nor is he as capable as his older brother, Ralph, who is duly favoured by their father. A tough upbringing has left Locke short of confidence, but his every effort remains focused on making his father proud.

Ramsey – A decorated war hero. In his valiant efforts to defend the capital during the Verderan siege, Ramsey sustained injuries that left him with one eye and long-term damage to his right leg, hindering his mobility. Ramsey was subsequently awarded a lordship and, with it, Ardlyn Keep, a castle granted to the Warden of the Northern Fells.

Ralph – The eldest son of Lord Ramsey and brother to Locke. Ralph is a very capable warrior and has followed his father's footsteps, gaining captainship of his own.

King Cyrus – At heart, Cyrus is a storyteller who grew up in the Low Country with his adoptive sister, Francine. Cyrus saved Fran as a child when their village was attacked, and they grew up with their adoptive family in Corhollow. Cyrus later learned that he was the son of the late King Anselm and the dowager queen, Adaline. He succeeded the throne from his twin brother, Augustus, who was killed by the late King Ferdinand of Verdera. On his deathbed, King Simeon of Auldhaven decreed that his nation would cede to Easthaven after forming an unlikely friendship with Cyrus. Cyrus is now the first king of the newly formed nation of Peacehaven and has ruled for ten years.

Queen Marcia – Originally a maid in Eldred's Keep, Marcia met Cyrus during his time impersonating Augustus. Even though Cyrus deceived Marcia about his identity for a time, their bond grew through a mutual love of storytelling. They were married following the Battle of Highcastle.

Adaline – The dowager queen. Adaline was married to King Anselm and mother to Augustus and Cyrus, though Cyrus did not grow up with them. A treaty with the late King Simeon required that any second-born son of Easthaven be ceded to Auldhaven, so Adaline and Anselm secreted Cyrus away to the Low Country rather than hand him over. Adaline is much-loved within Peacehaven and a source of comfort for her remaining son, King Cyrus.

Thaddeus – Thaddeus is a wise old man who mentors King Cyrus as he did Augustus and Anselm before him. He can be relied upon for sage advice. He and Garrett, King Anselm's late Chosen Shield, convinced Cyrus to stand in for Augustus, mentoring him when his twin was missing.

Broderick – Charged with upholding peace and justice in Peacehaven, General Broderick coordinated the defence of Highcastle during the Verderan siege and has since ascended to the role of High Commander.

Seth – Chosen Shield to King Cyrus. Responsible for the king's wellbeing, Seth previously helped free Cyrus when he was captured by Simeon's men and was central in reuniting Cyrus with Francine. Seth was subsequently appointed as Chosen Shield to King Augustus, only to be taken unaware when the Verderan king, Ferdinand, killed Augustus.

Wendell – Easthaven's late Master of Coin, Wendell conspired with the Verderans to kill King Anselm and end his family line. His actions were borne out of unrequited love for Adaline and jealousy toward her late husband. In an attempt at redemption, Wendell freed Cyrus, sacrificing his own life to damage the enemy camp with blast powder.

Roscoe – An old friend of Garrett's, Roscoe is a notorious pirate who first met Cyrus when he travelled to Verdera, impersonating his brother on a mission to entreat for peace. Nowadays, Roscoe wishes only to make an honest life for himself after Cyrus named him Magistrate in Kingsport, Peacehaven's largest coastal town and port.

Verdera

King Alonso – Son of the late King Ferdinand, and twin brother to Rafael. Alonso and his brother conspired with Wendell to assassinate King Anselm before laying siege to Highcastle in a battle where Rafael ultimately lost his life. After his brother's death, Alonso led the Verderan retreat from Highcastle, returning to his own capital, Casarossa, where he has since reigned in peace.

Other

Patch – Patch was a nameless "Shadow" orphan with limited speech, who had fallen in with a rebel force in the mines of Auldhaven led by a dangerous man named Shep. Patch was so named by Cyrus when the prince was held captive in the mines. Though he was involved with Cyrus's imprisonment, Patch grew sympathetic to Cyrus, and when Cyrus was freed, Patch was offered a life beside the pirate, and new Magistrate of Kingsport, Roscoe.

Simeon – The late king of the former Auldhaven. After Cyrus injured Simeon's leg to save his own life, the king eventually succumbed to his injuries some time later. Before he died, however, he and Cyrus forged a mutual respect, and since Simeon had no heir, he ceded his kingdom to Cyrus.

Lambert – Simeon's former right-hand man. Now a General of Peacehaven, he is Broderick's counterpart, stationed at the western city of Ravensward, the former capital of Auldhaven.

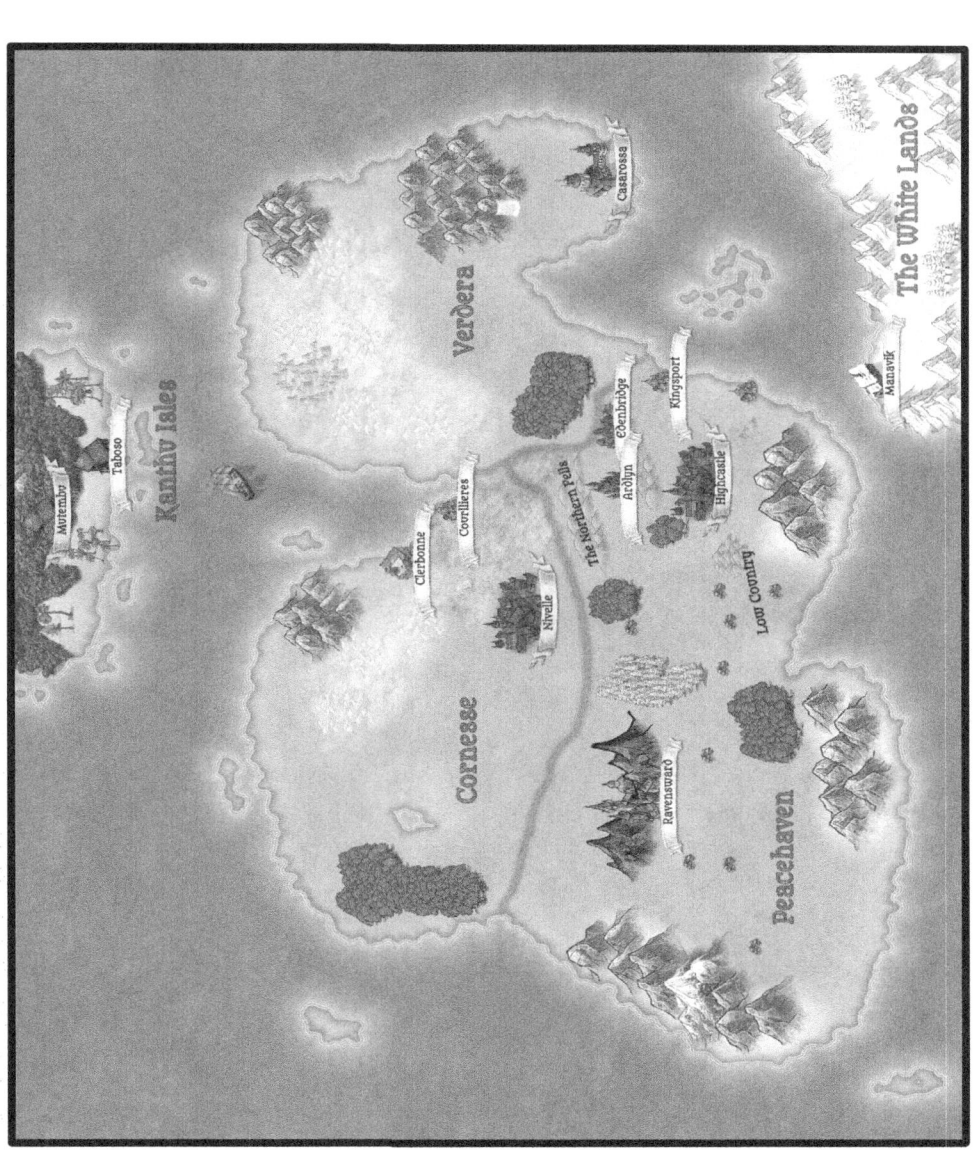

For the readers…

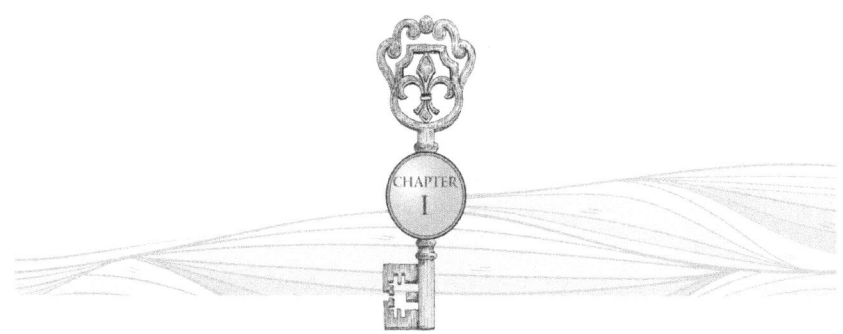

Francine

It was a bright autumn morning in Nivelle, dew clinging to the lawns lining the Cornessian capital's many boulevards. Sunlight was beginning to creep through the clouds, dispersing the cool chill of a morning mist.

"It really is a beautiful time of year," said Queen Mathilde, turning in her saddle to face her chosen shield, Fran. "Of all the seasons, I think autumn is my favourite. The mornings are cold, but the days turn so warm and bright."

"It certainly beats winter," Fran answered, her horse drawing level to walk alongside Mathilde, hooves clip-clopping on the cobblestones below. "Of all I miss about Peacehaven, I won't include the weather. Summer is fine enough, but even thinking of the dark months still gives me the chills."

Mathilde laughed, and an unexpected breeze caught the back of Fran's neck, causing her to draw her scarf a little tighter for comfort. "I'm glad that there is something you love about this country," said the queen. "Is it five years you have been with me now? I should hope there is more to your enjoyment of Cornesse than the weather alone." She fixed Fran with a warm smile, drawing her horse to a stop. Fran stopped beside her. "I can't imagine how much you must miss your family," Mathilde said, "but know that you are a part of mine now. I'm not so bad, am I?"

Fran straightened her back to sit upright in the saddle. Her eyes narrowed and her lips pursed theatrically as she considered the question. Mathilde's face was fixed with expectancy. "I think," Fran began, goading the queen, "that you are a bit like an autumn day: not always so easy in the mornings, but you tend to warm up around lunchtime."

There was a beat of silence before they both laughed, and Mathilde reached to nudge Fran's shoulder playfully before setting off in their intended direction, two horsebound guards following in their wake.

"I'll take that," said the queen. "Besides, I hear that the much-loved king of Peacehaven should arrive this afternoon. Not much longer now until you're reunited with your dear brother, but until then, you're stuck with me."

Their path ran parallel to the Vassonne River, which carved the city in two, and Mathilde pointed out a family of swans bobbing in the water. Aged fishermen lined the banks or dangled their feet from one of many bridges that connected Nivelle's two main districts.

It was a beautiful part of the city, one Fran knew well from regular visits at the queen's side. To their left stood a fashionable row of narrow houses built in the contemporary style, five storeys high and with colourful plastered walls intersected by thick wooden beams. The avenue, called Promenade Charmande, was popular among the young lords and ladies of the city and was a wonderful place in which to spend a morning. The idyllic location was perfect for a stroll or for a glimpse of the famous old bell tower, which stood among a vista of grandiose contemporary masonry as a humble reminder of time past. Chock full of dazzling white stonework buildings of governance and trade, the industrious heart of the city was to provide the foundations for Nivelle's bright future. By comparison, Promenade Charmande was an oasis of calm. This appeared not to be lost on Mathilde, who slowed to a halt, seeming to wince at the hint of government looming in the buildings in the distance.

"We really should get moving," said Fran, her eyes fixed on the magnificent clock face of the bell tower. Mathilde was the queen, of course, but she was yet a young monarch, and she was expected to balance the fine politics of her council, comprised of entitled nobility, all born into their position and—without exception—male. Fran knew exactly what had delayed their trip to parliament, even if Mathilde didn't want to discuss it.

"I know, I know," said the queen wistfully. "It may surprise you to hear that I don't much care for these assemblies." Mathilde blew out her cheeks, turning to Fran once more. "It's always the same subject of conversation, and I fear I am running out of both patience and excuses."

Fran took a moment to think over her reply, using the tricky navigation of this particular thoroughfare as an excuse for her momentary silence. She turned to the guards behind them and fired a hot look in their direction as the two of them chattered idly, no doubt restless at the queen's procrastination. Truly they were two of the most complacent individuals Fran had had the misfortune of working with. She hadn't learned their names yet, but she didn't expect them to remain in Mathilde's employ long enough for this to become an issue. When it came to the queen's safety, Fran knew she could only rely on herself.

"I don't envy you," Fran said as they emerged from the bustling traffic, "but you are the queen, and it is no safer to make enemies of your council than it would be for you to walk the streets frivolously." She paused to smile as a kind-faced man ambled past, sweeping golden leaves from their path. "You are much loved, my queen, and it is my job to ensure that this remains the case. But don't take my word for it. I ask you, what would Lucien tell you?"

The question made Mathilde chuckle, colour returning to her cheeks. "Ah, Lucien. Yes, what would that great oaf have to say from his comfortable seat beside the fire?" she said fondly, her smile warm. "His concern still echoes in my head, but that problem belongs to his wife and those poor children these days. I know very well what he would say…" She shook her head. "He would advise me that attack is the best form of defence, before telling me to march in there with my head held high and take no nonsense from any of them. Your vigilance is noted, dear Fran. I pay you for your sword, but it is your company and your counsel that bring me the greatest comfort. You're not entirely unlike Lucien, you know? But it's your brother, King Cyrus, of whom I am truly reminded," she continued as the horses trotted onward. "I lose track of the number of times I have saved that man, but your presence here in Nivelle goes a great way toward balancing the scales. I feel a good deal braver with you at my side."

Fran blushed. "You are too kind."

"And you're too modest," said Mathilde. "But enough of this talk. We have business to attend to. Oh, and Fran," she added unexpectedly, "I assume we are safe from danger, or is it normal practise for the queen's guards to fraternise with passers-by?"

Fran's smile fell into an immediate scowl. The guard in question must have overheard their conversation for he was already making his apologies to a young lady when Fran's glare fell upon him, the other guard's laughter only making matters worse.

"Oh, I'd say we are safe for now," she said, her brows narrowed intently. "These two are a danger, but only to themselves."

Nivelle's new parliament building never ceased to set Fran's imagination alight. She was no student of architecture, but the dazzling white stonework, grand colonnade, and ornate gabled roof dazzled Fran, seeming beyond the craft of human competence. And it was not just the building's façade, either, she had thought for the millionth time as she walked through the doors at Mathilde's side, crossing into the main chamber to take a seat behind the queen. The domed ceiling of the vast room was decorated with colourful murals depicting winged angels and mythical birds soaring through clouds so realistic that they seemed only moments away from emptying upon those in attendance.

Fran oftentimes found herself arching her neck to peer from the golden sun on one side of the ceiling to the haunting moon on the other, the spectacular composition interrupted by a star-shaped window from which light poured into the chamber. It was like a scene from one of Thaddeus's dusty leatherbound books back in Eldred's Keep, Fran thought, but on a scale so grand that she couldn't help but feel captivated.

And today was no exception.

The awe-inspiring building was almost a year old now, and Fran had visited many times at Mathilde's side, but she found herself marvelling once again at the advances in design and build, the sound of the gathered assembly fading momentarily away. This grand building felt a world away from the Low Country village in which she had grown up, and as Fran's gaze moved from the rows of important-looking politicians before her in their wooden benches to the queen, sitting in her stiff wooden chair with a determined look upon her face, Fran found herself struggling to believe just how far she had come from those days of her childhood.

"So, to our final piece of business," said the white-haired orator, Clement, whose nose was decidedly beak-like. Fran had no mind for politics, but nevertheless, she scolded herself for daydreaming about architecture and old memories. She cast a supportive look in the queen's direction as Clement continued to speak as though neither of them were there. "That is, the ongoing question of our beloved Queen Mathilde's succession. It is a matter we have debated on a number of occasions, and with no male heir to the line of King Maxim, it is one that we must consider if we are to avoid the disastrous fate of Auldhaven. We wouldn't want to repeat King Simeon's failings."

A deep rumble of "hear, hear!" echoed around the room. Mathilde seemed to sink deeper into her chair. Fran was tempted to reach out her hand to squeeze the queen's arm in reassurance, but she knew Mathilde wouldn't want to appear as though she needed it, so she refrained.

Clement continued, "Our queen is no longer a young woman. Time is of the essence, and I say to you, Queen Mathilde," he turned, finally acknowledging Mathilde's presence, "that it is high time you selected a suitable husband, thus securing our nation's future."

Another round of applause broke out, and Fran shifted uncomfortably at the sight of her friend and queen being treated like a mule at market. Fran bristled at the assertion that thirty-one was apparently considered "no longer young." Mathilde was the strongest and fiercest woman Fran knew, but in these matters, it seemed her fire had long since been extinguished, her ambitions tempered by the responsibilities of state.

"Are you all right?" Fran mouthed in the queen's direction as the assemblymen chattered to each other. Mathilde ignored her question, however, and as the queen rose unexpectedly, throwing her chair back forcefully, Fran was rushed to do the same, placing a hand on the hilt of her sword. The councilmen looked over at Mathilde, seemingly surprised to see her there.

"Thank you for those kind words, Clement," Mathilde opened assertively as the white-haired man lowered himself back into his seat, eyes narrowed. "You are not alone in thinking that things might have been much simpler had I been born with the same, shall we say, equipment as the rest of you. And though this is not the case, I might remind you that I have a perfectly good set of eyes and ears and a wonderful memory for retribution to boot." She paused to flash a menacing smile in Clement's direction. Fran was the only one who chuckled quietly; the rest of the room was filled with the sound of quiet contempt.

"I cannot fault your passion for our country and its future, Clement," Mathilde continued, "but it is worth reminding you that Cornesse is a woman. She is a figure of great beauty and experience, one who possesses a spirit that is not so easily tamed. I expect that much of this is probably lost on you," she continued, opening her attention to the wider assembly, "but I will not be freely given any more than Cornesse herself would be. I have heard your thoughts on the matter, and I will continue to consider my own, but until then, I suggest that you consider the matter closed. I've no doubt that the extra time will be better spent tending to other matters of state that are, I'm sure, more pressing and more interesting than this."

Fran reached down, grabbing Mathilde's chair to put it right, and the young queen nodded in appreciation before sitting down, clasping her hands primly in front of her. "Now, was there any other business?" she asked in a sweet voice, a small smile that belied deep satisfaction curling her lips. When no answer was forthcoming, the sound of midday bells gave them all the much-needed excuse to leave.

"Well now I've seen everything!" said Fran, racing to keep pace with her queen. Mathilde showed none of her earlier hesitancy, casting the wide wooden doors of the parliament building open, where the two royal guards stood waiting, bathed in sunlight and seemingly eager to regain favour.

"Your horse, my queen," said the taller of the two, a broad young man with curly blonde hair who, at a glance, reminded Fran of her brother. The other guard was clearly keen to follow suit. He kneeled, pressing one knee to the ground as though to give Mathilde a boost into the saddle. The queen, who Fran thought might usually make a teasing comment about this behaviour, simply accepted the man's help as she climbed onto her horse's back.

"Come, Fran," said Mathilde sharply, leaving Fran to frown at her unexpected change in mood. "We don't want to keep your brother waiting. Besides," the queen continued, her face expressionless and her voice strangely flat, "the weather has turned rather warm. If anything, it is too hot for my taste."

Fran's frown deepened as she pondered the queen's melancholy, and she pushed the curly-haired guard away scornfully to climb upon her own mount without assistance. Mathilde had already set off, Fran noticed with a tremor of panic. She pressed her heels lightly into her own horse's sides, causing him to follow along after Mathilde.

"Wait up," she called to the queen, as both guards scrambled to keep up behind them. Mathilde was setting a frantic pace as she retraced their path up the tree-lined boulevard, and revellers were already stopping to catch a glimpse of their much-loved queen. After a moment, Mathilde seemed to come back to herself, slowing to a trot and allowing Fran to sidle up beside her.

"Men, eh?" Fran ventured, the empty rhetoric buying time to catch her breath. She hoped that maybe her light tone would bring things back to normal with Mathilde. "Thank god the crown is yours," she continued, "if that's the best of our nobility. The way they speak to you! Ignorant idiots, every last one of them."

Fran thought she saw one corner of Mathilde's mouth shift ever so slightly, but then her face settled back into an apathetic mask. Fran's own face flushed pink as she realised that her effort at nonchalance had fallen wide of the mark.

"You shouldn't call them idiots," said the queen sternly. "Ignorant, maybe…but only because they have never found themselves in this situation before, with a young, unmarried woman on the throne."

Fran persisted, "But the things they say to you…"

"Not nice at all," agreed the queen, her mouth a hard line. "Do I think that they would have spoken to my father in the same way, made demands of him? Of course not. I do not care for their methods, and our beliefs may differ, but I don't doubt the passion those men hold for this country. We have a whole lot of battles to fight in this life, Fran. It's about knowing when to draw arms and face them. I am, after all, a Queen—with all the responsibility that title entails."

The pair continued forward, and Fran remained silent. She had the uncomfortable feeling that she had embarrassed herself in some way in her efforts to reassure the queen.

"I've too many reasons to hate my father," said Mathilde unexpectedly, "yet in this, we might have found some common ground. I wanted my parents to be happy. I wished for it every day, but as I grew older and more aware, I began to see things for what they were: obligation and duty." She paused. "I'll never forgive him for his drinking or his temper, but is it any wonder that they were so miserable, stuck as they were in such an institution?"

The question sat heavily between them as they rode, and Fran's heart quickened with the need to offer words of comfort to her queen. From stories, Fran knew that the late queen, Arielle, had passed quickly with the arrival of a swift and deadly pestilence when Mathilde was only a child. As for King Maxim, it was not to his famously unhealthy lifestyle which he had finally succumbed, but rather a freak hunting injury. Sad and untimely in both cases. Since Fran had never met either of Mathilde's parents, she found herself coming up short. "But you're the queen," she said, with all the optimism that she could muster. "Surely you can change things?"

Mathilde gave a sad smile. "It's a nice idea in theory, but there are limits to what a queen can do. Perhaps one day we will see kings and queens voted into power, selected for their admirable qualities and ability to lead, but for now, it is all in a name. And with that name comes the responsibility of passing it on to the next person who will be burdened with the crown without a say in the matter." She paused to shake her head, and when she resumed, she seemed to have plastered on a brighter voice. "Besides," she said, "I'm the only thing standing between the Cornessian people and that bunch of 'idiots' you were talking about, so perhaps it's not all bad!"

By now they were both smiling again, and Fran was grateful to move the conversation forward. They continued along the boulevard toward the castle at a gentle canter, and while Fran glanced over at Mathilde a few times as she remained level at her side—checking to make sure that the queen really was all right—her mind had already wandered to the impending royal visit. Her brother would be waiting for them, and with him, he was sure to bring news from home.

Sunlight flooded into the throne room, the fanfare that greeted King Cyrus outside little more than a blur of noise to Fran, who stood at attention in an effort to contain her excitement. He wasn't her brother by blood, but Cyrus was the closest thing to family Fran had ever known. He was the only real link to the life she had left behind in Peacehaven. However, Fran had lost count of the months since she had last seen her brother and his family. Mathilde was a fair queen and a good friend to Fran, but she was known for her remarkable work ethic. Indeed, much of Fran's work during Mathilde's reign thus far had been spent on horseback, as the queen visited her people and worked hard to maintain peaceable relations with their neighbours. She was a force of nature, someone Fran admired more every day. It hadn't been easy for Fran to leave Highcastle, but she had long yearned for such an opportunity, so she had taken it with both hands. Now, her utmost priority was to ensure that she never fell short of the queen's expectations. Her own expectations. But the anticipation of seeing Cyrus again made Fran nostalgic for those childish times, his many stories, and their long journey together.

She straightened herself, her face schooled into one lacking expression or emotion, with Mathilde to her left sitting upon a golden throne behind which several of the queen's favoured dignitaries gathered. The throne room was a feast for those with a hunger for details. An expanse of ornately embroidered carpet left no inch of stonework uncovered. Three steps ascended the dais where Mathilde sat waiting. Above them, an extravagant gilded ceiling added to the grandeur while an enormous, low-hanging chandelier sparkled in the sunlight, drawing Fran's attention to the centre of the room, where the delegation from Peacehaven were now arriving.

Fran turned to Mathilde and saw that the queen was smiling warmly back at her as though looking forward to seeing Fran's reaction to the reunion. This moment had been a long time coming. The anticipation in the room was palpable, yet Fran would be, first and foremost, professional. She decided to respond to the queen's enthusiasm with a subtle nod, but by the time she turned to face the new arrivals, she felt her lips curl irresistibly, all hope of control lost.

"Aunt Fran, Aunt Fran!" sounded a small voice as a blur of curly red hair dashed across the throne room. Fran's eyes widened, but she had little time to think as her nephew, Peacehaven's prince, threw his short arms around her waist, squeezing tightly as fond laughter echoed around her.

Fran looked to where her brother stood smiling, his hand locked with Queen Marcia's, while Marcia's other hand rested lightly on the swell of her stomach. Fran's counterpart in Peacehaven, Seth, stood ever vigilant on Cyrus's other side.

"Well, that's the formalities done then," said Mathilde with a laugh, and Fran ruffled the prince's auburn hair. He gave her a toothy smile before relinquishing his enthusiastic grip in his haste to give the Cornessian queen a similar greeting. This was, Fran thought, a welcome distraction from the morning meeting at parliament, and Mathilde's worries seemed to fade away as the boy prince hopped up the stairs and onto her lap.

"My, my Prince Leo," Mathilde said, holding him at arm's length and pretending to survey him with shrewd eyes, "you must be twice as tall as when we last met. Keep this up, and you'll outgrow the king in no time!"

Leo giggled, giving rise to a bout of infectious laughter around the throne room. While Cyrus did his best to restore order, Fran noticed Marcia ribbing her husband, enjoying every moment of the mockery. They really were a perfect couple, Fran thought, relieved to see her brother looking carefree and contented. She and Cyrus had been through so much together. She had been no older than Leo when her brother had found her in the woods and delivered her to safety. For all their adventures since—and whatever titles he now held—Fran still remembered Cyrus as the boy who had taken her hand and pulled her to safety time and time again, never letting go even when it would have been easier to go on alone.

"It's good to see you," she mouthed at her brother, who responded with a nod of agreement and a smile. The laughter ceased for a moment, and Leo hopped down as Queen Mathilde stood to address the new arrivals.

"King Cyrus and beautiful Queen Marcia," she began, her arms outstretched in greeting. "It seems our warm northern weather has treated you well. I trust you enjoyed your time on the coast. Courlliers is very beautiful at this time of year." She paused to breathe deeply in through her nose, as though sniffing deeply. "I can almost smell the sea air upon you, and if the young prince is any indication, I see that the sun was no stranger during your visit."

Prince Leo had, by now, returned to his father's side, and the small boy scrunched his face as Marcia reached to brush his sun-kissed cheeks.

"It was a most welcome break," said Cyrus, turning to face his queen with a brief smile before turning back to Mathilde. "These past ten years have been the busiest of our lives. We have been very lucky with Leo, but with another on the way," he placed a delicate hand on Marcia's stomach, "it seemed only right to take some time as a family. Your villa was a home from home and greatly appreciated, as is your kind offer of refuge during our lengthy return journey."

Mathilde smiled warmly and, if only for a moment, Fran was able to fully relax and enjoy the proceedings. It seemed Mathilde was momentarily lost in thought, and a brief silence followed before she cleared her throat and said, "You are most welcome. No doubt you are exhausted by your travels. Our guest quarters stand ready for your arrival, as is Fran. There are few who know the castle better than your sister." She turned to glance at Fran, addressing her. "Perhaps you could be so kind as to escort our guests to their chambers? In fact, why not take the afternoon for yourself? I am expecting Amare, the envoy from the Kanthu Isles, any time now, and there is no need to bore you with details of trade."

Fran smiled. It was all she could do to stop herself from rushing to hug the queen as her young nephew had done. "You're absolutely sure?" she asked, her voice lowered for only the queen's ears as she approached the throne.

"Quite sure," came the queen's response. "Oh, and Fran," she called as Fran turned to face her family. Fran noticed the queen eyeing little Leo almost wistfully. "Maybe it *is* time to start thinking about my future after all?"

Fran's smile widened. "Let the search begin!"

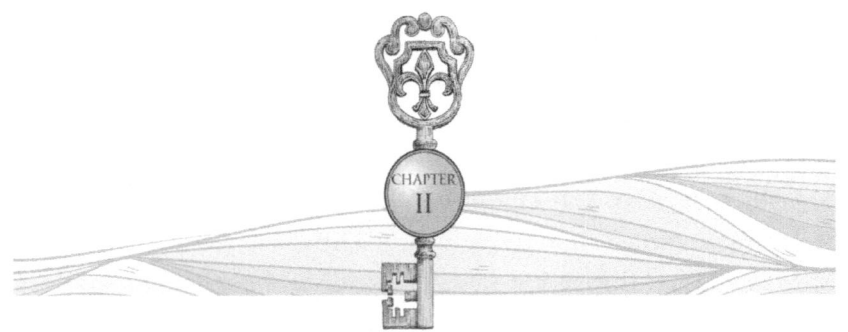

Locke

Locke turned his body, sending Ralph's practice sword whistling past his face. "Good, good!" their father shouted from the base of an oak tree. His wounded leg was stretched out before him, his back propped against the trunk as he watched on through his one remaining eye. "Now don't let up, Ralph. Press your advantage."

It seemed that their father lived their every cut and thrust. It had been many years since he had last raised a sword in malice, but the instinct still seemed to live within him. Ralph responded to his father's order, forcing Locke onto the back foot.

"You're going down," Ralph snarled, jabbing forward with a fierce blow. There were three years between them, and Locke's older brother was making the most of this advantage.

"Too slow!" he joked as he smashed his sword into Locke's knee.

"Too weak!" he continued as Locke raised his weapon feebly, the wooden blade smashed loose from his hands, leaving him unarmed.

Locke fell to the ground in defeat.

"Too quick to give up," Ralph finished, dragging Locke's sword toward him with his boot. Ralph's weapon was still trained on Locke, but it was his brother's disdainful expression that Locke feared the most.

Their father laughed as he hauled himself to his feet and reached for his walking stick. "Good show, Ralph. We'll make a warrior of you yet!"

He said nothing to Locke, whose attention had already drifted. A gentle breeze made the long grass dance around them. The trees swayed, and a scent of lavender wafted from fields nearby. A moment of calm. To Locke's relief, there were no spectators to witness his poor showing.

Ralph gave a dismissive laugh as Locke dusted himself down. Their father hobbled over to join them. *Now the storm,* Locke thought, knowing what was coming.

"I'm sorry, Father," Locke muttered with his head lowered, trying to stave off the inevitable conversation.

"Sorry?" his father snapped with contempt. "A lot of good that'll do you if you ever face someone who really wants to hurt you." He paused to sneer. "Was it apologies that helped me to crush the Verderan advance on Highcastle? Was it regrets and empty words that saw me recover when my body was broken in battle?" He raised his eyebrows, but this wasn't the first time they'd had this conversation, and Locke knew that silence would be his best defence from here on out. "No!" his father barked predictably. "It was hard work, courage, and good old-fashioned pride, something of which you seem to know very little."

Locke let his head fall even lower, hoping that would be the end of the monologue.

"Ralph," his father continued, "pass me your sword. It's time your brother learned a lesson."

Locke's heart sank as Ralph returned Locke's discarded practice sword with a kick and then moved to pass his own to their father. Locke glanced over warily as their father exchanged his walking stick for Ralph's weapon, and an inevitability washed over him.

"We don't have to do this, Father," he said.

But his father scoffed, and Locke noticed that townsfolk were beginning to gather in the field around them, watching on with intrigue. He knew them all of course: Aled the butcher and Tristan the blacksmith to name but two. To Locke's dismay, he noticed Garrick the farmer also amongst them, his son Jerald stood at his side. Of all the boys in Ardlyn, Jerald was the one Locke admired the most. The farmer's son was strong, brave, and popular with the girls. He was perhaps the only boy who could match Ralph in combat, and that alone made Locke want to befriend him.

"Life is full of hard lessons, boy," Locke's father continued. "It's my job to see that you learn one of them here today. Now prepare yourself. I won't be going easy on you like that brother of yours."

Locke stepped back, wooden sword weighing heavy in his hands. He imagined what the onlookers must have been thinking. Anticipation, perhaps to see a decorated war hero in action? Maybe concern for Locke, a boy mismatched against such an illustrious opponent? In either case, Locke wouldn't begrudge them their thoughts. What they didn't know, however, was that the storied Captain Ramsey had died on the battlefield many years before. The man before Locke was a ghost of his former self. Looking at the townsfolk, though, Locke saw concern on their faces, leaving him to wonder if he was the only one to realise the change in his father after all.

"Begin," his father screamed, lunging forward clumsily, his bad leg proving to be a weak support. The stale smell of drink seemed to radiate with his every movement, and Locke grimaced as he dodged the blow with ease.

"Your feet are almost as smart as your mouth, boy," his father snarled through shallow breaths. He flourished his sword in an act of defiance, and Locke maintained the space between them, hoping his father would see sense and stop this display.

"Show him, Father!" said Ralph, encouraging their father and thereby worsening Locke's predicament.

"Oh, I'll show him!" their father snarled, striking at Locke with a series of heavy, if clumsy, blows. Locke's wrist was already beginning to ache from the onslaught, but a subtle side-step blindsided his father to afford a welcome respite. Sweat poured from his father's brow. "Fight back!" his father demanded. Everyone in earshot could hear how frustrated the great Captain Ramsey sounded.

Locke's chest heaved with exertion. "You win, Father," he said, more out of hope than expectation. He noticed more and more people were continuing to gather around them, and his own face glistened in the midday sun.

"That isn't for you to decide," his father answered through gritted teeth. "Come!" he snapped, his sword raised. "Let's end this!"

There could only be one outcome, Locke knew, and he winced as he intentionally lowered his guard to present his father with an opening.

"You want more of that?" his father sneered with excitement, colour rising in his face. He slammed his sword into Locke's knee, just as Ralph had done.

Locke wanted nothing more than to buckle, to hit the ground and see the contest ended before anyone got hurt, before anyone's pride was wounded. He wanted to go home and spend time with his mother, but his father would never allow it. He wanted to see this charade of a contest through. He wanted to make a point. Locke raised his sword a final time, his heart sinking as he did.

Locke had to fight back, or at least appear to do so. His father's appetite for conflict would not be sated otherwise. In the back of his mind, Locke also wanted Jerald to hold him in high esteem, and a brief glance confirmed that the boy was still watching. Perhaps there was still a chance to make an impression and earn the friendship Locke keenly sought. Locke resolved himself as he moved to meet his father's renewed attack.

Swords clashed together, wood splintering on impact. Locke could tell that his father was enjoying himself; his spirit seemed to have reignited like an ember that had once burned within. "Good," he shouted, his words serving to stoke Locke's own enthusiasm. This was perhaps the only time he could remember holding his father's attention in a positive manner, and just for a moment, Locke lost himself to the challenge.

Back and forth they went as the crowd sounded their approval, cheering and groaning at the appropriate intervals. His father was unsteady on his feet but ruthless, and Locke focused to employ all he had learned both from Ralph and their father, back before the Battle of Highcastle had changed everything. His confidence grew with every strike, and he was just starting to share his father's enjoyment when the older man gave a sudden grimace, and his injured leg folded underneath him, leaving him splayed in the dirt.

Locke winced, rushing over to offer his hand in assistance. "Are you all right?" he asked.

His father snarled, "Get away from me," and their audience gasped as he swiped Locke's hand away in disgust, standing on his own. Locke could see that his injured leg was trembling, his sword discarded on the ground beside him. He raised his chin to growl, "Don't be a coward. Finish it, you fool!" His eyes were full of stubborn pride, and Locke froze, counting his regrets before instinct told him to turn and walk away. *Leave it, please leave it…*

"Are you listening to me, boy?" his father continued, speaking to Locke's back. Ralph's eyes were wide, and the world shrank to the patch of grass before Locke as he braced himself for the consequences. If only his mother were here. If only he'd just let his father win. If only King Cyrus had chosen a different captain that day during battle. His father was right—Locke *was* full of empty words and regrets. His face fell as a long shadow stretched to envelop him, the silhouette of a weapon lowering from above. He gritted his teeth, snapping his eyes shut as he did his best to prepare for the punishing impact his father dealt out.

⚜ ⚜ ⚜

Locke woke with a start, his father staring back at him, now several years older than he had been in Locke's dream.

"Prison Master Locke, sleeping on the job?" he asked, his raised eyebrow accentuating the deep lines on his forehead. Locke struggled to shake the images of his adolescence away.

"No, Fa—" He stopped, remembering himself. "No, Captain Ramsey, sir, just closing my eyes for a moment." He rocked forward in his chair and paused to rub his eyes. "It's all the dirt and dust down here, sir. It won't happen again, I promise."

"See that it doesn't." His father scowled, his glare threatening to burn a hole straight through Locke. "And for your information, I am Lord Ramsey, Warden of the Northern Fells." He leaned in to continue with a private whisper. "I didn't get you this job so that you could make a fool of yourself. Pull yourself together, boy!" He stepped back from Locke, straightening his jacket, and turned with a smile to face a group of new arrivals.

"Prison Master Locke," said Ralph, or *Captain* Ralph as Locke was so often reminded. The cycle was complete, with Ralph's ambitions realised, bestowed as he had been with the same title that had served their father so well. Unsurprisingly, neither brother nor father was prepared to forego the formalities, especially not for Locke's sake.

Locke inclined his head reluctantly. His brother had matured to realise every ounce of his early promise. The new captain was regarded as one of the most eligible bachelors in Peacehaven, his tall, muscular build complemented by the same long, flowing dark hair their father had once sported. To make matters worse, Ralph's jaw looked as though it had been chiselled from granite, and the thick stubble upon his chin put Locke's wispy effort to shame.

"Prison Master," came another voice, and Locke sprang to his feet to welcome High Commander Broderick with his very best salute. It seemed Locke had woken from one nightmare and walked straight into another. A disapproving father, a condescending brother, and now Broderick, the High Commander of Peace and Justice, a legendary general of Peacehaven's armies. Locke knew that Broderick had fought alongside his father in the Battle of Highcastle and that their time fighting shoulder-to-shoulder had engendered in them a deep camaraderie. It seemed that the High Commander trusted Locke's father implicitly, yet Broderick was apparently entirely unaware of Locke's relationship to the Warden of the Northern Fells—and Locke was under strict orders to keep it this way.

"High Commander Broderick, sir," Locke said with all his remaining composure. "It is an honour, sir. What brings you to this part of the castle?"

Broderick smiled as he surveyed their surroundings, a single cell in the bowels of Eldred's Keep, where only the most dangerous or high-profile prisoners were detained. It was a dark, grimy, moss-covered space with only torch flames for light. Low ceilings did little to brighten the mood, and Locke currently had only one other person for company: a shrunken old prisoner and long-time detainee named Walt, who sat huddled in the corner of his cell, mouthing the same incoherent gibberish he'd been peddling relentlessly in the two weeks since Locke had arrived.

"You smell that?" asked Broderick, leather breastplate squeaking as he walked over and rapped the handle of his sword against the wooden cell door, silencing Walt for once. Broderick paused to inhale deeply. "That's the smell of justice, and there is no sweeter smell anywhere in the castle. Delbert, bring in the prisoner!"

Locke turned as the door opened behind him. One of Broderick's stooges shoved a man with short, dark hair and a thick, scruffy beard into the centre of the room.

"Here he is, the very reason for my visit!" Broderick continued with outstretched arms. "Prison Master, meet your new resident. This is the notorious Finnian, a troublesome brigand, though I've no doubt his reputation precedes him."

"We captured him on the Great North Road," said Ralph before Locke could respond. Ralph sauntered toward the prisoner, whose hands hung before him, shackled by chains. "He has been terrorising carriages for months, a killer and a thief. A reputation surpassed only by his plunder, I should imagine."

Broderick stepped forward to place a hand on Ralph's shoulder as Locke's father looked on with lips upturned in a broad smile, his eyes full of pride. "But those days are over now, thanks to the young captain here. A man of great promise if ever I've seen one!" Broderick laughed jovially, looking at Ralph as though he were a son of his own. He turned back to Locke. "Finnian will be joining you for the foreseeable future, Prison Master. It will be for the king to decide his fate, though I suspect that this brigand's plundering days are over."

Locke's father stepped forward, a broad grin still etched upon his face. "Perhaps you might like to detain the scoundrel, Prison

Master? I think this man has had more than enough of our time already, don't you?"

"Of course," snapped Locke, reaching forward to drag Finnian by his chains. He paused at the door and fumbled with his keys, a nervous sweat developing on his forehead under the scrutiny of those gathered in the room. "Ah, there we are!" he said, more excitedly than he would have liked. The heavy key was recognisably gold in colour with the distinctive shape of a three petalled flower cut into the handle. To Locke's relief, the key glided into the lock, sparing him from further embarrassment, and he gestured the brigand toward his new home before turning to face the others. None of the men were even looking at Locke, and he realised he had been nervous for no reason.

"Are we done here?" Ralph asked their father, his eyes rolling with impatience.

"I should think so," Locke's father said, making for the exit. "You're no good to the people in this foul place."

Broderick nodded before following in the same direction. "I trust that everything is under control here, Prison Master?"

"Yes, High Commander," Locke said, smiling by way of agreement. Before he knew it, he was alone but for the prisoners once more. And Walt had started mumbling again.

"So let me get this straight," said Finnian, one hand gripping the bars of his cell as he leaned back casually, his face turned in an easy smile. "You work as a jailer, and your name is Locke?"

Locke blew out his cheeks with frustration, determined to ignore his prisoner.

"I mean, surely you see the humour in that?" Finnian continued. "When are we expecting your colleague 'Key' for the night shift? Come on, that's funny stuff!"

Locke pinched the bridge of his nose as Finnian doubled over laughing. What a day it had been. Not content with disowning and humiliating him in his waking life, it seemed his father and Ralph were now a permanent blight on even his dreams. The same memory had been haunting him for weeks now, a nightmarish reminder of his youth, though little had changed between the three of them in the intervening years.

"It is spelled with an E!" snapped Locke, though he knew he sounded like a petulant child. He huffed, frustrated at the circumstances in which he found himself. His father had wanted Locke to achieve something of his own, some level of personal success without the patronage of the family name. Locke understood that he would never have his brother's natural charm or athleticism, but had it really needed to come to this? A life in the bowels of Eldred's Keep with only half-crazed lawbreakers for company?

Of all the jobs, Locke thought with a sigh as Finnian cackled on at his own jokes. He'd hated the beatings his father had doled out, but he understood that his father knew no other way. *Tough love*, that's what people called it. That kind of discipline had elevated his father to the role of captain and decorated war hero thereafter. Locke understood that he had never met his father's expectations, something for which he would always despise himself, but his father's punishments had been severe, and it seemed that this job was as much a reminder of his failings as anything else.

"Shut up!" Locke finally yelled at Finnian's incessant laughter, throwing his heavy wooden baton at the bars, where it clanged noisily before falling to the grimy floor. Finnian went quiet for a moment, and Locke frowned as he realised how much he had sounded like his father in that moment. He rose from his chair and walked to retrieve his weapon. The prisoners remained quiet, and as Locke gazed upon them, he contemplated how he must look to them—ruled by anger, short-fused, frightening. His face dropped. He knew the men to be Walt and Finnian, prisoners in a cell, but their fearful expressions seemed plucked from his own childhood. Locke had only ever wanted to make his father proud, but Captain Ramsey was a tough man to please, and when Locke had failed as a child, there had been only one place for him: a heavy wooden door that opened into the cellar. His own personal prison cloaked in suffocating darkness.

A door hinge creaked behind him, and Locke twisted to welcome the end of his shift. "Prison Master Boyd," he said, raising his voice to quell Finnian's earlier joke. "What good timing. We have a new arrival, and he has finally decided to do the decent thing and grant us some peace."

As if in response to Finnian's newfound silence, Walt's nervous ramblings began once more, his gentle voice echoing quietly as Boyd stepped into the room.

"Nice job, newcomer," Boyd answered with his usual arrogance. "I suppose you'll want to get away then. Let's get this handover done, and you can leave me with some peace of my own."

⚜ ⚜ ⚜

Of all his daily duties, the handover was Locke's least favourite.

"Come on, in you go," said Boyd. Locke stepped beyond the cell door, baton extended, gesturing Walt and Finnian to their feet.

Locke's shift was over, but he would not be permitted to leave until a thorough search of both prisoners had been completed.

"Arms raised!" Boyd instructed, and both men obliged, allowing Locke to inspect them for weapons or any other contraband. This process always seemed a bit invasive to Locke, but despite his rather fragile appearance, Locke knew that Walt had been imprisoned for a handful of gruesome murders some decades ago. Only the late King Anselm's mercy left Walt still breathing. Some life that was, though, shut away in the darkness. The knowledge that Locke would play his part in it all served only to worsen his already sour mood.

"Pockets!" Boyd yelled for a second time, startling Locke as he returned to face Finnian.

"You're enjoying this," the brigand sneered.

Locke rolled his eyes. "Very funny. Just keep quiet and this will be over in no time," he said in reply. Both men went silent as Locke completed his checks before exiting the cell, closing the door, and bolting the lock behind him. "All set," he said, edging toward the door, but Boyd called to him at the last moment. Locke paused in the doorway, itching to leave.

"What is it?" he asked, fingers tapping on the woodwork.

Boyd fell into the rickety chair and folded his arms. "I heard we had visitors today. Important visitors?"

"Oh, that."

"Yes, that," said Boyd, his voice laced with anger. "Two weeks in the job and already rubbing shoulders with nobility, and that's without mentioning the High Commander!"

"It was all for Finnian," Locke mumbled.

Boyd's eyes narrowed. "Seems a bit excessive if you ask me. I'm not sure what it is about you, but something's not quite right." He paused to fix Locke with a deathly stare. "Just remember, if anyone asks, it's Boyd that taught you everything you know, right? Now get out of here," he snapped. "I'll see you in the morning."

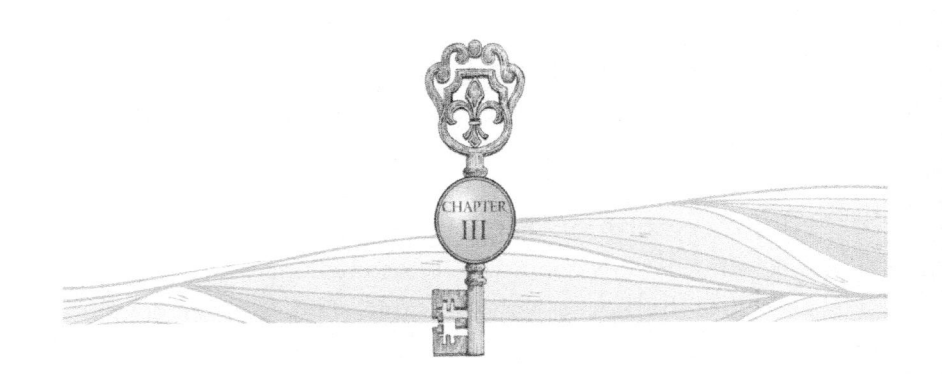

Francine

Fran knew the royal visit would be painfully brief. It seemed to her only moments ago that Cyrus and his family had arrived in Nivelle, but as Fran sat, nudging a sweet pastry around her breakfast plate, she knew that her brother would soon be on his way.

"And you really must go?" she asked on a whim, unable to stop herself as she looked at Cyrus across the table. Fran could already hear the hurried movement of castle staff in the corridors as they readied the royal carriage for Cyrus's departure.

Cyrus smiled sadly, confirming what she already knew, and her lips gave a subtle tremble. By way of response, Prince Leo declared, "I'm going to miss you, Aunt Fran," through a mouthful of bread and jam.

Mathilde had been right; the young prince grew so much between each visit. Fran recalled her own childhood, and though she gave no thought to the tragedies she had endured, she wondered if someone had shown Leo how to make bracelets from flowers and whether King Cyrus was finding time to tell the young prince stories as he had always done for her. Had she made the right decision leaving all of that behind? Would a life in Highcastle have been so bad after all? She reflected on the irony that where Cyrus had pursued adventure into the castle, she had sought her own journey outside of the walls of Eldred's Keep.

"Don't be sad," said Queen Marcia, reaching to place a hand on Fran's. "We'd love to stay, but this child will arrive before we know it." She placed her free hand on her stomach, smiling briefly. "Besides, I think your brother has someone he is itching to get back to?"

"Adaline?" Fran asked, confused by Marcia's accusatory tone.

The queen laughed and then frowned at Cyrus. "You'd think so, wouldn't you? No, I'm speaking of his prized mare, Adagio, of course. He's done nothing but fret over her since the moment we left!" She shook her head. "But that's another matter. Try not to worry, Fran. You'll be an aunt again in no time. Perhaps Mathilde will give you leave to come and meet your new niece or nephew when the time comes."

"She's right," said Cyrus, smiling. "You're welcome home anytime, but there is little to report in Highcastle at present. My council are complaining about taxation as always, but when aren't they in a twist about something? Anyway," he continued, "Mathilde has need of you for now. It's a shame we can't stay. I gather that the first throng of potential suitors arrives today?"

"You're right," she conceded, knowing Mathilde would need her today more than ever. "Look after each other. I see how the nobles get to Mathilde. They're not to be trusted."

Seth cleared his throat from the corner of the room. "That is why you and I have our jobs, remember?" he asked her, his brow arched.

Fran didn't respond but gave a forced smile instead. After a sigh, she softly said, "I'm going to miss all of you, you know?"

"I know," said Cyrus, his head inclined. "Eldred's Keep isn't the same without you."

⚜ ⚜ ⚜

The royal carriage grew ever smaller as it moved into the distance. Fat tears rolled down Fran's cheeks. In the end, she hadn't had the heart to face saying goodbye. She had wanted to carry Leo out to the carriage on her shoulders and chase the big wheels down the road, waving them off until she couldn't keep up any longer. She had wanted to savour every last moment with her family, but it had felt like her heart was being torn from her chest, so it was the best she could do to stand at Mathilde's window, the queen's hand resting supportively upon Fran's shoulder as those Fran loved most dearly left her behind. But this wasn't a new feeling. She'd been here before. It never got any easier, though Mathilde's comfort was a consolation and a reminder of the duty Fran owed her queen.

"Are you okay?" Mathilde asked, a softness to her voice that wasn't usually there.

Fran gave an ugly sniffle and wiped her eyes with her sleeve before nodding silently, giving the queen permission to turn and walk away. She took a few steps and then paused. "I know this isn't the right time," Mathilde said, hesitating, "but be honest. What do you think?"

Fran breathed in deeply to steady herself before turning to face the queen. She'd seen Mathilde negotiate trade deals with King Alonso and the Verderans, seen her face down pirate hordes in the northern seas. She had seen her friend battle with Clement and the council for the past five years, but in truth, she'd never seen the queen look as nervous as she did in this moment, looking anxiously down at her dress.

"You look…" Fran ventured thoughtfully before her face broke into a genuine smile, one which contrasted greatly with the red puffiness under her eyes. "You look wonderful, my queen."

Mathilde's shoulders visibly relaxed, the simple yet elegant blue gown sitting perfectly upon her lean frame. "And you're not just saying that?" asked the queen. Her hair was interlaced with delicate white flowers, set in a single large plait at the back of her head. "I feel stupid. This is a terrible idea, isn't it?"

The sting of Cyrus's departure was already beginning to fade, and Fran was glad for the distraction of the royal suitors this afternoon. She wasn't sure if it was a good idea or not—nor whether she was the right person to ask for fashion advice—but Mathilde had made her decision, and it was Fran's task to help her see it through.

"There's no harm in trying," Fran said. "If nothing else, it might appease Clement and the others for a time. You never know, the perfect man for you might be just around the corner. Or right inside the castle, as it were."

Mathilde sniggered. "My perfect man just rolled away with his child and his pregnant wife. I know you don't want to hear it, but that's my luck in a nutshell."

Fran knew Mathilde only too well and thus knew that the queen wasn't joking. She rolled her eyes at Mathilde's mention of her unrequited love. "Well, perhaps there's someone even more perfect," she said, keen to change the subject. Fran was by no means an expert on matters of the heart, but if what she'd heard from everyone in her life was true, then there was someone for everyone, especially a powerful, brilliant woman like Mathilde.

"Perhaps you're right," said the queen, walking to examine herself in a full-length mirror. "If nothing else, it will be fun finding out!"

⚜ ⚜ ⚜

In the end, it was no fun at all. It was another warm day, and the throne room was stifling as a constant stream of perfumed dandies paraded before the queen, singing, dancing, or reciting poetry while Clement and his lackies watched eagerly on. It reminded Fran of a cattle market she had attended with her adoptive father, Osbert, as a small child, only this time, Mathilde was the one looking to buy.

Fran made sure to keep a close eye on the queen as each new suitor arrived before her. It was at least mildly amusing at first: the grand entries, the increasingly flamboyant ensembles, the unfaltering confidence from an assortment of boys who were likely incapable of looking after themselves, let alone a country. As time went on, though, Fran noticed Mathilde wilting in the afternoon sun. The queen was not one for small talk, her eyes drooping and head sinking into her hands as Clement chided her at every possible opportunity.

"Well, that's that then," said the white-haired nobleman. "Fifteen men, the very best our country has to offer. My boy Hugo is quite the catch, is he not?"

Judging by Mathilde's incredulous sneer, Fran would guess that Hugo was not what Mathilde would consider a catch at all. The queen slumped further into her throne in frustration, and Clement's expression fell with her.

"It has been a long day," intervened Georges, a nobleman who worked closely with Clement. Fran knew the two men to be aligned in political matters and was both surprised and wary to see the bald man detach from Clement's hip as he approached the queen with a different tack. "It is a heavy decision for one so delicate. Perhaps the queen would rather defer to her council so that we might...share the burden?"

Georges might as well have flatulated in that moment, such was the embarrassment he had caused himself with his assertion. Mathilde's face soured, and the bald man backed away gingerly, as one might do when moving away from something explosive.

"Your offer is greatly appreciated," said the queen, her head tilted, her voice turned sickly-sweet, "but I've seen every suitor you have, and none of them is of interest. If that is the very best that Cornesse has to offer, well, then we have even bigger problems than I thought! No," she continued her voice full of frustration, "I've played my part, but it seems that your queen is destined to be alone. That is, unless you have any other fine ideas?"

The room went quiet, which Fran found unsurprising given Mathilde's dangerous tone of voice. Clement was normally good for a smart suggestion, but even he seemed short of words. They really were a rather loathsome bunch, Fran reflected. A meddling gaggle of old men more concerned with their own standing than anything else. Fran smiled to see them shrink beneath Mathilde's scorn, but just when she thought they must be done for the day, a man stepped forward unexpectedly, a wide smile stretched across his face.

"Great queen," came his heavily accented voice. His face was unfamiliar to Fran, but there was a kindness in the man's eyes, and Fran found his dark skin beautiful and exotic. She realised this must be Amare, the envoy from the Kanthu Isles.

"I have watched from afar, great queen," the man continued, now knelt before them, his bright eyes still fixed on Mathilde. "I have seen the boys that these men offer you, yet I see no king among them." He rose to his feet as Mathilde gestured him to continue. "You invited me here to trade in precious goods, great queen. I have shown you our diamonds, our gold. It's true that the Kanthu Isles are full of riches, but perhaps there is one jewel that you might yet consider?"

The room was somehow even more silent than before, a silence so absolute that it was almost deafening. Fran noticed that Clement, despite his sudden loss for words, seemed to be doing some quick thinking and scheming, his eyes twitching.

Mathilde sat up straight with interest, addressing their guest. "Do go on, Amare," she urged. The atmosphere was uncertain, but perhaps for the first time, it seemed that the queen was interested in what one of the men in the room had to say.

"As you wish, great queen," the envoy continued, his face serious and determined. His eyes, however, were alight, belying his excitement at Mathilde's encouragements. "As a student of history, you will know that the complex geography of our island nation has led to years of wars that have ravaged our lands. You are not without your own conflicts, of course, but decisions in the Kanthu Isles are made with bows and spears more often than with conversation." He paused to scratch his neck, and Fran noticed a long, fading scar that seemed only to illustrate his point. "We are a proud people, but our history runs red with blood. Our land is divided into many factions, lines drawn by men that would be kings and kings that would be gods. But the world is changing, *our* world is changing, and there is one man above all others who is keen to see the change."

Mathilde narrowed her eyes. "Your king, I presume?" she asked.

"The very same," said Amare, nodding. "You are as smart as you are beautiful, great queen Mathilde. King Othelu is ever grateful for your patronage, but perhaps there is yet more to be bargained for. With his own hands, King Othelu has introduced order to our islands, while still honouring our ways and traditions. The clans are finally united, and new trade lines have been established in the southern port of Taboso. It is King Othelu's vision to see the fruits of our lands exported around the world. He desires to see new wealth and new ideas introduced to the people, and with them, an end to the skirmishes that have defined our history."

"And what does any of this have to do with the queen?" asked Clement impatiently as all others watched on.

"A fine question," answered the envoy. His smile never wavered, and Fran couldn't help but admire his ability to hold court. "King Othelu's power grows with every day. He is a man of great fortune, one who is happy to share his wealth. A father to six sons, King Othelu has seen his princes marry to secure the peace he has created."

"Six sons?" asked Mathilde with an approving nod. "Impressive."

Amare smiled. "Indeed. But there is one son who is yet unmarried. Prince Taiwo is Othelu's second son, and the most coveted bachelor in all the Kanthu Isles. The boy is of a similar age to you, great queen—a strong, handsome warrior with a desire to travel the world. Taiwo is his father's most cherished treasure, yet King Othelu remains keen to see his final son married to an equally impressive woman. I would be remiss in my duties if I did not propose a...*solution* to your current predicament."

"You would have me marry your prince?" asked Mathilde. It seemed the heads of everyone in the room moved in unison, back and forth from Mathilde to the envoy, following the conversation as closely as possible.

"I would only ask that you consider it," said the envoy. Sounds of hushed speculation began to echo out around the room. To Fran's ear, most of these whispers sounded indignant.

"Preposterous!" yelled Clement, stepping forward to find his tongue and giving voice to Fran's suspicions. "You cannot be seriously considering this, my queen. It is one thing to trade with these people, but to bargain your throne? How do we know they can be trusted?"

To Amare's credit, he never flinched, even when Clement had referred to his countrymen as "these people." As Mathilde sat forward with a sneer, however, it seemed she was prepared to take offense on their guest's behalf. "It is a rather unusual suggestion, I grant you," Mathilde began, looking not at Clement but at the envoy instead, her lips pursed. "I'd begun to think that all my searching was in vain, but perhaps there are treasures as yet uncovered. Clement…" she called to ensure the man's attention, "is it not your intention to see your queen married? Your primary aim to ensure the future of Cornesse for your children and generations to come?"

"Well, yes but—"

"Would it not seem prudent to at least consider this foreign prince?" she asked, cutting the old man short. Her eyebrows were raised, and Fran couldn't help but enjoy the nobleman's discomfort as Mathilde toyed with him. "You want your king," she continued, "Othelu wants his peace, and it has always been my ambition to improve trade with the island nation. It seems…" She paused, narrowing her eyes in thought. "It all seems very logical, if you ask me. A far cry from a storybook romance, to be certain, but we all have our obligations."

The envoy's smile widened, and he clapped his hands together once in jubilation as Clement turned to join his peers, his face set in a mask of fury.

"Then it is settled, great queen," said the envoy. "I will return home at once and send for a portrait of the prince, so that you might—"

"No, no that won't be necessary," said Mathilde, raising a palm to interject once more. "Your gesture is appreciated, and I am open to your suggestion, but this queen is not so easily bought and sold. Francine," continued the queen, turning to draw Fran's full attention. "Your sword at my side is most appreciated, but in this I require the benefit of your judgement, which I know to be impeccable. Our envoy, Amare, will return to the Kanthu Isles at first light, and I would ask that you travel with him to meet this prince, Taiwo, before escorting him to our capital in person so that the two of us might meet to discuss a potential match. I know this may seem unusual," she added, her voice lowered as she addressed Fran to the exclusion of all others, "but this task requires someone I can trust. I will not command this of you, but please consider my request and let me know when your decision has been made."

The room remained silent as Mathilde's final words echoed out. All eyes were now on Fran, who nodded wordlessly, unsure as to the correct response.

"Well, that's settled then," said Mathilde, as if to spare Fran's unease. "I thank you all for your time today. Oh, and Clement," she paused as the nobleman turned around from his hasty pursuit of the exit. "I just wanted to thank you. This might not have been such a bad idea after all."

The old man cursed as he turned away. The queen sat silently, her delighted smirk growing more pronounced with each step Clement took away from her.

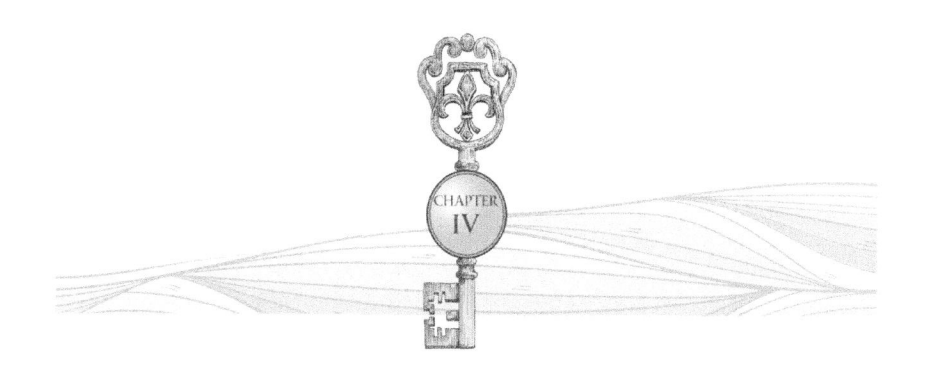

Locke

Locke dragged his weary body through the streets of lower Highcastle after his shift at the prison, longing for his bed. His back ached, his neck was sore, and he wondered why nobody had warned him against the perils of spending all day sitting down.

He stopped with a grimace, applying pressure with his hand to a sore spot on his spine. He was in a lively part of the city, a short step from the western quarter, which had been largely rebuilt since the war. Laughter sounded nearby, and he attributed the hubbub to a touring comedy ensemble, whose performance, *To Kill a King,* was said to provide a farcical account of the death of King Rafael during the battle of Highcastle. The production was the talk of the lower classes and a welcome distraction from daily life, but Locke knew better than to trivialise war and suffering. He walked away from the sounds of mirth and continued toward home, his thoughts consumed by the injuries his own father had suffered during the conflict.

Like the rest of the city, lower Highcastle was a jumbled mess. What the capital lacked in uniformity, it made up for in character and charm. The streets were narrow and sprawling, fringed by small, ramshackle houses with extended families packed tightly inside. It was a far cry from Locke's upbringing at his father's keep a day's ride north of the city, in the small town of Ardlyn. Captain Ramsey had ascended to nobility shortly after the war, during the king's reform: an effort to unite the two former nations of Auldhaven and Easthaven. In his wisdom, King Cyrus had awarded a lordship to the head of each noble family, with discretionary honours for those making exceptional contributions to the new nation's future. The aim was to form an improved council to meet the needs of all, while the honourable Lord Ramsey had received a small castle and stewardship for the vast fells that connected Peacehaven with Cornesse in the north.

His father had been like a caged animal in the early days, and though Locke's memories were fraught with sadness, he still harboured happy memories of his rural upbringing. The capital was exciting and unpredictable, but even though Locke had only been in Highcastle for a few weeks, he already yearned for home.

A door swung open nearby, the sounds of lively music spilling from a tavern. The hinge must have been rusty because the door closed slowly, giving Locke a peek at the raucous patrons, arms locked as they stood singing bawdy songs at the tops of their voices. The whole scene seemed so wonderfully carefree to Locke, who marvelled at their wide smiles and spirited, if tuneless, voices. He wondered what it would be like to live without the weight of expectation resting on his shoulders, or how much ale it would take to create the illusion, if only for a time.

He was only a few short steps from the slow-closing door. He was tired, but perhaps he would return sometime. He considered the prospect of truancy, or better still, simply leaving his wretched job to pursue an altogether different life. A life where he was one of those befuddled singers, a different man, stood among friends. A life of carelessness and fun. It seemed to Locke that the prisons of Eldred's Keep existed before him, and they'd still stand long after his passing. His mind had started to spiral with a world of possibilities when reality resurfaced, and his father's disapproving visage appeared in Locke's mind. *That's not my world*, Locke thought to himself sadly. *Like it or not, I've a job to do…*

To make matters worse, Locke winced as his temple gave a sudden twinge. It had been two days since Finnian's arrest, and the brigand's constant blathering had served to ensure that Locke's back was not the only source of his physical suffering. To some extent, Locke had appreciated Finnian's humour, yet there was something about the brigand that left Locke unsettled. The man was a notorious lawbreaker, and his only future surely laid either in death or in lifetime imprisonment. He hadn't started muttering to himself yet, like his colourful cellmate, Walt, but there was a startling confidence about Finnian that made Locke uneasy: the confidence of a man with a secret—something Locke knew all about from his own efforts to conceal his relationship with his father, Lord Ramsey, from those who knew him in Highcastle.

As Locke rounded a corner, another door opened, and he was home. The Eagle was primarily a tavern, one popular for tall drinks and cheap food. It was rowdy at the very best of times, but Rufus the landlord was an old friend of Locke's father, and with prison master wages being what they were, Locke had had little choice but to accept a small but affordable room in the loft. Above all else, Locke's father had spoken of Rufus's discretion; Locke's secret was safe here.

"Welcome back!" called the landlord, hand towel waving in Locke's direction. Locke's head was now throbbing, but the pain and exhaustion didn't prevent him from a courteous nod in Rufus's direction before making for his room.

Three weeks in the capital already felt like a lifetime. The Eagle was cheap but offered little respite from the bedlam beyond. An insatiable grime seemed to encumber Locke no matter how frequently he washed, and the people were often sharp and hurried, leaving him lonely in the confines of his four claustrophobic, paper-thin walls.

He forced down the alluring vision of the rowdy tavern he had seen on his walk back to The Eagle, along with the thoughts that the spectacle had caused him to entertain. He knew he was here to make a name for himself and to do his best to make his father proud. Giving up was not an option, but Locke could never have imagined things would be so difficult. He missed his mother's cooking, the familiarity of the keep, the small river just outside of Ardlyn where he would sit and watch the water wheel turn methodically, revelling in his peaceful surroundings. This life, by comparison, was such a joyless existence, and Locke could hardly contain his surprise when he arrived to find welcome company waiting at his bedroom door.

"You're late," said Grace, and Locke smiled as all his troubles seemed to fade in an instant. If there was one positive thing to come from his time in the capital, it was Grace, the fair-skinned barmaid with dark hair and bright red lips. He'd noticed her the moment he'd arrived at The Eagle, and though their time together had thus far been fleeting, he felt drawn to the warmth of her beautiful smile, wondering over and over again whether she might feel the same.

"I didn't realise we had plans," he said, pausing at the top of the staircase. He was aiming for relaxed and aloof, but her appearance really was unexpected, and he fought to mask the excitement in his voice.

Grace smiled, and Locke felt his knees go weak. "We don't," she said playfully. "Well, we didn't anyway, but Rufus has given me the night off, and it is still only early, so I wondered…" She paused to purse her lips, and Locke realised he'd been holding his breath in anticipation of her every word. "There's that performance that everyone is talking about, the one about King Rafael."

"*To Kill a King*," Locke finished with a nod. He was tired, and his head was thumping, but she was right, it *was* only early evening, and he wasn't going to let his day worsen by passing up an opportunity like this one. "I think it might have started already, but maybe we can still make the final act?"

Before he knew it, they were heading back toward the laughter, and Locke realised with a giddy jolt that he really was going to be part of the scene he had imagined himself in, just one of the revellers enjoying himself. An enormous crowd was crammed into the small square, and Grace giggled with mischief as she dragged Locke through the masses until the stage was in sight. A smile crept across Locke's face. Maybe he was capable of being careless and fun, after all.

"I'll be taking that crown of yours!" yelled one of the actors, a dwarf in imitation Verderan armour. It was clear that the dwarf was intended to portray the villain, King Rafael, while his opposite, King Cyrus, was played by a giant of a man with a dazzling great sword resting in one hand.

The actors began to dance around, King Cyrus holding his opponent at arm's length, much to the amusement of the crowd. It was a ridiculous showing, and Locke's grin faded quickly to leave him humourless as the Verderan dwarf king fell to the floor, defeated, and another dwarf in identical costume tumbled forward to skewer the defeated Rafael with a sword of his own. The crowd roared with applause, and Locke forced a fresh smile as Grace turned toward him, her face bright and scrunched with laughter. He wanted to enjoy the show and lose himself in the moment with Grace, but the vivid memory of his father's own injuries from the Battle of Highcastle still haunted him, their repercussions tormenting him to this day.

Grace's face faltered. "Do you want to go?" she asked, as if sensing his discomfort. She didn't look disappointed but rather genuinely worried at the look on his face.

The crowd was already beginning to thin, and Locke nodded, gesturing Grace to join the throng. *I think she likes me*, Locke thought to himself, his mood lifting as they retraced their path into the backstreets. *Don't mess this up*, he urged himself silently, but he knew that this would be easier said than done.

⚜ ⚜ ⚜

They had been walking for some time when the conversation eventually turned to family.

"Dead," said Grace, straight-faced. "Mother and father. They were both killed during the Battle of Highcastle."

Locke stopped in his tracks. "That's awful," he said, shaking his head.

"It wasn't the childhood I'd imagined," Grace answered with a sad smile. "We were never rich or anything, but we had our own little house, not too far from here actually." She paused and gazed off over the rooftops wistfully. "It was the catapults that did it for them in the end. I'll never forget the way those rocks tore through our walls like parchment. I guess I was the lucky one. I was small enough to escape through the rubble, but I was too small to help them…my parents, that is. Mother died instantly, but father was trapped under a wooden beam and a pile of bricks."

"He was still alive then?"

"For a time," said Grace, and her face fell. "I tried to free him, but I couldn't, no matter how hard I tried. I wanted to stay with him, until the end, but the king's men were in the streets rounding up survivors. I can still hear Father now. 'Don't worry about me, go, get out of here!'" She mimicked her father's voice while sharing her last memories of him. "He was always stubborn, but his tone was different in that moment, no longer defiant but accepting. That was when I knew that I had to go. The king's men took me to the castle."

"The castle?" asked Locke, wondering if their paths might have crossed far earlier than either of them had realised. He considered the possibility, but then he pushed it away quickly. He had never known suffering the likes of which Grace had described.

He had been cocooned in the rural safety of Ardlyn during the siege and had only visited Highcastle after the battle had concluded. The image of his father's broken body appeared in his mind momentarily. That was a day that he would not soon forget.

"The castle," Grace echoed, and she gestured them forward. "Can't say that I attended too many balls or banquets while I was there, but it was safe."

Locke followed, deep in thought, captivated by her story. "Then what happened?" he asked, hoping the question wasn't too personal.

Grace sighed. "Nothing good. We'd won the war, but I'd lost everything. The king sent food to help those who needed it, but I had no money, no home. Countless nights spent in derelict buildings as the city was rebuilt around me." Another sigh, this one more pronounced. "But then I met Rufus," she said, and her smile reappeared as though it had never left. "It wasn't much, but he gave me a job and even let me stay at The Eagle for a while."

"That's great," said Locke, before stumbling to correct himself. "The job that is. I'm sorry about your family."

Grace raised a hand and waved him away dismissively. "It's fine," she said, and her tone assured Locke that she meant it. "Besides," she continued, "look at me now. I get to clear sick and spit from a tavern floor! I guess you could say it all worked out in the end."

They laughed together, and Locke changed the subject as they walked on into the night, avoiding any question of his own lineage. He'd been taken with her from the moment they had met, but this felt different. Grace was unlike any of the girls he had met back in Ardlyn. She was fun, confident, and funny too, he realised as their collective laughter echoed in the narrow streets, drawing murmurs of disapproval from residents whose restful hours had been unwillingly interrupted. Best of all, Grace laughed *with* him, not *at* him, as was more commonly the case—at least with his father and Ralph, anyway.

For those few hours, things were different. Locke was different, lighter somehow, and his woes faded in significance as he embraced the moment. What did he have to worry about anyway? Nothing compared to Grace's heart-breaking story. He marvelled at her courageous enjoyment of *To Kill a King* in the face of all she had experienced and took great comfort in the fact that she had been able to put the past behind her, moving irrepressibly forward toward a brighter future. He wondered, could he do the same?

It seemed that the night would never end, until Grace finally offered to walk Locke home, rebuffing his own attempt at chivalry. Highcastle was a maze that lent itself to aimless wanderers, and stars twinkled in the night sky as they returned to The Eagle, Locke's face aching from smiling.

They paused at the doorway, and Grace turned to take Locke by the hand. "I had a really nice time tonight," she said, grinning. Her eyes sparkled in the moonlight, and Locke's heart raced as she closed the gap between them. "I mean it," she continued, her tone sincere. "I haven't had a lot of luck with men, but you...you're different somehow."

Locke's smile widened as her words about him mirrored his own thoughts about her. His hands were clammy with nerves, but nothing was going to ruin the evening now. "I feel the same," he ventured, barely recognising the voice as his own. "I can't say I've enjoyed living in Highcastle thus far, but maybe I'll find something to love about the capital after all."

A moment of silence descended upon them. Locke's heartbeat quickened, and his smile faded as Grace stepped away dismissively, dropping his hand so that it fell at his side like a lead weight.

"I—" Grace started, before stopping herself abruptly. "I'm sorry, Locke. I had a nice evening, but maybe we shouldn't do this anymore."

"But Grace!" he protested, baffled by the abrupt change of tack.

"No, I'm sorry, Locke. I know you're lonely here, and you need someone for company, but I'm not that girl. Maybe we shouldn't have done this. I should never have let myself get carried away. You're one of Rufus's customers—it's unprofessional, and I can't afford to lose my job over this." She looked down, shaking her head, and when she faced him again, she was wearing a sad smile. "I had a nice time, but sometimes these things are just moments. I'm sorry. I'll see you around, okay?"

She turned and disappeared into the backstreets, leaving Locke standing there, his hand still dangling at his side, warm from its contact with hers only seconds before.

Locke looked to the sky and found a full moon. He was embarrassed to find that he had to choke back tears as he tried and failed to understand how he'd managed to make such a mess of things.

⚜ ⚜ ⚜

Locke stomped through the tavern, ignoring Rufus's greetings to ascend the stairs and fumble for his keys, pausing a few steps from the top as he did so. He was ashamed and entirely confused by Grace's actions. It had all seemed to be going so well, until...

He stopped, his train of thought grinding to a halt. He'd found his keys, but his eyes widened with shock as he realised that his door was already ajar. A gentle suggestion of movement sounded from within, and Locke's heart raced once more, his hand reaching for the heavy wooden baton that was part of his work uniform. *You idiot*, he thought as he grasped for a weapon he knew to be elsewhere. He was not permitted to take his baton with him when he left the prison. He considered returning downstairs to alert Rufus, but the landlord was a busy man with a short supply of patience. Locke couldn't afford to lose his room at The Eagle, fearing the repercussions from his father if he were to return home with his tail between his legs.

But who was in his room? Locke had kept to himself since arriving in the city and had no notable enemies from his former life. His mind turned to his colleague, Boyd, but scornful though his fellow prison master might be, Locke's very presence at The Eagle meant that Boyd was otherwise occupied in the dungeons of Eldred's Keep.

Another sound of movement set Locke's nerves on edge. He climbed the last few steps noiselessly and crept forward, wincing in anticipation as he leaned forward to peek through the door.

"Are you coming in or what?" came a familiar voice, startling Locke. He pushed the door wide and composed himself, stepping into the room to find his father smiling back at him.

"You took your time, didn't you?" his father asked from a seat in the corner. He crossed his legs and flashed a knowing smile. His eyebrows raised accusatorily as red wine swilled in the glass in his hand. It had been quite the night for unexpected visits, Locke thought.

"I'm sorry, Father. I wasn't expecting you." The end of his statement lilted up in question.

"I can see that." His father paused to take a long drink, lips darkened from the wine. His expression turned to a smile. "I suppose I should take this as a good sign?"

"Huh?"

"Your evening with the barmaid," he answered, rolling his remaining eye. "I presume it went well?"

Locke felt his cheeks redden. "Oh, that. Yes," he began, and then his thoughts caught up with him. "Wait, how do you know about that?" His own eyes narrowed.

His father laughed. "I arranged it, of course," he said, and his face was suddenly full of amusement.

Locke's expression fell, and, in that moment, he wished that the dingy ground would open up and swallow him whole. "You did what?" he asked angrily.

"I arranged it," his father repeated nonchalantly. "I can't imagine Finnian is giving you an easy time, and I thought you might be lonely. Wait you didn't think…?" He left the question hanging.

Locke seethed with anger. He'd known it was all too good to be true. Why would a girl like Grace ever look at someone like him? Their awkward departure was beginning to make more sense.

"I thought I was doing you a favour!" his father continued with a shake of his head. "Honestly, you try to do something nice,

At the very least I'd expect some thanks. The whole thing cost me enough!"

Locke threw a fist into the door, splintering the wood. His father jumped with surprise, some of his wine splashing onto the wooden floor as Locke began to snarl, no longer able to contain his emotions. "You paid her?" he asked with a grimace. "What is this place, a brothel?"

"No, not a brothel," his father answered dismissively, placing his glass upon a nearby table. "It's a tavern, you know that. But everyone has their price."

Locke turned away, placing his head in his hands in an attempt to achieve some composure.

"Your colleague, Boyd, has been asking around about you," his father said, conveniently changing the subject and throwing Locke off-guard yet again. "I told you to keep a low profile, avoid undue attention. This change will be good for you, but it's important that you do it alone."

"What do you mean?"

"I mean that you need to start being more sensible. Don't give Boyd any further excuse to question or doubt you. Get your head down, keep yourself to yourself. You're responsible for an infamous brigand, Locke. This could be the very making of you." He paused to retrieve his glass. "I'll have words with the girl…"

"Grace." Locke clenched his jaw. "There's no need to—"
"Yes, Grace, that's it," his father chortled, cutting Locke short. "I'll have words with her. I did hope you were able to maintain some…discretion. It would be a shame to see our secret so freely given." He halted and massaged his injured leg, before standing with the aid of his stick. "Get yourself some sleep, Lockey. You look

exhausted." He patted Locke on the shoulder and left without another word, without any hint of an apology.

Locke collapsed onto his bed, staring up at the uneven ceiling, his eyes fixating on a mouldy spot in the centre. Grace's parting words echoed in his mind, mingling with those of his father, and he wondered if anyone in the world had ever felt as worthless as he did in that moment.

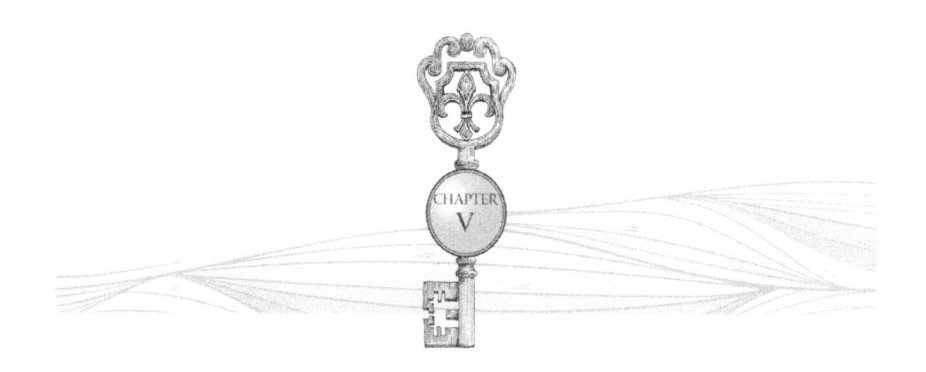

Francine

Fran folded the last of her clothes and placed them into her trunk. She was tired and nervous, but a pervading sense of adventure kept her moving as the sun rose beyond her window. It was a little after daybreak, and the birds were in the midst of their morning song. She rubbed at her eyes, yawning deeply. Fran closed the trunk, sitting down on its lid as she took a final moment to look around and appreciate her quarters: a spacious, if simple, room with bare stone walls, polished oak floors and understated hand-carved furnishings before the hearth.

Wasn't this what she had always wanted? To travel to frontiers unknown, to venture further than even Cyrus had journeyed? At the thought of Cyrus, her stomach fell as she considered that she might not make it back in time for the birth of her new niece or nephew. She had missed the day that Leo was born. It had been not long after her arrival in Nivelle, and Mathilde had requested her presence for a hunt in the woods nearby. Fran was no expert with a bow, and the queen had called it beginner's luck, but Fran could still remember the feeling of satisfaction as she carted a heavy boar back to the castle with her head held high. It had been a fine day all told, and the news of Leo's birth should only have heightened her mood, but the sense of guilt still burned now as it had in that moment. Everything else had suddenly seemed insignificant: the hunt, the boar. She should have been there in Highcastle, for her new nephew, the new prince, and for Cyrus.

She wondered if this mission to retrieve Prince Taiwo was only yet another attempt by Mathilde to distract Fran from the feeling of homesickness that had weighed on her since her brother had departed Nivelle. It was not in Fran's nature to question the queen, and her doubt in Mathilde's motivations faded as quickly as it had risen, as she realised that she herself had encouraged Mathilde in her search to find a suitor, after all. She shook her head to halt the spiral that she had started. The Kanthi prince sounded like he had the potential to be a fine match for Mathilde, and it was an honour to be trusted with such a task as being Mathilde's judge by proxy of this man's character. Fran's overwhelming feeling was one of duty, yet she had always viewed the queen as something of a sisterly figure, and it was more than a little reassuring to find that Mathilde clearly felt the same.

To Kanthu then, she thought silently. In all honesty, there had never been a decision to be made. Mathilde had asked, so Fran would go. She hopped from her trunk as two young squires appeared expectantly in her doorway, and though she couldn't fault their application, she struggled to suppress a smile as the two boys shuffled her luggage awkwardly in the direction from which they'd arrived.

Her passage through the castle was a sombre one, and although Fran felt her heart beating with excitement, her thoughts were divided with the dread of yet another goodbye, even if it was only temporary. She knew that Mathilde was made of tougher stuff, so it was no surprise to find the queen waiting, straight-backed, by the carriage as Fran emerged into the early morning light. The birds continued to sing their cheerful songs, but as Fran saw the last of her belongings hoisted onto the carriage, her mood was tinged with apprehension. Amare would be her companion for the journey, and she noticed that the envoy already sat in the carriage, ready to leave.

"The lengths we'll go to for our country!" said Mathilde by way of greeting, her voice uncharacteristically jovial given the time of the day.

Fran blew out her cheeks. "Or for duty to a queen, at least."

At this, Mathilde gave a half smile. She raised one hand to place it on Fran's shoulder before continuing, "I hope you know how much this means to me. I never dreamt of marrying a stranger or even entertaining the idea, but if I absolutely must, I'd like him to be someone of whom you approve."

It seemed, then, that Fran was to be a royal matchmaker now in addition to her duties as the queen's shield, and if the sadness of her departure wasn't heavy enough, she had this added weight of responsibility to carry on her journey.

"Your opinion means the world to me," Mathilde added gently. "Besides, I think this journey will be good for you. Go, see the world. Don't worry about me. I'll drag Lucien out of retirement while you're gone. Queen's orders." She smiled. "Get yourself back to Nivelle safely, and we can discuss your extended leave. I presume you'll want to see the baby?"

Fran smiled as the thought washed over her. "Of course, thank you, my queen."

"Well, good. I know your brother is keen to have you with them. At least this way, I might have someone other than Lucien to talk to while you're gone. If your journey proves successful, that is."

"You think Prince Taiwo will want to talk to you?" asked Fran playfully.

"Probably not," said Mathilde, "but when has that ever stopped me?"

⚜   ⚜   ⚜

For all that Fran had grown to admire the grandeur of Nivelle, there was some comfort in seeing the cityscape fall away behind her, giving way to quiet countryside. Her childhood had been spent in the woods and fields of the Low Country, long days exploring in nature, her imagination brimming with thoughts of exciting new worlds just around every tall tree or across any meadow. She loved the openness of these landscapes, a sense of freedom that was often stifled by the towering buildings and dark shadows that came with city life. The air here was free of smoke and the stench brought on by humans, and as she pushed her head through the window to look out, a contented smile gave a tug at her cheeks despite her conflicted feelings about her journey.

They were but four in number: Fran, accompanied by the Kanthi envoy, Amare, and two drivers, who rode facing away from them upon a raised seat at the front of the carriage. They had not long left the city, but the horses drew them at some speed across the well-developed track, and Fran revelled in fields of green as far as the eye could see. The road was flat as it carved through the countryside, and as the sky seemed to grow larger above them, the appearance of farmland reminded Fran even more powerfully of home. It seemed that there was no escaping this feeling, this deep yearning for the place from which she had come. To her right, she spotted the first of many sprawling vineyards where the famed Cornessian red was produced. This was Cyrus's favourite, a taste he had inherited from his father, the late King Anselm, though Cyrus hadn't realised it for some time. Fran forced down the loneliness as it crept up to meet her at yet another thought of her brother. She drew back inside of the carriage as her hair began to blow wildly in the breeze.

"It is a beautiful landscape," said Amare softly as Fran fidgeted with her hair. The kind-faced man sat on the bench opposite, and Fran assumed that he must have been watching her as she looked outside. In close quarters, she noticed that he had dimpled cheeks, accentuated by a bright, youthful smile that made it very difficult to estimate his age. His air of wisdom and position of responsibility brought Fran to conclude that he looked well for his years but was likely of a similar age to her parents. A sudden pang of lingering sadness manifested itself in an empty sigh. *Well, the age that they would have been, if things had been different…*

"It has a certain charm," she said eventually, forcing down her feelings. "I'm sure it is nothing compared to your country, though. I have read that your jungles are wild and dangerous and that your beaches are carpeted with fine white sand, like sugar or snow."

Amare laughed. "Well, I am no expert in the substance that you call snow, but I'm sure you will find our islands to your taste. I can't imagine that anyone could be disappointed with the Kanthu Isles. The water is crystal blue, and the sun shines almost without exception. Enjoy this moment, though," he said softly, "for there is no sight more beautiful than home."

Amare sat back in his seat as the carriage continued ever forward. Fran finished tying her hair back and glimpsed out of the window once more, seeing a small boat floating on the river. Traders with goods bound for the city, she knew. Tall reeds swayed in the breeze at the riverbank, and Fran spotted an elegant chateau perched on a hill. It was a perfect moment, and all was silent but for the turning of their wheels, the gravel track churning beneath them as they edged toward the coast. *It is beautiful*, she thought to herself, considering Amare's words. *It could well be the most beautiful place in the world, but it's many miles from Cyrus and his family, and it certainly isn't home…*

"So, what is he like?" asked Fran, fearing that she might be seen as unsociable by Amare. "The prince, that is. Will Mathilde like him?"

The question seemed to pluck Amare from a daze, and his smiled reappeared in an instant. "He is Othelu's second born and most handsome son, the deepest desire of all Kanthi women. He is a strong warrior and will make a wonderful husband with the strength to protect your queen."

Fran nearly choked with laughter at his grand speech. "I think she's quite capable of looking after herself!" Her face turned serious, and her eyebrows narrowed. "Will she *like* him—I mean, to talk to?

The queen is a great woman, and she deserves true happiness, not just a would-be protector or a good alliance."

"Hmm," muttered Amare, pressing a finger thoughtfully to his lips. "I can see that you care for your queen, but you cannot save her from all of life's dangers. I hope she will see good in Taiwo and find love in his arms, but that is not for us to decide. Try not to worry," he continued, with a glint in his eye. "Life is a journey. You must learn to enjoy yours from time to time!"

Fran nodded as she turned away. Green fields had turned to rivers of gold in the distance, and while there was no doubting the envoy's gift with words, talented as he clearly was at turning people's thoughts the way of his own tides, her own mood had blackened with a prickling feeling of doubt. She wouldn't judge the prince before meeting him, but her priority was to protect the queen, and this meant that Fran's own enjoyment would always fall second to duty and vigilance.

⚜ ⚜ ⚜

A sharp jolt drew Fran from her slumber. She reached to massage her aching neck and stretched out the tightness in her shoulders as her eyes adjusted to the low light of a setting sun.

"Welcome back," said Amare with his customary smile. The man looked as fresh as the moment they had left the city, and Fran wondered if he had been awake the entire journey, his back upright against the rear of the carriage. Fran hurriedly wiped a string of saliva from the side of her mouth.

"Where are we?" she asked, her voice slightly slurred. She'd forgotten that Amare was their guest, her thoughts blurred from sleep, and addressed him in a familiar, casual tone that she wouldn't normally use when speaking with an envoy of a neighbouring nation.

"Nearly there now," Amare answered, and as Fran's senses began to return, she heard gulls cawing overhead and smelled sea salt heavy in the air.

She returned to her familiar spot at the window and leaned forward to follow their path with her eyes, leading toward the port town of Clerbonne.

A far cry from Mathilde's lavish villa in Courlliers, in which Cyrus and his family had only recently sought relaxation, Clerbonnne was a working port with a pebble beach at the base of a rocky precipice. A smattering of limestone buildings lined the clifftop, and a steep incline ran down to the quay, where traders hollered back and forth, handing produce between them. It couldn't have been more different to the setting of Cyrus's rejuvenating family jaunt, and Fran felt the flame of responsibility reignite as Amare shifted restlessly in his seat, showing the first signs of fatigue. Fran had not seen the envoy's composure slip even an inch until then, and she wondered if the prospect of sea travel was not to Amare's liking.

"We're here," announced one of the drivers from his position beyond view. From the window Fran saw several well-built, seafaring men approaching their carriage as they slowed to a halt. The men wore dark breeches and light shirts stained from sweat and grime. Their thick forearms spoke to the toil of life at sea, and a colourful collection of piercings and tattoos brought pirates to

Fran's mind. She reached for her sword on instinct, but her grip soon relaxed as she heard the driver jump down to meet their welcome party with some familiarity before opening the carriage door.

"I hope your journey was comfortable," said the driver, reaching to offer her a hand which Fran declined politely. The man had a handsome face, and strands of dark hair protruded from beneath a tricorn hat. "Please make your way to the vessel," he continued, as Fran took her first steps from the carriage. "These gentlemen are here to help with your luggage. Your belongings will be taken directly to your quarters."

Before she knew it, Amare had also clambered from the carriage and was at her side once more. He gave a nod in the direction of the quay, and they both covered the remaining yards to the clifftop before descending a flight of crude steps cut into the rock face that led toward their ship.

"Ah, the freedom of life at sea," said Amare, but his words seemed distant as they arrived at sea level and Fran was overwhelmed by the craft that sat before them. The ship was everything she had imagined from Cyrus's old stories. Comprised of multiple decks, the galleon carried four masts, with a raised stern and a prominent beak from the bow.

"Like the Dirty Dagger," she whispered, giving voice to her favourite of Cyrus's stories. She recalled details from her brother's early adventures with the wily pirate, Roscoe, and though the latter had since retired to the comparatively tame role of Magistrate in Kingsport, Fran surged with excitement at the prospect of an adventure of her own, perhaps one to rival Cyrus and Roscoe's all those years ago.

"Excuse me," came a voice, and Fran stepped away from Amare as a man pushed past with the first of her belongings. The young man moved with admirable urgency as the wooden boards creaked beneath his feet, his pace never slowing as he climbed the gangway and stepped aboard. He was clearly a practised hand at efficiently loading a ship.

"And this ship belongs to your king?" Fran asked Amare. The sun continued to set, now only a sliver of pink light against the darkening sky, and she hugged herself to keep warm in the shadow of the impressive ship.

Amare laughed, and Fran's skin turned suddenly hot with embarrassment. "This ship? Oh no. Our boats are made for short journeys between the islands and through our lagoons. They are long, narrow vessels in hollowed-out trees. This ship—" he repeated, pointing to the galleon before him, "well, this ship belongs to traders from the port of Taboso. King Othelu paid for our passage with gold. Relax," he added, winking. "Here comes the captain now."

Fran turned her gaze as a man appeared on the gangway. He was little more than a silhouette in the fading light until his boots touched down on the wharf. He was still some distance away, but Fran noticed a head of thick, dark, curly hair, and at first glance, he seemed surprisingly young to hold such a lofty title.

"Good Captain," called Amare, spreading his arms out in welcome. Apparently he used such ostentatious greetings with everyone, Fran thought.

The wooden slats beneath them continued to rumble as men ran past with the last of their belongings, and it was only a moment before the captain arrived before them. His skin was tanned from days in the sun, and as he smiled to make his introduction, Fran was left speechless as a strong memory hit her.

"A pleasure to see you again, Princess Francine," said the captain, and Fran remained silent as the young man kissed her softly on the hand. She would normally object to such a show of affection while she was in her duty to the queen, but she was too taken aback to even consider doing so.

"Patch?" she asked, reaching to uncover his name from the thick marshes of her memory. It had been six years since her last visit to Kingsport, and the man before her was some distance from the stringy adolescent that had served at Roscoe's side back then. "Is it really you?" she asked with a developing smile. She reached even further back to their first meeting at Cyrus's coronation, and though she'd found him to be an exciting curiosity, she could never have predicted that sea air would treat him so well.

"You remember," said Patch smiling, his tone warm. "It's Captain Goldhand these days, but you can call me whatever you please."

"Captain Goldhand?" Fran scoffed before grinning. She looked to his hands but found nothing unusual.

"Long story," said Patch, shaking his head.

"You two know each other?" asked Amare with raised eyebrows.

Fran smiled. "You could say that, though it has been some years since we last saw each other. It has also been a while since anyone called me 'Princess Francine,'" Fran continued, standing up taller. "I'm Queen Mathilde's chosen shield now."

"Is that so?" said Patch, his lips pursed, head nodding in a way that suggested he was impressed, if not entirely surprised, by this news. "Well, anyway, I know you've had a long journey already. The roads are fine from the capital, but Amare for conversation…I wouldn't wish it on anyone!" He paused and flashed a mocking smile at Amare, who gave a playful grin in return. Why don't we get you onboard and in the warm?" He finished, moving to wrap a strong arm around Amare's shoulders, embracing him like an old friend as they turned to walk toward the ship. The captain's identity had taken her by surprise, and as she fell into step a couple of paces behind the two men, Fran cringed with embarrassment at her girlish role in their initial exchange. "Captain," she called, keen to add something as she followed along the quay. "Your ship, is this the Dirty Dagger?"

"The Dagger?" he responded turning back with a smile. "Well, that takes me back. No, Roscoe got blind drunk and lost the Dagger in a game of cards years ago. Lucky for us, he won a ship called the Bronze Blade in a drinking contest the same night, and this, well this is our newest vessel, the Silver Sword."

Fran did her very best to maintain a straight face.

"Anyway," said Patch, oblivious to her amusement, "let me show you to your quarters. Time and tide wait for no woman, not even a princess." He paused. "Or the queen's chosen shield."

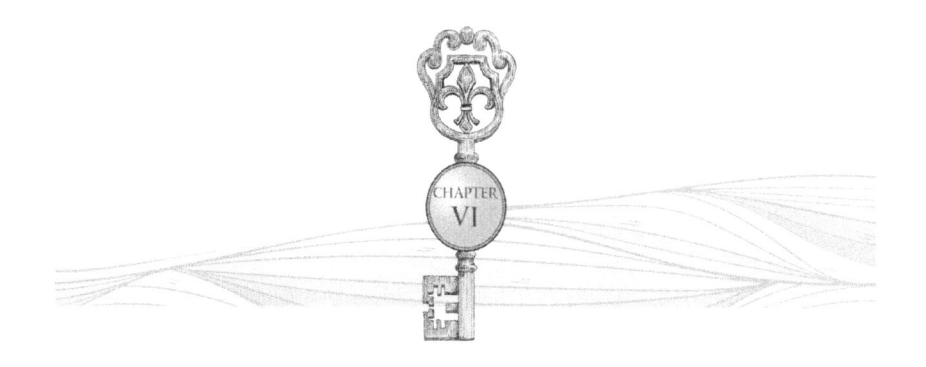

Seth

Seth paced the corridors of Eldred's Keep. His face was expressionless, but his thoughts were overtaken by a nagging frustration. He had returned to the capital with King Cyrus and his family only days previously, their journey back from Nivelle free from incident. The royal family was home safely, and Seth had succeeded in his duty as chosen shield to the king.

So why did he feel so restless?

The grey stonework of the castle was little more than a blur as he continued onward, no particular destination in mind. To either side, myriad doors remained unopened, exciting opportunities forever hidden or perhaps just closed away. As he so often did, Seth thought unbidden of his daughter, taken by King Simeon's men along with her mother, Felicia. His wife and daughter might be long gone, but they would never be forgotten. The castle was a safe space like the thick woollen blanket he used to wrap around Eve at bedtime. He could still hear her giggling as he tucked her in tightly. The blanket had been a happy place where her dreams had come to life. Her world had been full of opportunities until the door slammed upon her, a life ended all too soon. That was not justice, Seth thought fiercely, even a decade later. He smiled sadly and turned his thoughts to Cyrus and Marcia, who were busy living dreams of their own.

But what is it that I dream of these days? Seth wondered, his smile slowly fading as he stopped in his tracks. The king's sister, Francine, had given Seth purpose for a time, the girl's presence like an echo of his own daughter's interminable spirit. Sure, Fran could be sullen and demanding at times, but she had started out as a fish-out-of-water in the capital, and in aiding her to realise her desire to learn swordwork and carve her own path, Seth had seen that he could make a difference.

Long were the days that they had worked together, building her strength and technique until Francine had absorbed all that he had to offer. A lifetime of experience had been distilled into those lessons. Then Mathilde had come calling, and Seth realised what he had known all along: Highcastle was too small to contain a spirit like Fran's. She left, chasing greater dreams elsewhere. Once again, he was all alone.

He fidgeted with his belt, grimacing as the rough material cut into the soft paunch of his ever-expanding waistline. He knew he'd indulged a little during the trip to Courlliers, but his body was testament to years of neglect. Was he even the same man anymore? Where was that sharp, young blacksmith and swordsman who had travelled from village to village, charming women and besting their men in regional contests of swordsmanship? It all seemed a distant memory now, his ambitions faded, his sharpness dulled.

Another pain twinged at him, a little higher this time, on the crest of his stomach. This was a constant reminder of his failings a decade ago. He'd made one simple, seemingly unimportant decision: to leave King Augustus alone with Ferdinand, the Verderan dog, for a handful of moments. A simple decision that had cost Seth his honour and King Augustus his life.

To this day, Seth could hardly believe his luck at the second chance King Cyrus had given him. The king often extolled the virtues of forgiveness, yet scarcely a day had passed in the last ten years without waves of guilt troubling the peaceful sands of Seth's mind. It had been, he knew, an unforgiveable lapse of judgement, one from which there was no return. No way to truly make things right. It was true that Augustus had been reckless, perhaps even dangerous, but the boy had been too young to die. Another life lost to the ambitions of a hateful king and the decisions of a careless man.

He sighed as he walked, somewhat comforted by the thought that at least King Cyrus now sat upon the throne. Seth had witnessed first-hand the courage and bravery of Garrett, who had served as King Anselm's legendary chosen shield. Yet another injustice, Seth thought bitterly, that Seth had survived his own wounds to continue in the role of chosen shield while Garrett had succumbed to death on the battlefield. Seth didn't think he would have been fit to sharpen Garrett's sword, and though he felt strangely jealous every time the king nostalgically mentioned Seth's predecessor, Seth knew that Cyrus deserved better.

The king's kindness still echoed in Seth's mind: *You want to do good, and more than anything, you are keen to learn from your mistakes.*

Deserving or otherwise, Seth had been granted the opportunity to prove himself.

He sighed, pacing toward his private quarters, another privilege that he was yet to earn. These mental spirals were not unusual; Seth's mind was a busy instrument capable of both great and terrible things. His thoughts turned to his very first meeting with the king and how they'd made a daring escape from the hands of Simeon's men. The king had been unaware of his royal lineage at the time, tied hopelessly to a tree at Seth's side after sustaining a knife wound to the back. An unexpected smile formed on Seth's face, accompanied by a brief swell of pride, before it fell once more. Seth had fought bravely that day, using his skilled hands to fashion a lockpick that saw Cyrus set free from what had seemed a dire situation. He considered that day his proudest after the day Eve had been born. But for all he knew, Cyrus might have found a way to escape without Seth, had he not been there. It had been Seth's own foolish desire for revenge that had alerted the guards, after all, putting Cyrus at greater risk during his escape. Perhaps they would all have been better off without him.

King Cyrus had overseen a tenure of great peace and prosperity. The boy Seth had met shackled to a tree had grown into a historic king loved by his people, and for very good reason. It sometimes seemed there wasn't a man in the land who would see King Cyrus come to harm. This was folly, of course. Seth knew that there would always be someone who would yearn to seize power. While Seth was glad that no hint of harm had yet reached his beloved king, he was still desperate for a chance to make good on

Cyrus's faith in him. The absence of an opportunity left him feeling strangely and selfishly redundant. He hated himself for even thinking it, knowing a chosen shield should be content with the continued safety of his king.

He arrived at the door of his chambers, closed his eyes, and let his head rest gently against the ornate wooden door. He had no reason to resent the king, but Seth felt as though his own position was an act of charity, another example of King Cyrus's unyielding selflessness, pity for a man who had failed to shield himself, let alone another.

What if Cyrus had judged things wrong and would be better off without him? Maybe he'd be doing the king a favour by leaving, by allowing Cyrus to find a better, worthier chosen shield. It had been a while since Seth had entertained the thought, but his head suddenly swam with an ocean of new possibilities. Perhaps it really *was* for the best that he should walk away and pursue dreams of his own, or at least figure out what his own dreams might be. He wasn't as quick as he once was, but he had experience on his side that would make him a formidable competitor with a blade. His mind came alive at the prospect. He would have to start small. He'd heard of vicious, unsanctioned knife fights in poorer areas of the city, dangerous contests that captured the imagination of the lower classes. They were risky, potentially fatal, but how he longed for the roar of the crowd! He found his blood racing at the thought, a savage grin crossing his face for the first time in years. It all became clear to him in that moment. He would use these fights to flatten his curves and sharpen his edges. He would make a new name for himself and then travel to compete in the Low Country, perhaps in the former Auldhaven or even farther afield in Verdera, where he still had some scores to settle.

With his new ideas, Seth felt alive again, a newfound purpose burning inside him with an intensity he thought he had forgotten. He saw it all play out in his mind, glorious and dangerous, before puffing out his cheeks with another sigh as he bumped his forehead stiffly against the doorframe to bring himself back to reality. What was he thinking? He wasn't a young man anymore, however much he might like to think otherwise. The fantasy had been nice while it lasted, but Seth knew that no number of petty victories would bring Augustus back to life or restore Seth's honour. He felt embarrassed at his moment of weakness and foolish self-pity. He would never let himself be accused of desertion. He would remain in his post at the service of the king. The fire inside of him dwindled in acceptance that he would rather face a pitiful life of anonymity, forgotten in the stories told around campfires, than betray the faith of yet another king to whom he was sworn. A king whose faith he would always stand ready to repay. There were many in far worse positions than he, he reasoned. These peaceful times were a blessing, and he only wished that they had come about sooner.

He straightened himself and cleared his throat. As he reached for the door handle, the voice in his head added in a whisper, *Never forget how lucky you are.*

⚜   ⚜   ⚜

Seth had just gotten comfortable in his favourite armchair by the window when an enthusiastic knock sounded at the door. He sprang to his feet, years of vigilance yet unhindered by his inflated frame.

"Yes, what is it?" he called, opening the door to find a fresh-faced squire, his cheeks pink and his brow glistening with perspiration.

"I—"

"I'm sorry, can I help you?" Seth said in a kinder voice, correcting his unnecessarily abrupt tone. He could see in the boy's wide eyes that he was nervous. There was no doubt that the fire still burned inside of Seth, however deep down, and he surprised himself by seeing how quickly it could be brought to the surface. He wondered what the squire had come to tell him. Was this the call to action Seth had been waiting for?

"The king sent me," the boy stuttered eventually, pushing his wispy blonde fringe out of his eyes. "He says he needs you, now!"

Seth's mind unfurled with possibilities. *Is the king in danger? Perhaps there is some new frontier to explore?* Cyrus had often stated his intention to travel to the White Lands in the south, where vast ice sheets were punctuated by jagged mountains and tribes worshipped monstrous snow bears. Already, Seth's imagination was racing again, imagining himself climbing up sheer walls to icy peaks in aid of his king.

"Where is he?" he asked excitedly. It had to be the White Lands, he told himself, and his grin broadened at the prospect of travel, adventure, danger.

"The throne room, sir," said the squire nervously, his voice barely perceptible as Seth pushed past him to charge through the castle.

There was a newfound spring in his step, similar to the rush he had felt when thinking of his fantasy life only moments before. He puffed out his chest and was surprised to feel a subtle give in his beltline, as though the very possibility of adventure had stripped away the weight of complacency. He moved quickly, his mind already fixating on luggage—what would Seth and the king need to bring with them on this adventure? This would be no pleasure trip, like their time in Courlliers; he would need his sword, his knives, and perhaps it was even time to forge that hand-axe Seth had long coveted. Would he have time before they set out?

It seemed no time at all before he arrived at the throne room, frantic as his thoughts had been. Two guards stepped aside, raising halberds to allow Seth entry.

"You needed to see me, my king?" he said, each word brimming with enthusiasm. He expected to find Cyrus pacing impatiently, perhaps flanked by Thaddeus, the old man whose counsel served as the very wheel to steer the king in matters of state. At the very least, Seth had expected to see young prince Leo, a boy full of mischief and curiosity in equal measure. But to his surprise, none were present except for the king, Queen Marcia, and someone else, a woman Seth didn't know who appeared similar in age to Seth himself.

"Ah, Seth. Yes, come in, there's someone I'd like you to meet."

Seth's eyes narrowed as he approached the quiet gathering. King Cyrus was not upon his throne. Instead, he stood at the foot of Isidore's Chair with the others. On closer inspection, Seth found the unknown woman to be of kind, if unremarkable, appearance.

She was dressed in a practical, earthy green dress, and her hair was tied in a tight, purposeful way.

"This is Lillian," the king continued, and Seth corrected his posture, suddenly conscious of his appraising gaze.

"A pleasure to meet you," he said in a polite tone.

"And you," came Lillian's reply. She had a twinkle in her eye that lit up her plain appearance, and Seth couldn't help but smile before turning his attention back to the king, his eyes questioning.

"It will not be long now until three becomes four," Cyrus continued, nodding at Queen Marcia's abdomen. "The trip to Courlliers was a much-needed respite, but the queen is now facing the late stages of her pregnancy. You know the troublesome scale of Eldred's Keep as well as anyone," he added, gesturing around the echoing expanse of the throne room.

Seth nodded slowly in response, trying to piece together where this conversation might be leading. Though Seth's imaginings of adventures in the White Lands were becoming increasingly improbable, he was no closer to surmising the king's true reason for summoning him.

"Prince Leo's birth was not easy for the queen," Cyrus began again, "and I would not see her suffer any more than is necessary. Lillian will be joining our household to assist with Marcia's needs in the coming weeks. She will be an important member of our extended family, and it is vital that she is brought up to speed as quickly as possible."

He paused to place a hand upon Seth's shoulder. "The castle is a confusing place to new arrivals, but I thought…" He paused again to remove his hand and place it in Queen Marcia's. "*We* thought you could help Lillian to settle in. Show her around the castle a little, help her to help us. It's going to be a very busy time, and you'll be seeing a lot of each other."

The king ended with a smile, and Seth returned the gesture out of courtesy.

Just another example of the king's unyielding selflessness, he thought, chuckling to himself before stepping forward to accept the request graciously. It seemed that King Cyrus fancied himself as a matchmaker now, and the aim of his unconventional request was not lost on Seth, no stranger to the king's subtle manoeuvrings after many years of close service.

"It would be my honour," Seth added, nodding courteously in Lillian's direction.

"Just as I thought," said the king, gesturing to the exit with a wry smile.

Lillian cleared her throat as she followed Seth back towards the great doors, moving out of earshot of Cyrus and Marcia. "You're Seth the Blacksmith, aren't you?" she asked timidly.

Seth nodded. He certainly had been, once upon a time.

"I thought so," Lillian continued. "And a great swordsman too, if I remember rightly. You competed against my late husband before the war. It was just an exhibition, but I remember him telling me that you were the best he'd ever fought. 'Lightning fast, and deadly with a blade!'" She chortled as she attempted to mimic her husband's voice. "It's an honour to finally meet you," she finished with a glint in her eye.

Seth stopped to smile back at her, lost for words at her enthusiasm. *Would a peaceful life in the castle really be so bad after all?*

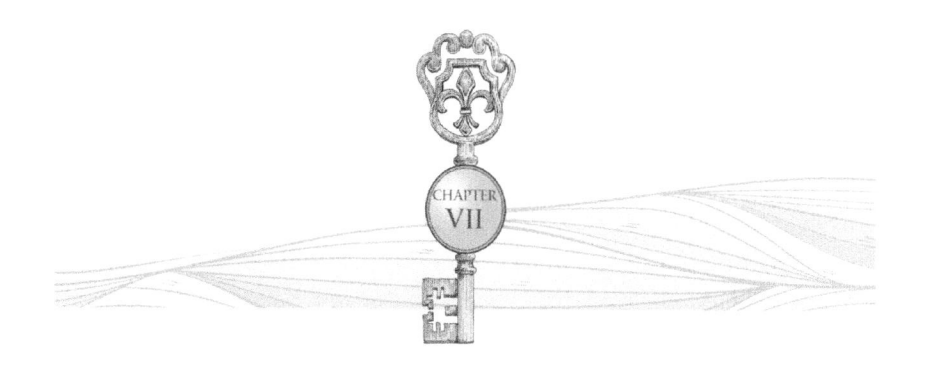

Francine

Fran's first two days onboard the Silver Sword had passed without incident. The ship was a fine vessel, and the weather was clear, barely a cloud in the sky. For Fran's part, she did her best to mix with the colourful crew, and for the most part, she found that she was well received. She was the only woman onboard, perhaps the only woman the crew had ever travelled with. But Fran knew she was much more than that and would not be taken for some damsel. She was a skilled warrior and served as chosen shield to a powerful queen. Fran had learned much from her experience watching Mathilde do battle with her council in Nivelle. The crew of the Silver Sword would take Fran seriously; she would make sure of it.

Patch had told Fran and Amare that the journey would take four days with a good wind, and life onboard quickly fell to its own routine. While Fran was glad to have her own space—a cosy den of dark oak with a bunk, a desk, and a small porthole—she felt drawn out of her private quarters to the bustling upper decks, where it seemed everyone had a part to play.

It was a truly impressive operation all told, the workforce onboard somewhat surprisingly reminding Fran of Mathilde's pastime for beekeeping back in Nivelle. The crewmembers seemed to buzz about the place with a sense of undeniable purpose, and whether scrubbing the decks or arranging the sails, there was no place for idle hands as their vessel moved ever forward toward the Kanthu Isles. He may have been the queen bee in Fran's analogy, but it soon became clear that Captain Goldhand, as the men all called him, was no joke. The ship was akin to a floating castle, yet Patch was somehow always visible, driving his men forward, laughing with them during quiet moments, and putting his own calloused hands to work when needed.

Fran felt like a bit of a spare part but made sure to help where she could. Though skilled as a warrior, she soon conceded that successful seafaring required a very different set skills that seemed to be beyond her learning in such a short space of time. Fortunately, there was no shortage of manual tasks to keep her busy, and she was often called upon as an extra set of eyes on lookout. The tasks were simple and a little tedious, but they were preferable to her time assisting the ship's cook or scrubbing the deck as part of cleaning duty. Fran was keen to be regarded as a team player, but she feared that certain tasks were less likely to help her achieve her desired standing among the crew.

Life at sea was not one that Fran had ever considered, so she was surprised to find that it felt both natural and alluring. There was an undeniable freedom to be found in the never-ending horizon and an infectious quality to the camaraderie of their crew.

And there was no shortage of personality onboard. Fran mostly knew her compatriots by face alone. At their worst, they were a spitting, smoking cloud of body-odour. Yet, as time wore on, she found herself warming to their yellow smiles and crass songs, their simplicity a refreshing change after life at court. It seemed that she was already beginning to find her place onboard, and Fran felt increasingly welcome by all except their quartermaster, a grizzled old buccaneer that the crew called Teeth, so named for his mouth of gold—an ominous moniker if Fran had ever heard one.

The quartermaster was Patch's right-hand man, and his responsibilities included food and supplies, though Teeth's remit also extended to issues of justice and punishment onboard. It seemed obvious to Fran which duties the old man favoured. His clear, if unfounded, vendetta toward Fran was becoming something of a hobby for him.

She'd known his type before, of course. The clothes were different, but behind his eyes, Teeth held the same contempt for her that Fran had come to know in Clement and the rest of his stooges back in the capital.

"Out of the way girl!" he had yelled as the ship rolled in tall waves on their first day of sailing.

"I—" Fran's feeble reply still rankled her a day later. Teeth's contemptuous emphasis on the word "girl" was not lost on her, but Fran was more cutting with a sword than with words. She'd been gathering rope at the time, and stood mouth wide, searching for a suitable response as some of the crew watched on and Teeth snarled back at her.

"I, what?" he had asked, face scrunched in a look of revulsion. "I'll tell you what you are: a hindrance, always in the way. Wherever I look, you're there, playing your silly little pirate fantasy. Well, let me tell you…" Red-faced, he had pointed an accusatory finger angrily in Fran's direction. "You aren't in the safety of your pretty palace now, *girl*. This isn't a game. It's a matter of life or death, and the sooner we get to Taboso, the better!"

That Teeth had found the time to scold her so thoroughly—for what, she still wasn't exactly sure—given their present danger amazed Fran. She kept this to herself, of course, dumbfounded by the quartermaster's behaviour and lack of respect. Didn't he realise that he had no authority over her? She wondered if that was the core of the problem after all. In all other matters, his command was absolute. He was second only to Patch, and Teeth held the crew in the palm of his hand.

But Fran was nothing if not stubborn, and the harder she applied herself, the further she seemed to fall from his favour. The quartermaster mirrored his captain's ability to appear unexpectedly, and Fran felt as though she were walking on eggshells as she adapted to life at sea, at least when Teeth was around.

Fran sometimes considered simply retreating to her cabin and bolting the door shut to avoid Teeth and his wrath. It seemed that there was no pleasing her detractor, and she wondered what she stood to gain by pleasing him anyway. At the root of it, Fran liked to be liked, having always taken great pleasure in winning people over, but the issue with Teeth was nothing more than a distraction from the task at hand: retrieving and assessing the Kanthi prince. The weight of the responsibility of Mathilde's prospective marriage still sat heavily on Fran's shoulders, and though she had no idea what Prince Taiwo looked like, her thoughts often turned toward him. What kind of man should she expect to be waiting for her at the end of the voyage?

Fran's earlier suspicions had been realised; the Kanthi envoy, Amare, had been largely absent from day-to-day activities since they had come aboard the Silver Sword due to debilitating seasickness, and though Fran had a head full of questions, she felt somewhat relieved that she didn't have to bear his presence around the clock.

Instead, Fran found her days rather pleasingly punctuated by brief moments shared with Patch. It all seemed so very private and personal at first: a joke here, a glance there. She was acutely aware of Teeth's growing disapproval but found herself unable to resist seeking Patch out at every opportunity. Years ago, when Fran was only a girl, Cyrus had given her a small silver mirror, and she found herself consulting its reflective surface more often than she ever had to check her appearance, trying fruitlessly to tame her unruly hair.

It came as no surprise, really, when the wolf-whistling began. Their catcalling was all done in good spirit as far as Fran was concerned, and no one crossed the invisible line into rudeness or complete impropriety. Fran, who typically stood in the shadow of a beautiful and impressive queen, was not used to getting this sort of attention. Still, her efforts were only meant for one.

She couldn't help but wonder if Patch was prone to similar thoughts. She noticed one day that he removed his linen shirt in the midday sun, his muscular torso a welcome distraction, and she found herself thinking that perhaps he had done so for her benefit. After a few seconds spent appraising the captain, however, she forced her attention elsewhere, knowing that standing around staring at Patch was unlikely to earn her any lenience from Teeth.

She may have just been overthinking things, but Fran began to worry that the attention she was paying Patch had become all too obvious and the attention she was getting from the crew had become somewhat embarrassing. Her journey was simply a means to an end, she reminded herself, and it had always been her intention to blend in with the crew. It had certainly started well, with Fran making great strides to integrate herself into life onboard. But when, on the afternoon of her second day onboard, she found herself wrapped in Patch's arms as he stood behind her, demonstrating the proper technique with which to scrub the wooden deck clean with a mop, her hard work was soon washed away, jeers and wolf-whistles ringing in from around them. This was everything that she had hoped to avoid.

"That's it, get your woman working!" called Redbeard, the appropriately named boatswain, drawing laughter from his peers.

Fran had invited Patch's instructions with enthusiasm, but as ridicule sounded out, her cheeks flushed pink, and she was quick to pull away. This had only served to draw further wisecracks, and though Fran had come to appreciate the banter onboard, she felt she needed to take a step back to avoid looking overly keen at best or, at worst, pathetic.

The evenings, however, were very different. After a day's work, Fran was relieved to retire to her cabin, where she'd find a very welcome pail of hot water and small vials of scented oils. She would fuss with the clothes in her trunk and curse herself for leaving far better options behind before joining the captain in his quarters for drinks with Patch and Teeth. Despite the quartermaster's aggravated feelings toward her during the working hours, even Teeth was courteous during these evenings. The three of them would while the time away sipping rum or bitter wine, gathered around Patch's gnarled old desk, before the old man retired for the day. This felt like Fran's cue to leave, yet the captain's wry smile suggested otherwise each evening, and the two of them had spent a couple of long nights talking, laughing, and recalling old times. It was only reluctantly that Fran would retire to her cosy bunk, but she did so in the knowledge that if she didn't, neither she nor Patch would have the energy to face the next day.

⚜ ⚜ ⚜

Fran's eyes jerked open to the unmistakeable sound of fists beating on her doors.

"You in there, girl?" called a voice Fran thought belonged to Redbeard. Fran had hoped by now that the crew might respect her a bit more; sure, it was only her third day onboard, but she thought that by now they might not resort to banging crudely on the door to wake her up. And at the very least, she might have expected them to use her name!

"Yes, yes," she grumbled, stumbling out of bed to make herself decent. She hadn't expected breakfast in bed by any means, but a glance out of her porthole window told her that the sun was still rising, and she had no official duties, after all. Was it really necessary to rouse her at this hour?

Redbeard continued to bang on the door, calling for her. "Hang on," she added irritably, pulling on a jacket. Redbeard was hardly the most eloquent, but Fran's eyes still narrowed at the boatswain's tone and the unexpected nature of his wake-up call.

After a few clumsy moments, she finally opened the door. "And a good morning to you too!" she ventured, hoping to make a joke. It was Redbeard outside of her door as expected, but her quip failed to provoke the reaction she had sought.

"You're needed up on deck," said the leathery old seaman, no lilt of humour to be found in his voice. "Teeth wants to see you." The five words Fran had dreaded most.

Fran's heart sank, and her brain reached for any idea as to what she could have done to draw Teeth's ire this time. The quartermaster had been perfectly amiable in the captain's quarters only hours before, yet his long memory for previous indiscretions reminded her uncannily of Mathilde's.

"Right now?" she asked, attempting to buy time, but when Redbeard's face remained stern and unmoving, Fran stepped forward to join him, closing the door behind her.

The ship was uncharacteristically quiet as they made their way onto the main deck. It was still early, but Fran had expected to encounter the normal hubbub, and her nerves only worsened to find the crew gathered in anticipation of her arrival. A quick glance around told her that Patch was nowhere to be seen.

"Thank you, Redbeard," said Teeth, stepping forward to greet them. The rest of the group remained silent. "How nice of you to join us," Teeth continued, a devious look in his eye. "I should have known you'd be trouble, but this? You'll be the death of us!"

Fran stepped back, her narrowed eyes darting around quizzically as the crew hollered in support of the quartermaster's baffling allegations. "What do you mean?" she asked, realising that she'd left her sword behind in her haste. "I wish no harm on any of you. I just want—"

"I don't care what you want," Teeth interjected, and Fran bumped into Redbeard as Teeth stepped forward to snarl in her face, forcing her backwards. "Your words offer little protection against the curse," he continued menacingly. "You might be the queen's girl, but I will not put my men at risk!"

At these words, Fran's breathing steadied, and it was all she could do to stop herself from laughing. "A curse?" she asked sceptically.

"Yes, a curse," snapped Teeth, and to her dismay, Fran noticed that no one else was laughing. She didn't say anything but instead looked around at all of them, questions in her eyes. Her heart sank. With no sign of Patch or Amare, she was on her own.

"It's the food," said Redbeard, speaking out from behind her. "Three days into the journey, and our food has all turned rotten. I've never seen such luck. It's just not natural."

Fran realised immediately that the situation was serious, all traces of laughter fully faded from her face. Ridiculous as the idea of a curse was, she knew fear to be a dangerous kindling, and when she looked to the chef for even a hint of reassurance, the large old man turned his face away from her as though he couldn't bear to look at her.

"But this is madness," Fran pleaded desperately, hands raised as though poised to reason with the crew. "How could the food supply problems have anything to do with me? I've hardly visited the storeroom or the galley, and when I did, it was only to help."

Teeth scoffed, "Spreading your pestilence, more like. Some of the men have taken ill already. We checked supplies first thing this morning. The fruit is brown and full of maggots, and the meat is turning putrid. We've been able to salvage a share of our inventory, but we'll yet suffer for this. It's a bad omen is what it is. The situation has already gone too far."

Fran's body seized up as two of the crew reached for their knives, and she noticed a third carrying a length of heavy rope. She knew she had to think fast, but with her only weapon back in her quarters, she wasn't sure what she should do, sure that if she called out for help from either Patch or Amare, she would be quickly silenced. Instead, she felt frozen, like the many deer who had roamed outside of Corhollow when she was a girl. Those deer had always fallen stock-still in the split seconds before her brother, Edgar, had let loose his arrows, and Fran felt as though she were in a similar predicament now. It came as no surprise that Teeth had sought to hurt or humiliate her, but a curse? It seemed she had underestimated the quartermaster, who seemed intent on blaming her for their every misfortune. She looked around at the crew, who gazed back at her blankly or whose eyes wandered to avoid her stare.

Cowards, she thought, reflecting on her efforts to befriend them. She had wanted them to respect her, and yet it seemed that respect came second to fear. Nobody, it seemed, knew that better than Teeth.

"I'm sorry," Teeth continued, though he didn't sound sorry in the slightest. "I take no joy in this, but there are many legends that warn against the perils of carrying women to sea. In truth, I should have seen it sooner. It is my job to secure safe passage for the crew after all." His words were like those of someone tasked with an unfortunate job, like putting down a family pet, but the relish with which he spoke betrayed him. Then, no longer able to maintain his apologetic pretence, he snapped, "Anyway, enough of this talk. Tie her up, boys. Let the captain decide what will become of her."

Fran's instincts kicked in as her first attacker rushed to meet her. He was of an imposing build, but Fran deftly turned his wrist, sending his knife skidding across the deck as the man cried out in pain. His face was full of surprise, but Fran wasted no time in landing a crunching fist on the bridge of his nose. Blood exploded up her sleeve, and though her knuckle throbbed from the impact, she moved quickly to evade an arching fist from a second assailant, slamming a shoulder into the man's chest, folding his body in two. In the previous days, she had begun to learn faces and names, but in that moment, Fran couldn't have said who any of these men were. She knew only to defend herself.

Let the captain decide what will become of her, she recalled as her mind raced to catch up. Patch would surely see sense, but he was still nowhere to be seen, and she needed to survive the immediate threat until he showed up. Knives *were* knives after all, and Teeth had shown himself to be dangerously unpredictable.

She considered moving to reclaim the discarded knife but knew that would only serve to escalate matters. Her every instinct told her to fight, but she would still have to travel among these men for at least another day, assuming she was alive to do so. It was bad enough that they suspected her of cursing them without also killing their crewmates in plain view. *I have to buy myself some time*, she thought. *The time for respect has passed. Let them fear me instead.*

She knew that none of these men would be a match for her, and a smile tugged at her lips as, for the first time since coming onboard, she found her hands set to a task they knew only too well. She had studied under some of the finest warriors in the

Quadripartite. Her years of training with Seth and Thaddeus in Highcastle before Mathilde's tutelage in Nivelle seemed to flash before her eyes as she dodged time and time again. The third man advanced on her with an apprehension the other two had lacked, and from the corner of her eye, Fran noticed Amare appear on deck, beyond the sight of the baying crowd. The envoy had likely been roused from his cabin, his refuge during his seasick days. In that moment, his eyes were wide, though he stayed silent, not attracting notice. He turned quickly to descend belowdecks, and Fran silently hoped he would return with Patch in tow.

"Well, come on!" she called out, encouraging her attacker, the man who had initially carried the rope, toward her in an act of bravado. He had long since dropped her intended restraints, and though his fists were tightly clenched, he remained hesitant. Fran used the time to turn and drop the second of her enemies with a vicious knee to the head. For all of Teeth's encouragement, it seemed none of the other crewmembers were prepared to join the melee. The look of dejection on Teeth's face told Fran that she was winning, and she laughed as she bared her teeth to hiss at the final combatant, giving over to an almost animalistic side that came with the territory of doing battle.

"Get her, you fool," Teeth chided. "What are you waiting for?"

As Teeth's insults became increasingly more abusive, the man flinched against these words. His bald head had dropped, as if regretting his decision to face Fran down in the first place, but he continued to advance, if only to save face. Fran wondered if she should take it easy on him, but Patch was still nowhere to be seen. Like her opponent, she had little choice. She'd spent two long days working to show the crew that she was not weak. She had their attention now, and she wasn't going to waste it.

A distant memory suddenly echoed in her mind. Wendell's words, from their time together in Highcastle. "Earn their attention," he had said to her, back before she knew how to wield a sword but desperately wanted to learn. Wendell had turned out to be a liar, one who had conspired against her family nonetheless, but Fran knew his advice to her had been sound. For the first time in a long time, she thought with frustration about Wendell's betrayal, and her rising temper at the men onboard swelled uncontrollably. For better or worse, her instincts took over. Fran closed her eyes, took a deep breath, and let her hands go free.

Her attack was like lightning, and the bald man stood stunned as Fran launched an uppercut to rattle his jaw. He offered a clumsy counterpunch, but Fran was frighteningly fast, dodging to land a second blow to his neck, sending him stumbling away as his breath caught in his throat, coming out in ragged gasps and coughs. The end was in sight now, but Fran knew better than to leave anything to chance. The man was off-balance, and she leapt to wrap her arms and legs around him. His eyes were wide with fear, but this was no time for mercy, and Fran gave a savage headbutt to claim her second broken nose of the day.

The man toppled like a felled tree, his body landing hard on the deck to break her fall. His eyes were already rolling in his head, but Fran needed to teach him a lesson. She'd show them all what she was capable of.

Memories came flooding in as her fists beat down, opening fresh wounds in the man's face. She thought back to her first kill in Highcastle, the would-be assassin who had been sent to end

Adaline's life. Fran had been so young and so scared, but her instincts had made her act and attack to save Adaline's life. The same approach was serving her well today, albeit in pursuit of saving her own skin.

Her fists continued moving of their own accord, the voices of the crew a distant blur as her hands, swollen beyond recognition and entirely numb, became coated in blood. Rough hands grabbed her shoulders unexpectedly, and Fran lashed out, almost feral, as an almighty yell barrelled out of her chest. Despite her protestations, she was finally pulled away by whoever had appeared behind her. Her hands swiped at the air before thick forearms drew tight around her, and her legs flailed as she was lifted effortlessly from the ground. She froze for a moment, and her eyes widened at the bloodied mess that she had created. She let her arms fall limp in her futile struggle, and as the red haze began to clear, she noticed the crew parting before her, Patch finally appearing among them with Amare at his side.

"Calm down, just calm down," said Redbeard, his grip loosening as he spoke.

Before she knew it, Fran was back on her feet. An innate feeling of embarrassment surfaced briefly before subsiding to the incontrovertible truth: Teeth was the aggressor here. Fran had only ever defended herself. Her fate rested in the captain's hands now, though, and she hoped he'd see sense.

"What in the hell is going on here?" he asked, eyes narrowed as Fran's defeated enemies groaned at her feet.

"It's the girl," said Teeth, stepping forward predictably, no hint of shame in his face. "There's a curse upon us, and when we tried to ask her about it, she attacked my men like a thing possessed!"

"He's lying," came Fran's instinctive reply, but Patch raised a hand to silence them all. He chewed his thumbnail as he considered the mayhem before him, looking back and forth from Fran's bloodied form to the men she had decimated.

"A curse, you say?" he said finally, looking at Teeth. "On what basis was Francine assumed to be the cause for this curse, and why wasn't I informed?"

"I'm sorry, Captain," said the quartermaster pleadingly. "It's our food. The meat and veg has turned rotten already. It was clearly the work of a curse, a powerful one at that. I only meant to rid us of our misfortune."

"By that you mean our guest, Francine?"

"Well, yes, but—"

"But what, quartermaster?" Patch asked, cutting him short. "I hold no fear in curses and superstition. In fact, I find that most things are better understood with a little common sense. I presume you bought our produce from the Cornessian, Arnaud, as instructed?"

"Well, not exactly—"

"So, no then?" Patch snarled, his patience disappearing before their eyes. Fran watched on in silence, her breath returning to normal as her eyes shifted between the two men. Patch continued, "To be clear, Quartermaster, you are not only guilty of disobeying a direct order from your captain, but in doing so, you have endangered the life of the crew and the wellbeing of our guest. A guest, I might add, of the very man who commissioned our passage."

Perhaps for the first time, Teeth seemed lost for words.

"And to top it all off," Patch continued, stepping forward to jab a finger at the older man's chest, "you had the gall to pursue this folly behind your captain's back, waking our guest at the break of dawn to avoid my detection. Well, that," he said, turning abruptly away, "*that* is mutinous behaviour if I've ever seen it. Redbeard, remind me how I am supposed to punish this type of transgression?"

"Well sir, you've got flogging, marooning, dunking, the plank…"

"Correct," Patch interjected, halting the boatswain's list and fixing Teeth with a deathly stare. "You are a valuable member of my crew, Quartermaster, but that will only buy you so much favour. If it isn't clear already, let me tell you that there will be no second chances. I am the captain around here, and yours was a very serious error of judgement, one that will not go without consequence. The rope…" he snapped, pointing to the length of thick cord that had been intended for Fran. "You intended to bind our guest presumably?" He did not wait for Teeth to reply. "I must thank you, then, for helping me determine your punishment. You will spend the remainder of our journey belowdecks in irons."

Teeth nodded silently, apparently still lost for words. It was far less than he deserved to Fran's mind, but Patch had the unenviable task of maintaining harmony among the crew or else risk all out mutiny. Teeth, she supposed, was an experienced crewmember who would be hard to replace. The damage to his reputation would be perhaps the most severe consequence of all.

"But before that," Patch continued, with Teeth's gaze cast down toward his feet, his shoulders slouched dejectedly. "You will apologise to our guest for the error of your judgement. The rest of you, clean yourselves up."

Just as the others began to make their way silently away from the scene, Patch added, for all to hear, "By the way, Quartermaster, you're on half rations until Taboso. I expect to see your takings from the food budget returned within the day."

Chapter VIII

Locke

"Arms up," Locke ordered without enthusiasm. Both prisoners raised their arms, and Boyd began the handover inspection that signified the end of his shift. Walt could have been concealing a giant axe for all that Locke cared in that moment. Locke's eyes were puffy, his head was sore, and he'd barely slept, his thoughts overtaken by the incident with his father the night before.

What was he thinking? Locke asked himself silently. He'd slipped past Grace on his way to work that morning, shame burning in his chest, threatening to make him heave. He considered last night's events, approaching the situation from all angles. Perhaps his father's intentions were entirely innocent. Locke *had* been lonely, after all. Maybe this was his father's way of trying to help.

Locke had moved to the city to make a name for himself and prove his independence. He'd tried his best, with the weight of his father's expectations resting heavy upon his shoulders. He was sure he hadn't revealed his true identity to anyone along the way, but he'd need to be more careful around Boyd in future. For whatever reason, it seemed that Locke's distrustful colleague had found reason to doubt him. Boyd's questions were yet to reveal anything of interest, but news of the prison master's clandestine enquiries had made one thing very clear: Locke's father had eyes and ears everywhere.

"All done," said Boyd, smiling as he stepped from the cell to slam the door behind him. "What's wrong with you today?" he asked, but before Locke could even try to come up with an answer, Boyd shook his head in disbelief. "We get the most infamous brigand in years, the attention of the nobility, and you're dragging yourself around like the walking dead. Seems my instinct was right about you, *newcomer*." Locke's eyes widened. "You're just another jumped up country boy with none of the backbone required to succeed in a job like this."

Locke breathed a sigh of relief as Boyd secured the cell, clicking the lock shut, and then handed Locke the keys.

Boyd continued, "Keep your focus today. People are watching."

Locke folded into his chair as Boyd left, a spring in his step as he headed out of the grimy prison and back into the world outside. It looked like Boyd's suspicion had turned to scorn. Would Locke's incompetence actually pay off? He shuffled in his chair with a grimace of discomfort. His back was already killing him, and the day had only just begun.

⚜ ⚜ ⚜

Despite what it might look like to an outsider, it hadn't been easy growing up in Ardlyn Keep. As a child, it hadn't taken Locke long to realise that his brother was taller, faster, stronger, and more handsome than he was. He accepted the fair criticisms that came from his father, a decorated war hero, along with the unfair ones. He learned at an early age to swallow his pride. He was far from perfect and was often reminded of that fact. Looking back, he hoped that the experience had hardened him and that he had become, if nothing else, resilient.

Then he met Finnian.

"You really are in a mood, aren't you?" the prisoner asked, the umpteenth iteration of the same question he'd been asking all day.

Locke rolled his eyes yet again, turning in his seat to face the other direction, adamant as he was not to give Finnian the time of day. Besides the heavy wooden door, Walt and Finnian's cell comprised of floor-to-ceiling iron bars. In theory, it meant that Locke could monitor the cellmates without obstruction. In practice, it meant long hours of the tiresome brigand's insolent questions, the man's cocksure face pressed to the gaps between the bars.

"Oi, Locke, did you hear me?"

"That's *Prison Master* Locke to you!" Locke snarled, still not looking at Finnian.

The brigand laughed, and Walt remained quiet in his corner. "Sorry, *Prison Master Locke*," he said, voice laced with impertinence.

"I assumed we were disregarding good manners, what with you ignoring me all morning!"

"Well, think again," Locke answered sternly, finally turning toward Finnian, his face like thunder. "My mood is none of your business, nor am I obligated to show you any politeness whatsoever. Now, quieten down in there."

Finnian scratched his chin wordlessly, making no effort to conceal the mischief on his face. Locke could tell the brigand was planning his next words, so he lowered his hands to feel for his wooden baton, fingertips resting upon the handle in preparation for whatever was about to come out of Finnian's mouth.

"It's just," Finnian started tentatively, "don't get me wrong, you're a grouchy bastard at the best of times, but you're a right misery today. The way I see it is that we're stuck here together. Might as well share a bit of conversation. You know, lighten the mood." He tilted his head to one side and gave an infuriating grin.

"I'm fine," Locke spat in an attempt convince himself as much as anyone else. "It was just a rough night. I don't want to talk about it, and I won't be needing any pity from you."

Finnian scoffed, seemingly unperturbed. "Pity, eh? Now you've got my attention. Let's see, you've got a job. I know you hate Boyd, but you don't see much of each other, so it can't be that…" He had scrunched his mouth to one side and tapped his cheek with a single finger, as though wracking his brains.

"Finnian…" Locke said with a warning growl.

"You're not much of a looker, but you seem healthy enough, so I'm assuming that isn't it."

"I'm warning you, inmate." Locke's fist clenched more tightly around his baton.

"Family problems, perhaps? Am I getting warm yet?"

Locke swallowed but said nothing.

Finnian went on relentlessly, "It could be a girl, but I don't think you've got it in you. To tell the truth, I'm not sure you even favour girls, the way your fingers linger in my pockets during handover…"

Locke's patience snapped, and he sprang from his seat to grab Finnian by the collar of his shirt, tearing the filthy material as he did so.

"I told you to stop," Locke yelled, their noses nearly touching.

Finnian's expression turned scornful. "I'd take your hands off me if I were you. You don't know who you're messing with, boy."

Locke already regretted his impatience with Finnian. He wanted to step back and turn away, but he knew he needed to earn the brigand's respect, lest his days be condemned to the same infuriating questions. "I know exactly who you are, inmate," he started with confidence, Finnian's shirt crumpled in his ever-tightening grip. "You're a low life, murderous thief who'd rather spill blood and steal from good people than work to earn an honest wage of his own."

"You know nothing," came Finnian's reply, and his expression soured, suggesting that Locke had managed to hit a nerve at last.

Locke smiled, feeling buoyed by Finnian's discomfort. "Oh, I know plenty. I know that you're just another hateful bit of scum from the provinces. Notorious brigand?" He scoffed as he looked down his nose at Finnian. "You attacked carriages, killed innocent people, and stole from them. Oh, you've earned yourself quite the reputation. But unlucky for me, you got caught. What I do know is that you'll face a lifetime in prison at best. Things are going to change around here, or you'll have me for an enemy, and I can promise that that's one grouchy bastard you won't want for company."

He stopped abruptly, blood racing. It was the most exhilarating outburst of Locke's life, and it had come not a moment too soon, just when his confidence in himself had been spiralling. But he'd done it. He'd stared into the eyes of a dangerous brigand and faced him down. He felt pride swelling deep in his chest, and he wished for all the world that his father had been there to see it.

Then Finnian started laughing. Not a nervous laugh but one of supreme confidence, one entirely lacking fear, full-bellied, loud. "You have no idea, do you?" he asked with a smirk, raising his hand to grab Locke's shirtfront, mimicking the way Locke was still holding his. "You think you have all the answers, but you don't. I may be a thief, but at least I'm truthful about who I am." He paused, and Locke recoiled at the veiled threat in those words. "You think you live in a perfect little world, but you don't, *Prison Master Locke*. There are villains far worse than me out there—of that you can be sure—and the sooner you realise, the better."

It took every inch of Locke's courage to maintain his composure. He knew that there were guards in the corridor just the other side of the main doors, but he'd come this far, and this was one battle he needed to fight alone.

"You're going to die for your crimes," Locke said spitefully.

Finnian's smile was completely sadistic now. "I wouldn't count on it."

Before Locke could come up with a response, Finnian yanked him forcefully against the iron bars. Locke's eye-socket exploded as it crunched into the metal. Unable to stop himself, he shouted in surprise, his hand flying up to his eye.

"I told you to take your hands off me!" yelled Finnian, yanking him forward by the collar once more.

Locke tried to scrabble back in desperation but was forced to call for help as he was still stuck in Finnian's ironclad grasp. His arms had fallen limp at his sides, his head was pounding, his vision was a blur, and Finnian's stale breath was making him nauseous.

The world was foggy, but Finnian's grip finally relented, and the brigand stepped back, arms raised, as two of the King's Guard rushed to step between them.

"Are you okay?" asked a third guard, lowering Locke into his chair. Locke's tongue was thick, and he couldn't find the words to answer, but a smile appeared at the sight of Finnian on his knees with halberds primed upon him.

"I'm okay," Locke uttered, his voice sounding almost drunken.

But the guard stepped back, shaking his head. "I don't think so. You'll need to see the surgeon."

⚜ ⚜ ⚜

So, this was how to make a bad day worse.

Locke's head hung between his legs, a strip of thick bandage folded and pressed to the wound on his head, stemming the flow of blood. So much for fighting his own battles and winning Finnian's respect, he thought bitterly. The brigand might have killed him if not for the timely intervention of the guards. In the end, they'd had to drag Locke away, bloody and broken, Finnian's laughter echoing in his wake. His legs were unsteady, and his head was throbbing, but it was the shame that stung worst of all. He'd lowered his eyes as he was hurried through the castle, through a baffling series of stairs and corridors, until they had abandoned him in this room.

Locke straightened gingerly in his chair. He winced as his head levelled and a bout of dizziness caused him to sway. He was in a banquet hall of some description, in the centre of which stood a long oval table with seating for ten. Elaborate candelabras lined the walls, and rich tapestries provided contrast against the dark grey brickwork. Locke recognised the colourful images as crests representing several of the highborn families. There were wyverns, griffins, and other creatures of myth, powerful beasts to signify the prominence of these oldest and most highly regarded households. His father often lauded himself for the honour of having ascended their family to such esteemed company.

"Not bad for a soldier, eh?" he'd said so many times that Locke couldn't count. At this, Locke would simply smile. He found it hard to believe that his father had the diplomacy required for political office and often marvelled at the fact that he had ever been made a lord. He certainly didn't show such patience at home.

"And who do we have here?" came a voice, drawing Locke out of his revery.

Locke turned to see a young woman moving purposefully towards him. Her skin was bronze, and her hair was dark though largely obscured by a pure white headscarf. He wondered if she was a woman of religion, appraising her black, full-length robes that skirted the tiled floor.

The newcomer smiled as if reading his thoughts. "You were expecting the surgeon?"

Locke nodded, bandage still pressed to his head. He winced slightly at the movement.

"Well, you can blame your timing for that. The surgeon is with the queen, unless you think your eye is more important than the progress of a royal baby?"

She paused and smiled, and Locke returned the gesture. "No, no, of course not," he managed. He supposed that explained why he had been taken to this random hall instead of the doctor's study.

"Good. Well, let's have a look at you. It's Prison Master Locke, isn't it?" she asked, placing a basket onto the table.

Locke nodded again. "As far as I can remember." He smiled, but the woman before him remained focused on her task at hand.

"Well, I'm Mary," she said, gesturing for Locke to remove the blood-stained bandage. She took it gingerly and set it aside, turning back to look at his wound. "Oh, that is a nasty one," she said under her breath, as though speaking to herself.

Mary reached for fresh cloth and a bottle of vinegar, dowsing the fabric in the smelly liquid before cleansing the wound. Locke clenched his jaw, sucking air in through his teeth to stop from swearing. This hurt almost as badly as the injury itself, but Locke kept his reaction to a minimum, keenly aware of the nurse crouched over him. Her face was almost as close as Finnian's had been during their altercation, and despite the acidic scent of the vinegar and the stinging pain, Locke found himself smiling once more.

"So, am I going to live?" he asked, his voice infused with humour that had appeared so rarely since his move to Highcastle. He hoped she might find this quip more entertaining than his last.

Mary pursed her lips playfully. "Hmm," she said, eyes narrowed, "only time will tell now. I hope you've said your goodbyes, just in case?"

Locke's smile widened, and the nurse pulled another small jar from her basket, the corners of her mouth twisting slightly as well.

"We won't need to sew or burn the wound," she continued, applying a thick paste that smelled like honey. "It's going to hurt for a few days, and you'll have a bruise like you've been kicked by a horse, but you'll be fine soon enough. Don't worry, you'll lose none of your good looks!"

"That's a relief. I don't have much to lose!"

Mary smiled. "Don't be so hard on yourself."

If Locke's face had already been red from injury, he couldn't imagine what colour it became in that moment. Mary turned away, as if sensing his self-consciousness, and as she fumbled with her basket, a vision echoed in Locke's mind. He found himself recalling that night in Eldred's Keep ten years ago when his father had nearly lost his life. The tragedy of war remained close in his memory, and as he watched Mary in fascination, he was a young boy once more, awestruck by the power to heal. The power to repair.

Locke cleared his throat, shaking his head slightly as if to make these morose thoughts go away. He momentarily wondered how his life might have been different, considering the various choices that had led him to this point. Perhaps he could have been the healer, rather than the healed. He'd had dreams once, dreams inspired by the surgeons who had helped his father. Who was Locke helping in the dark depths of the dungeons of Eldred's Keep?

"You must love your job," he said. "Healing people, that is, making a difference. It must be so rewarding."

Mary turned, facing him once more. "It has its moments." She paused to give a sad smile. "You'll live to fight another day, but there are some injuries that can't be healed. I can't save them all."

The door swung open behind them, and Locke inwardly cursed as he twisted to find High Commander Broderick silhouetted against the corridor. "What's been happening here?" Broderick demanded.

Locke immediately launched into the story of the evening, recounting the events to explain why he'd abandoned his post in the middle of his shift, skirting around the insults Finnian had thrown at him, to which he had risen against his own will, like a moth to a flame. His eyes shifted a few times to Mary as he spoke, wondering what she would think of him. He tried to make it sound as though he had merely been standing near the cell when Finnian, in some sort of rage, had reached out and grabbed him without provocation.

"Hmm," Broderick responded. "It sounds as though you've learned your lesson: never stand so close to the bars without back-up. That eye looks sore, so take a few days and get yourself together. This is your first and only warning."

"Yes, High Commander," said Locke, his voice full of reverence.

Mary picked her bag up from the table and smiled. "You're good to go."

Locke smiled back at her, wondering if he would see her again. An unexpected pang of guilt came over him. *Grow up*, he thought reflexively. *Grace never liked you. It was all just a job.*

His smile faded as he turned to leave. His thoughts moved to a more pressing matter, his heart pounding as he reached the door. How was he ever going to explain this to his father?

Francine

Surrounded by countless smaller, sandy atolls, the vast archipelago of the main Kanthu Isle was a welcome sight when it appeared on the horizon. Fran's hands still throbbed from her violent bout of self-defence, but it was the distance of her crewmates that truly hurt the most. She wondered how things had even ended up this way. Teeth had targeted her without reason, hiding behind old superstitions, and though he had been mutinous in his actions, Teeth's subsequent imprisonment had rendered him something like a martyr among the crew. She had believed the crew had followed Teeth through fear that would fall away in Teeth's absence, but for all her efforts to fit in, it seemed her progress had been undone. As her smiles began to be met with contempt, Fran recalled the first days of their journey with wistful nostalgia. The crew, meanwhile, avoided her as though she really was the curse they'd described, and Fran winced when she saw that a few who had fought her now had faces blooming black and blue.

The long days had seemed only to grow longer, and Patch was notable only in his absence as their precious moments in the same place slipped away. Fran understood his predicament, but even though he had done his best to help her by punishing Teeth, she couldn't deny feeling frustrated with the way that things had turned out.

As the port of Taboso began to form before them, her hands slammed on the balustrade in resentment. Fran could not free her mind from the trap of the previous day. She was so angry with Teeth, and underneath that, she felt a slight annoyance with herself. She had needed to defend herself, but had she gone too far? It had been many years since her last "frenzy"—as she called these spells of red—and she doubted there was a dress in the world that could make the captain forget the brutality he had found in Fran on the deck of the Silver Sword.

She breathed deeply as their sails flapped above her. The mast creaked in a way that had become reassuringly familiar, and bare feet thumped on the deck as the first mate called orders to bring them into port, all of them moving around Fran as though she were not there. A mass of ships had emerged before them, and Fran's worries were eased momentarily by the array of magnificent galleons on view. Beneath them, the water was as blue as sapphire. The port was littered with wooden huts along its open shore, and traders hurried on white sand as ships dropped anchor to berth at long wharves that stretched out into the ocean.

"Prepare yourself for arrival," said Patch curtly. Fran had not heard him approach, and by the time she turned, he had already gone. In his place, Amare appeared before her, and after a day spent in silence, Fran was grateful for his company once more.

"How are you?" he asked, his expression uncharacteristically sullen. "The ocean can be both rough and unpredictable, but we are approaching calmer shores, of that I can assure you. I'm sorry…" he said, his tone serious. It seemed the appearance of land had made a world of difference to his seasickness, and before Fran knew it, he had joined her at the balustrade, standing by her side like an old friend. He didn't wait for Fran to respond before continuing, "King Othelu is a man of peace, and you were invited here in the same spirit."

"It's done now," said Fran, and her voice croaked from the lack of use. Her anger still burned bright inside, her temper somewhat assuaged by the imminent prospect of their arrival on land. Besides, the attack had not been Amare's doing. In fact, without Amare, Patch would never have been summoned to see the situation resolved.

Amare nodded graciously. "You are both kind and forgiving. I have spoken with the captain, who will deal with the culprits in his own way. I have no doubt our return journey will be less eventful and only hope we can put this ugly situation behind us." He paused and looked eagerly to the shore with a light in his eyes Fran had not seen before. "Does it meet your expectations?" The question was clearly intended to change the subject, and a light-hearted lilt had returned to the man's voice.

"It's quite something," said Fran, her enthusiasm not what it might have been under different circumstances.

Amare's smiled widened. "That it is. What you see is the port of Taboso. The port receives visitors from all over the world, seeking to indulge their worst vices, but don't worry, we will not stay here tonight."

"No?"

Amare shook his head slowly as if to emphasise his point. "I think not. The port is full of dangerous men, more dangerous perhaps than the ones on this ship." He paused. "I can't expect you to protect me from all of them!"

Fran's scowl faded and a breath of laughter escaped her as the Silver Sword drew alongside the jetty. "To the king we go, then," she said with a hint of feigned enthusiasm.

"To Mutembu," said Amare, correcting her with the name of the king's royal settlement. "And an audience with the great king, if our luck prevails."

⚜ ⚜ ⚜

Fran had been through her fair share of horrors, but nothing could have prepared her for Taboso. No sooner had she set foot on land before the smell alone had her longing for the fetid yet familiar stench of the Silver Sword.

"What is that?" she asked Amare, her nose wrinkled.

"What, the smell?" he answered straight-faced. He inhaled deeply, his nostrils flaring. "Well, that could be the liquor, the opium, or the whores—it's hard to be more specific. Still living up to your expectations?" He grinned before continuing on his way.

Fran chased along behind him. A drunken pirate lolled toward her, and she slammed the man's pawing hand away, rolling her eyes as her assailant fell, off-balance, into a stagnant puddle.

The bright welcome the coast had provided from a distance already seemed a memory. Visions of white sand and palm trees had been replaced by dusty tracks and tumbledown shacks with evidence of the vices Amare had mentioned in every direction. She wondered if this is what the Kanthi king had imagined when he endeavoured to introduce new cultures to the islands. At the shoreline, local fishermen waded waist-deep in the water to retrieve enormous nets, but the streets before her, in contrast, were choked with weather-beaten freebooters of all nationalities.

Fran looked back, hoping to catch a glimpse of Patch in the crowd, but the quayside was awash with activity, and the unfortunate thing about pirates, Fran thought, is that they all look much the same.

"Don't worry, you'll see him again soon enough," called Amare, turning his head back in her direction, though Fran noticed he never broke stride. She felt momentarily embarrassed that Amare had caught her looking around for Patch, but she quickly shook the thought off. There were more pressing matters at hand. She could tell that Amare was in a hurry to reach Mutembu, but her curiosity was piqued by the unusual pleasure port and its people. She wasn't sure if she was intrigued or disgusted. She concluded that it was probably a bit of both.

Fran was some distance from the comfort of the capital now, she thought, and though she remained mindful of her tenuous immediate surroundings, she felt her sense of adventure returning with every breath, pungent as the air might be. A small cart whizzed into her sightline drawn by two of the crew from the Silver Sword, though she didn't know their names. Despite her newfound thrill of excitement, she found herself relieved to know that their belongings were following closely behind, in this of all places.

"Tell me the plan again," she called to Amare, making strides to catch up. The commotion of Taboso was now largely behind them, and the landscape had turned green in the shadow of a precipitous jungle.

"Just a little longer on foot," said Amare warmly. His skin seemed to be glowing from within, such was his newfound energy since returning to his home island. "It won't be long until we reach the boat, and from there, you can relax."

"Of course, another boat!" said Fran, blowing out her cheeks. They arrived at the treeline, and Fran peered ahead, her eyes taken by an array of strange plants and colourful flowers scattered among the trees, as if to welcome them.

Amare smiled before producing a large knife from a leather scabbard that Fran had not noticed until that moment. She assumed he intended to cut his way through the tropical forest but reached for the pommel of her own blade just in case. Events aboard the Silver Sword had left her on high alert. She was probably overreacting, but she wouldn't be caught off-guard and unarmed again.

"Not far now," said Amare, his jovial tone reassuring her. "Enjoy the scenery. Oh, but try not to touch anything. It would be a shame to see you killed after coming so far!"

Fran rolled her eyes, her arms tucked close to her sides as they entered the jungle. She had expected the canopy to offer respite from the midday sun but could not have prepared for the stifling humidity she encountered instead. A sheen of sweat formed on her upper lip in an instant, and she felt as though the canopy roof pressed in on her, leaving insufficient space to breath, a wave of nausea threatening to overcome her before Amare offered a steadying hand. She nodded gratefully at him, and then he stepped away once more. For all the clothes she had brought with her, Fran felt foolishly underprepared and overdressed for these conditions. She loosened the neck of her dark blue tunic. Amare retained the formality of his linen shirt and leather doublet coupled with a belt of gold. It was an ensemble better suited to the royal courts of the Quadripartite than the Kanthi jungle, but he otherwise looked very much at home.

She'd known the forests of Peacehaven and Cornesse well, but she had never imagined wild, untamed nature on the scale that now appeared before her. The trees themselves seemed to reach for the heavens, bark as thick as armour, ancient and imposing with roots that forced their way above ground to mingle with the undergrowth. Thick vines seem to climb on every surface, and colourful insects scuttled along the surface of mighty leaves wilted with moisture. It was a wonderland, but one full of dangers, and Fran followed the dirt path hastily to keep up with her guide.

"What about our luggage?" she asked, with Amare only a few strides ahead of her. The cart had been close behind but would no doubt struggle on this new, narrow track.

"Don't you worry," said Amare, cleaving a low branch that hung in his path. "They will meet us at the riverside. You are to have the rare privilege of travelling in a Kanthi dombosu for this journey. It is like your rowing boats but longer and narrower." He stopped briefly to tap his blade on an enormous trunk that towered over them. "The hull is carved from the base of a single tree and our oars—that is your word, correct?" he asked, interrupting himself, his eyes narrowed as he considered her.

Fran nodded.

"Yes, oars," he continued. "They are a different shape but...well, you'll see."

Amare turned on his heels, setting off at a pace once more, and as Fran followed along, her eyes were drawn to the treetops, where brightly coloured birds whooped and whistled to one another. Every sight, smell, and sound was new to her, and she thought sadly how much Mathilde would have enjoyed seeing this new, vastly different region. She wondered how she would ever explain it properly to the queen, but she soon felt foolish at the thought. Such descriptions would be Taiwo's job now. If all went to plan, he would be her conversation and her counsel. She and Mathilde been a team of two for some years. It was Fran's job, of course, but they had grown close, and the queen had become like a sister to Fran. The sister she had never had. Fran would continue in her duty after Mathilde was married, but Taiwo's very presence would secure the queen against her greatest dangers: Clement and the nobility. Taiwo would, first and foremost, be the one to defend her when it was needed. Fran wished only good things for the queen, and though she questioned if the heat was affecting her, she couldn't help but wonder how things in her life might be about to change.

"Over here," called Amare, and Fran realised she'd fallen behind. Though little more than trodden earth, the path was clear in its singular direction, and the sound of moving water became more prominent with every step. Finally, Fran broke free from the thicket and into a clearing beyond, where she found Amare waiting for her.

"Thought I'd lost you," he said, grinning back at her.

Amare made for the boat, but Fran hung back for a moment, panting slightly with the relief of fresh, riverside air now that she was out from under the close, green ceiling of trees. The river itself was maybe twelve feet in width. Unlike that of the ocean, this water was not crystal blue but rather a muddy brown, and earthy banks climbed toward the treeline on either side in a way that surprised Fran by reminding her of the wide boulevards in Nivelle. Though the water moved with unexpected current, the dombosu was tied to a small jetty, and Amare stood alongside their oarsman, who had one foot inside the craft in a hint at his readiness to leave.

Fran grimaced, apologising as she rushed toward the boat. Their latest companion gave little in the way of reaction, and Fran wondered if he spoke any of her language at all. He was only the second Kanthi man she had met, with Amare being the first, and though Amare had been keen to provide Fran with an insight to their culture, she couldn't help but marvel at the oarsman's fascinating ensemble, silent though he was.

The oarsman was probably a couple of years older than Fran, tall and muscular, his dark skin marred by scattered, well-healed scars upon his arms and legs. His earlobes had been stretched to create large circular holes, and his hair was plaited tightly against his head and tied off with multi-coloured thread, while his body was covered by a sleeveless garment running from shoulder to knee. The material looked like hessian to Fran, its light colouring contrasting with the deep brown leather of the man's woven, open-toed shoes. It was mostly an entirely practical creation but for the rows of sparkling gems upon his fingers, which had enchanted Fran's eyes as soon as she spotted them. Gilded bracelets extended far up his arms, and a colourful, braided necklace sat tight upon the lump in his throat.

Amare watched her eyes rove along the oarsmen's jewellery. "You see that we have many treasures," he said before pausing to embrace the younger man, whose face lit up as Amare spoke with him in the local language. "This is Amehlo," said Amare, mirroring the oarsman's smile as he stepped back to gesture with an outstretched arm. He halted and looked back toward the path from which he and Fran had arrived. "Oh, and what timing, our belongings have arrived!"

The weight of Fran's trunk was shared by the two crewmembers she had seen bringing the luggage from the port. Sweat-drenched, the two men emerged from the treeline, no doubt pleased to be free of its suffocating embrace. The dombusu dipped deeper into the water as the trunk was lowered into the hull, and as Fran considered her own journey through the stifling jungle, she grimaced at the thought that they had completed at least some of the distance without the cart to lighten their load. She couldn't help feeling a little guilty for the sheer weight of her belongings.

But there was no time for rest as the men went in pursuit of the next piece of luggage. Fran smiled tentatively at Amehlo, who remained straight-faced in waiting. It might have been Fran's imagination, but he seemed somewhat annoyed by the luggage. He certainly kept glancing at it, almost as though it were a loathsome fly.

"Not long now," said Amare, who opened his mouth to speak again but was interrupted as more of their luggage began to appear through the trees. Two large sacks were lowered slowly into the boat before Amare asked, "Is that everything?"

To Fran's reckoning, it probably was. It needed to be with space in the dombusu already running out. But before either of the young men had chance to answer, a rustling noise sounded from behind them, and a twig snapped underfoot as another man stepped into view. Patch.

"Just one more," he said, a smile lighting up his face as he lifted a final piece of luggage, a sack of his own. Relief flooded Fran's stomach at his friendly appearance. They'd spoken little since the incident, and Fran's eyes widened at the sight of him, her skin turning inexplicably hot under the young man's gaze.

"Ah, good Captain," said Amare, stepping forward to meet him. "So glad you decided to join us. It has been sometime since your last visit to Mutembu. The great king will be joyed to see you, I'm sure."

Patch dropped the sack, running his hands through the mats in his curly hair. "A pleasure as always, Amare. Besides, I couldn't possibly leave you alone with this one." He pointed in Fran's direction, and she imagined her skin must have turned somehow redder still.

"Well, you are most welcome either way," said Amare. "As to you, young lady…" He turned to Fran, inclining his head toward the waiting dombosu. "Departure is upon us. Your vessel awaits!"

⚜ ⚜ ⚜

The river was called the Anwatu, a word that literally meant "fast flow" in the Kanthi tongue, or so Amare told them. In their boat shaped like a spearhead, the four of them cut through the water at exhilarating speed, and Fran's face was fixed in a nervous grin as Amehlo harnessed their momentum, steadying the boat with a short-handled oar shaped like a ladle.

"Everything okay?" asked Patch, turning to face her. They sat single-file, with the luggage stacked at the back of the dombosu. The front of the craft sat high in the water, and Patch's eyes shifted to where Fran clutched nervously at the side of the boat.

"I'm fine," she answered curtly. She decided to change the subject. "Do you always show up unannounced? First in Clerbonne, now this?"

Patch laughed, and their forward momentum sent a breeze through his hair. "I like to be unpredictable. Besides, I was always meant to meet Amare in Clerbonne. It's you that was unexpected!"

His quip deserved a smart answer, but the dombosu suddenly jumped jarringly on the water, a bit like a skipping stone, and Fran managed little more than a churlish half-smile before settling onto her perch once more, steadying herself.

"Careful," said Patch, calling over his shoulder. "There are a hundred ways to die in this jungle, and most of them are in the river." He grinned as he turned back to face the front of the boat. "Forget those fools back on the Sword—I suspect a river snake might provide somewhat sterner opposition."

This was the first time Patch had mentioned the incident, and Fran sat quietly as the dense jungle passed them in a blur. There was no doubting the change between them, but his presence and light-hearted nature only served to ease Fran's concerns. After all she had been through, his joke was inappropriate. But was it really Patch that she was angry with? Either way, he had something about him that would make Fran's anger a challenge to sustain.

"Everyone okay back there?" yelled Amare, arms wide as he stood to call to those behind him. Unlike onboard the Silver Sword, where he had been plagued with seasickness, Amare seemed to thrive in the water transport native to his homeland.

"We will be coming to a fork in the river soon, and then we will reach the slow water. Not long now," he said, and he waited for Fran to give a subtle nod before returning to his seat.

As always seemed to be the case, Amare was right. It was only moments later that Amehlo began positioning them toward the left bank and their course took them down a small drop into a slow-moving, meandering tributary with trees curling overhead.

"Still, okay?" asked Patch, but Fran's eyes were taken by the impression of movement in the trees. The question echoed out in their newfound silence, and Fran squinted as a line of men appeared from the thicket on their right. Her blood began to race immediately, imagining pirates or thieves. She noticed with unease that they were all armed with spears and bows.

"Do not worry," said Amare, waving his hand at the men in a gesture that seemed almost dismissive, causing them to shrink away as quickly as they had arrived. "They are Botosi's men. Suspicious sorts, no doubt, but you face no danger while you are with me."

Fran's heart was still pounding as the last man disappeared into the treeline. Their dress had been similar to Amehlo's, but their weapons had been cause for concern. "Botosi?" she asked curiously.

"A clan leader," said Patch, swivelling to speak. "He was Othelu's main rival for the throne. You could say there's history there."

"Exactly, young man," said Amare appearing at Patch's side. "But *history* is the right word. We are a nation of peace these days, and with Taiwo's soon-to-be engagement to the great queen—well, we can all look forward to a bright future."

The envoy smiled broadly, and Fran returned the gesture for ease if nothing else. It was the first time Amare had mentioned the reason for their journey in quite some time. She'd started to wonder if anything was actually as it seemed with the envoy, and her face fell as her mind drew similarities between the smiling man before her and manipulative old Clement and all the other nobles back in Nivelle, fearing that she, and indeed Mathilde, might be being taken for a ride.

"Don't worry," said Patch, misreading her concern and trying to ease her previous worry about Botosi's men. "We're here. Look, that's Mutembu just up ahead."

Indeed, another small jetty had appeared in the distance. Drawing closer, Fran noticed two men with sharp spears and fierce eyes awaiting their arrival. Despite Patch's reassurances, the thought of Botosi's men still lingered, and she startled as the men stepped forward to begin shouting in their direction as the dombosu edged closer.

Fran reached for her sword and leapt forward to ask, "What are they saying?"

But as usual, Amare only smiled. "They're saying 'welcome back friends, you've found your way home.'"

Fran sagged back onto her seat, relieved that she had misinterpreted the cacophony of voices for violent instead of friendly. She dreaded to think how a threat might sound.

Amehlo slowed their craft as they crept toward the jetty. Their arrival was greeted with smiles all around, and the oarsman rose from his seat to throw a heavy rope around a post, speaking in animated Kanthi. Fran stood as Amehlo gestured for them to disembark their boat, and Patch stepped aside as she sprang to join Amare on the bank.

"Don't forget the luggage," she called back in mockery.

"But of course, Princess," said Patch, bowing as he reached for her trunk. It seemed to Fran that Patch always had everything well under control, so she couldn't believe her luck when the dombosu listed unexpectedly as the last piece of luggage was removed, dumping the captain into the river waters.

She struggled not to laugh as she made her way to the riverbank. "Are you okay?" she asked, attempting to sound concerned. Truthfully, she *was* a little concerned; like Patch said, there were all sorts of deadly things in the water. But Fran just couldn't get past the image of Patch flailing in mid-air before landing in the water with a satisfying plonk. She extended her hand to him as a gesture of goodwill to make up for her unforgiveable facial expression, which did not wholly conceal her smile.

Patch took her hand, dragging himself upright before sprawling in a stretch of long grass, presumably hoping to dry himself in its blades. "Never better," he answered breathlessly, and despite all that had just happened, Fran begrudgingly admitted to herself, in the most private recess of her mind, that he still looked every bit as handsome as before, even with a dark mop of wet hair.

"Well, what a relief," said Amare, making to stand over Patch. "Remember what I always tell you. 'There are a hundred ways to die—'"

Patch rolled his eyes. "Yes, yes, I hear you. Now…" He rose to his feet once more, water dripping from the tips of his hair. "Why are we still standing around? Othelu will be waiting."

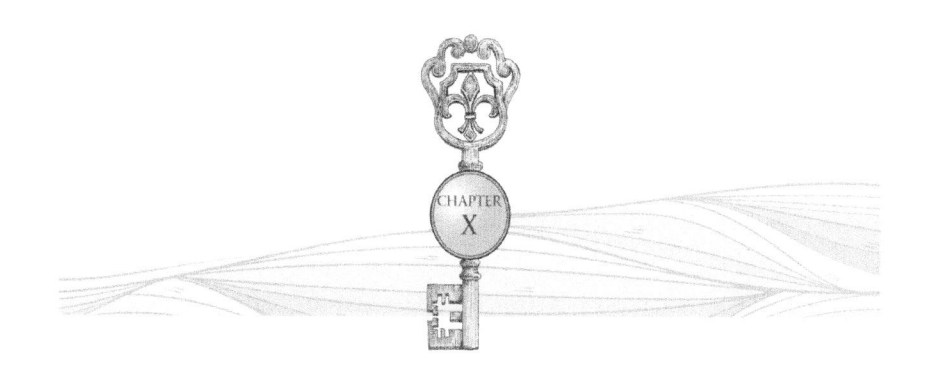

Francine

During the short walk to Mutembu, Patch made little fuss about his recent riverside mishap, but Fran couldn't help but grin at the amusing squelch of his sopping wet boots. When Amare was out of earshot, she sidled up to Patch to speak in a low voice so as not to be overhead. "So, you've met King Othelu?" she asked.

"A few times, yes," said Patch. "And Prince Taiwo too, of course. The clan is full of good people, I wouldn't worry about them. If there's anyone among them you should worry about pleasing, it's Zimbeza."

Fran's eyes narrowed. "Zimbeza?"

Patch smiled back at her. "You'll see."

Fran furrowed her brow but didn't press him any further. They continued through the jungle in silence. Amare led the way, with Amehlo at the rear, and the two Kanthi men who had greeted them at the jetty trailing some way behind, toiling with the luggage.

"Here we are," announced Amare unexpectedly.

And as Fran rounded the corner, she saw her first glimpse of Mutembu through the trees. She hadn't known what to expect, but this was so much more than she could have imagined. The settlement itself was built into an enormous clearing. The ground was dusty, but intricate walkways wound between the buildings, marked with intermittent paving stones. At the heart of the town stood an impressive construction that Amare called a longhouse. Like almost every other structure Fran could see, the longhouse sat high upon thick wooden stilts with an entrance accessed by a set of stairs. The impressive dwelling was a feat of carpentry, and though it was all very different from the grandeur of Nivelle, Fran was no less impressed. Her eyes were drawn to the longhouse's gable roof, built with what looked like thin, interlocking tree trunks, and she noticed a wonderful uniformity between this central building and all the other shops and houses in sight. Every man-made structure seemed to be carefully constructed to be in keeping with their natural surroundings, and a few structures here and there were even built into the canopy of the trees that remained, a series of rope bridges ensuring that the community remained connected throughout.

"You have to see it to believe it," said Patch, leaning closer to her to offer his thoughts. "The islands get terrible rainfall in the wet season, so the buildings are raised to avoid flooding."

Fran shook her head in disbelief. "It's beautiful. Things are so crowded in the capital, but this…" She trailed off, her eyes wide with admiration. It felt like Mutembu was truly at one with nature, like it had grown as a natural addition to its green surroundings, and though it was bustling with townsfolk, the settlement was something of a hidden sanctuary in the heart of the jungle.

Amare ushered them forward, and Fran followed on, her head still swivelling this way and that to take in this strange new place. Though the colours and faces of Mutembu were different to anywhere she'd been, there was something reassuringly familiar about the town. The people smiled as they passed each other, and the sound of livestock and laughing children filled the air.

Amare called for her to keep up, and their group followed a path toward the longhouse, passing a large campfire along the way, where a group of Kanthi women were gathered and speaking in the local language. They each carried a basket of different food, from which Fran noticed delicious looking flatbreads and an assortment of local fruits.

"We've arrived in good time," said Amare, calling over his shoulder. "It had not occurred to me, but our swift departure from Nivelle means that we have returned in time for the celebration. Othelu's youngest son, Bakiri, has come of age."

"A celebration?" Fran questioned. "Is it not customary to bring a gift?" Again, she felt unprepared. A trunk full of clothing, but did she have anything suitable to wear?

Amare's carefree smile soon calmed her. "Worry not, young lady. Your presence is gift enough, though the prospect of Taiwo's betrothal will also be welcome. It is an occasion for fun, and we will mark it in traditional Kanthi fashion, with drink and sport."

Patch scoffed. "More drink than sport for you, I'd imagine."

Amare stopped in his tracks, turning to face Patch with a smirk. "I like to play to my strengths," he said with a wink before continuing on.

"And what of the other princes?" enquired Fran. "Taiwo's brothers, will they join the celebration?"

"Unlikely," said Amare without ever breaking stride. "Two of the middle sons, Kabiru and Emeka, live with their wives on the smaller islands, shrewd matches arranged by the king. These bonds ensure fealty from the formidable peoples of the sand isles, while their brother Dayo resides with the mountain people."

Fran nodded as she followed. "And the eldest prince?"

"Zakari," said Amare. "You are right to think that the heir would usually live at his father's side, but the king himself could not conquer Zakari's hunger for travel. It is true that Taiwo is the strongest and most handsome of the king's sons, but Zakari is the most charming, and it is this charm that helps maintain King Othelu's peace. Prince Zakari travels tirelessly upon the main island and to the sand and stone isles beyond, with the authority of his father's voice."

"Your king is not short of envoys then?" Fran asked in jest.

Amare laughed. "I fear Zakari is destined for greater things. He is his father's son, though, and he will continue what the great king has started. It is a shame you will miss him, but with six sons comes many an opportunity for celebration. Today is Bakiri's day, and all being well, Taiwo's too. We shall see what the future holds for Othelu's second son."

Fran marvelled at the way the verdant green jungle pressed in on Mutembu's edges at every border, and she reflected wryly that the jungle was much easier to admire from a distance. To the north, she saw a steep incline, trees growing steadily as if attempting to envelop the mighty mountain range beyond.

As they climbed the stairs to the longhouse, Patch moved closer to her side, his voice dropping low. "Now, try not to worry," he said, his words having the absolute opposite effect. Fran swallowed hard as Patch continued, "Remember, it's not Othelu you need to worry about it's—"

He paused mid-sentence as a large Kanthi man with a thick, dark beard appeared at the door of the longhouse. He wore a similar knee-length, sleeveless garment to the other men Fran had seen, yet his was made from shimmering blue silk with patterns of gold thread along the neck and shoulder. Fran noticed that the lavish material pinched around the man's middle, tested by his bulging stomach. He looked them over, and then his face broke into a smile. He spoke the common tongue, in an accent like Amare's. "Captain Goldhand, my dear friend. What a wonderful surprise." He extended his arms in welcome, and Fran's eyes fell upon the crown on his head. She realised with a start that this must be King Othelu. She straightened her back imperceptibly, wanting to make a good first impression no matter what Patch said about not needing to impress the king.

"Great king," said Amare, falling to one knee. He tugged at Fran's sleeve, but before Fran could follow suit, the king burst into cheerful laughter.

"There's no need for the lady to kneel," Othelu said, waving his hand.

Fran instead lowered her head in reverence. "A pleasure to meet you, good King Othelu."

Patch took Fran's other hand, tugging her the last few steps toward the longhouse.

"It has been too long since my last visit," said Patch. He dropped Fran's hand and reached toward the king instead, gripping his arm in a tight, familiar way. Fran felt a little out of place, not sure what to say or how to address this impressive new presence.

Othelu's laughter subsided as his eyes fell upon Fran. "And who is this treasure, a lady friend?" he asked, brows raised as he pushed Patch playfully away. Fran wasn't sure if she had ever felt so embarrassed, both by the question and by her own eagerness to hear Patch's reply.

"No," said Patch unequivocally. Fran tried not to let her disappointment show in her face. "This is Francine, a princess of Peacehaven and chosen shield to Queen Mathilde of Nivelle."

The king nodded his approval. "I must say, that's quite the introduction. I am King Othelu Bengatu the First, High King of Kanthu and clan leader to all in the shadow of the brown mountains." He lifted her hand to kiss it softly, and Fran thought that the king must have been a real charmer in his youth.

Fran, whose cheeks were still slightly hot from Othelu's question to Patch, cleared her throat to try to shift some of her self-consciousness. "Most kind," she stuttered, curtsying awkwardly, and cursing herself for never quite getting the motion down. It was something Mathilde teased her about whenever the need arose for such formalities, which, to be fair, was not often since Fran was usually stationed at Mathilde's side, clad in armour. She knew the movement looked particularly stupid given that she was currently wearing trousers.

Sparing Fran from further awkwardness, Patch said, "We've come to speak about Prince Taiwo."

"Why, what has he done now?" the king asked, his voice almost exasperated.

"Oh, nothing," interjected Amare, stepping forward unexpectedly. His face shifted into a mischievous smile. "It is a question of what he might do next."

⚜   ⚜   ⚜

The longhouse was every bit as beautiful inside as Fran had anticipated. The floor was covered with exotic animal hides, and the walls were decorated with enormous wooden shields, oval in shape, which seemed far more logical to Fran than the circular design she was used to. The door opened at one end of the impressive building, and Fran strode forward, keeping pace with King Othelu as he led the way toward the opposite end of the large open room.

"I trust Amare has looked after you?" the king asked Fran, taking her by surprise. She had thought he would want to get right to business, discussing Taiwo and not much else. "He is my ambassador," Othelu continued, "but one who spends too much time in lavish surroundings. I fear he remembers little of Kanthi hospitality."

Fran thought it best not to draw out her answer. "Our journey here was a pleasant one," she said, not altogether truthfully, glancing over at Amare as she did. "I feel very fortunate to be here, though there is much for us to discuss."

"Of course, of course," said the king, continuing toward the far end of the longhouse. Shards of light poured through small, square windows, and for the first time, Fran noticed two large wooden thrones. In one of them sat a most beautiful Kanthi woman, bands of gold covering the length of her arms. Othelu stepped forward, taking his place in the unoccupied chair and looking at Fran. "To business then," he said. "You all know who I am, of course, but this," and he turned to face the woman at his side, "this is Queen Zimbeza, High Queen of Kanthu and...well, you know the rest."

"Great queen," said Amare predictably, dropping to his knee once more. Patch inclined his head, and Fran mimicked him before her eyes fell upon the queen. To her surprise, Zimbeza was even more beautiful than she had appeared from afar. Her skin was dark and radiant like obsidian, her hair plaited tightly to rest upon the nape of her neck. Perhaps most striking, however, were the queen's dark, piercing eyes, which seemed capable of reading Fran's every thought. It was clear even while she was seated that Zimbeza was a tall woman, and her lean body sat in great contrast to Othelu's, whose bulbous stomach rolled onto his knees as he sat forward.

Imagine looking like that as a mother of six, thought Fran in silent admiration, her tangent interrupted abruptly as the king began to speak.

"Is she not the most beautiful woman you have ever seen?" he asked, reaching to place a hand upon Zimbeza's, his voice oozing affection for his wife. "I, too, could spend days gazing upon her, but I feel certain that there are other reasons for your visit."

Amare cleared his throat before explaining his proposal. Fran noticed a narrowing in the queen's eyes as the envoy proceeded, and though Othelu seemed warm and gracious, Zimbeza's expression remained incredulous, keeping Fran on her guard.

"So, you see," said Amare, drawing to his conclusion. "This union would provide great benefits to all involved. I hope you do not think me too forward, great king, but you did ask me to build relations during my time in Nivelle, and, well," he paused to chuckle, seemingly delighted by his own ingenuity, "there is nothing better for that than a royal wedding, as I'm sure you'll agree."

The king sat back, a smile lighting up§ his face. Fran had never doubted Amare's strong ability to influence others, but she had not expected things to be so simple and straightforward, the king's head nodding in approval as he rubbed his hands together expectantly.

"A very fine proposal indeed," said Othelu, and then he shook his head and laughed at his unintended wordplay. "This is fine work, Amare, though you will understand that this decision does not rest with me alone. It is wrong to favour any one of your children, but Taiwo is our dearest son and the apple of his mother's eye. Zimbeza, my queen, what say you?"

All eyes turned to Zimbeza. Patch nudged Fran softly, and she glanced over to see him giving her a shrewd look that plainly said, "I told you so."

Fran looked back to Zimbeza, holding her breath as she waited to see what the queen had to say. Zimbeza straightened herself, her very presence demanding attention. Though she had yet to speak, Zimbeza pursed her lips in thought, and Fran was overcome with intimidation as gold bands rattled on the queen's arms when she sat forward to answer.

"Not bad, Amare, not bad," she conceded, her voice as smooth as silk. "So, the queen of Cornesse gets her king and access to the riches of our lands. This…*girl*, Mathilde…" her voice turned a bit rougher, "…is able to maintain control of her council and deliver a Kanthi prince to her chambers like a commodity. It all sounds like a very fine deal, but tell me..." She paused to fix Amare with an icy glare. "How does any of this benefit your king?"

The question cannot have been unexpected, so Fran was surprised to find Amare momentarily silenced, presumably the result of Zimbeza's sharp tone. The queen's love for her son was there for all to see, and her passionate words were reminiscent of Mathilde's own marital discussions with her nobles back in Nivelle, an irony not lost on Fran. Nevertheless, she felt her heart beating faster, her skin prickling at the queen's contempt. *That girl?* Fran thought. *How dare she speak of Mathilde in that way?* she thought as Amare floundered. She realised she could not let it pass.

"How does it benefit your king?" asked Fran, eyes narrowed, and lips raised in a sneer. She had pushed aside her feelings of intimidation, and her words flowed freely as she did what she was best at: defending her queen. "Mathilde is a powerful and formidable queen, and her beauty is legendary. She holds the utmost respect throughout The Quadripartite and is a woman no one could fail to admire." She paused, shaking her head in disgust. "She at least has the decency to meet someone before judging them, which is why she sent me here to bring Taiwo back to meet her in person. I wonder whether this...*boy*, Taiwo, deserves her!"

"Strong words," said Zimbeza, "And yet your queen did not see fit to grace us with her *formidable* presence?"

"She's back in the capital, caring for her people, as she should be," came Fran's reply. "Her father died when she was young, and she still took her place with grace, despite her age and gender, proving wrong all those who believed she could not do it. She has spent her adult life working tirelessly for the betterment of

Cornesse, and I travelled here hoping to repay that with some hope of happiness. I must say," she paused, lifting her chin high so that Zimbeza seemed to reduce in size below her, "I'm starting to question the wisdom of my journey." She stepped back and glanced over at Patch, whose eyes were wide with shock.

"I think what she means is—" Amare began desperately, but his words were cut short when the queen's hand raised to stop him in his tracks.

"Mathilde's chosen shield?" she asked. Fran nodded defiantly, refusing to relax her posture. "Hmm," she uttered thoughtfully. "It seems then that you would know the queen as well as anyone. You're right that I have been quick to judge, but you understand that the fate of both my son and my land depends upon this decision."

Again, Fran nodded, her heartbeat beginning to slow to a dull thud as Othelu gazed upon his queen suspensefully.

"It is a shame that I will not meet Mathilde here today," Zimbeza said, "but it seems Amare is not the only skilled envoy in the room, though perhaps he is a bit more adept at diplomacy." She paused, her expression breaking into an amused half-smile. "You asked for my opinion, great king," she continued, turning to Othelu. "I think that if Mathilde leads her country as she chooses those with whom she surrounds herself, then this might be a very fine match indeed. Amare," she snapped suddenly, "send for Taiwo. It seems tonight might well be a double celebration."

Othelu smiled as he sat back contentedly in his chair. Just as Fran, Patch, and Amare were about to leave, Othelu called, "By the way, Captain Goldhand, will you dry yourself off? You're making my throne room smell like fish."

⚜ ⚜ ⚜

Their luggage arrived as they exited the longhouse. They had decided to leave Taiwo's family to discuss their decision with him alone, with Othelu insisting that Fran take time to recover and refresh before the evening's festivities. Her lodging was a house on the outskirts of the settlement that was typically reserved for high-profile visitors, a thought that tickled Fran, not least because of her sweat-stained, dishevelled appearance. The house was a simple, spacious construction, decorated with ornate wood furnishings and animal hide rugs upon the floor.

Fran had bustled quickly into the house when they arrived, desperate to get settled and change clothes. Patch had been granted similar lodgings nearby, but he had accompanied Fran this far. Fran became acutely aware that this was the first time they had been alone since the incident on the Silver Sword. Though her mood had subsided, she didn't want to appear as though she were trying to linger with Patch. She sought out the partitioned bedchamber and closed the door behind her, turning to find her trunk inside and sighing with relief.

"That was quite something," came Patch's voice from the other side of the thin wall that separated them.

Fran's blood was no longer racing with adrenaline, but she felt a deep contentment in her actions with Zimbeza and a surge of pride at having surprised even herself. She sat down on the bed, which was covered in soft blankets. Though she had been so looking forward to getting cleaned up, she found her eyes growing heavy as fatigue finally caught up with her.

When Fran offered no answer, Patch said, "Anyway, I'll let you rest."

"Thanks," she mumbled, but her eyes were now closed. The last she heard was Patch quietly closing the front door behind him.

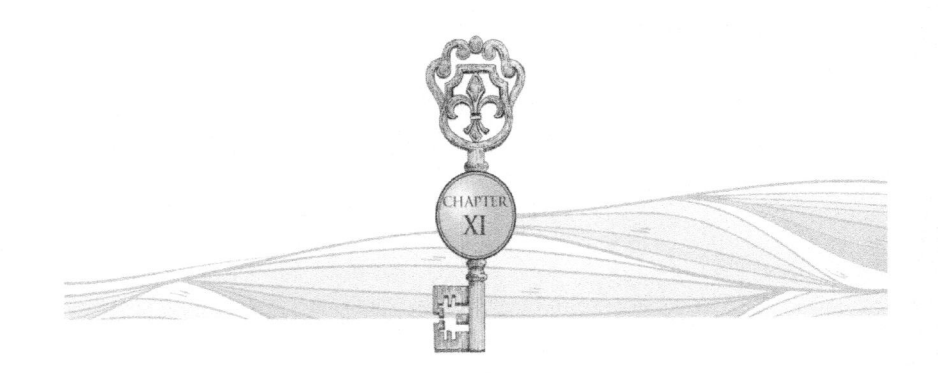

Locke

Five minutes in The Eagle told Locke that he would rather face the familiarity of his father's disappointment than the newfound awkwardness that existed with Grace. It was likely that his father would find out about the incident with Finnian anyway, so in the end, he reflected, it was the lesser of evils.

And so, it was decided. Locke paid for the services of a horse and departed the city the following morning, tracing the River Aramere past Dalhart Forest into the open valleys beyond. The weather was mild, and the smell of fresh grass carried on the breeze, which would have been pleasant but for the stinging pain of the wound to his eye. Though fear of his father's reaction lingered in Locke's mind, there was some comfort in breaking free from the oppressive feeling that accompanied him in the city. The promise of home pulled him ever onward, and his hired horse appeared to share his urgency, driving ever forward until the landscape became more dramatic, vast peaks and deep ravines marking the border of the northern fells.

He was home.

The towers of Ardlyn Keep loomed in the distance, silhouetted by the afternoon sun. Fields of lavender brought a new, welcome scent to the air and Locke began to think of his mother, his spacious quarters, and the good, kind people who lived in the town from which their home took its name. His cheeks pinched with a smile before thoughts of his father loomed once more like a cloud full of rain. He set his horse off at a gentler trot, each step heavier in anticipation of his father's scorn. Soft earth crumbled under his horse's hooves as Locke descended an uneven track that wended toward the town. Forge, fire, and food filled the air, the nostalgic sounds and smells of rural life.

It had only been three weeks since Locke had left home to move to Highcastle, so it was no real surprise to find everything exactly as he had left it. It felt far longer than that to Locke, though, so he had almost expected his home to be as changed as he felt, somehow wearier or battle worn. There was no grand welcome waiting for him, no pomp or ceremony, and his quiet arrival was lost to the hubbub of the weekly market.

"Mutton, get your fresh mutton!" called Aled the butcher. Old Tristan sat sharpening blades at the door to his smithy, while two mischievous girls snuck apples from Audric, whose attention was lost in his negotiations. Locke smiled as he dismounted to follow the main path toward his family home. Carts hurried by, and he spotted familiar faces, their earnest welcome showing little regard for the cut and bruising that decorated his left eye.

"Welcome back, Locke," said Millicent the baker. Her hair was tied into a tight bun as always, and she removed her hand from the pocket of her dark green apron to wave with a broad smile.

I suppose it's nothing unusual, thought Locke, recalling his father's frequent hard disciplines when Locke was growing up. He dropped his eyes, wincing at the pain the quick movement had brought him. Remembering the many beatings he had taken over the years, however, brought about more pain than his injury ever could.

⚜ ⚜ ⚜

The portcullis stood open as if Locke's arrival had been planned. He found the appearance of two guards on the battlement to be less welcoming. It was no match for the majesty of Eldred's Keep, but Ardlyn Keep was a castle nonetheless and had once provided a stronghold against incursions from neighbours to the north. These days, the presence of armed guards seemed needless to Locke, but he knew the thought would get short shrift from his father. *You can take the man from the army, but you can't take the army from the man...*

"Lockey, what a nice surprise!" called Tanner, one of Locke's father's longest-serving men. The man was abrasive at the very best of times, an ex-soldier whose obvious yet unfounded dislike of Locke was one of many similarities he shared with Locke's own father.

"It can't be Lockey. Back already, young man?" said Willard, his father's other lackey. The guards were two peas in a pod, forever encouraging one another. Stranger still was that they looked very much alike, both bald with scarred faces. It had always seemed as though Locke's discomfort was their only source of pleasure, but Locke was in no mood to add fuel to their fire today.

"Just a short visit," he answered, hoping that would be end of it.

Almost predictably, Tanner laughed. "Nothing to do with that shiner on your face then?"

"You've not lost that job already, have you?" added Willard with a distinct lack of actual concern. Locke imagined that this interaction would be the pinnacle of their day.

He winced before stepping beyond the gatehouse and into the courtyard, where a young squire rushed to take his horse.

"Welcome back, sir," said the boy, his voice heavy with the sort of reverence that Locke might have expected from Tanner and Willard if they weren't so impertinent, spurred on by his father's open dismay at Locke. Even now he could hear them behind him, continuing to speculate over his unexpected appearance and the injury to his eye.

"Your father is at market, sir," the squire continued. "He might not be back for some time."

Locke was flooded with relief at having a bit more time before he had to face his father, but he kept his face neutral, not wanting to show the young squire how much he was dreading facing Lord Ramsey. He thanked the squire before making his way inside. The smell of fresh bread greeted him in the doorway, and Locke rushed toward the kitchen with expectancy, hoping to see his mother. For all that their life had changed since the war, Locke's mother still liked to cook, clean, and fuss over their family. She'd been uneasy with the addition of staff that came with their new position and home in Ardlyn and had taken to treating them as friends or an extension of the family, never asking anything of them that she wouldn't do herself. Though the changes in Lord Ramsey had not been easy, Locke's mother had always been their unyielding bedrock, forever seeking the good in people, and Locke admired her for it. He knew his mother wasn't perfect, but she was humble, hopeful and the one constant that reminded Locke of happier times.

"Mother, are you here?" he called, blustering down the corridor and into the pantry. "Where are you, Mother, are you—" He stopped abruptly, the sound of old wood creaking underfoot.

A fresh loaf sat cooling on the shelf, and the walls were lined with bottles, pots, and pans, though Locke's thoughts were firmly elsewhere.

He grimaced as he stepped back and peered down at a dark oak door with iron forging set into the floor, which Locke knew all too well led to the cellars below.

His father's voice echoed from his childhood, as clearly to Locke as if it were today.

Why can't you be more like your brother?

You're no son of mine…

There's only one place for you…

The breath caught in Locke's throat as he saw a clear vision of his own small hands banging on the underside of the door, eyes stinging with tears, knuckles raw and head pounding with the sound of his own screams. All he'd ever wanted was to make his father proud, but the darkness in the cellar had given him time to think, and he'd come to see himself for what he really was: a failure. Staring at the door today, years later, Locke knew deep down that nothing had changed.

He knew his father wasn't perfect, but the man was a celebrated hero. What had Locke ever done but disappoint those around him? In the end, the cellar was the very least that he deserved, he thought. He had become a better man for it, at the end of the day, maybe slightly less of a failure than he would have been otherwise. Yes, a better man—and one who would never forget.

The sweet smell of warm bread wafted through the room, pulling Locke back into the here and now. He tore his eyes away from the door and steadied himself, shaking his thoughts away. He knew his mother would scold him, but Locke was hungry from his travels, so he accepted that he would have to seek forgiveness rather than permission on this occasion. He looked around surreptitiously a final time, and then he stepped forward to tear the heel of the bread away. It was crusty on the outside but soft and spongy within, perfect but for the absence of one thing...

Now, where is the butter? It must be around here somewhere, he thought, inspecting the shelves unsuccessfully. It was as though his mother had planned it all along, suspecting his misdeed before he'd even arrived. *She always was one step ahead of me...*

He smirked and stuffed a hunk of bread into his mouth, skirting the cellar door and continuing into the dining hall beyond. At the centre of the room was a long rectangular table. Above it, an ornate chandelier lined with candles hung low from the beamed ceiling, golden arms polished to sparkle in the sunlight. He paused to gaze at the portrait of his father above the fireplace. A younger Captain Ramsey in full uniform, his expression full of pride, chest protruding as if swollen by his victory. It was still the most magnificent piece of art Locke had ever seen, and it was a wonderful depiction of his father's triumph during the Battle of Highcastle. The brushwork was incomparable, and his father's likeness bore no indication of the injuries that had befallen him. This was a version of his father that Locke could scarcely remember.

"I thought we'd be seeing you," came a sudden voice, startling Locke and immediately making his stomach drop. He raced to swallow the last of the bread with an audible gulp, the idealised depiction of Captain Ramsey appraising him through two healthy, whole eyes.

"Father, you're back," Locke said, turning to face the painting's real-life counterpart.

His father stood blank-faced in the doorway. "So, I am," he answered, without a hint of humour. "Your mother is still at market, but she'll join us soon enough."

"And Ralph?" Locke asked, though more out of courtesy than interest.

"Touring the north in search of new recruits for our armies," his father responded curtly, chin raised a little higher than before. "These are peaceful times, but war is only ever just around the corner. The threat from Verdera is ever present, and things can change very quickly." He paused to halt his tangent. "Honourable work is what it is. Your brother works tirelessly for his country. It's enough to make a father proud."

"Father, I—"

"No!" his father snapped, shocking Locke into a momentary silence. "I gave you one task, Locke. One!" he repeated, raising a finger to illustrate his point. "I put myself at risk to get you a job, a house. Your brother hand-delivered the most high-profile brigand in years right to your doorstep. All you had to do was sit tight and stay out of trouble, yet for some reason you decide to fight with the prisoner. And worse still…" His voice dropped lower, as though he were embarrassed to even utter the next bit loudly enough to risk someone overhearing. "Worse still, you lost."

"But, Father—"

"No, Locke, I don't want to hear it," his father interjected once more. "You were always a very tough child to love, you know that? Your mother, well, she's softer than I am, more patient. She told me to give you a chance and filled my ears with fantasies of how you would grow to surpass my expectations." He paused to purse his lips, head shaking with disbelief. "Now look at you. Your eye is a mess, and your reputation in an even worse state."

Then came the words Locke feared above all others.

"You've disappointed me, and not for the first time. You've let us all down, and the only consolation is that nobody in the castle is as yet aware of our association."

The blood drained from Locke's face. "That you're my father, you mean?"

His father scoffed and turned away. "Whatever, boy. It matters little now. What's done is done, and you're lucky I am a man who believes in second chances. And third and fourth and five hundredth, apparently…" His voice trailed off.

Locke was silent for a moment before cautiously saying, "So, you forgive me?"

His father turned to face him once more, an unexpected smile creeping across his face. He paced towards the centre of the room before reaching into his pocket to retrieve a parcel of dark cloth. He placed the tiny bundle on the table with a gentle clang. "That remains to be seen, boy," he answered, leaving Locke on edge. "You want to make amends, I presume? To make up for your mistakes and make your family proud?"

Locke nodded fervently.

"And you would do anything to make it so?"

"Of course."

"Good," his father said gently. "Then there is a task I would have you complete for me. I need this parcel delivered to someone."

Locke's eyes lit up at the idea that such a simple task could fix things with his father. "Of course, Father. I can—"

His father raised his hand, and Locke fell silent once more. "Wait, boy. Wait. This parcel, I need it delivered to someone *discreetly*. You trust me, don't you?"

"Yes, Father."

"And you'd do this without question, knowing that I have always done what is best for our family and for our country?"

"Of course…"

His father collected the parcel and walked across the room, where he placed it in Locke's hand. "I believe you," he said with a smile. "I believe you, and I believe that you can do this."

"Anything, Father, but where do you need it delivered?"

His father narrowed his eye, and his expression steeled. "The castle, son. I need this delivered to Finnian."

⚜ ⚜ ⚜

Two swift knocks echoed at his chamber door.

"Are you in there, Locke?" his mother's voice called from the corridor. "Your father told me what happened to your eye. I can't say I'm not happy to have you home."

A sad smile appeared on Locke's face. "It's only temporary, Mother," he called through the thick wood. "I'm fine, just a little misunderstanding. It looks worse than it is, really." He paused, and a deep breath steadied him. "I'm just getting cleaned up. I'll be out in a minute."

"If you say so," came his mother's response, and Locke could almost hear her rolling her eyes. "Don't be long," she called out. "I've made bread, your favourite. You won't want it to go cold!"

The room fell silent once more, and Locke glanced down at the parcel, which he had unravelled on the bed beside him. His heart was pounding, and his head was wracked with a thousand thoughts.

It must look worse than it is, he thought, trying to convince himself that all was well by repurposing his words to his mother.

In the centre of the cloth lay a thin piece of metal with a small hook at one end, key-sized and crafted for the same purpose. Locke had been tasked with delivering a lockpick to one of the country's most dangerous men, his own most guarded charge.

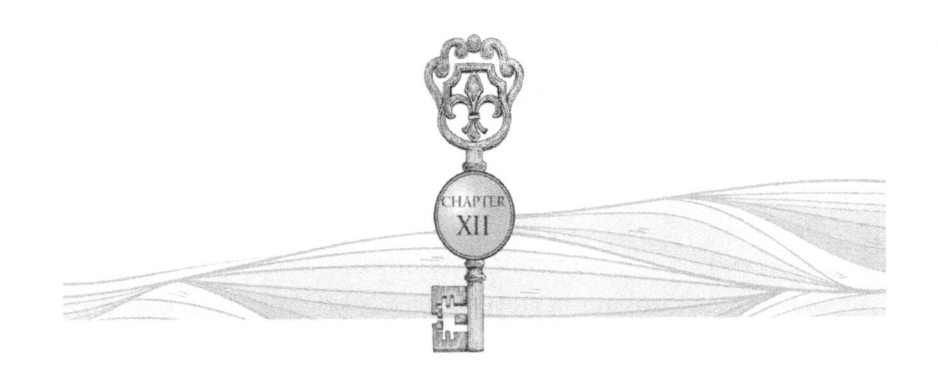

Francine

Fran's eyes popped open as she reached to swipe what she knew, even in sleep, was an insect from her face. "Get off, get off!" she yelled, jumping to her feet. The room was half dark, the only light that of torches beyond her window.

To her surprise, Patch called out, "Everything all right?" His voice was full of concern, his words muffled by the two doors between them. She wondered how long he had been waiting.

Fran pulled the hair away from her face and moved away from the bedchamber to open the front door. She found Patch, his curly hair mussed with sleep. "I'm all right, just a bug, I think," she said. "Did we oversleep?"

"Looks that way," said Patch with a deep yawn. He paused and smiled at Fran's own unruly waves of hair, which she still fought to control. "They'll be waiting for us, but it seems like you might need a moment," he said playfully. "They've waited this long, what's another few moments?"

Patch turned and left, and Fran decided she had better make herself more presentable. She washed quickly from a bowl of water that had been left for her and then tied her hair back, changing into a light linen shirt, boots, and fresh breeches. She rolled the sleeves of her shirt before descending the stairs to join Patch on the stone pathway below. She had no idea whether her ensemble was suitable, but it was the best she could do with what she had, and her efforts, however hurried, had her feeling a whole lot better about herself.

The town was far quieter than it had been during their arrival. It seemed everyone had gathered about the campfire, and the sound of music grew louder with their every step. As they moved closer, they saw large shadows dancing on the side of the longhouse.

"It's quite the party," said Fran, her eyes still heavy with exhaustion.

"You haven't seen anything yet," answered Patch. "Let me get you a mug of bombota. You'll need it."

He disappeared into the throng, and Fran shook her head, wondering what bombota was made of. The flames of the campfire climbed into the night sky, and while everyone around her was celebrating, Fran couldn't keep her mind from wandering to a similar gathering many years ago, her childhood friends clustered together to listen to Cyrus's storytelling. Beyond them, Osbert's face had appeared among the revelry, his broad smile turned upon Fran and Cyrus's adoptive brother, Edgar, who grimaced as he fought to free himself from their father's tight embrace. Her lips twitched in remembrance before a gentle breeze drew smoke from the fire into her eyes. She blinked to clear her vision, but when they opened, the memory had gone.

"Everything all right?" Patch asked her for the second time that evening. He'd appeared at her side with two mugs of dark, frothy ale.

Fran grabbed one and consumed the contents in one. She wiped her mouth with the back of her hand as Patch looked on with wide, impressed eyes. "I am now," she said, grimacing as a belch escaped her.

"Good," he said, his tone suggesting he wasn't sure whether it was indeed good or not. "Well, come on. I think Othelu's about to break the news."

Patch smiled and took her by the hand, and Fran tried desperately to tamp down the fluttering in her heart, knowing that Patch meant nothing by this small gesture. The music stopped and conversation faded as they arrived to see Othelu gesturing for silence.

"What's he saying?" Fran whispered as the king proceeded in Kanthi, his voice booming out for all to hear.

Patch raised his eyebrows. "I'm sorry, do I look like Amare?"

Fran rolled her eyes. "I thought you might have picked up the language on your many visits here. You certainly seem to know the king well enough."

Patch shook his head distractedly, listening on even if he didn't know the language. "He just mentioned Bakiri. You'd know that if you listened," he said with a wink. Fran searched her memory, going through all the new names she had learned that day, and remembered that Bakiri was Othelu's youngest son. The celebrations this evening were in his honour.

While Othelu orated, he wore his customary smile, Zimbeza standing at his side, her neck adorned with gemstones sparkling in the firelight. Their language was unlike anything Fran had ever heard, abrupt and almost rhythmic. She hadn't been in Mutembu long enough to understand the king's words, but Bakiri's name sounded out mid-sentence, and she joined the assembly in timely applause as the young prince appeared to stand beside his father.

"It's his sixteenth birthday," Patch said quietly. "Today, Bakiri becomes a warrior."

"I see," said Fran pausing as Amare emerged through the crowd toward them. The envoy had replaced his customary doublet with local dress, and a twinkle of excitement in his eyes assured Fran that he was only too happy to help Patch and herself to better understand proceedings. He stood at their side and leaned in to continue where Patch had left off.

"Like his brothers he is already promised in marriage. He is to wed a girl called Osanti, whose father holds great standing among the clans to the east of the island. It is another smart match that will unite the families and add further support to Othelu's kingship. Another pillar of peace, you might say," he ended with a smile and a wink.

Fran nodded in understanding as a young Kanthi girl appeared on cue. With her was a middle-aged man Fran presumed must be her father. Another round of applause broke out as Othelu embraced the new arrivals, and Fran smiled at how obvious it was that Bakiri and Osanti felt a great affection for one another. Perhaps a marriage of convenience *could* develop into something more. It gave her some hope for Mathilde and Taiwo.

"So, what next?" she whispered to Patch, unable to look away.

"Sport," he said. "All for fun, really, but the Kanthi are proud warriors, so you never know quite what to expect. Anyway, shh," he said with a gentle nudge. "Here comes Taiwo." He inclined his head.

Fran turned as the prince approached and wrapped Bakiri in a full-bodied embrace. The younger man was wide-eyed and starved of breath, so tight was his brother's grip, before Taiwo relented to flash a luminous smile at the admiring crowd.

"We will continue in the common tongue," said Othelu, his eyes searching to settle on Fran, "for we are fortunate to share this fine occasion with friends from afar. Please join me in welcoming Francine, chosen shield to the queen of Cornesse, and of course the good Captain Goldhand, who is already well known to many of you."

Fran's cheeks flushed as all eyes fell upon them. She noticed that Patch's hand was now resting on the small of her back, but she was more concerned by the familiarity with which he was greeted by the female contingent.

Are there no ugly girls in Mutembu? she wondered. She scolded herself for even thinking it and wondered why it bothered her anyway. She smiled at the crowd as she stepped aside to free herself from Patch's touch.

"But this is no normal visit," the king continued with excitement in his voice. "For with them, our guests deliver the prospect of yet another royal wedding!" He paused as many in the crowd gasped, and Fran grimaced in the knowledge that Mathilde would still need some convincing, thinking that Othelu might be getting ahead of himself. Nevertheless, Taiwo stood beside his father, positively beaming. They had the same infectious smile and kind eyes, though the prince was lean and muscular with a jawline that Fran couldn't help but appreciate. She found herself smirking as the king continued on, explaining their arrangement to all in attendance. The prince's smile never faded, and Fran began to relax a little, casting an approving nod toward Amare, who was to be commended for his inventive matchmaking.

"But before all of that," Othelu said, "we will first admire the warrior spirit of the Bengatu bloodline. Taiwo," he called summoning the prince, "will you meet your brother's challenge in combat?"

"I will," said Taiwo, his voice deep and confident, his shoulders drawn back, and his head held high.

"As I expected." Othelu reached out to raise Zimbeza's hand into the night sky. "Let the games begin!"

⚜   ⚜   ⚜

The contest was a total mismatch, man against boy. Despite Bakiri's obvious enthusiasm, he was no match for his brother's superior size and strength, the ten-year age gap compounded by Taiwo's admirable wrestling technique.

Fran finished off another mug of bombota and grimaced as Taiwo grappled with his brother, sending him flailing into the circle of the crowd. The onlookers jeered as the young prince landed awkwardly. Fran was reminded of that same night many years before, back in Corhollow, her brother Edgar strutting like a peacock as Cyrus lay similarly sprawled.

"Get up," she muttered under her breath, not knowing if she was talking to Bakiri or Cyrus. *You could be king one day*, she thought, willing Bakiri to his feet. She remembered dragging Cyrus back to their house that night, hurt and humiliated. The king had been practically just a boy himself at the time, but he never gave up. He never stopped fighting, and when flames razed their village to the ground, it was Cyrus who had been there to save her. She reached to swipe Patch's drink from his hand as the heat of the campfire tormented her once more, bringing back visions of that horrible night.

"You could have asked!" Patch exclaimed, half a laugh escaping his mouth.

Fran nodded but didn't respond, and then she emptied yet another mug of the sour brew. Her face was expressionless as the crowd swelled with excitement. She felt totally unable to join in with their clamouring. Did they call this sport? Patch was soon distracted by the action, unaware of her melancholy next to him, and Othelu stepped forward as Taiwo fixed his brother in a chokehold to bring the contest to a close.

"A fine exchange, I'm sure you'll agree," the king said, his eyes sparkling as he stepped between his sons.

Taiwo offered his brother a helping hand, drawing Bakiri close with an affectionate grip, before, all of a sudden, his attention turned to Patch, his eyes fixed on the captain. "Another contest, Father," Taiwo announced with a grin. "We wouldn't want our visitors to feel left out. Captain, dear friend, what do you say?"

Fran startled at the sudden turn of events. She reached for excuses on Patch's behalf, but felt her jaw widen as her words fell on deaf ears. Patch leapt forward with enthusiasm to meet the challenge unquestionably.

"I knew you couldn't resist," said Taiwo, grasping Patch's forearm like an old friend.

Fran rolled her eyes at the rather shameful show of masculinity, wondering if she would ever understand why men operated in such strange ways. She told herself there was no need to stay and watch this contest; after all, it had no bearing on the evening's occasion. Just as she had resolved to walk away, however, it became apparent how heavy her legs had become, her thoughts slow and fuzzy in the warm evening air.

Might as well stay then, she thought as Patch swiped Taiwo's leg to send them both crashing into the dirt. It wasn't so bad, she supposed. They were both...*gifted*, in their own way. But Patch was clearly the stronger of the two, his thick, sinewy arms straining as he fought to ensnare the prince. What Taiwo lacked in strength, however, he made up for in cunning, and Fran smirked as Patch snatched at air, Taiwo twisting to safety before turning to pin his opponent face first into the dusty ground.

"Good show, good show," said Othelu applauding both men. Fran clapped along with a smile and a mental note to talk Patch through his errors later, something she knew would irritate him.

Though her drinking slowed, the night continued in a blur of spear throwing, stick fighting, and rock lifting that lasted many hours. A tiredness still lingered for Fran as a result of their travels, but just as she felt herself wilting, Othelu eventually returned to take centre stage.

"Impressive stuff," the king said with a proud smile, addressing all in attendance. "But war is not won with brute strength alone. Let us now see what you can do with a bow!"

The king backed away as two men appeared with a circular target made of compacted straw. Behind them, a third man held a longbow, which he extended to Bakiri. The young prince accepted it with a smile.

"A little display, for fun," added Othelu, patting his son on the back.

But Bakiri needed no encouragement, and he wasted no time firing the first arrow, which landed wide right of the dark circle at the centre. The crowd applauded, and another man stepped forward to fire in a similarly wayward fashion before Amehlo, who Fran recognised from their dombosu journey, appeared to provide the best shot so far. It was a commendable effort, and Fran pursed her lips with approval as Taiwo teased his kinsman, mouthing "not bad," before taking up position of his own.

There was no doubting the prince's confidence, and while Fran might have thought him arrogant, there was something about Taiwo to suggest that his assured disposition was not without cause. She watched as he steadied himself and was unsurprised when his arrow thudded into the outer edge of the dark centre circle, the crowd erupting as Taiwo threw his hands high to bask in their vociferous applause.

Fran smiled and inclined her head as the prince's jubilant expression fell upon her. It was a fine way to end the evening, and Patch was already turning away when the crowd silenced suddenly. Fran had been about to follow Patch, but she turned her head, wondering what had caused the silence, and found that Taiwo was clearing his throat to speak once more.

"Leaving so soon?" he said playfully to the captain. "This is your chance to level the score." He paused to offer the bow before his eyes narrowed with mischief. A smile appeared on the prince's face, and he turned to face Fran instead. She shifted uncomfortably, her legs heavy.

"On second thought," the prince continued, a finger pressed thoughtfully to his lips, "it would be wrong for you to have all of the fun. Francine," he called, extending the bow in her direction. "Please, do me the honour of taking part. It is a special occasion, after all."

Fran's eyes squeezed shut as applause rippled all around her. Words of encouragement sounded out, and hands nudged her back and shoulders, motioning her forward to meet the challenge.

How has it come to this? she wondered wordlessly. Here she was, only travelling to meet Taiwo at Mathilde's behest, yet it would be her—Fran, of all people—to face the scrutiny of the crowd. She cursed Mathilde for all that had transpired since she had left the capital, none of which she would have been subjected to if Mathilde hadn't sent her on this outlandish errand. She'd had every intention of maintaining a low-profile after the incident aboard the Silver Sword, but with a longbow in one hand and an arrow in the other, she doubted whether things would be so simple.

"Good luck," said Taiwo with a goading smile.

Fran smirked churlishly, wishing that the prince had included her in the wrestling instead. This really was the worst-case scenario: she was representing Cornesse, a nation known for its archers, but Fran was perhaps the least skilled among them, instead sharing Mathilde's penchant for a blade. She shook her head as if to flush out the excuses. The bow was larger than she was used to, the light was poor, and if she was perfectly honest, she was drunk. It didn't help that the target was moving—or was it?

She nocked the arrow, working to steady an involuntary shake in her legs. Her eyes narrowed as she strained to focus on the target, and she gave a silent prayer to any god that might happen to be listening. *Just don't let me embarrass myself,* she thought, drawing the bowstring to ready her aim. Taiwo's arrow sat proudly at the edge of the central circle, and Fran took a sidestep before setting herself right once more.

"Here goes nothing," she muttered to herself, closing her eyes. She swallowed deeply before releasing the bowstring. The world went silent. The next thing she heard was a gasp.

"What?" she asked weakly, her eyes readjusting to the firelight as she opened them.

The explosion of noise was startling, her attention drawn to Taiwo, whose face had fallen quite unexpectedly. Patch appeared before her, his face wild with glee, and Fran groaned as she was hoisted high into the air, fighting back a wave of nausea at the sudden movement.

The crowd had descended into deafening mayhem, but Fran's gaze fell upon the target, and her face cracked into an instinctive smile, her roiling stomach momentarily quelled. Beyond them, her arrow was lodged proudly in the centre of the circle. Beside it, a splintered stump—all that remained of the prince's near-perfect shot.

⚜   ⚜   ⚜

"Let me down," she yelled to Patch, her voice lost to the din of music. Tall wooden drums resounded on the walls of the longhouse, and it seemed that the entire town was drinking and dancing, while Fran fought to keep the bombota down. For all that she admired Cyrus, her brother had always had a weak stomach, and she was determined to demonstrate a little more decorum, however much the acidity was burning in her throat.

"I'm sorry," said Patch, their eyes now level. "What a shot, though! You're full of surprises, aren't you?"

Fran shrugged. "I'm full of something," she groaned, and she covered her mouth as another belch escaped her.

Patch laughed, his face settling into a warm smile. "It has been a long day. Are you ready to head back?"

Fran made to answer, but the crowd parted, and she paused as Taiwo appeared to interrupt their departure yet again. She was more than ready to escape the commotion, but the prince seemed determined to speak to her, and it was her job to get to know him, after all.

"Not bad," Taiwo conceded, his smile retracting to form a hard line. "It's one thing to take me away from my country and my family, but to embarrass me in front of my people…" He trailed off to pinch the bridge of his nose in thought. "I don't know you, girl, but *you*, Captain, you are supposed to be a friend!"

Patch recoiled, his body language perfectly illustrating Fran's own surprise. "Come on, Taiwo, it's just a little fun!" Patch said. His jovial tone should have ended the discussion, but the prince lashed out to push him back unexpectedly. Fran stepped forward on instinct and realised that there was more than bombota now burning in her chest.

"It's all right," said Patch, placing a hand upon her shoulder. "It's late, and we've all had too much to drink." He stepped beyond her to stand face-to-face with Taiwo. "We were just leaving anyway," he added flatly. "Maybe best if we continue this in the morning?"

Taiwo nodded, and they both turned without further discussion. The prince was absorbed back into the crowd, and Fran scowled as Mathilde's prospective husband swilled bombota clumsily, his hands pawing at an attractive Kanthi woman who had the misfortune of standing nearby. He had seemed impressive and warm earlier, Fran thought, but she could clearly see that he could not handle his drink.

"What an ass," she said through gritted teeth, giving voice to her anger.

"He has his moments," Patch said, nodding. "Anyway, that's more than enough fun for one day. It's time to get you home."

The evening had deflated so quickly with the prince's actions. Her optimism for his union with Mathilde was waning, but Fran reminded herself that this was why she was here in the first place. It was an unusual task, but the duty remained the same: Fran's priority was, first and foremost, to protect the queen.

"Of course," she said, following Patch toward their respective lodgings.

The prince had shown a different side of himself, but Fran resolved that she would think things over in the morning with the benefit of a clearer head.

⚜ ⚜ ⚜

Fran had never been much of a drinker, and as she stumbled through the dark paths of Mutembu, she began to remember why.

"Here, take my arm," said Patch, his forearm extended. It was a bit cliché for Fran's tastes, but the uneven surface was hazardous, and there was nobody else around to see them, so she consented to swallow her pride, taking his arm.

"He's not always like that," Patch continued, guiding them forward. "Taiwo, he's just a kid really, sheltered by his father's reputation."

Fran wondered briefly how Patch had known that she was fixating on Taiwo's behaviour, but she scoffed at his words. It was Bakiri, not Taiwo, who was turning sixteen, with those days far behind Mathilde's would-be consort. Her hopes for the prospective match dropped further still. Mathilde had stood up to her duty at a much younger age and would not suffer excuses the likes of which Patch had offered for Taiwo's behaviour.

"If only life were so easy," she answered eventually. Flashes of her own childhood filtered through her memory: homes burned; families lost. "We've all known suffering," she snapped in frustration, snatching her arm away. It occurred to her that she couldn't even remember her birthparents' faces anymore. Her only memory now was that of her mother's golden hair and the smell of freshly baked bread that followed her father wherever he went.

"Okay, okay," sighed Patch, realising he had made a misstep. "People deal with things differently, Fran. Some sink where others swim. I know you've been through a lot, but not everyone is like you. You, well…you're special."

They both stopped, Patch's face partially illuminated by a strip of moonlight through the canopy of trees. Her cheeks flushed as she saw him flash a coy smile in her direction. Her face was still obscured by darkness, and if he sensed her embarrassment, he didn't let it show. Fran gave a half-smile, if only to mask her shame. She knew all about Patch's upbringing from Cyrus's diaries, with pages dedicated to the voiceless boy Cyrus had discovered in the Auldhaven mine.

Amazing how he always seems to say the right thing these days, Fran thought, marvelling that there had been a time when Patch could not form words, much less the sentences he articulated now. She grimaced in embarrassment at having taken out her bad feelings toward Taiwo on him.

"You're right of course," said Fran, reclaiming Patch's arm. "About everyone being different, I mean. I just want the best for Mathilde. I'm meant to solve her problems, not create them."

Patch laughed. "You're doing your best for your queen. You can't say fairer than that." He slowed as they arrived at their neighbouring houses. "There's more to Taiwo, I promise you. Give him a chance. He might surprise you yet."

Fran nodded, an unexpected nervousness rising within at their close proximity. She could easily reach out and touch his face, but she refrained.

Patch grinned, a little shiftily. "Well, goodnight," he said.

She felt her breath hitch. "Yes, goodnight," she replied.

Patch inclined his head across that small space between them, landing a soft kiss gently on her lips. "Get some rest," he said in little more than a whisper, the light of a sky full of stars reflecting in his dark eyes. "Tomorrow is a new day, and Amare is keen to return to Nivelle to present the prince. He does not wish to make the queen wait."

Chapter XIII

Francine

Her head was beating like an echo of the drums from the previous evening, but Fran nevertheless woke with a smile on her face. The morning sun was warm and bright, but it was last night that dominated her first thoughts. She yawned deeply, stretching like a starfish in an ocean of thick blankets lining the bed. She recalled her exchange with Taiwo, the arrow, the celebration, the kiss. Her breath caught momentarily at the thought, and then she internally chastised herself for feeling so giddy. It was nothing, probably just a show of friendship, and it was probably best that it stayed as such. Yes, Patch was handsome and charming, but her duty was to Mathilde and Taiwo, the queen of Cornesse and her prospective king. Her buoyant mood subsided as she replayed her conversation with the Kanthi prince. The memory was hazy, and she grimaced at the taste of bombota still lingering at the back of her throat.

Give him a chance. He might surprise you yet, Patch had said.

Whatever their relationship, Fran knew she trusted Patch, and her smile returned as she thought of the day ahead.

A knock sounded on her front door. "You about ready?" called Patch, as if reading her thoughts.

Despite her excitement at hearing Patch's voice again, Fran rolled onto her side. *Just a few more minutes,* she thought groggily.

"Fran, it's time," he insisted.

Handsome and charming as he might be, Patch was relentless. She sighed heavily, crawling to gather her belongings. "Ready," she grunted unenthusiastically. While she could have done with a few more minutes—or hours—of sleep, Fran reminded herself that she needed to get home. Her mind turned to Cyrus and the imminent arrival of the new baby, her new niece or nephew. Excitement washed over her, and she woke up properly, packing with renewed purpose as she thought of all that waited for her at home.

⚜   ⚜   ⚜

It seemed all of Mutembu had gathered to bid Taiwo farewell. A smile had returned to the prince's face, and the outpour of emotion from the rest of the clan comforted Fran. Maybe Patch had been right about the prince after all.

"Take care of him," Zimbeza told Patch, stepping forward to wrap her son in a tight embrace.

"He'll be fine," Othelu added, his voice full of ease. "He is not so different from his brother Zakari—and his father too, of a time. We Bengatu men were made to travel and to lead." He gripped

Taiwo's forearm as the prince escaped his mother's grasp. "Amare," he continued, turning to the envoy once he released his son. "Send our best wishes to Queen Mathilde, and tell her that we hope to see her in person next time, perhaps as a daughter."

Amare inclined his head. "Great king."

"Fran," said Zimbeza, reaching to take her by the hand. "A gift, for you." She stepped back, and Fran opened her fingers to find a delicate silver necklace resting in her palm. "It is a small gesture, a trinket purchased from a trader who visited Mutembu many years ago."

"It's beautiful," said Fran, holding the chain up to the light.

"It had a name," Zimbeza continued, head shaking as her eyes lowered in thought. "I no longer remember it, but the wearer is said to be blessed with clear thought and purpose." She laughed softly, stepping to place an arm around her son once more. "It is probably a foolish tale, but it would comfort me to know that you have it. It may not be precious, but you travel with my greatest treasure after all." She nodded toward her son.

Fran smiled and turned to find Patch wearing a similar expression. "You have been most gracious hosts, as always," he said to Zimbeza and Othelu with a subtle bow. "Look after that wife of yours, Othelu, and Bakiri," he turned to the young prince, whose bride-to-be stood at his side, "train hard. We both owe your brother a lesson!"

The young prince nodded, a smirk playing up his features, and Amare led the group away from Mutembu and back into the jungle, sounds of farewell from the villagers and Taiwo's family growing distant in their wake.

⚜ ⚜ ⚜

They found Amehlo at the jetty waiting as impatiently as ever.

"The rainy season is coming," said Amare, lifting his head to inhale the humid morning air. "The sky is full of water," he continued, and he pointed toward at a gap in the canopy. "You see the mist? We must pray that the weather holds, or it may be some time before we leave, and I do not wish to keep the queen waiting. Taiwo is eager to meet his match."

Taiwo added nothing more than a grunt to Amare's words, and Fran suspected that the prince's eagerness was being somewhat overstated by the envoy, based on their previous interaction. Whatever her thoughts, though, Fran knew Mathilde well enough to know that the queen appreciated efficiency in all things. She hated to wait, and Fran knew that in a delicate matter such as this, long days of procrastination could very well lead to a change of heart. It would be a stretch to say that Mathilde had been enthusiastic about the situation in the first place.

Focusing on the more immediate problem at hand, Fran followed Amare's sightline, and her heart sank at the fog that was already collecting in the treetops. The branches were dusted with white as though the clouds had descended upon them, and she thought of Cyrus and Marcia. Would a delay cause her to miss the birth of the new baby?

"We should get going then," she snapped.

Amare smiled as the luggage arrived to join them. "After you, young lady. Your carriage awaits."

⚜ ⚜ ⚜

They arrived to Taboso in the late afternoon, and Fran breathed deeply as she stepped forward to break free from the humidity of the jungle.

"What is that smell?" she asked, her relief short-lived.

Amare shrugged with a simple smile. "Welcome back."

"It's not looking good," said Patch, appearing beside them. "I'll speak to Redbeard and the others, but my gut tells me we should wait before setting off."

"A night in Taboso?" Taiwo asked enthusiastically.

Patch scratched his chin in thought, looking at Taiwo with wariness in his narrowed eyes. "Maybe," he sighed. "We'll see."

He left in pursuit of his crew, and Taiwo followed him. Amare suggested that Fran might be more comfortable at a nearby inn, and though the port seemed anything but restful, Fran followed him with few other options. She wished that she had followed Patch too, but she wasn't overly eager to see the crewmates from the Silver Sword again until she absolutely had to.

Their temporary home was to be The Shipwright, a dilapidated if characterful inn. As they approached, the doors swung open, sending an unruly patron tumbling to land at their feet. The man's deep red tunic might have been valuable at some point, but the garment was full of holes that revealed a stained undershirt. His hair was long, unruly, and grey in colour, though his moustache had been tainted yellow, presumably by the effects of pipe smoke, a smell that followed him closely. Fran wrinkled her nose. She stepped back, her hand instinctually moving towards her sword just in case she found herself in need of it, but when she glanced over, she found Amare smirking.

"Is Davey working?" Amare asked, sounding as if he already knew the answer.

The patron climbed to his knees. "I was just speaking with him," he said, pausing to inspect his mouth for missing teeth. "He's in one of his better moods. You'll find him behind the bar."

Amare nodded and flipped a gold coin in the man's direction. Their luggage arrived, and the envoy moved past the man, climbing the stairs to arrive at the swinging doors.

"You're in for a treat," he promised Fran with encouragement. "This is the best place in town. Relax, I'm sure the captain will send word soon."

It was hardly the most inspiring endorsement, but Fran consented to follow, joining Amare among the hubbub of the crowded tavern.

"If it isn't my old friend, Amare," a booming voice called, welcoming their arrival.

Fran stayed close to Amare and ever vigilant. There wasn't an empty seat to be found, and those present competed with one another to yell or sing across long rectangular tables, causing a din that did nothing to improve Fran's headache. Meanwhile, a cloud of smoke seemed to gather above them, drawing Fran's attention to the low ceiling and supporting beams, where patrons had carved their names and drunken messages into the woodwork. The white walls were stained yellow and brown by smoke, like the man's moustache, and the tavern gave Fran a claustrophobic feeling, assaulting her senses.

Fran correctly guessed that the booming voice belonged to Davey, who Amare had been looking for. Davey was, Fran thought, an imposing landlord who was built a lot like a bull. The large, white man had thick forearms covered in ink, and his shirt was open to the navel, exposing a broad chest covered in curly grey hair.

"Good to see you again," said Amare, calling across the bar to Davey. The innkeeper paused his conversation with a bearded pirate to join them and return the sentiment.

"How long has it been? And you've brought a friend to visit me?"

A large man with a limp pushed past Amare, momentarily knocking him. He steadied himself. "I have," he said, his doublet straightened, a smile returned to his face. "This is Fran, chosen shield to Queen Mathilde of Cornesse. She's with me on very important business."

Davey inclined his head. "Well, you're a very important man." His words had a hint of mockery that made Fran feel warmer toward him. The innkeeper turned his attention upon her. "If it wasn't for Amare, I'd have never met my wife."

"Is that so?" she asked, raising her eyebrows at Amare, who smiled back at her. It seemed that the envoy had a real fondness for matchmaking, and it occurred to Fran for the first time that it was interesting that Amare had no partner of his own, at least not that he had spoken of. She wondered whether years of devoted service had left Amare unable to pursue his own personal interests, and thoughts of Patch surfaced unexpectedly in her mind. It was clear that Amare was devoted to King Othelu, just as Fran was devoted to Mathilde, but was a life of service really enough? Would it be enough for Fran? Her heart beat a little faster at the startling realisation that her short time with Patch was already cause for her to ask such questions. *It was just a meaningless kiss, stop getting ahead of yourself...*

She shook the thought away as a tall Kanthi lady with braided hair appeared on the other side of the bar. Fran noticed the way her hand swept over Davey's shoulders as she brushed past him to grab a bottle of brown liquor.

"That's Okah," said Davey, confirming Fran's thoughts. "She's my partner in all things. Amare is a good man with a kind heart. You're in safe hands with this one."

"Think nothing of it," said Amare.

Davey shook his head at Amare's modesty. "Okah made an honest man of a devious old pirate. She made me want to do better, to be better..."

"We saw Peyton on the way in," said Amare with a grin. Fran could only assume that this was the man who had landed at their feet outside the tavern.

Davey swiped at the air contemptuously with a big hairy hand. "No less than he deserves. The foolish old drunk is always causing problems. This place isn't perfect, but we're working at it. With peace in the islands and ambition like Othelu's, there's money to be made, and money means opportunities."

"Taboso doesn't seem short of opportunities," said Fran, thinking of the array of questionable activity she had seen on her arrival to the island.

The innkeeper gave a satisfying chuckle. "You're not wrong. But we take measures to maintain certain standards in this establishment. In time, I hope more people might see fit to visit us with their important business. But here I am, talking away while the two of you are dying of thirst. Fran, what can I get you?"

"Oh, I'm fine," said Fran, raising an apologetic hand. She doubted she could keep a drink down if she tried.

The innkeeper's brow furrowed, and Amare cleared his throat to interject. "Nor for me, but there is something else we need your help with. The rooms in your loft, are they still available?"

Davey nodded. "Aye."

"Good," said Amare, and he paused to look around them before retrieving a few gold coins from a small leather pouch, which he handed across to the innkeeper. "We shouldn't be here longer than one night, perhaps less. This should cover it."

Davey's raised his hands, this time in protest. "I couldn't," he said, turning his face to dismiss Amare's money. Whatever your business, I will not profit from it. I owe you one. Besides, it is not every day that you have the chance to host a royal dignitary. Please, make yourself comfortable." He paused to reach into his pocket for two faded silver keys. "You will forgive our humble lodgings, Fran. The rooms are basic, and I wouldn't trust the food from our kitchens, but the ale is fresh, and you are both very welcome."

"Thank you," said Fran, who found her frustration at the weather somewhat lessened, accepting that Amare had chosen The Shipwright well. Despite Davey's intimidating appearance, it seemed he was as honest and decent as she could hope to meet in Taboso. The tavern was a den of smoke, drink, and general debauchery, yet Davey seemed kind, and he made no fuss handing over the keys before leading them to the loft space above.

"Get some rest," said Amare as they parted at the top of the stairs. "I expect you need it after all of the excitement last night!"

Fran's eyes widened and her skin turned hot. Did he mean the archery or her walk back with Patch afterward? *It was just a silly little kiss*, she thought shaking her head as Amare closed his door behind him. But if that was the case, why did she keep thinking about it?

Davey had called the room basic, but Fran had never imagined that this could be an overstatement. A small, rickety bed and desk were joined by a three-legged chair that threatened to fall over whenever she walked on the loose floorboards. Night had not yet fallen, but Fran had no desire to explore the sights of Taboso, and even if Amare had intended to embarrass her, he was right about one thing: she did need some rest.

She fell onto the bed and squeezed a thin cushion tight to her ears as a band of musicians struck up an untimely tune below. She wondered what news to expect from Patch, and though music reverberated on the walls all around her, her thoughts soon faded, giving way to much needed sleep.

⚜   ⚜   ⚜

Fran's eyes opened to unfamiliar surroundings. Her mind retraced their journey from Mutembu, and she sighed at the delay caused by the fog. Her room was windowless, but her intuition told her it was already after dark, and her brows furrowed at the frustrating lack of news. She swung her legs over the side of the bed, feeling exasperated. Then again, she thought, Patch didn't normally keep her waiting. What if he was hurt, or perhaps worse? Her priority was to find Taiwo, since he was her charge, but would the crew of the Silver Sword even take them on as passengers without their captain? A pang of guilt struck her for even considering this possibility. However hard she tried to deny it, Patch already meant more to her than that. She shook her head, knowing she was probably letting her worry get the better of her.

Lively music continued below, glasses clinking without a care in the world, making Fran wonder how she had managed to sleep at all. Fran tied her hair and boots purposefully and slipped from her room in silence, knowing Amare would never sanction a solo journey into the belly of Taboso. She descended the stairs to find the tavern much as she expected: wizened buccaneers with gold teeth and hoop earrings, women of all shapes and sizes perched upon their laps. Fran marvelled at the mixture of so many peoples and races in one room, even if most of them identified as pirates. A cloud of pipe smoke passed over her, and though Fran swiped at the air to scour the room, there were no familiar faces to be found.

She waited until Davey was distracted with a crowd of clamouring patrons requesting refills and chose her moment to sneak past the barkeep and into the street beyond. It was every bit as dark and murky as she had envisaged, and she rubbed her eyes, willing them to adjust.

Where do I go now?

She grimaced, immediately questioning her own judgement in leaving The Shipwright. A full moon did little to brighten Taboso's dingy backstreets, and Fran's eyes twitched with the prickling feeling that she was being watched. At any rate, she knew better than to stand still. The path to her right was fringed with a row of well-lit, if questionable looking, drinking holes. She buried her hands in her pockets, lowering her head as she moved like a moth to a flame, resolving herself to search for Patch and his crew.

The Black Barnacle, The Drunken Sailor, even the Come On Inn. Fran left no stone unturned, her annoyance rising at the apparent disappearance of the crew of the Silver Sword. It seemed each tavern was somehow darker and grimier than the one before, and though she placed scant value on luxury, Fran became increasingly thankful for The Shipwright after all.

This is useless, she thought, stepping back out into the mist for what felt like the hundredth time. The streets seemed to darken a fraction more as she left each tavern without success, and she dodged two bleary-eyed revellers to step into an alleyway and rest against a lichen-covered wall. She berated herself for ever thinking she would find them. Taboso was too big and too labyrinthine, a cesspit where the winding streets sprawled like tentacles, yearning to draw in those foolish enough to wander without aim.

Fran's head lolled in defeat for a moment, but then her anger subsided as a sudden thought occurred to her. "The Silver Sword," she muttered, bringing her palm to her forehead with a loud smack. It seemed obvious now. Patch had very likely gone aboard the ship itself to meet the crew. After all, it would make more sense for them to live onboard even in port rather than spend out at various taverns and inns. She smirked at her own foolishness, but she managed only a single step before a familiar voice caused her smile to fade, stopping her in her tracks.

Laughter resounded in the street beyond. She peered toward the sound and saw Patch and Taiwo, arms draped around each other's shoulders, with a woman at each of their sides. Fran crouched in the shadows, cursing quietly as the unsteady clique stumbled away from The Shattered Cup and into the haze beyond. To think that she'd been worried about them. To think that she'd suffered the indignity of entering every other godforsaken hellhole in this part of town, and all the while, Patch had been drinking away like an inconsiderate man-child. What a wild time they seemed to be having, and here she was squatting in a puddle of what smelled suspiciously like piss. Her fists clenched at the shame of it. Fran remained still for a moment to let her temper settle. At the very least, this meant the end of her search. She sneered as Taiwo's voice echoed in the distance, yet as his last words faded, she realised that she was not alone.

She started as a thick hand reached to cover her mouth. Wiry finger hair bristled at her nose, a second arm clamped tightly around her, constricting her defence.

"Bit late to be out by yerself, isn't it?" came a man's voice, breath hot in her ear. "I've been watching you," he continued menacingly. "Not many like you around 'ere."

His excited laughter filled the air. His stale breath nipped at Fran's nostrils, and her eyes watered. She gritted her teeth and pushed outward to test his resistance. Her attacker was just another faceless street-thug, but Fran felt as though she were back in Highcastle a decade ago, her small, twelve-year-old body powerless in King Rafael's grasp. The Verderan king had captured her and threatened her life in front of Cyrus before agreeing to an ill-fated duel that had seen Rafael perish at the sharp end of a Cornessian arrow. She stilled, a fiendish smile spreading over her face at the memory. It was time for this new attacker to share a similar fate.

Her jaw chomped down, crunching her teeth into his knuckle. The man yelled, unable to stop himself, and his grip weakened. Fran used his moment of weakness to throw a vicious elbow flying into his ribs, where she heard a distinct crack.

"You bitch!" he called, and she knew she'd make him regret it. A backward kick sent him stumbling, and Fran turned to face him at last, seeing that the man was not much older than she was. He had a big, crooked nose, dark deep-set eyes, and patches of flaky skin around his mouth and chin. His fearful expression put a fresh smile on her face.

"Who are you?" he asked in terror, but Fran ignored him, knowing that the time for words had passed. She stepped forward, sending him scuttling across the filthy ground in fear. Fran caught up with him and swung one of her feet between his legs, her heavy leather boot leaving him writhing in pain.

"Who I am is none of your business," she snarled, kneeling to pin his arms with her legs. She knew she could leave him and walk away, but could she allow that? Was that even what she wanted? Her answer was instinctive as her fists began to pound into the flesh of his face, flecks of blood spraying into the night air around her. She'd promised herself she would never allow another person to overpower her, and the man in front of her became a blur of Rafael, the superstitious men on The Silver Sword, and every other brute who had ever made the mistake of underestimating Fran.

The world became distant, her fists blood-red, her attention zeroed in on the man's face. She could feel his legs twitching slightly below her, but his face had gone blank. Eventually, Fran sat back, resting on the man's torso and panting with exertion. He was not moving, and as Fran looked away from the mess of a man to the mouth of the alleyway, she startled, realising that a woman was standing there watching her. How long had she been there?

"I don't doubt he deserved it," came the woman's voice, snatching Fran's breath with surprise. Fran rocked back on her knees, standing up to find the woman, who had hair that looked copper in the moonlight, walking toward her, surprisingly nonplussed by the mess Fran had created. "My name's Sabina," the woman continued. "How about you?"

Fran's eyes narrowed. "Fran. Do you know this man?"

"Well enough. Let's say that we work together." Sabina shrugged. "He had it coming to him. Any chance he'll live?"

Fran leaned down toward the man, where she heard gentle breaths whistling between his broken teeth. "He'll live," she said. "Is there somewhere we can take him?" Apart from not wanting evidence of her latest rage splayed on the streets of Taboso, Fran figured it was the humane thing to do.

Sabina opened her mouth before pausing to consider her answer. "No," she said, seemingly uninterested in her supposed colleague's fate. "I think this is all part of his lesson. Let's get you out of here and get you a drink."

"Are you sure?" Fran asked, quirking her brow in question.

"Oh, honey," said Sabina with a devilish grin, "I'm not known for making jokes."

⚜ ⚜ ⚜

They walked through the streets, Sabina a few strides ahead and Fran in hot pursuit. Fran could tell that Taboso held no mystery to Sabina. She moved quickly and surely before halting at the doors to a place called The Salty Dog.

"We're here," she said, with the faintest suggestion of a smile. Fran nodded before following, her face expressionless as she fought the urge to place her hand on her sword. This was becoming something of a habit, visiting unsavoury establishments, and she wondered vaguely how any town could sustain so many inns.

The tavern's interior was nothing new or exciting, displaying the usual grime and debasement Fran had seen in the other hole-in-the-wall places she had spent her night visiting. Sabina led the way to a perch at the end of the bar.

The landlord must know her, Fran thought, because he said, "Coming right up," before Sabina had ordered a thing. The drinks arrived so quickly that Fran wasn't fully seated by the time they slid along the bar, leaving a wet ring in their wake. Sabina's drink was gone before Fran could draw breath.

"So, what brings you to Taboso?" Sabina asked. Fran guessed Sabina was probably in her forties. Her red hair, which was brighter in the light, was tied tightly, and her face featured a prominent jawline and fading scars upon her cheek. She tapped her fingers on the bar, and the barman promptly placed another small glass in front of her, filled with a clear liquid.

Fran considered the question, trying to decide how much to give away to this anomaly of a woman. "I came to find someone," she answered carefully. She made to take a sip of her drink, but she nearly fell from her stool, startled as Sabina began to laugh.

"Find someone, you say? What is it that you're looking for?"

Fran rolled her eyes. "It's not *what* as much as *who*."

"Ah," said the older woman, reclining with a smile. "A boy then? Well, look how well it worked out with the last one."

"Huh?"

"Selwyn, my colleague you attacked in the street." She paused to once again down her drink in one. "Do keep up."

Fran slouched forward as exhaustion caught up with her. "It's not like that," she said, once again conflicted as to how much she could share. For all Fran's vigilance, she couldn't deny her anger with the evening's events. She was pleased for Sabina's timely company, and if she had meant Fran harm, there would have been no better opportunity than the one she had passed up in the dingy alley in which they had met.

"I travelled from Cornesse to collect Prince Taiwo," she continued, with some hesitation. "The prince is to meet Queen Mathilde and discuss the prospect of marriage. It's my job to get him there safely."

"I see," said Sabina, drawing out her words. "And how did getting attacked fit into your plans?"

Fran shrugged. "It's all part of the job, apparently. I stepped out to keep an eye on the prince and, well, you know the rest."

"So, this prince is giving you the run-around?"

"You could say that."

"Well, I don't blame you for what happened back there," Sabina said with a supportive nod. "I grew up with brothers, and brute strength is really the only language they understand."

Fran smirked, remembering times when Cyrus had fallen foul of her wrath. "If only things were that simple," she said sadly. "Mathilde is queen of Cornesse and the most powerful woman I know, yet so many of her decisions are still made by a council of men." She felt guilty saying it, but Sabina was a good listener, and she seemed to understand Fran, or at least Fran's frustrations, in a way no one else had since her departure from Nivelle.

Sabina shook her head with disapproval. "Not on my watch. I don't know this queen of yours, but it sounds like she needs some backbone. You're a friend of hers, though, I presume?"

"Chosen shield."

"Right. And what part of the job involves chasing a boy across the world on her behalf?"

Fran finished her drink before slamming the glass down. "Exactly!" Just hearing the words made her feel vindicated. "The prince is an idiot anyway, just like all the others. Maybe this fog is for the best. Perhaps Taiwo will run home to his mother or, better still, drown himself."

"You're planning to leave already?" Sabina asked, turning in her chair.

"Tomorrow, I think, with any luck," Fran sighed, a yawn escaping her lips. "The weather caused delays, but our ship is stocked and ready; well as far as I know. Anyway, I'm sorry, I'm rambling."

"It's fine," Sabina said as she smiled. "Sounds like you've had a hell of a day. Barkeep, put these on my tab, will you?" She placed a hand on Fran's shoulder. "Come on, I'll show you the way back."

⚜   ⚜   ⚜

They came to a halt with The Shipwright in view.

"This is where I leave you," said Sabina. And whether from drink or fatigue, Fran found herself smothering her new companion in a warm embrace.

Sabina smiled as they parted and gave a courteous nod before turning to leave. She took no more than a few steps before the fog enveloped her, and Fran turned to make her way toward the inn.

What an evening, she thought, slowing to delay her arrival, her mind playing over the night's events, from Patch and Taiwo's exploits to her run-in in the alley, to her drink with Sabina. Maybe she *had* been a little harsh on Mathilde, she thought with a twinge of guilt, but Sabina was right: strength *was* the only language men understood. Whatever happened to the feisty young queen Fran had grown to love and admire?

She continued toward the foot of the tavern's outdoor staircase. One thing was certain: Sabina would never have never allowed her to be played by Patch. All those moments onboard the Silver Sword, their time in Mutembu—sweet words, subtle looks, the kiss. Fran shook her head as anger swelled within her. It was all just a game to him, a distraction maybe, and when all was said and done, he was no better than Taiwo after all. No wonder he had been so quick to tell Fran to give Taiwo another chance; they were birds of a feather!

She climbed the stairs quietly and nudged the tavern doors open, sneaking around like a child after dark. The tavern was empty, but candlelight still flickered in the wagon wheel of candles hanging from the ceiling, and Fran closed the doors before turning the key in the lock.

"Where have you been?" asked Amare, his voice startling her. The envoy rose from his place in the shadows, and the landlord, Davey, remained seated, a jug of ale hovering halfway to his mouth.

Fran scowled at their inquisition. "I am not required to answer to you, Amare," she reminded him, "but if you must know, I have been out searching for the prince. That idiot is still out there somewhere, and we should be on our way home."

Davey sipped his drink before placing it on the table. "We were only worried," he said, and his warm tone made Fran feel a little guilty for her sharp response.

"This is not a good place," added Amare. "There are many dangers."

Davey counted them on his fingers. "You've got the opium barons, the brothel-keepers, the pirate captains. Firemane's crew has been causing problems left, right, and centre, and—"

"Enough!" snapped Fran, her eyes rolling in frustration. Though she felt bad snapping at Davey, she was at her wit's end. "That all sounds very frightening, but I'm chosen shield to the queen of Cornesse, not some defenceless *girl,* and I will not be locked in a room at your every whim. Besides," she continued, wondering what Sabina would have made of her outburst, "the captain promised news. He said he would update us, and I've heard nothing. I mean, where is he? The taverns are closed! Am I to believe he's still out there, skulking around in the darkness with that foolish prince?"

She stopped pointedly, Amare's jaw hanging loose with surprise, clearly not sure what to make of Fran's abrasive tone. She wondered, belatedly, if he was thinking of her blind rage onboard the Silver Sword.

"Why don't you sit down?" offered Davey, pulling a barstool from the table. "The captain came by with news earlier. He said you'd be leaving in the morning."

Fran's stomach burned with the embarrassment of her outburst, but even more so with the shame that she had been traipsing around Taboso all night looking for Patch when he had already come by the tavern to leave word. Why hadn't she just asked Davey if he had seen the captain before she set out on her foolhardy excursion?

After a pause, she asked, "So, we're finally going?" She took the seat Davey had offered her.

Amare poured her a drink and smiled. "We leave at first light."

Locke

"**L**ocke, are you listening? Hello?"

Locke grunted, "Huh?" and his daydream parted to be replaced by Boyd's impatient expression staring back at him. Locke had been thinking of the lockpick and the request his father had made of him. Even Boyd's appearance was a welcome momentary distraction from Locke's waking nightmare, but the man's arms were crossed, and his shoulders were raised questioningly at Locke as he shook his head.

"Well, get up!" Boyd continued, grabbing Locke's arm to pull him from his chair. Once Locke was standing, Boyd gestured toward the cell door. "It's time for handover. I know Finnian gave you a beating, but I had hoped he might have knocked some sense into you. No such luck from the look of things!"

Locke stood and hesitantly followed Boyd to the cell, where Finnian was standing in his customary position, the thief's face pressed between the bars.

"He's been even stranger than usual today," said the brigand, scratching at the thick crop of dark stubble on his cheek. "He's been distant, like his thoughts are elsewhere. Hasn't said a word to me all day. You know, I don't think he takes this job as seriously as you do."

"That's enough," yelled Boyd, pointing angrily and silencing the brigand. Boyd turned and shook his head in Locke's direction. "He's not all wrong, though," he continued, his voice lowered for Locke's ears only. "I don't know, three days' leave for a sore eye, and you're still a waste of space. I'm going to have to speak to High Commander Broderick about you—"

"No!" Locke snapped, cutting his colleague's threat short. "I mean…no, there's no need, I'm just a little distracted is all."

Boyd's eyes narrowed as he opened the cell door. "Fine. Well, let's get this over with. And you…" he said, turning to Finnian, "no funny business, understood? Arms up. Same for you, Walt, and cut the nonsense. We're going to have a nice peaceful evening."

Locke nodded, though Boyd's insults fell on deaf ears. He stepped into the cell wordlessly, hands shaking, beads of sweat already forming on his brow, as his fellow prison master closed the cell door behind him, watching from the other side of the bars.

How has it come to this? Locke wondered, approaching the prisoners. His father had given him no further insight to his plans, and Locke knew better than to ask. He'd spent the remainder of his visit to Ardlyn Keep being coddled by his mother, who had been more concerned as to whether he was sleeping or eating properly.

"You're a bag of bones!" she'd said, Locke's laughter cut short by his father's lurking presence. In the end, he'd returned to the capital with more problems than he'd had when he left in search of respite. Instead, he'd left Ardlyn Keep with a head full of worry and something far more dangerous tucked inside his pocket.

"I said arms up!" Boyd's forceful voice echoed against the stone walls. Against his own will, Locke cringed slightly at the reverberation.

Locke's hand brushed against his pocket for the hundredth time that day. The parcel was still there, an ominous reminder of the task ahead. He'd spent days thinking about the best way to do it. In truth, it had been a struggle to think of anything else. He considered simply handing it to Finnian through the bars, but he knew Walt was watchful and had no idea if he could be trusted, though Locke's gut told him not. It would be too dangerous to let himself into the cell without Boyd there as backup, so in the end, Locke had concluded handover would be his best and only option, though that wouldn't make it any easier.

"Well, come on," Boyd called brusquely. He folded his arms and tutted loudly. "These two may be here for life, but there's no need to take all night for something so simple."

Locke turned at this. "Life?" he asked. "So, Finnian has been sentenced?" It occurred to Locke that he was simply looking for an excuse to delay handover—and thus his task—but he did find himself genuinely curious as to the brigand's fate.

"I am here, you know?" said Finnian indignantly, but Boyd raised an eyebrow, and Finnian fell silent.

"He was taken for sentencing in your absence," Boyd answered eventually. "He's lucky that King Cyrus is merciful.

Lifetime imprisonment for this one. The world didn't stop because you were off taking a break, you know?"

Locke nodded and turned, letting another insult pass without comment. Instead, he looked over at Walt, who stood mumbling to himself quietly, both arms raised while Finnian flashed a cocksure smile.

"Well, come on then. Let's get this over with," said the brigand, raising his arms routinely.

Locke felt Boyd's attention hot upon him as he began searching Walt. His hands moved instinctively, but his actions were blurred as his mind began to wander over the same subject that had troubled him for days. *Why Finnian?* This was a man his father had personally delivered to be put in chains. The man was an infamous thief, and Locke's brother, Ralph, named Finnian's capture among his finest achievements to date, which was really saying something, as Ralph had no shortage of achievements for which to laude himself. Finnian was a dangerous swine who deserved his sentence, so why set him free?

Locke inspected Walt's pockets to conclude the search. He could delay no longer and knew he would simply have to trust his father's plan, whatever that might entail. Whatever shortcomings he might have had in Locke's upbringing, the man was considered a hero for a reason, after all, and he had asked for Locke's faith. What right did Locke have to question a man like that? What did he know of the world? This wasn't for him to judge or decide. It was a chance to earn his father's respect and make a difference. In the end, there was no decision at all. It was not a question of would he or wouldn't he. It had to be done.

He stepped toward Finnian, whose arms had begun to sag. "Arms up," he barked, carefully expressionless in the face of the brigand's roguish smirk. The search began at Finnian's collar, moving to the prisoner's underarms and across his chest before an inspection about the waist. Finnian's smell was one of stale sweat, and Locke used the excuse of the stench to turn away, grimacing at Boyd as he reached into his own pocket to lay a hand on the parcel.

"Just get it done," said Boyd, and he rolled his eyes theatrically, clearly unimpressed by Locke's apparent reaction to Finnian's odour and unaware that Locke had surreptitiously moved the parcel from his pocket to his sleeve. Whatever Locke thought of his fellow prison master, the man certainly did seem to take the job very seriously. Boyd's attention remained fixed on Locke as he returned to continue the inspection, and Locke thought he saw Finnian's eyes flicker briefly, the smallest hint of a question in his eyes, to Locke's sleeve.

A moment of understanding passed between them, and the corner of Finnian's mouth curled into a grin. Finnian wasn't a renowned thief for nothing, Locke thought. Sleight of hand would be second nature to him.

'What's that?" Finnian called unexpectedly, his eyes widening as he gestured frantically across the room.

Locke startled and turned to face Boyd, who twisted toward the door with his baton raised. Understanding dawned on Locke as he felt Finnian's hand fly almost imperceptibly to Locke's sleeve, pulling the parcel free as Boyd scoured the room. By the time Boyd turned to face them once more, the act was done.

Boyd's eyes narrowed. "What's what? I warned you, no funny business, inmate."

To his credit, Finnian persisted with the finesse of an experienced performer. Locke stepped to one side as the brigand's neck arched, his eyes darting about the room. "I guess it was nothing," he concluded, his tone sounding genuine even to Locke's ears. "Perhaps Prison Master Locke is contagious and I've caught his madness."

Locke bit his tongue, his heartbeat slowing with a sense of relief as Boyd chuckled to himself, apparently unable to ignore Finnian's wit at Locke's expense.

"Okay then," said Boyd, finally lowering his baton. "Well, when you're ready, Prison Master Locke. I'm sure you must have some sort of home to get to. You certainly spend more time there than here."

Locke stepped beyond the cell door, where Boyd stood ready to meet him. "Keys," said the prison master, opening his palm expectantly.

Locke obliged and then made for the exit. His body was slick with a cold sweat, and a wave of regret suddenly crashed against his conscience.

Right or wrong, the thing was done, a voice in his head told him. It sounded oddly like his father's.

⚜   ⚜   ⚜

Upon leaving the prison, the implications of his actions hit him immediately.

Locke rushed through the streets in a daze, a blur of faces seeming to watch him, judge him, their arms reaching to haul him back and subject him to a king's justice. A light drizzle filled the air, and strands of his hair soon plastered themselves to his forehead; he lowered his eyes as pathways turned to mud underfoot. He was desperate to get back to his room at The Eagle.

He tried to focus on imagining the proud moment when he would tell his father he had achieved the task that had been set for him, tried to envision the look of pride and vindication for the faith that he had placed in Locke. He'd done everything that had been asked of him, but the feeling was not one of relief or triumph but instead of fear and regret. He was a traitor to the crown, he realised, and the very thought of returning to the castle sent him nauseous with dread. He felt his nerve wavering.

Maybe I should hand myself in, confess my crimes?

He stopped in the middle of the path, the even heavier rain now causing his boots to fill with water. All the possible outcomes played in his mind: death or perhaps a lifetime sentence of his own. A lifetime spent on the other side of the bars with Boyd and his smart mouth his only company, besides his new cellmates, Walt and Finnian, that is. And what about the questions he'd be asked if he confessed? An investigation would surely uncover his relationship with his father fairly quickly. The inquest alone would destroy their family's reputation, putting their hard-earned status at risk, never mind what would happen if anyone realised that Locke's father was the one who had given him the lockpick. They could lose their home, their livelihood, and for what, other than the easing of Locke's conscience?

He shook the rain away and continued for home. *This* was the true test, he thought, the moment he would rise to meet his father's expectations and those he'd placed upon himself. *This* is where he would need to be resilient and repay his father's belief. He just needed to get home and maintain a low profile. Tomorrow was a new day, and there was no telling what Finnian was planning with his father's help. Boyd hadn't seen a thing, and there was nothing incriminating to connect Locke with Finnian's escape. The sequence of events played in his mind, and his heart suddenly raced. He held no love for Boyd, but he feared the repercussions that his actions might produce for his colleague. An escaped prisoner was one thing, and Locke knew that Boyd would hate to be the one on duty when Finnian got away, but what if an even worse fate awaited Locke's fellow prison master? What if Finnian's notoriously merciless reputation was true and Boyd became a casualty of the thief's escape? Could Locke live with that blood on his hands?

He pushed through the front door and into The Eagle, shaking rain from his hair.

"Locke!" He looked up to find Grace, her timing more than a little unfortunate, and her appearance caused a rush of embarrassment to pool in his stomach even though there were much more pressing matters at hand.

The barmaid rushed forward to meet him. She placed a hand on his arm, but Locke pushed it away and stepped past her into the cacophony of the tavern. Musicians were playing, and Rufus was laughing with one of his regulars as though it were any other night. Locke, of course, knew otherwise.

"Not now, Grace!" he snapped. The bar area was as busy as ever, and Locke navigated through a maze of stools and tables, making for the door in the corner that led to his room, Grace trailing after him. "It's fine," he continued dismissively, thinking that she would leave him alone if her guilty conscience was eased, but then his emotions got the better of him. "I understand," he said. "It doesn't even surprise me, really." He arrived at the door, stopped, and turned. "I mean, why would someone like you ever look at someone like me anyway?"

Grace sighed, her face looking tortured. "It's not like that, Locke," she pleaded. "Things aren't always so black and white. I like you. I do…but—"

"But what?" Locke scoffed.

Grace lowered her head, a blush creeping up her neck. "Money, Locke, I needed the money! Surely you must understand? I'm not asking for your sympathy, but it's like I told you, I'm here in this city alone. Rufus pays me what he can, but it is barely enough to put food on the table. Is it wrong to want more for my life?"

She paused for a moment, and Locke realised that she was shaking. He felt a sudden, unexpected pang of guilt for the way he had treated her. Whatever her motive for spending time with him, the story of Grace's family was surely too tragic to be a falsehood. It had been many years since Locke had wanted for money—or anything material, really—but he knew the extent of Grace's suffering and couldn't blame her for accepting his father's request, however much it hurt Locke's pride.

"Then Lord Ramsey turns up," Grace continued, her voice lowered. "I didn't want to do it, not for the money anyway. I meant what I said: I really do like you. I said no at first, but he's a lord. How do you deny someone like that? How does someone like *me* deny someone like that?"

Locke made to answer, but his mouth stilled. He considered Grace's circumstances and compared them to his own. Would he have done anything differently in her position? A vision of Finnian's soon-to-be escape and Locke's own role in it played in his mind, and he sighed. Was Locke really the victim here? No more so than Grace, he concluded, or Boyd, who would likely be held responsible if Finnian were to succeed in breaking free. In the end, they were all just pieces in his father's game, and Locke realised in that moment that he needed to know why.

"It's fine," he repeated, and this time his words rang sincere. He reached out to squeeze Grace's hand briefly before dropping it once more. "I understand, and I'm sorry. I like you too. It's just…it has just been one of those days."

Grace gave a half smile. "I'm sorry. I just wanted you to know. I was hoping maybe we could do it again sometime, but not under false pretences next time…" She trailed off and blushed again before adding, "Anyway, try not to get too down. You seem to have friends in high places. It can't be all bad."

Locke scratched his wet hair. "You'd think so, wouldn't you?"

"What's the deal between you two, anyway? You and Ramsey?"

Locke opened the door to signal his departure. "That," he said, turning to face her just inside the threshold, "is a long story." He closed the door behind him, unwilling to let Grace even further into his mind than he had already allowed her to venture.

⚜ ⚜ ⚜

"You're back," Locke's father said, his bloodshot eyes twitching nervously as he stood to greet his son.

Locke jumped at the unexpected voice. "Father?" he asked, his own brow furrowed with concern and annoyance. Couldn't he have a moment of peace? He followed his father's gesture into the room, slightly resenting being welcomed into his own quarters, meagre as they might be, as though he were a guest. His father lowered himself to sit in the same chair he had used during his previous visit, and Locke was left standing. Despite his annoyance, he felt a modicum of relief that it was only his father waiting for him here. He had feared the threat of the King's Guard, and his nerves settled as his father's head tilted to take a long swig from a bronze hipflask.

"It's done then?" his father asked, drying his mouth on the back of his hand. Lord Ramsey had never been one for small talk, but Locke sensed an urgency that rendered his relief short-lived.

"Well come on, boy, spit it out!" his father snapped, startling Locke even further.

"You mean the—the parcel?" he stuttered, struggling to find his tongue.

His father rolled his eye. "Yes, the parcel, of course. What else would I be talking about?"

"Yes," Locke answered quietly.

"What?"

"Yes!" Locke repeated, raising his voice in a way he normally wouldn't with his father. Sweat rolled down his back and his stomach twisted with anxiety. What was his father worried about? Was it related to the parcel, and if so, what had Locke gotten himself into?

His father nodded. "Good," he said, and a half smile appeared on Lord Ramsey's face as his index finger tapped rhythmically on the arm of the chair. "That's good. I shouldn't be here, but I had to be sure you had gone through with it."

Locke's nerves finally shattered. "Gone through with what, exactly?" he demanded, unable to stop himself.

His father stood in silence and hobbled to the window, leaving Locke with clenched fists.

"Father, what did you have me do?" he tried again, but his father remained quiet, his back turned, twitching the makeshift curtain to peer into the dark streets beyond. "It was a lockpick, wasn't it?" Locke persisted. "In the parcel, I mean. It was a lockpick, but why? And why Finnian of all people? He's—"

After a flurry of unexpected motion, Locke gasped as his back hit the wall, leaving him breathless. His father's hand was tight at his throat, and the smell of liquor was heavy in the air between them, the scent so strong it made Locke's eyes water.

"Lower your voice, boy, or I'll see that tongue removed," he growled. His grip loosened incrementally. "Why Finnian, you ask? Do you really want to know?"

Locke nodded, as much as was possible given his father's hold on his throat, which was still tight.

His father sneered. "You're even stupider than I thought. Let's just say that there is more to the brigand than meets the eye. Your brother arrested him, yes, but the two of them are…shall we say, acquaintances. Men of mutual interests."

Locke's eyes widened, unable to believe what his father was telling him. Could this be? Or was it some sort of trick? That seemed more likely than Ralph—perfect, shining star, Ralph—being in league with Finnian.

"We put Finnian in that cell, and before you ask, yes, I made sure beforehand that you would be the one to watch him."

"But why?" Locke choked.

His father stepped back, shaking his head. "Because brave men fight for what they believe in. You see this eye?" He pointed to the mound of scar tissue on the left side of his face. "I made this sacrifice for my country. A sacrifice that was meant to see Easthaven free of its enemies."

"But the war is over. We won—"

"Pah!" his father snapped, swiping the air dismissively. "We won nothing. *My sacrifice* was for nothing. You think I gave my eye so that we could allow the Verderans to walk out of Highcastle with their heads? You think I put my body on the line so that our beloved king could see his wealth and reputation swelled by a union with *Auldhaven*?" He spoke the last word as if it were a swear word, and he spat on the ground as he said it.

"Father, you don't know what you're saying," Locke pleaded. "What about your title, our land?"

His father's laughter cut him short. "No, boy, it's you who does not understand. My title is a mockery, a worthless gesture intended to keep me quiet. Do you really think that the highborn nobles of the council are interested in the opinion of a half-blind, hobbling old soldier?"

Locke had no idea what to say.

A sad shadow crossed his father's face. "I fought at Broderick's side during the siege of Highcastle. General Broderick, that is, the king's High Commander of Peace and Justice. It was my sword and soul that drove the Verderans from the capital, yet that old fool is revered as a hero while I'm retired to a worn-down old castle in the provinces like an embarrassing drunken uncle."

"But—"

"No," his father continued, undeterred. "You were there, after the battle. When I laid there broken and bleeding. Where was the king? Where was Broderick, my commanding officer? You know the answer! They were off celebrating *their* victory, *their* future. But what about my future?" He finally snapped, throwing his hipflask against the wall in anger. "I was there at the Battle of Yarlsford when King Simeon tried to outmanoeuvre King Augustus. I fought to defend the king that night while his chosen shield, Garrett, died. During the siege of Highcastle, it was me, Captain Ramsey, who found the king unconscious in that tunnel under the city. It was upon *my* back that King Cyrus was carried to safety. Then orders were given, and I rushed to join the battle. I put my body on the line for this country, and I should be the hero here. This is my story, and I will gain the happy ending I deserve."

Locke's eyes widened with terror. "What have you done?" he whispered.

"No more than was necessary," his father answered calmly. "Finnian is a man of many talents. Imprisoning a famous brigand was no problem, but giving him the freedom of the castle, now that took a little more planning."

"You mean…"

"I knew you'd catch up eventually. Your act will enable Finnian to complete his end of the bargain. He was a good soldier once, believe it or not. He served under Broderick, not that the High Commander would remember. Another forgotten man forced to take matters into his own hands."

"And the crimes," snapped Locke. "Did he even commit them, or is this all more lies?"

"Oh, he's a brigand, all right," his father answered flatly. "I find that lies are easier to swallow when served with truth. There is no denying that Finnian had lost his way. I cannot condone his every act of violence, but men do what they must to get what they need. There is little money in soldiering at the best of times, and even less in times of peace. It is something I have tried to discuss with the council on a number of occasions, but would they listen? No, of course not." He scoffed as Locke shook his head in disbelief. "They're all too busy lining their own pockets, the fools. Men like Finnian provide the perfect distraction from their endless, all-consuming greed. Another scapegoat to make the king feel safe in his palace of gold. It was the perfect plan," he added with a self-satisfied smile. "The wheels have been turning for many years, but when your brother captured Finnian, the final piece finally fell into place. In Finnian's eyes, I saw my own hunger and desires reflected. The man shares our vision, Lockey." His eyes widened excitedly. "Finnian knew that we could not keep him from prison, but he wanted to help, to make a difference, and we were able to give him that opportunity. Things will change, and we will have need of men like Finnian.

Locke could only gape, but his father had hit a stride now and left no room for him to speak anyway.

"The king has grown complacent, just like his father before him," Lord Ramsey continued. "He trusts too much and will be made to suffer for it."

"You're going to kill the king?" Locke asked, his heart threatening to burst from his chest.

His father clapped mockingly and smiled. "Finally, he gets there. You know, I wonder if you're mine sometimes, I really do. Don't suppose I could blame your mother, really, all those years I was away with the army, must have been lonely for her—"

"Stop!"

"What?"

"Just stop," Locke pleaded, unwilling to listen to his father's insulting suggestions about his mother and choosing instead to veer the conversation back to the matter at hand. "There has to be another way, surely? Ask for an audience with the king, help him to see…" He was desperate to reverse the series of events that he himself had set in motion, at his father's behest.

"Such a romantic view of the world," his father answered, shaking his head as though full of sorrow, his words thick with derision. "The time for talking is over. There are others of a similar mind: warriors, men of honour. Good men who ride for Ardlyn Keep as we speak. Prince Leo is too young to rule, and Peacehaven will need strength and stability lest we fall victim to Verderan ambitions, of which they have already revealed themselves capable only ten short years ago."

He stepped forward to place a hand on Locke's shoulder. Locke thought how much this gesture of reassurance would have meant to him under different circumstances, how unbelievable it would have seemed to him that his father would have extended him this small show of kindness.

"The council exists to push money around a table, not to rule," his father said. "There are many who still fear the Verderan threat. The king's murder will be attributed to King Alonso, and the people of Peacehaven will welcome a show of strength in their pursuit of retribution. Our family will provide that show of strength, Lockey. My voice *will* be heard in council, and your brother will be the man to lead our armies."

"So, war then?" Locke asked, his heart sinking even deeper into his chest. "You would bring war to our country to further your desire for coin and justice?"

His father sighed as though the thought of war brought him pain, but Locke could see a manic fire in his eyes that suggested otherwise. "It is often the only way," his father said. "Don't you see, boy? I am a warrior of the old ways, a relic in the king's eyes. This new world holds no place for my kind."

The room fell silent. Locke's head fell into his hands. The implications finally dawned on him. He had let an assassin loose in the castle and instigated a new war. His father had asked for his trust, and against everything his past had shouted out for him to do, Locke had given it to him. And this is how his father had repaid him. Locke had spent his entire life trying and failing to please the man before him, but finally, at long last, Locke saw Lord Ramsey for what he was: a coward controlled by drink and a need for power and vengeance.

"You set me up!" he said, pushing his father's arm away. "Finnian will kill Boyd, and the blame will fall on me. You never believed in me or wanted me to succeed on my own. You distanced yourself to avoid the finger of blame and prepared me as your lamb for slaughter. Will you deny me when I'm in chains, or when the noose is around my neck? Are you so heartless that you would disown your own son?"

"My son?" his father answered angrily. "We might share blood, but you are no son or heir of mine. You are what you have always been: a disappointment. I gave you a chance to redeem yourself, and you dare to question my actions? This is how you win, Locke, in life and in war. He who strikes first strikes last. Your brother sees it, and that is why he will lead this country one day." He paused, seemingly to let his temper cool, and when he spoke again, his voice was lower. "There is still hope for you, but I will not tolerate your scorn, your...judgement. You care for your family, don't you? For your mother?"

Locke nodded and let his arms fall, feeling the fight go out of him as tendrils of his father's manipulation began to tighten around him. What choice did Locke have after what he had done at the castle?

"Good," his father began once more. "I'm sorry. We all say things we regret sometimes. I only want what I..." he stopped to correct himself, "what *we* deserve. This is for the best, for our family and for the country, but I need you to keep it together."

"Keep it together?" Locke asked, the word *family* still echoing in his mind.

His father smiled. "Yes, that's right, son. Sleep, eat, go to work, and act as though everything is normal. News of the king will spread, but I'll protect you." He spoke with such conviction that Locke started to believe him. "All eyes will turn to Finnian, but plans have been made. I've told you everything now. I've shown trust in you, son. I just need to know that I can rely on you." His hand reached into his jacket, where he grasped the hilt of a small knife, its metal edge glinting in the light. "I can rely on you, can't I?" he asked again, as though seeking reassurance.

Locke thought of his mother. His quarters at Ardlyn Keep. The fresh loaves of bread in the kitchen, kneaded by her hands. The beautiful lavender that surrounded the town and the people he had known his whole life within. His heart sank as the word escaped him, but there was only one answer. "Yes."

He watched as his father turned and limped toward the door, the scars of war still haunting his every step. *There are some injuries that can't be healed*, Mary, the healer had said to Locke as she dressed the wound on his eye. It was only in that moment, watching his father hobble away, that Locke fully understood the truth of her words.

Thaddeus

Moonlight illuminated Thaddeus's quarters. He rolled onto his back and gazed at the ceiling. *Not time to get up just yet*, he thought, but old habits die hard, and Thaddeus smiled at the fading memories of daybreak training with Cyrus, and Augustus before him, and Anselm before them both.

The early bird catches the worm, that's what Thaddeus's father had always told him. Thaddeus had worked hard to find his place in the castle and forge three kings into the very best they could be. *Trust, commitment, and dedication*, that was the ethos. In practice, it was all about setting a good example. He favoured an early night these days, but hadn't he earned that right? He wasn't a young man anymore; in fact, he hadn't been for some time. Nevertheless, he was still the first to rise each day, setting out while Eldred's Keep was still cloaked in the silence of the wee hours. A quick visit to the kitchen before bread began baking. A brisk walk around the courtyard to keep the old joints limber. Above all else, Thaddeus valued the importance of people and relationships. He made it his priority to know the names of all those who worked within the castle. From squires to seamstresses, cooks to chambermaids. There really weren't enough hours in the day, all told. Besides, if he didn't keep himself busy, he might never leave his bed again, such was the danger of old age.

He rolled onto his side to gaze out of the window. Stars still twinkled in the night sky, and he breathed a sigh of deep contentment. There was some comfort in knowing that his work was done, at least until Prince Leo grew older anyway, though time was probably against Thaddeus on that front. He still missed Anselm dearly, but Cyrus had grown to become a great king in the strangest of circumstances. Peacehaven wasn't perfect; the same power struggles existed within the new council as with the old, parts of Highcastle still carried the scars of war, and the melding of Easthaven with Auldhaven had put great strains on food and other resources. King Cyrus wanted every man and woman of Peacehaven to share the bounty of his bright future, but the new nation was a large sprawl, so some were bound to slip through the cracks. King Cyrus was but one man, after all.

Besides, Thaddeus took comfort in the idea that there was always room for improvement. And if nothing else, he reasoned, the country was at least a place of peace once more. Strong relations had led to thriving trade across borders, and King Cyrus had done a fine job rectifying Augustus's mistakes while simultaneously continuing the great work their father had begun years before.

King Cyrus had proven himself a fast learner, and though Thaddeus was old, he was no fool. He knew the king deferred to him out of sentiment and courtesy rather than any real need. Great kings never turn from wise counsel, and Thaddeus was happy to help as called upon, as a confidante or voice of reason in Cyrus's ear. The king was smart, considered, and a fine swordsman, if a little short of what Augustus could have been with the right application. Cyrus was a true king. A man who had lived among his people and risen to lead them against overwhelming odds. He was idolised by his son, Prince Leo, and the family line would only be strengthened by the arrival of another royal baby any day now. Life was good, he reflected, and Thaddeus was proud to have played his part in how things had turned out. His was a mind for planning and logic, but Cyrus had been a gamble that had paid off.

At this thought, Thaddeus smiled at the memory of his old friend, Garrett, without whom Thaddeus would never have taken the risk on Cyrus. The king's late chosen shield had been an insatiable fool whose love for life was surpassed only by his sense of duty. Garrett had given everything for his king without question, and as Thaddeus looked back on his own long life in the castle, he was proud to say that he had always tried to do the same. He wished, a little wistfully, that Garrett had been given more years, but he was comforted by the fact that his friend had done everything he could to do himself proud in the time he'd been given.

But how much longer do I have? Thaddeus wondered as a cool breeze wafted through the room. He pulled the bedcovers to his neck and shifted uncomfortably, not so much for himself but for Cyrus, wondering who would counsel the king in Thaddeus's inevitable absence. He knew he could never walk away, but good planning is about establishing contingencies. He was seventy-six years old, or was it seventy-seven? At any rate, time had positively flown by, and it showed no sign of slowing. He momentarily considered Broderick's suitability as his successor. After all, he had ascended to the lofty position of High Commander, but Thaddeus soon disregarded the notion, knowing the former general to be too hot-headed, too…impulsive. His mind next moved to Seth, who had provided great comfort to the king through the years, but Cyrus's current chosen shield was another warrior whose fire was not easily tamed. Thaddeus himself had started out with a sword in his hand, yet he had never been as impulsive or fearless, instead favouring the art of swordplay. Not just the technique but the mind games and subtle tactics he had learned to repurpose for altogether different fields of battle these days, be those challenging political negotiations or the fierce arena of Peacehaven's council. No, try as his mind might to find another successor, Thaddeus knew there was only one viable option…

His cheeks twinged as they always did when he thought of Francine. The king's sister had always been Cyrus's steadying influence. She was a whip smart girl whose swordsmanship was without compare. He'd have loved to have more time to mentor Fran, but the princess was born to travel, hungry as she had been for her own great adventure, and her time with Mathilde made her more suitable still to someday fill Thaddeus's shoes.

Yes, he thought with a sense of deep satisfaction, *Fran is the only option*. She could protect her brother from the dangers faced by a king. The imminent arrival of a new niece or nephew for Francine would likely see the princess return to Highcastle for a visit. If Thaddeus couldn't convince her, he hoped the baby might.

He closed his eyes and smiled. He would speak to Fran when she arrived for the special occasion, make her see the sense in his plan.

Another problem overcome, but for now, perhaps a little more sleep…

⚜   ⚜   ⚜

Thud.

Thaddeus's eyes snapped open, and he sat up on instinct, heart racing. He couldn't have been asleep for long because it was still dark outside his open window. The candlestick beside his bed flickered under another breath of cool air, but Thaddeus threw the covers back and stepped slowly toward his doorway with curiosity. It had probably been just another clumsy guard, but Thaddeus knew better than to assume. The memory of an assassin's attempt on Adaline's life was still fresh in his mind as though it had happened yesterday, and though ten years had passed, one could never be too careful, he thought.

He raised his candle and reached to open the door. His feet were bare, and he gasped as a viscous wetness spread from the hallway into his quarters, running between his toes. He looked down, already knowing what he would find there. *Blood.*

His worst fears had been confirmed. This couldn't be happening, not again, he thought desperately, but his survival instincts prevailed, and Thaddeus threw the door open to find two guards sprawled on the floor, a third man rushing away, sword in hand. He wanted to call out but feared drawing Adaline or any other innocents into the swordsman's deadly path. His quarters were tucked in a secluded corner of the castle—a mark of respect for his station—and he thought it unlikely that anyone would hear him anyway.

No, this one's mine, he thought, stooping to collect a sword from one of the fallen guards. He cleared his throat, and the assassin turned back toward him. He had dark, scruffy hair with a beard to match, and as Thaddeus squinted in the half-light, he recognised the intruder as Finnian, the infamous brigand imprisoned for a life sentence. A smile appeared upon Thaddeus's face. *That sentence might be shorter than you think,* he thought viciously. Thaddeus flourished his sword.

Finnian sneered, apparently unbothered by Thaddeus's display. "You really want to do this, old man?" he asked.

It was an insult, of course, purely meant to throw Thaddeus off-balance. Thaddeus had been around too long not to recognise Finnian's jibe for what it was. But as he stretched out his old, tired limbs, he wondered if he could really answer the brigand's slight with any confidence. In the end, he only nodded. Words had become his primary weapon in recent years, but it had not always been so. There were some questions in life to which diplomacy wasn't the answer, and this was one of them, he decided, gritting his teeth. *This* was the moment to let his sword do the talking.

Finnian leapt forward without delay. Thaddeus raised his sword to block instinctively and backed away from danger, his mind racing to catch up. *A soldier?* he mused, studying Finnian's form and speed. There was no denying his movement, the grip of the sword, the discipline in the brigand's stance. This fight would not be easy, but life so rarely was.

One more for old times' sake, he thought, forcing a menacing grin of his own onto his face as he stepped forward to meet his foe.

Back and forth they went, Thaddeus twisting and turning as he rolled back the years. Every clash sent new energy jolting through his body, and laughter fell from his lips as he explored and exploited Finnian's every weakness. The brigand was good—but not good enough. His guard was slow, and his attacks were predictable. Thaddeus had trained men like this, and he probed to nick Finnian with warning strikes. A small tear in his shirt. A neat cut on the top of his thigh. Thaddeus was toying with his opponent and enjoying it, a thrill he hadn't felt in decades racing through his blood. He'd admonished students for less, but he wondered what harm it could do. His only hope was that he would be granted the opportunity to continue without interruption. When the time was right, he'd end the contest in style.

"Tired, young man?" Thaddeus goaded as Finnian stepped back with his eyes lowered and chest heaving, reaching for breath. Thaddeus strode forward to maintain the pressure, and it dawned on him all of a sudden that he was fighting in his nightgown as a breeze rustled the soft cotton fabric, which swept at his ankles. He continued onward, pushing the slightly embarrassing thought aside and moving freely across the cobbled floor as his opponent stopped to halt his retreat.

"You don't have to do this, old man. I'm warning you."

But Thaddeus gave a victorious smile. "Thanks for the warning. It's already done."

His next strike almost cleaved Finnian in two. A reactive block saved the brigand, but Thaddeus kept on, unrelenting, each angular jab troubling his opponent until Finnian's shirt was drenched with a nervous sweat. "Your time is at an end," Thaddeus grunted, knocking the sword from Finnian's hand. The contest was over, and he almost wished he had an audience as he grabbed the brigand's neck, driving his sword into his shoulder.

It wasn't a killing blow, but Finnian turned white nonetheless. His face was pale, his eyes now wide, and his jaw hung loose with surprise. Thaddeus stepped back to let blood gush from the wound. The moment had arrived, and he braced himself to bring their exchange to an end.

"You gave it your best," he said, out of habit as much as anything else. His father's words. He thought back to the regional contests in which he had competed as a boy. His father had lived every cut and thrust as though he were the one competing, living every victory and loss with a deep pride in his son, as Thaddeus had earned his reputation. Thaddeus smiled down at the bleeding brigand, and he raised his blade for a final time. But as he stepped forward to force the end, Finnian lashed out unexpectedly, and a shove to Thaddeus's chest drove the air from his lungs.

"What did you…?" he began, but Finnian just stared back at him, one hand pressed to the wound in his shoulder.

Something was wrong. Thaddeus wheezed, his knees buckled, and everything went silent. His chest was suddenly tight, too tight. Pain coursed through the left side of his body and into his arm. He tried to speak again, but it was no good. He staggered, and the sword fell, clattering to the cobbled floor. His mind swam, whether from fear or dizziness he was no longer sure, and he dropped to his knees. Finnian remained before him, wide-eyed with surprise. Each shallow breath felt to Thaddeus like the sharp end of a thousand tiny blades, and beads of sweat rolled down his face as the world slowed. Thaddeus folded to land face first.

"You can't..." he uttered with the last of his energy. His fingers reached out ineffectually. His hand fell limp, and the sound of Finnian's boots clattered by, becoming gradually more distant. He was all alone but for the bodies of the two guards sprawled out before him. He thought of the pain their families would endure when they heard the news, and then of Cyrus, a pang of guilt coursing through Thaddeus's body at the realisation that he had failed his king.

Then his father's voice echoed. *You gave it your best, son...*

The pain subsided, his heart slowing more and more by the second. He closed his eyes for a final time, let his head rest as though tucking in for another well-earned few hours of slumber, and never woke again.

Francine

Fran rolled onto her side, Zimbeza's necklace hanging loose in her hand.

"Welcome back, girl," Redbeard's voice had boomed when she'd returned to the Silver Sword. The crew had been assembled in a line on deck to greet them on arrival, a motley honour guard, their best effort to appease Fran following the events of their previous journey together. Teeth had done his very best to present a picture of humility under his captain's glare, but Fran had noticed the gentle twitch in his jaw as he bit down to contain his true feelings. If he was anything like her, he would not forget so quickly.

She had smiled and thanked them, of course. Amare had seemed most humbled by their efforts, while Taiwo seemed perfectly at home with the formality. In Fran's case, the sight of them all, but particularly Patch, had left her cold. Their return to the

Silver Sword had offered little in the way of joyful reunions, and she'd made her excuses to spend the better part of her first day onboard brooding in silence in her cabin.

A sigh escaped her as she thought yet again of Patch. The journey to retrieve Taiwo should have been a simple task, like fetching bread from the bakery. She knew better than to form emotional connections, attachments that would only weaken her and lead to heartache in the end. So why had she let it happen? Her sigh soon turned to a groan of frustration. She regretted what she had seen in Taboso, but worse still was how much it bothered her. She replayed the image in her mind, Patch, effervescent in the clutch of his swooning admirers, strolling along with Taiwo without a care in the world. She hated that he had made her feel so foolish, but she knew she couldn't confront him about it—or wouldn't, anyway. The ship was no place for such talk, even if she had wanted to. Her heart sunk realising that they would part in Cornesse within four days, their time together so fleeting. *It's probably for the best*, she thought. So why did the prospect of farewell fill her with such dread?

The wood panelling of her cabin creaked as their vessel ploughed ever-forward in pursuit of home. She regretted the brevity of her time with Sabina and scolded herself for not having shown more interest in her confidante's own problems. Come to think of it, she hadn't even asked what Sabina did for work.

Probably something impressive, Fran thought with a smile. But that was all behind her now, the romance of travel replaced by routine, service, and discipline, the only life Fran had known as an adult. She had travelled across the Quadripartite at Mathilde's side, of course, but this had been her first true journey independent of the queen. It had not been without its ups and downs, but the feeling was no less exhilarating, with the benefit of hindsight anyway. It had been the type of journey that those in Peacehaven no doubt imagined when speaking of Fran's exciting life of adventure since moving away from the capital. She remembered the feeling when she had left her family in Highcastle to pursue the life of excitement that her position with Mathilde had promised. Fran would be happy to see the queen when she returned to Nivelle, and Cyrus, Marcia, and Leo once she made it to Highcastle for a visit. But she'd had a taste of adventure now; she'd experienced life outside of city walls and overcome every challenge that had been thrown at her. With Sabina's devil-may-care attitude still fresh in her memory, Fran wondered, *Can I really go back to the way things were before?*

Someone knocked loudly at her door, startling her from her thoughts. *Probably Patch again*, she thought, having ignored his previous attempts to make contact. She couldn't escape the image of him winding drunk through the streets of Taboso with Taiwo, a pair of women staggering at their sides. If nothing else, she thought, she was pleased to have seen him for who he really was, apparently nothing more than a drunken scoundrel.

Her eyes narrowed as the thumping knock sounded again. Their journey thus far had been routine from what she could tell, and she stashed the necklace in her pocket as a similar thud echoed above. *Running on deck?* she thought, as raised voices called, adding to the hubbub. They were still days from Cornesse, and whatever was going on, it seemed to have created quite a disturbance among the crew. Her curiosity, as it so often did, got the better of her. She sprang from the bed, fetched her sword, and made her way above deck to meet the mayhem. The ship's passageways were as empty as they had been when Redbeard had marched her to meet Teeth's summons during their journey to Taboso. The same thought washed over her as it had that day: *Something isn't right...*

"What's going on?" she called out as she emerged on deck. Then it registered in her mind.

The grey skies were thick with fog, and her crewmates were scattered and frantic as they rushed to intercept an attacking force, the identity of whom was as yet unknown to Fran. Her first thought was of pirates, despite the fact that she had been forced to keep quite unsavoury company onboard the Silver Sword and knew that her own crewmates were just as likely a source of the chaos. She squinted through the fog. Another ship was nestled alongside the Silver Sword, gangplanks and grappling hooks allowing the new arrivals to flood the deck, a mass of wild-eyed men, descending upon them in a blur of scars, beards, tattered clothes, and raised cutlasses. Teeth and Redbeard rushed forward to enter the melee, the deck beneath them already blood-red from the early exchange.

A hand gripped her shoulder unexpectedly. "Are you all right?" asked Patch, wincing at a thin cut across his cheek and panting from exertion.

Despite the seriousness of the situation at hand, Fran could not help but flinch away from his touch. He seemed not to notice, stepping past her to drive his sword into the belly of a previously unseen assailant.

"Could be worse," Fran said gruffly, summoning as much composure as possible. Her eyes swept the area around them; for the moment, they were free of any immediate threat.

"These pirates, who are they? Where did they come from?" she asked, drawing her own sword in readiness.

Patch wiped the blade of his sword on his breeches. "The fog masked their approach. We didn't see them coming until it was too late." He paused, and his own eyes flickered beyond Fran to where the fighting continued. Fran's face twisted in confusion as she saw Patch growl at the sight of something behind her and heard what sounded like a woman's voice calling his name.

"Firemane!" he snapped in response, bristling with agitation. Fran's skin prickled with memory. She recalled the name from her night at The Shipwright. Firemane, a pirate captain so fierce that the very mention of the name had put Davey, the sizeable innkeeper, on edge.

Fran whipped around, and though she'd come to expect the unexpected, nothing could have prepared her for who was staring back at her. *It can't be*, she thought with a sharp intake of breath. Red hair and a wicked smile, the captain that everyone called Firemane was none other than Sabina. This was not the reunion Fran had imagined.

Without further word, Patch lunged to meet Sabina's advance.

Fran raised her sword and surveyed the scene. The deck was already flooded with Sabina's men, but the fighting had broken into small, deadly skirmishes, as both crews fought for every inch of the deck.

But where was Taiwo? Her grip tightened around the handle of her sword. She'd come too far to lose him now, too far to fail in her duty to her queen.

She gave another quick glance, but the prince was nowhere to be seen among the mayhem. It seemed Sabina's men were everywhere now, but the crew of the Silver Sword continued to fight back in an attempt stem the tide. Bodies were already strewn across the wooden deck, and Fran knew that there was not a moment to waste. She had to find Taiwo before it was too late.

Before her, Patch's sword crashed against that of a skinny man with a pointy beard. For all her bluster, Sabina remained safe behind a line of her own advancing fighters, and as Fran rushed to Patch's aid, one of them extended a menacing axe in her direction.

"Let's see what you're made of girl!" he bellowed.

The man's bulbous belly bounced as he closed the distance between them, and he never slowed before hefting his axe in a swing that threatened to part Fran's head from her shoulders. She didn't have time for this man, but he left her no choice. Concern for Taiwo weighed heavy in her mind, but she was no good to him toying with this oaf. *I'll show you what I'm made of,* she thought as she ducked his next clumsy attack. Her blade tore a red line in the man's left thigh, sending him to his knees. His cry of pain was surprisingly high-pitched, but Fran's blade in his back soon silenced him.

Another wail sounded, and Patch's opponent fell to share a similar fate. Patch never paused before continuing forward, but though he hacked and slashed to get to Sabina, the pirate's smile only seemed to widen behind the protection of her men.

Fran yearned to follow him and wipe the smile from Sabina's face, but Teeth and Redbeard had arrived to join the action, and as Fran twisted to avoid an arrow, she spotted Taiwo locked in battle with two of Sabina's men at the front of the ship.

Hold on! she thought, though she never shouted it. Nobody would have heard her above the din if she had. It was some relief to see him alive, but Taiwo was cut adrift from the heart of the battle, and though his sword was raised, his aggressors were forcing him back with every step. It was only a matter of time, so she sprinted to his defence. A pale man with bright pink cheeks rushed to meet her, but Fran smashed the sword from his hands before running him through. It would take more than that to see her slowed.

Getting to Taiwo would not be easy. Bodies littered her path, and there were yet more of Sabina's men who seemed to want to join them.

A bald man with a thick moustache and a dagger. A dark-skinned Kanthi man with a curved blade and a stump of flesh in place of one ear. Fran stained her sword with both of their blood as she closed in on Taiwo. She ducked and rolled, cut, jabbed, and slashed. She knew the prince to be a capable warrior, but Sabina's greater number was starting to make a difference. As Taiwo twisted to drop one of his opponents, two more rushed to take their crewmates' places.

When at last she reached them, Fran was breathing heavily. She stepped back to avoid a vicious swipe from a foe wielding two knives and felt another blade whistle so close to her head that it would not have surprised her if she had turned to find strands of her own curly hair fluttering to the floor. There were five…no, six, of Sabina's men now circling them. Fran was unharmed, but as another man crashed to the deck, she was relieved to find Taiwo standing over him.

The smell of smoke filled the air, but Fran could only focus on the task at hand. She dashed forward to meet a blade that had been destined for the prince's back and heard the pirate gasp with surprise as his sword ricocheted off Fran's unexpectedly. Thaddeus had always told her that a man's next movement was betrayed by his eyes. But Fran was too fast, too deadly to worry about her opponent's actions, and if the same rule applied to women, it didn't seem to be helping this pirate. She punctured his ribcage, withdrew her sword, and rushed to stand at Taiwo's side.

"I wondered when you'd turn up," said the prince, through heavy breaths.

Fran rolled her eyes and raised her sword as they both braced for the next onslaught. "Just glad to find you alive," she grunted, contrary to her foolish outburst with Sabina in Taboso. Despite all the other distractions around them, Fran's chest burned with shame. To think that she had let her guard down and invited this danger. To think that she had put Taiwo's life at risk, despite all the faith Mathilde had placed in her. Though the fighting continued in every direction, Fran knew she had to make things right.

"We must get you to safety," she growled. She and Taiwo were outnumbered three to one, and she wondered if their enemies had grown complacent in their greater number. But how would she escape with Taiwo? Her head pounded at the thought. The odds were stacked against them, while Patch and his men had been forced back across the deck. Nowhere was safe on the Silver Sword anymore, and Sabina's ship was less appealing still. *Perhaps we can find a rowboat*, she thought wildly. It might be the only way. But she was no more an oarsman than Taiwo. They were a day from Taboso, and being in the open sea alone would only make them an easier target for Sabina's archers.

Her thought was short lived as a man lunged at Taiwo. A song of steel sounded out, and Fran parried a blow meant for her own chest as their aggressors surrounded them in a half-circle of death. The edge of the ship was close at her heels to prevent any further retreat. Sabina's men were limited but organised, and they prodded at Fran and Taiwo like cornered animals, sniggers echoing out, their faces fixed with menacing grins. Thoughts of escape would have to wait, Fran realised. They'd need to fight their way out of this first…

An old pirate with a grey beard never saw it coming. The ferocity of her attack left a red gash the length of his chest, and he fell to the floor shaking.

She had hoped to make a lesson of him, but her attack only seemed to rile his crewmates. Another two stepped forward, and she snarled as Taiwo grunted with exertion beside her. Suddenly, it felt as though there was no battle anymore, no fire, or smoke, or the sound of gulls. The whole world retracted to the small space around them. Together, they stood and fought for their lives.

Down went another of Sabina's men as Fran parried a cut before slicing off the man's hand at the wrist. His cry of agony only added to the cacophony, but Fran was left breathless as one of Sabina's men barrelled into her with his shoulder. The unexpected attack made her stumble, and though she thought she had regained her footing, she tangled with Taiwo and fell awkwardly to the floor, releasing her sword.

The next thing she heard was Taiwo calling to her. She sat up, urging the prince to focus, and then groaned as one of Sabina's men seized the opportunity to leave a neat cut in Taiwo's arm. *You fool,* she snarled, remembering two of Seth's most basic lessons: never turn your back on an enemy, and never lower your guard. She scrambled as she tried to return to her feet, but her attacker was upon her, and a heavy boot in her back sent her tumbling once more.

Who's the fool now? she wondered, enveloped by her enemy's shadow. It was Fran's job to save and to shield, and yet here she was, hopelessly unarmed. She considered what Mathilde would think of her in that moment, and her heart sank lower still as Taiwo's blade crashed to the deck beside her.

It was now or never. She had to fight back...

A swift kick to the knee caught her foe off-guard. The man yelped as he fell, and Fran pounced to turn his own sword upon him. The weight of the blade was comforting, and a new energy rushed through her as she sprang to her feet to meet the attack of another. Their swords met in the air and ground together. Neither was prepared to give an inch, and they both snarled as the man leaned in to make his weight advantage count. By this time, their noses were almost touching. Her legs strained and his bloodshot eyes widened. She knew she couldn't beat him with strength alone, and she pivoted to turn his sword away before lashing out with an attack of her own. The man was no fool and would not fall easily. His long black hair danced on his shoulders as they went back and forth, a handful of Sabina's men watching on. From the corner of her eye, she saw the hilt of a sword crash into Taiwo's temple. The prince fell to the deck, lifeless as a rock. She sidestepped to avoid her enemy's jab before scything him down with a backhand slash.

Her path was clear, and she made to cover Taiwo, heavy drops of blood falling from her blade with every step.

Well come on then, she thought as Sabina's men encircled her. Small fires had appeared all over the deck of the Silver Sword. Flaming arrows jutted from the main mast, and cabin boys were rushing to douse the flames with buckets of water as Sabina's archers traced their every step. Rising smoke restricted her vision, which was not helped by the ever-present fog. Fran saw no sign of Patch, Teeth, or Redbeard. She also realised she had seen no sign of

Amare, whose fate she considered for the first time with a pang of guilt.

She knew in that moment that she couldn't save them all. Sabina's men edged toward her like a five-pronged pitchfork; a man with a dark beard peppered with grey, another with a large hoop piercing his nose. At either end of their advancing line, two younger men with blond hair tinged red with blood—twins, she thought, from the look of them.

Yet, it was the fifth man among them who decided to make a move. His white cotton shirt was stained with sweat, and his pocked red skin glistened, drawing attention to the large white pimple on the end of his nose.

"It's the end of the road, girl. Now, how about you come quietly?"

Fran's eyes narrowed at the suggestion. She didn't know what puzzled her more, the fact that they were intending to take her, or the idea that she would let them.

She rolled forward and countered the man's feeble attack before driving the tip of her sword into his gut. The other men were slow to react, but Fran lashed out to attack one of the twins with all her might. Though he managed to block, the blond man fell back from the pressure. His brother cried out and rushed to his defence, but his anger made him reckless, and Fran dodged easily before raking her sword down his back.

Two remained, but they'd circled around behind her. The man with the peppered beard was crouched over Taiwo, while the other with the hooped nose ring stared back at Fran.

"That's enough," he barked, his rough accent like nothing Fran had heard before. "No more silly business, or your friend gets hurt."

The bearded man grinned as he lowered a knife ominously over Taiwo's throat. Fran scolded herself for leaving the prince unattended, but what other choice had she been given?

For all her skill, there was no hope of saving Taiwo with force. "Okay, take it easy. Let's not do anything hasty," she said, lowering her sword only to flinch as a hand tightened around her shoulder from behind. *The other brother*, she realised as a blade pressed threateningly against the small of her back.

She prepared for the worst, knowing that the man must want revenge for his brother's life. Her eyes fell on Taiwo once more and her chest heaved with regret. For all her efforts, she had failed, and it seemed she and Taiwo would both pay the ultimate price. In that moment, her mind moved to Cyrus, and then Mathilde, feeling she'd let them both down. But regrets wouldn't save her; she'd need a miracle for that. Then an unexpected voice sounded through the din.

"Wait!" snapped Sabina, rushing over to join them.

The blond man tutted, but his grip on Fran's shoulder loosened immediately. Fran breathed a sigh of relief and stole a moment to search for her crewmates. She saw that Patch and Redbeard were locked in struggle as Sabina's men forced them back, but she was powerless to help them. Sabina had arrived with two further men.

She cleared her throat and then said, "Fran, darling, so sorry we had to meet like this." Sabina's tone was conversational, as if they were sitting back at the bar together, talking over a drink. "I did, however, want to thank you for making my life so very easy. Don't get me wrong, I enjoyed our little chat, but," she shook her head, "you really must learn to keep your mouth shut."

Fran wanted to lash out at Sabina, but the threat of the sword still lingered behind her, stilling her in place. "You won't get away with this, Sabina," she said through bared teeth, though she had little faith in the sentiment.

Sabina smiled. "Oh, but I think I will." Her eyes flickered to the man at Fran's shoulder, "Renshaw, see her bound and gagged, will you? The same for the prince. We got what we came for. Let's not overstay our welcome, eh?"

Fran's shouts of protest were muffled as Renshaw covered her mouth with a piece of rancid cloth. Her arms were tied behind her, and she was released to stumble toward the gangplanks and the promise of Sabina's waiting ship. She turned to see Taiwo lifted from the deck and carried by two of Sabina's men, one at the prince's ankles, the other at his shoulders.

Are they here for me? For Taiwo? she puzzled. Whatever the answer, it was her own carelessness that had caused this situation. Quite outside of the immediate predicament her idiocy had put them all in—including the deaths of many men onboard the Silver Sword, possibly including Patch—she also burned with the shame of every bad word she had said to Sabina about Mathilde. The queen would have never let her emotions get the better of her the way Fran had when she met Sabina, and Fran's mistake had now put Mathilde's match in jeopardy, along with the prince's life, and—she realised with a jolt—her own.

She walked as slowly as she could, hoping for some kind of salvation, a sort of miracle. The deck of the Silver Sword was obscured by a drifting cloud of smoke, with the sound of fighting continuing behind them, blades echoing in chorus with the cries of dying men.

She had by no means enjoyed her time on the Silver Sword, but this was not the way she had intended to go. She began to accept that she and Taiwo would be taken as prisoners, her mind already plotting methods of escape, when the silhouette of three men appeared suddenly through the haze.

A sense of hope piqued within her, fading as quickly as it had appeared. It was Teeth and two of his cronies.

"Are we going to have a problem here?" asked Sabina, eyebrows raised.

Teeth and his companions moved toward them, their cutlasses already stained with death. The quartermaster halted as Sabina's men stepped forward to meet them. His eyes narrowed as he looked at Fran before surveying the deck, perhaps searching for reinforcements, though Fran had no reason to believe she understood Teeth's reasoning or actions.

"Oh, I don't think so," he said with a hint of a smile, lowering his weapon. Fran's jaw clenched with anger, and Sabina smiled smugly.

"Come on, boys," Teeth continued, turning to his crewmates. "The prince and the girl have been taken. We did all we could to save them, of course, but someone will need to tell the captain."

Sabina nodded, and Fran struggled, finally forcing the gag from her mouth. "I'll kill you for this!" she cried in Teeth's direction.

The old man grinned at her before winking and turning away. Then, the hilt of a sword came crashing into Fran's temple, sending her spinning into darkness.

Chapter XVII

Francine

Fran's eyes opened to find Taiwo staring back at her. "Good, you're still with us," he said with a half-smile. "Get ready, she'll be here any moment."

Fran rubbed at her eyes and looked around. They were in a dark cell with a wooden floor and iron bars, and her hands were heavy with chains. Her head was throbbing. "Who'll be here?" she asked. But at that moment, a door clicked open, and Taiwo shuffled on his hands and knees, scrabbling over to rest beside Fran.

"Ah, Fran, my dear. What a relief," said Sabina, simultaneously answering Fran's question and instantly reigniting the rage Fran had felt before she had gone unconscious. "Sorry about earlier, only you were about to start running that big mouth of yours, and I was keen to get back to my own ship. Things were really starting to…*heat up* on yours." She paused to laugh. "But wait," she snapped, a level of seriousness returned to her voice, "you'll be wondering why you're here. Why the infamous Captain Firemane has taken time out of her busy schedule to retrieve you and the prince. Any thoughts, Prince Taiwo?"

Taiwo's eyes narrowed in thought, but he gave no answer.

"Well, all right then," Sabina continued, keeping her eyes trained on Taiwo. "Why don't you tell Fran here about Makeba? You do remember Makeba, don't you?"

More silence from the prince. Fran couldn't tell if the name was unknown to him or if he was carefully schooling his face to look clueless. The name was certainly unfamiliar to Fran.

"Really?" Sabina began once more, red eyebrows raised. "Well, for your benefit, Fran, Makeba is the woman Taiwo was originally promised to. A beautiful young woman by all accounts, and the daughter of a rather menacing clan leader. I'm sure you have heard of Botosi?" She paused, and Fran took a deep breath as the implication dawned on her. "Yes, that's right," said Sabina, a smile spreading across her face as she saw Fran catching on. "It seems Taiwo's father has been building peace on a foundation of lies. Surely you didn't think you'd get away with this?" Her question was for Taiwo, her tone full of venom.

"That's enough!" spat Taiwo, but Sabina smiled as if the conversation was going exactly as she had intended.

"Temper, temper," she said, wagging her finger at Taiwo as though he were a small child. "I've always enjoyed a good wedding myself, but Botosi was not best pleased to hear of your arrangement, no…" she added, shaking her head, "not happy at all. So unhappy that he pledged a rather spectacular sum for the services of yours truly. My task of course, is to return you both to the island, only this time you'll be staying with Botosi. I always think it's important to see as much of a place as possible, learn all the different sides." She ended with another menacing smile.

"But our conversation in Taboso," Fran said feebly.

"Touching stuff," said Sabina, and her expression seemed to soften, if only by a tiny degree. "Look, I like you, Fran, but this should serve as a lesson. You spend far too much time worrying about others. I'm here today because I put myself first." She paused to press a thumb to her chest. "They call me a pirate queen, and I am about to gain a royal fortune because of you. Don't take it personally. It's just business."

"But—"

"It's just business," snapped Sabina. "Anyway," she continued, turning toward the doorway. "That's all from me until we reach land. You'll be pleased to hear that this trip will be full of reunions. Door!" she barked, and the door opened to reveal a man's silhouette in the corridor. "I'll let you two catch up, but play nicely. I've had enough drama for one day."

Fran's stomach dropped as the man stepped into the light.

"Fancy seeing you 'ere," said Selwyn, Sabina's "colleague" from Taboso, his face still black and blue from his previous encounter with Fran in the alleyways of the port town. "Dinner is served," he said, producing two crude wooden bowls. "One for you," he said, passing a bowl through the bars into Taiwo's outstretched hands. "And for you, a meal fit for a whore." He stopped to smile and tipped the gruel slowly onto the wooden floor. "I'll be back to see you later." He gave a gap-toothed grin before he left them in silence, Fran staring at the pile of sludge that should have been her dinner.

⚜ ⚜ ⚜

The only thing stronger than Fran's hunger was her resolve. Taiwo had been kind enough to share his bowl with her, but the portion was meagre for one person, let alone both of them. Her head was still throbbing, and she decided to rest in the hope that it might ease her pain.

But sleep did not come easily.

What fate had befallen Patch and the crew of the Silver Sword? For all that had gone before, she found herself missing every one of them in a strange, irrational way, even traitorous Teeth, and none more so than Patch.

Beyond this, Fran's mind was wracked with the thought of Selwyn's veiled threat, wondering what foul plans he had for her and what she might have in store for him if given the opportunity finish what she had started in Taboso. As time went by, her thoughts darkened. She wondered if her current predicament was any less than she deserved after her misplaced trust in Sabina. She turned to look at Taiwo, who was sleeping restlessly, and she lamented that the consequences of her mistakes would not be suffered alone. It dawned on her as she sat imprisoned on Sabina's ship just how sheltered her life had been, saved by Cyrus and nurtured by Mathilde every step of the way. She wasn't a child anymore, and she found her actions to be naïve and inexcusable as her stomach grumbled. The queen deserved better, and Fran drifted into fitful sleep with her head against the hard, grimy wall, trying desperately to figure out how she would make things right.

⚜   ⚜   ⚜

She woke a little later with no notion of the time. Lingering thoughts of Cyrus caused Fran to reach for her pocket, where she was relieved to find the mirror her brother had given her as a child. Sabina had taken Fran's freedom, but the mirror was something to hold on to, a token of hope. She weighed it in her palm and closed her grip tightly. The shame of their surroundings and Fran's own part in it left her with no desire to see her own reflection.

Their cell occupied the back wall of a dark, windowless room, their surroundings silent but for the sound of waves lapping against the hull. She assumed that they must be some way below deck. The fetid air's scent was only worsened by a waste bucket in the corner, far closer than Fran would have liked. Taiwo sat upright beside her, and Fran grimaced as she gazed once again upon the puddle of discarded gruel. The lumpy, porridge-like substance had congealed on the floor, to the delight of some rather voracious flies. Her stomach turned.

"You know, it really wasn't that bad," said Taiwo, rolling his neck with discomfort. "Once you got past the look, the smell, and the flavour it was quite edible." He gave a small grin, and Fran nodded silently, not forgetting the prince's behaviour back in the Kanthu Isles, both at his brother's birthday celebration and afterwards as he had wandered the streets with Patch. Taiwo's smile dropped, and his face turned sincere. "What you did for me on the Silver Sword…" he began tentatively. "I know they never planned to kill me, but you stood at my side when I was outnumbered and in grave danger. Your actions were very brave."

Fran scoffed. "It's all part of the job. Mathilde sent me to deliver you to the capital, remember? Besides, we were both passengers on the Silver Sword. Firemane's actions put us all in danger."

"I know you acted out of duty," said Taiwo with a serious tone that took Fran by surprise, "but you still came to my rescue when I needed it. You risked your life, despite my actions in Mutembu."

"It's nothing," she said, and though she tried to play it down, Fran found herself surprised at the prince's remorse. The way he had spoken to her after the archery contest was entirely unacceptable, she knew that, but it was somewhat reassuring to find Taiwo apologetic for his actions. Perhaps there was more to him than she had first thought.

"No," came Taiwo's sincere reply, "it's everything. I don't know what will happen next, but know that I am sorry. It seems you're as deadly with a blade as you are with a bow. Maybe we can still escape this?" He looked at her with an almost playful glint in his eye.

Fran nodded, not wanting to disappoint the prince or cause a panic, but she knew in herself that the outlook was bleak. "Maybe," she began, forcing an optimistic smile onto her face. "How's your arm?" she asked, gesturing to where the prince's wound was wrapped tightly with a blood-stained cloth.

"I'll live," said Taiwo, a jovial edge returned to his voice.

Fran crawled to test the iron bars of their cell and sighed. Escape wasn't going to be easy, she knew, sinking into the silence that comes with deep thought and planning.

⚜   ⚜   ⚜

Fran was just beginning to doze when Taiwo started speaking.

"So, tell me," he ventured, causing her head to snap upright. "You're a princess in your own right, sister to the king of Peacehaven?"

Fran sensed that he'd been waiting for an opportunity to ask. "Oh, that," she answered, waving a hand dismissively. "It's true, though that all seems irrelevant right now."

Taiwo pursed his lips, his head turned to the ceiling in thought. "But why are you even here?" he asked. "Surely you should be in Highcastle now with your brother, not working as another monarch's chosen shield. Was there really no one else for Mathilde to send?"

"You'd think so, wouldn't you?" Fran answered with a sad smile "No," she added, guilt still burning within her gut. "Mathilde is more than a queen. She's a trusted friend. I was happy to do this for her and honoured that she asked. It's true that my life might have been much easier in Highcastle. I could have spent my days at leisure, drinking fine wine, maybe even married a highborn man. But I've met my share of nobles and even a couple of princes…" She paused and raised her eyebrows at Taiwo, who smiled at her inference with some humility. "That will never be the life for me," she continued. "In Peacehaven, I am King Cyrus's sister, but in Cornesse I am chosen shield to the queen, a woman I have admired from the first day we met. In Cornesse, I am someone with purpose, with value. I can make a difference. Highcastle is my brother's story. I guess I needed to write my own."

"It isn't easy, is it, living in the shadow of someone like that? Take my father, the man that united the Islands, the first true king of Kanthu. Or even my charming brother, Zakari, who seems set to eclipse our father's achievements. How does anyone compete with that?"

"Exactly," said Fran, responding instinctively. "Or the great King Cyrus, who single-handedly brought peace to the Quadripartite and established the nation of Peacehaven. I know he wanted to close the book with me safely inside the castle walls, but what did safety ever teach us about ourselves? He used to tell me stories, you know, when we were little…"

Taiwo nodded with interest.

"He was a great storyteller, Cyrus. I suppose he still is. He loved to tell me stories of great warriors and kings, their valiant acts, victories in battle and triumphs against overwhelming odds. I loved those stories, every one of them. But as I grew older, I realised that I'd never seen myself reflected within them. There was no shortage of helpless princesses in towers or doting queens. But when we came to Highcastle, I met Queen Adaline, Queen Marcia, and then Mathilde too. I suppose I saw that women could do more and be more. They say that Highcastle would have fallen to the Verderans if not for Queen Mathilde's intervention."

Taiwo laughed. "You wanted to be a hero then?"

Fran shook her head dismissively. "Never a hero, no. I just wanted to write a story of my own. I realised that I didn't have to be another nameless girl in a castle. I knew I wanted more."

"And is this enough for you yet?" Taiwo joked, gesturing with his chained hands around their cell, the clink of the chains blending seamlessly with his light laughter. She could tell he was trying to lift her mood.

"It's getting there," said Fran, and for some crazy reason, she was smiling, even though she was somewhat disconcerted to feel a flutter toward the prince that she had never imagined possible in Taboso.

"I can tell she means a lot to you," said Taiwo, his voice lowered. "The queen, that is. I know you probably don't think much of me right now, but we're not so different you and me. I feel like every day is a blank page, and I'm just trying to find my way like anyone else."

Fran snorted. "You certainly know your way around the drinking holes of Taboso," she said. It was meant as a joke, but her tone betrayed her, and her eyebrows lowered as her effort garnered no response from the prince. "Maybe it's time to move forward and become the man you can be," she said, "The childish act can only last so long. You have to take responsibility, become accountable."

Taiwo nodded his head, his expression giving way to a sad smile. "All fair points," he said gently, "but for the right woman, any man is capable of change."

Fran started to tell him that he could change with or without the "right woman," but she stopped herself, knowing that he meant his words sincerely. She gave him a smile. He really was quite handsome, and she found that she was drawn to him for reasons she would never have been able to quantify in that moment—something entirely instinctual. She could feel the warmth of his breath upon her face, skin tingling at their closeness. Whether it was down to a lack of sleep, her anger with Patch, or simply the heat of the moment, something was drawing her toward him as surely as a magnet. The last few weeks all seemed jumbled and almost crazy, but a blank page is one full of opportunity. All logic escaped her. She leaned toward him...

Before she could second-guess herself, convince herself to stop, their lips were touching. His mouth was soft and inviting. Fran's mind emptied, focused solely on the feel of their mouths pressed together. A singularly perfect moment unfolded, seeming to move independently of time or intentions.

And then she felt Taiwo's hands pushing her gently away. An objection. A rejection.

"I'm sorry," he said in an awkward fluster, not meeting her eye.

"It's fine," Fran said quickly, but her face burned with shame. She was ashamed to feel a lump forming in her throat, and she told herself that if she cried—even just a single tear—she would never, ever forgive herself.

"I mean, you are very beautiful, but—"

"The queen, of course!" said Fran, her voice falsely cheery as her stomach churned with an even deeper guilt than before, a feeling only heightened by the prospect of telling Mathilde what she had done. She'd never kept secrets from the queen before, and her actions were tantamount to treason, not to mention the personal betrayal.

"Well, the queen, yes," said Taiwo, "but what about the captain. I thought—"

"You thought what?" snapped Fran, her mood changed in an instant, her embarrassment taking on an angry edge. "Is this just one big game to you two? Pitiful Fran, a bit of fun when there's no one else around, but the minute there's a better option or some drunken skirt on offer…" She trailed off, her heart beating in frustration.

"What are you even talking about?"

Fran shook her head, her jaw clenched. "That night in Taboso!" she shouted. "You, stumbling out of that tavern with Patch and those girls, or should I call him Captain Goldhand?" The name felt so foreign on her lips.

At this, Taiwo went silent. Fran had hoped to surprise him with her outburst, but the prince seemed unaffected and unexpectedly deep in thought. "The night in Taboso?" he said eventually, his brief silence followed by a wry smile. "You're talking about the night before we set off?"

Fran nodded, finding herself irritated by the fact that Taiwo was now shaking his head and laughing.

"I know it was dark," he said, "but you might want to look a little closer in future. It was not my finest night, I must confess, but the captain's only crime was that he didn't leave me behind!"

"What are you saying?"

"I'm saying that we went for a drink, one drink became two, and before I knew it, Captain Goldhand was carrying me home."

"And the women?" asked Fran, wondering how she had become wrongfooted.

"Pfft," he said with a grin. "They were opportunists, Fran. It's hard for a prince to go unnoticed in Taboso. As for the captain, his only vice is cards. He's a hustler, an expert player. The man never loses, and his victories earned him his name. Trust me, he wasn't interested in those women."

Fran remained silent, and in that moment, she wished that the ground would open and swallow her. She thought of Patch once more and hoped that he was still alive. She wondered if they would ever be able to talk things through.

"Goldhand was playing cards when I had a...disagreement at the bar," Taiwo continued. "The owner of the tavern is not a tolerant man, but Goldhand and I are well known to him, so he asked the captain to get me out before things worsened. Luckily for me, the captain never drinks when he plays. You must have seen us on our way out, but I'm still piecing it all together myself. I can't believe you'd think..."

"What?"

"Well, isn't it obvious? Goldhand, he thinks the world of you!"

Fran recoiled, and her skin felt hot. "No, he doesn't. His crew hates me, and their beloved captain spent most of the journey ignoring me."

"Ah, he told me about that," Taiwo answered with a nod. "But did he not take your side and punish the quartermaster?"

"Well, yes, but—"

"And do you think that he might have distanced himself to protect you? To help you find your place among the crew without his intervention?"

Fran sat in silence, and Taiwo smiled back at her.

"Your crewmates on the Silver Sword, how did they smell?"

"Huh?" Fran grunted with a grimace. "You know yourself, awful."

"Of course they did!" Taiwo answered immediately. "Hot water and scented oils are a luxury onboard a ship, reserved for those in command, the captain alone in some cases." He raised his eyebrows and ended with another telling smile as if urging her to get to the conclusion he was laying down for her.

"It was him, the captain—he sent me the water each day?"

Taiwo nodded. "When he told me, I thought it was a nice touch."

Fran suddenly felt very stupid as her mind raced over her time on the Silver Sword, wondering which of Patch's other actions she might have misinterpreted in her haste to assume he didn't care about her.

"There are many who would envy such attention, you know? He is strong, brave…" Taiwo paused to give his shoulders a gentle shrug and to swallow loudly. "Very handsome."

Fran's eyes narrowed. "Anyone I know?" she asked, unsure if she was once again misinterpreting things.

But Taiwo's silence was telling.

"But the queen," Fran continued softly. "You are to be married. I didn't realise that you were—I mean, that you—"

"Yes, well…" Taiwo interjected. "Do not worry, it is not quite that simple. Our people are taught to appreciate beauty wherever we find it."

"Even Teeth?" Fran joked, causing Taiwo to shake with laughter.

"There are some exceptions!" The prince lowered his head and continued, "You cannot control who you love, but I am my father's heir, and it is my responsibility to ensure the future of our family line. It was said that Queen Mathilde would never marry, yet here you are, bidding me to come and be her king. Perhaps we will not be so different after all, me, and this queen of yours."

"Perhaps not…" Fran uttered, and her lips pursed as, for the first time, she began to consider if things might just work out between Taiwo and Mathilde. There was, however, one question that still bothered her. "The girl, Makeba," she asked, "do you love her?"

Taiwo shook his head. "No—not really anyway. She is a good match, to be sure, smart and beautiful. But love… *love* is finding someone who can steal your breath and leave you speechless."

His words were unexpectedly tender, and Fran wondered how she had managed to misjudge the prince so badly. She thought of her first meeting with Patch all those years before. The mysterious pirate boy with dark curls and his smart black tunic. She, a young, clueless girl, newly a princess, wordless and smitten.

Their reunion on the docks, all those years later. Patch's tanned skin, still smattered with freckles, the way he had kissed her hand.

She, a young, clueless woman, wordless and smitten.

A pang of guilt came over her as she recalled the many occasions in which she had chided Cyrus in the past. Sure, he was the mighty King Cyrus these days, but Fran remembered an awkward boy who stumbled over his words when pursuing his future queen. Taiwo's words echoed in her mind, and it finally dawned on her. She'd been so busy fighting to preserve a fearless reputation, a sense of unyielding independence, that she'd failed to see what was in front of her all along. *I hope it isn't too late to tell Patch how I feel…*

"We need to get out of here," she snapped assertively.

Taiwo shrugged. "Yes, that is the problem."

Francine

Selwyn appeared in the doorway, returning as he had promised he would. Fran rubbed her drowsiness from her eyes as Taiwo snored loudly beside her. The pirate's key screeched as it turned in the lock, but Taiwo fidgeted only briefly before his rhythmic snoring began once more.

"I've been looking forward to this," said Selwyn in a low, almost hungry voice as he stepped across the cell toward her. There was an excited glint in the man's eyes that Fran didn't like, and his smile revealed what yellowing teeth remained.

Fran looked to her hands, still bound in chains. She'd been captured by the most feared of all pirate captains, Firemane, and was being held hostage by her savage right-hand man. The Silver Sword was surely long gone, probably nestled at the bottom of the ocean. The obvious dawned on her as she grimaced at Selwyn: there would be no escape.

"Let's get this over with," she said, accepting her grim fate. She used the wall of the cell to shimmy to her feet, and Selwyn encouraged her with a vicious-looking knife. The man's face was still a mess from their run-in, and Fran dreaded to think what Selwyn's vengeance might entail.

The walk to the cell door seemed to last a lifetime, though it was only a few steps. Selwyn locked up behind them, and Taiwo finally stirred just as Fran stumbled through a second doorway and into the corridor, yanked forward by her chains. In their wake, Taiwo called, "Where are you taking her?" but the prince was left in silence, unanswered. Fran might have liked to know the answer herself.

The ship itself was nothing spectacular, she thought, the same familiar wooden walkways and wet floors, the scuttling of rats and a pervading fug of rum and body odour. All was quiet, so Fran guessed it must be the middle of the night. Wherever Selwyn was taking her, she suspected she would find herself alone with him there. Her stomach lurched.

Then suddenly, the pirate stopped, and another familiar face appeared in the darkness. Fran dragged to a halt, and Selwyn nodded at Renshaw, who stood in the shadows armed with a one-handed crossbow, which he aimed toward them. To Fran's surprise and dismay, her situation had only worsened.

"Payback time," said Renshaw with no hint of humour. He lowered his weapon and used his spare hand to draw his long blond hair away from his eyes. "This bitch killed my brother. Why don't we just kill her now and be done with it?"

"You know why," answered Selwyn. "Firemane says we are to return them both to the Kanthu Isles, her and the prince. No matter what happens, we need to keep them alive, or on our heads be it. Lucky for her I am expert at what I do."

Renshaw's frustrated expression turned to a sick grin. "Make it painful."

"Oh, I will," said Selwyn. "By the time I'm done with her, death will seem like a kindness." Both men sniggered, and Fran's body went cold. She took no comfort from the news that they were not intending to kill her.

"I'll cover for you," said Renshaw. "Try to be quick."

"And my things?" Selwyn asked curtly.

"All waiting for you as requested."

"Good," said Selwyn, "I owe you one."

Renshaw gazed about them nervously. "With what she's got coming to her, I'm sure we can call it even. Now, you, move…" He raised his bow to gesture Fran toward an open doorway. Beyond him, she saw a room with a table at its centre and a single chair. A candle flickered upon the tabletop, illuminating an ominous wooden box like a small chest, closed so that the contents remained concealed.

"The chair!" Selwyn grunted, with Renshaw still hovering in the doorway.

Her hands were bound, but Fran managed to sit awkwardly while Selwyn glared back at her.

"Nothing stupid," he added, as if reading her mind.

It was a hopeless situation, but Fran's eyes still twitched around the room, searching for anything that might aid her escape. The walls were bare, and she noticed a length of rope only as Selwyn reached for it. He lowered himself slowly without ever breaking eye contact. He took the rope and asked, "Comfortable?" as he began to wrap it around her. A rhetorical question, of course, but Renshaw's aim remained purposeful, so she didn't dare utter a sarcastic reply. She'd bested Selwyn once before, but the element of surprise was lost, and where could she hope to escape to anyway?

A tight tug of the rope reinforced her grim reality. Selwyn tied a knot at the back of the chair, and Fran thought of calling out for someone—anyone—until Selwyn pulled a grimy strip of cloth from his pocket and forced it into her mouth. Fran let a deep sigh escape her, though the sound was muffled by the gag. She had missed her opportunity, and with it, any hope of escape.

"We'll be fine now," said Selwyn, turning to acknowledge his crewmate. Renshaw nodded and stepped back into the corridor, closing the door behind him.

"I thought we'd never be alone," Selwyn continued, his teeth bared with mischief. He brought a clutch of Fran's hair to his nose and sniffed deeply. "I hate how we left things, don't you? I thought I'd never see you again, but 'ere we are. Must be luck, or what's that word…destiny!" He turned away, and Fran's eyes glanced nervously toward the table. "Lucky me, eh? And, oh yeah, I nearly forgot. I brought you a gift. Would you like to see?"

Fran's eyes widened.

"I'll take that as a yes," Selwyn continued, still facing away from her. "It's all in this box 'ere," he said, lifting the lid on the small chest to begin removing the contents. "This one's really good for stripping flesh, or this one that's useful for breaking bones. What about this one?" he asked, turning to face her with a chuckle. "Great at pulling nails or teeth. A tooth for a tooth if you will." He placed the instruments on the table with gentle precision as Fran felt a damp sheen of sweat break out all over her body.

"I could just use a candle and simply burn the flesh away, slowly as you like," he continued, his voice almost tender. "Too many options and too little time—it's always the same problem, isn't it?" He raised his knife to inspect the blade in the dim light. "I love all my tools, but maybe we should keep things simple to begin with. You don't mind if we use this, do you?" he asked, pulling another piece of material from his pocket. "This will cover your head while I'm working. Nothing personal, I just find this makes things more…uncomfortable for you. I'm a perfectionist, you see."

Fran tried to squirm as Selwyn put the knife down and pulled the hood roughly over her head, plunging her into darkness. Fear pulsed through her in waves, but her arms were tight at her side, leaving no room for movement. She was desperate to deny her captor the satisfaction of seeing her visibly upset, so she remained as still as possible while she listened to Selwyn empty the last of his instruments methodically from the wooden chest.

One by one, she counted them by their dull thud onto the wooden table. She imagined that each device was more painful and terrifying than the last. Every instrument gave its own unique clang, and Fran's imagination ran wild, just as Selwyn had intended. Clang…clang, he continued. Clang…clang, then a pause. Her shoulders tensed as she listened on intently. Silence descended between them, and Fran's breaths grew heavy before a sudden thump startled her.

What was that? She wondered, heart racing, but the room fell still. For a few moments, she couldn't even figure out if Selwyn was still standing across from her. She knew that he was enjoying his moment, the power, the sense of control. Finally, the floorboards groaned, and she imagined his expression as footsteps began in her direction once more.

No pain, no fear, she thought. She was certain she could sense a body looming over her. She braced herself for the consequences, and her breath caught as an unexpected jerk of the hood sent light into her eyes once more.

"I could get used to this," said a voice too soft to be Selwyn's. Fran squinted, and her eyes adjusted. Her heart was racing, and her jaw dropped with surprise.

Patch?

"Well, look who it is," he said with a smile.

Fran's gaze shot around the room, finding Selwyn sprawled on the floor. "But how did you?" she tried to ask, her words garbled by the gag. It occurred to her that, for all her surprise at seeing Selwyn incapacitated, her greater feeling was the relief of seeing Patch.

"Still making as much sense as usual," said Patch. "I'm here to rescue you, but I don't suppose there's any rush."

Fran's eyes narrowed, and Patch smirked as he reached to remove the gag. She noticed a crossbow on the table next to the small chest, and she assumed that Patch must have taken it from Renshaw. How else could he have broken in to save her?

"I'm never going to live this down, am I?" she asked, already knowing the answer.

"Probably not," said Patch. "But I still need to save the prince. Help me out of here, and perhaps we can call it even?" He raised his hand to jingle a set of keys. Fran recognised them as Selwyn's.

"And the rope?" Fran asked, rolling her eyes.

"Oh yes," said Patch. He knelt to cut Fran's constraints and then used the keys to remove her chains. "Sorry."

Fran climbed to her feet and pushed past Patch, grabbing the keys and Selwyn's knife from him as she went. "There will be time for apologies later. You have yourself a deal."

Back in the corridor, Fran found Renshaw on the floor, as expected. The pirate was propped up against the doorway, almost peaceful as if sleeping.

"The Silver Sword…" she muttered, unsure how to phrase her question. "Is it, I mean, are they all—" She halted as Patch's hand landed on her shoulder.

"It's fine," he said, and Fran turned to find the hint of a smile tugging at his lips. "Roscoe always said she was the best he'd sailed on, and now I believe him. They tried to slow us by burning the mast and sails, but we managed to control it. Unlucky for Firemane, The Sword is made of tougher stuff. We lost a few good men, but the attack was only ever meant as a distraction. They left as soon as the two of you were taken."

"They came for Taiwo," Fran said with a nod. "He was promised to another girl, Botosi's daughter, Makeba."

"So that's who Firemane was working for…" Patch bit his lip in thought. "Well, I guess we'd better get the prince out of here," he continued. "There's a boat ready to take us back to the Sword. Best we don't keep them waiting."

⚜ ⚜ ⚜

The cell door clicked open. Taiwo briefly squinted against the faint light that spilled through the door, and after a moment, his eyes widened before a smile broke out on his face.

"I'm pleased to see you two!" he said, delight evident in his voice.

"And you," said Patch. "But we need to get out of here."

Fran stepped forward to unlock Taiwo's shackles. The prince's hands fell loose, and he massaged his wrists as Patch raised Renshaw's crossbow to keep guard.

"The crew are waiting," Fran said urgently. "The captain cleared a path. We just need to sneak out of here. Take this," she added, handing him Selwyn's knife.

"And what about you?" Taiwo asked.

Fran shrugged. "I'll be fine. Now let's go."

"There was one more thing," Taiwo answered with a grimace.

"What now?" Patch asked impatiently.

Taiwo looked to the ground. "Fran, I think you've stepped in the gruel."

⚜ ⚜ ⚜

Fran raised her head to find the deck blanketed with fog.

"See anything?" asked Patch.

She stared down at him from her place atop the ladder. "Nothing. Where are the others?"

"A small boat on the port side," Patch whispered as Taiwo watched on silently, his eyes darting between Fran and Patch as they spoke in hushed voices. "Just need to make it across the across the deck and we're home safe."

"As simple as that," Fran jested. "Who's with you?"

Patch's nose wrinkled. "Best not to ask."

Fran rolled her eyes and returned to keep watch, wondering which of the Silver Sword crew had consented to come and rescue her. Escape was within touching distance, though she doubted she'd be able to see her arm if she tried in this fog. That was a complication, but it also might help provide cover for their escape, she thought. Waves lapped gently against the side of the ship, and the only other sound was the occasional creak of timber or the squeak of ropes and rigging. It certainly seemed clear enough. She knew Sabina would have men on lookout somewhere on the ship, but it was unlikely that they would be searching for movement on deck given that they all believed Fran and Taiwo to be locked securely in the bowels of the ship. There were only three of them trying to make a break for it, after all, and if they stayed in the shadows, they'd be long gone before anyone noticed. At least that's what she told herself to help build up the nerve to make a move.

"Let's go," she said, encouraging the other two to climb the ladder. She crouched at the top and awaited their arrival, spotting a large barrel looming in the mist. She indicated them to follow with a wordless gesture, and the three of them moved quickly and quietly to take cover behind the barrel. They suddenly heard someone whistling and nearly startled, but they took care to remain silent as their heads swivelled around, looking for the source of the jaunty tune. Fran saw him first. One of Sabina's men was in the crow's nest above. She pointed wordlessly to him so that Taiwo and Patch would know he was there too. The man gave no impression that he'd seen them, however, and continued on whistling, apparently quite at peace with the world. It was the perfect opportunity, she thought, and a split-second decision hastened Fran forward, the sounds of the sea growing clearer with every step.

Faster and louder, her heart began to beat. They were going to make it—to freedom, to safety, *to Mathilde*. Fran was finally going home with the chance to make things right. *Still together and nearly there*, she thought through heavy breaths. She glanced back at Taiwo and Patch and smiled. Just a few more steps now and—

Fran's body slammed back onto the deck with an almighty thud. Her head was spinning, and the air had been driven from her lungs. What had she had run into? Something solid, immoveable.

"Going somewhere?"

The unfamiliar voice sent Fran scrambling backward across the deck. She rested at Taiwo's feet and grimaced at the prospect of the towering pirate glaring back at her. With arms like tree trunks, the man was a mess of bedraggled hair and beard, his cutlass appearing small but deadly in his enormous, meaty hand.

Fran saw Patch raise the crossbow above her. "Are you planning to stop us?" he asked, as Taiwo helped Fran to her feet.

The pirate stalled; his eyes narrowed, but his lips stilled with no attempt to call out. The world around them was completely silent, and it was then that Fran realised the whistling had stopped.

"Look out!" she called, as another pirate, this one with long, dark hair and a braided beard, appeared, wrapping his arms around Patch's neck in a headlock. The giant lunged forward to follow his crewmate's lead, and their silent standoff seemed a distant memory as Taiwo leapt in front of Fran to shoulder the massive man to the ground. Taiwo and the giant pirate landed awkwardly, the pirate's sword sent skidding across the deck. Taiwo twisted and tried to pin his opponent, but the larger man was too strong, and Taiwo cried out as he was pressed to the floor, both arms shaking as his own knife was lowered toward his chest.

Taiwo could fight, but the pirate was too big, too strong, and Fran dashed forward to wrap the larger man in a chokehold of her own as the knifepoint hovered threateningly. The act itself provided a momentary distraction. The giant arched his back and spared a hand to loosen Fran's grip, leaving Taiwo free to slam the knife away. Fran, however, was clubbed in the side of the head and left sprawled on the deck.

The impact left her mind a blur, but choking sounds echoed out behind her, and Fran turned as the crossbow crashed to the ground, Patch struggling to loosen the whistler's grip at his throat.

"Fran!" Taiwo called breathlessly through the mayhem. The giant was back upon him, huge fists knocking all sense out of Taiwo as his arms flailed helplessly. Fran climbed to her feet slowly and unsteadily. They were losing, and Sabina's reinforcements could arrive at any moment. There was no sign of help from the crew of the Silver Sword, and Fran realised that it was now or never. The moment was upon her. She let her fists clench, allowing the red haze that she so carefully avoided to fully take control.

Crack. Her fist slammed into the giant's jaw.

Another strike, then a sweeping hook before a vicious knee left him slumped on the ground, Taiwo motionless beside him. Her knuckles were covered in blood, but adrenaline coursed through her body, and she barely heard when someone behind her called out for help.

She turned to find the whistler grappling with Patch, who had somehow gotten free from his chokehold, on the deck. Patch was on top for the time being, but his opponent had worked his way free. Damn Patch's poor technique, she thought as she made to rush over to aid him. She needn't have worried, however. The whistler's freedom was short-lived before Patch sent his face slamming into the deck. He did not move anymore.

"We have to get Taiwo out of here," she called, rushing to help Patch back to his feet. Sabina's men could be heard stirring below deck, but the heavy mist continued to obscure Fran's vision, and they stumbled forward before Fran was left wide-eyed once more.

"Not so fast, little lady…"

The giant was back.

A smile appeared on his face as he licked blood from his split lip. His dark, deep-set eyes were full of malice, but it was the cutlass in his hand that Fran feared the most.

"Stay back," said Fran, leaving Patch and Taiwo with no choice but to follow her instruction. She stepped forward to face her enemy. He was big and strong, but his size also made him clumsy. She'd had fought his type before, and since he was all that stood between Fran and safety, she knew that big and strong wouldn't be enough to save him.

The giant growled as he swung his cutlass. He was quick for his size, but Fran dodged the wide, arcing attempt with ease, every muscle in the man's arms and shoulders betraying his deadly intent. She wanted to toy with him, to make him suffer for the damage he'd done to Taiwo, which was ironic, really. It wasn't so long before that she'd been tempted to trouble Taiwo with a punch or two of her own. But here they were: Taiwo on his knees, Patch encouraging him little by little toward the ship's railing, Fran defending them both. There was no more time for games, and the giant wasn't playing anyway. Fran braced herself as the cutlass jabbed in her direction once more. She ducked the blade and rolled beyond her enemy to where the one-handed crossbow rested invitingly on the deck. She fired the bolt on instinct, hoping for the best, and by the time the giant's glare fell upon her, she found that his enthusiasm had faltered, his expression suitably dropped.

"What did you…?" he croaked, falling to his knees. He reached to find the bolt protruding from his chest, wheezing as Fran stepped forward to floor him with her boot, the crossbow still in her grasp.

The fog remained as thick as ever, but there was no masking the sound of Sabina's crew emerging on deck. Fran hurried to the ship's railings, where Taiwo and Patch were propped against one another, and found a rope ladder hanging over the side. As she looked over the edge, she saw a most unwelcome sight: Teeth climbing to meet them.

"We need to get out of here!" spat Teeth, eyes darting beyond them in search of possible threats. "I brought what you asked," he said, looking at Patch, "but be quick about it, all right?"

Patch nodded and reached to take a small, lit torch from Teeth's outstretched hand. He helped Taiwo over the railing and turned to Fran. "Cover me," he said, before darting into the darkness.

Cover you with what? She wondered exasperatedly, half-tempted to run after him. She discarded the crossbow. She had no bolts, rendering it useless, and she had no sword. Dark silhouettes began to appear through the heavy gloom. Every step brought them closer. They couldn't know that she was there—after all, the fog limited their visibility just as much as her own—but the noise of their scuffle with the two pirates had evidently been enough of an excuse for Sabina's crew to decide to sweep the deck. What if they knew she and Taiwo had escaped already? What if they found the...

"Body!" called one of the men. "I've got a body over here."

He hadn't seen her, but Fran knew exactly where to look, knew exactly where the giant's fallen body lay. She backed away silently and clambered over the ledge, gripping hold of the ladder as a crowd of Sabina's men surrounded their dead crewmate.

"Must be the girl—the prisoner!" she heard the same man say. "She must be trying to escape. Quick, sweep the deck, all of you...move!"

Footsteps pounded on the deck as Sabina's crew broke off in search, and Fran knew it was only a matter of time before she or Patch—or both—were found. She looked down at Teeth, who gestured emphatically for their departure, and footsteps grew louder until a hand landed on the rails above her.

"See anything?" came a voice, and Fran's breath stilled.

The young pirate leaned forward and squinted at the horizon.

Fran couldn't remember ever feeling so desperate, so close to escape with such a thin line standing between life and death. Her mind was beating a tattoo: *Don't look down, please, don't look down...*

Then...boom!

The pirate fell back as the sky turned red, inky black being completely taken over by a vibrant crimson. Fran held tight to the railings as she slammed against the hull of the ship, and her ears rang. Somewhere, distantly, she thought she heard Teeth calling for her to leave. It was hard to hear him over the ringing in her ears, and she only had eyes for the vivid red of the sky.

She forced herself to snap back into the moment. She needed to go, but what about Patch? She couldn't leave him behind, but what if he'd been caught in the blast? What if they'd captured him already, or worse still, what if they had killed him?

There was no time to waste, she realised, and she raced down the remaining rungs of the ladder to join Taiwo and Teeth in the boat.

"What are you waiting for? Let's get out of here!" yelled Teeth, and the two remaining crewmembers who had been waiting in the boat raised their oars to start rowing. Teeth sat at the back of the boat with a sour snarl, and they all startled as someone jumped the rails above before descending the ladder toward them. Fran's heart raced. It was Patch. She was unable to stop her heart feeling as though it might burst out of her chest for two glorious seconds, and then she saw Sabina's men appear at the ledge in hot pursuit. Their boat was already pulling away and Patch had no choice but to launch himself from the hull of the ship into the icy water below.

Sabina's men had now gathered in force, and when Fran looked up from Patch's form swimming in the freezing water, she saw that Sabina herself had joined their ranks. Fran thought she heard Sabina call for bows.

"Give him your oar!" Teeth instructed frantically as arrows began sailing through the air and dropping like rain into the water. The waves were steady, and Patch swam to them quickly before taking the end of the oar offered to him by one of the crewmates, slumping himself into the boat, teeth chattering with the cold.

"If any of my men die because of you," said Teeth threateningly as he fell back into his seat.

Fran might have responded under different circumstances, but Teeth's men *had* been there to save her and Taiwo, and they weren't safe yet. The smell of smoke now drifted on the breeze, and arrows forced them to cower as the two oarsmen rowed their boat, slow and exposed, into the depths of the fog.

Moments passed before the arrows finally ceased and the sounds of Sabina and her crew fell too far away for their ears to pick up.

Fran turned to Teeth. "You were saying?"

But Teeth offered no reply.

"What now?" asked Patch, shuddering under a thick blanket, his skin looking worryingly pale.

"It's Teeth," Fran said in an even voice. "He's taken an arrow. He's dead."

Locke

Left foot, right foot. One in front of the other.

Locke repeated the instruction in his mind as he walked slowly. Slower than slow.

Small distances, that was all they were. From his room at The Eagle, the door closed behind him. Through the tavern, where Grace smiled at him hopefully, oblivious to Locke's despicable act of treason, which would make her never want to speak to him again. Out into the cold autumn morning, wet mulch beneath his feet and morning dew in the air. Left foot, right foot. One in front of the other.

Locke lifted the hood of his cloak to cover his head. His eyes followed his feet, and he pushed onward, always moving, lest he stop and find himself unable to begin walking once more.

Go to work and act as though everything is normal.

His father's orders left no room for negotiation or misunderstanding. Locke had made his decision the moment he handed the parcel to Finnian. There was no turning back now, no choice other than to see things through.

But how? How could he possibly be expected to face the consequence of his actions? Were there even any consequences to face? Perhaps Finnian hadn't managed to escape after all. Maybe the lockpick had failed, or Boyd's vigilance had prevented any such attempt. Maybe he would walk into work and find the insufferable brigand still locked in his cell, ready to annoy Locke all day long with his inane chatter. Locke tried to keep his mind on these possibilities as he passed into the shadow of Eldred's Keep.

At the portcullis, he found more men on duty than usual. Not just the regular guards but soldiers, men armed and purposeful. He wondered if they were Truth Seekers, the pride of High Commander Broderick's forces. The Seekers were established in the wake of King Augustus's passing: a highly trained force assembled to discover and quell acts of sedition. He paused, his heart seeming to fail, and his hopeful thoughts soon fell away. What had he been he thinking? He was party to an escape attempt, successful or otherwise. In the best of scenarios, Boyd had found the lockpick and would not hesitate to point the finger at Locke. Even if it hadn't been found already, there was little chance that such an object would escape Boyd's attention during handover.

But no, something was wrong. Something felt different.

Locke pulled himself out of the way as traders' carts and castle staff passed by, following the cobbled road toward the castle. They were being made to wait, subject to the scrutiny of the King's Guard, which dampened Locke's brow with sweat immediately. He had to pull himself together. He was expected at work and was no doubt late already. Despite the pressing need to hurry, he couldn't help but scan Eldred's Keep with his eyes, searching for the flag his mother had told him flew high above the castle when a monarch had passed on. But where was it now?

Locke thought of young Prince Leo and the not-yet-born royal baby, and a wave of guilt washed over him as he realised that his own actions might leave the children fatherless, maybe even worse. He tried to tamp down his guilt as he scanned around again and realised he could find no flag.

Had the king survived after all? If not, perhaps High Commander Broderick had ordered silence as his Seekers continued their investigations. Likely they were onto Locke already, but his failure to appear at the prison would only make matters worse. In the end, it seemed there was no choice but to trust his father's words and act as though everything were normal.

News of the king will spread, but I'll protect you, his father had said.

Only time would tell.

"Prison Master Locke," said the guard at the gate, addressing him with a curt nod. The young man had dark hair and a smooth face. His name was Hector or Humphrey, or something like that, but Locke was too preoccupied to remember.

One of the King's Guards stepped forward, and Locke's eyes were drawn to the halberd in his grip. "If you'd like to come with me, Prison Master," he said flatly, his choice of words suggesting that it was an option but his tone and serious facial expression letting him know it was an order. Locke's heart was beating fast, but there was a queue forming behind him that made him feel as though he needed to move quickly.

"Is everything all right?" he asked, with every effort to curb the tremble in his voice.

The guard nodded, his lips pursed. "Perhaps it is better to discuss this elsewhere. The rest of you..." He turned to address the gathering crowd with a booming voice. "The castle is locked down until further notice. Castle staff only. The king regrets that he will be unable to hold an audience today."

The king, thought Locke. *So, the pretence continues.*

Or, the voice in his head countered, arguing with himself, *the king lives.*

Grumbles of disappointment filled the air as traders turned around, heading back from wherever they had come, back to their lives, back to freedom. Locke followed the guard who had approached him, flanked on either side by further members of the King's Guard. He had no idea what he was walking into, what fate awaited him, but he had a feeling he would find out soon enough.

⚜ ⚜ ⚜

They arrived at the prison doors, and Locke's body went cold at the thought of returning. He had developed a thumping headache, beating like a drum behind his eyes. He massaged his temples, as if the act would make his troubles go away.

The guards at the door stepped aside. "Right this way," said the guard who had approached him first, and Locke proceeded onward into the familiar surroundings of the prison, where the High Commander was already waiting.

"Prison Master Locke," he began, his tone serious. He turned to face Locke, whose eyes were already scanning the room for answers, searching for any sign of Finnian. "I'm sorry to drag you in here like this, but there has been an incident."

"An incident, High Commander?"

Broderick's eyes lowered, and he shook his head. "A most serious incident, Prison Master. A plot to free the brigand, Finnian, and kill the king!"

Locke's eyes widened with practised surprise. "The king?" he asked naively.

"Yes, the king," Broderick answered sadly. "A treacherous deep-rooted plot it was as well. And it would have worked if not for…if not for…" He trailed off and turned away, hiding his face with his hands, apparently ashamed of such a display of emotion on his own behalf.

"If not for what?" Locke said, unable to stop himself from asking to sate his own curiosity, though relief flooded through his body. The king was alive then, he realised. But there was no sign of Boyd. He looked to the cell and noticed Walt muttering as usual in his corner, arms wrapped tightly around his knees. Who had interrupted Finnian's route to King Cyrus?

Broderick turned back to Locke, red faced, tears clouding his eyes. He cleared his throat to compose himself. "If not for Thaddeus. The man gave his life to save his king. He always gave his king everything."

Thaddeus? The king's mentor? But…

"It seems Thaddeus intercepted that dog Finnian on his way to the king's chambers. They fought, and the brigand was injured."

Broderick paused to sniffle loudly. "There's a trail of blood to attest to his injuries, and we believe he was forced to alter his plans."

"Alter them?"

Thaddeus nodded and composed himself. "Aye. He must have lost a lot of blood, but he's a cunning one, that Finnian. I take no pride sharing the failings of my men, but the brigand found his way to Prince Leo's chambers—"

"The prince is dead?" Locke asked, his stomach churning.

"No," Broderick answered firmly. "Well, not that we know of, anyway. The evidence suggests that the prince was taken. For what purpose, we don't know." He walked to close the gap between them, and Locke was suddenly reminded of the precarious nature of his position. "I wondered if Finnian had mentioned anything to you, or perhaps to Prison Master Boyd?"

Locke chewed his lip thoughtfully. "Nothing, High Commander, not that I can remember. And Prison Master Boyd, sir," he began, dreading the answer to the question he knew he had to ask, "is he...?"

"Dead, yes." Broderick's answer was terse, lacking any discernible emotion. When he saw Locke's face, which Locke knew must have gone paler than pale, Broderick added, "I'm sorry, I know the two of you were close. What I can say is that he died doing his duty, and we hold no suspicion toward the man."

"No, High Commander?" asked Locke, a powerfully nauseating sensation taking him over, making it hard to keep his voice level.

Broderick licked his teeth and waved his hand dismissively. "No, this is something deeper, something that has been bubbling for some time." He paused, and Locke's heart quickened as the

High Commander gestured for one of his guards to close the door. He dropped his voice. "You've heard of the Battle of Highcastle, Locke?" he asked.

Locke's chest tightened. "Yes, High Commander."

"The historic defeat of the Verderans," Broderick said, his eyes unfocused as though on a memory to which Locke was not privy. "I was there that day. It was a fine victory, but not one that came without suffering. Winners and losers, Prison Master Locke. While one man drinks, another digs. While one celebrates, the other suffers. Vengeance is patient, but in my experience, the roots of revenge can grow to prove most fruitful."

It was all Locke could do to stop himself from running for the door. He'd thought his act had been a convincing one, but Broderick clearly knew something, suspected something. His own father had served under the High Commander, and though Locke had never seen the likeness himself, he wondered if Broderick or his Seekers had made the connection between himself and his father. Walt's murmurings suddenly became words in Locke's mind: *guilty, traitor, liar.* Accusatory words, one after another, before the usual nonsense reconvened once more. Had Locke imagined that? He couldn't bear to look around to see if anyone else in the room had noticed, least of all the High Commander.

"Vengeance, High Commander?" Locke persisted, sweat causing his tunic to stick to his back.

"Of the most treacherous kind," Broderick confirmed. "Verderan vengeance, that is…" he added, and Locke finally breathed. "The king, Alonso, is clearly a snake just like his father and brother before him. I've petitioned King Cyrus to take proactive measures, but our leader is a man of peace. Quite how he will react to this, I don't know, but—" He halted abruptly. "I'm sorry, I've said too much. This is none of your concern, Prison Master, and I am sorry to burden you. I'm out of sorts."

"It's no problem," Locke answered meekly, and another jolt of guilt ran through him in the knowledge that Thaddeus's death at Finnian's hands was the main source of the High Commander's pain.

Broderick smiled. "You're a good man, Locke. You saw Finnian for what he was and tried to make him pay for it. It's a shame we didn't let you into the cell to finish the job!" He exhaled through his nose, half a laugh, and Locke let his shoulders relax. "This country was built on good men, hard work, and trust," Broderick continued, passion bringing his voice to life. "We will need more men like you for what lies ahead, I've no doubt. For now, though, the prison is under control of the King's Guard. You live in the capital?"

Locke nodded.

"Good. Provide details to the men on the door and go home, Locke. I know how difficult it is to lose a friend," he said, his voice thick with emotion as he fought back the tears pooling in his eyes once more. "Take time while my Seekers continue their investigations. Put this place from your mind, and we will send for you in due course."

Locke nodded again. He felt guilty knowing that Broderick pitied him, thinking that his source of unhappiness lay simply in the death of his so-called friend, Boyd, when Locke's mind was truly troubled with much more sinister deeds. "But what about Walt, High Commander?" he added.

"Oh, I wouldn't worry about him. He never even left his cell."

Locke looked to Walt, still muttering in his corner, his brow furrowed at the idea that the man had seen an open door and stayed put. "Huh," he said, turning to leave. But the more he thought about it, as he bid farewell to the High Commander, Walt's inability to leave his prison did not surprise Locke. After all, Locke knew all about remaining in a prison even after you're given the opportunity to run.

⚜   ⚜   ⚜

His composure only lasted as long as was necessary, taking him out of the prison doors and back into the streets of the capital, where he promptly vomited.

"Are you okay?" asked a passing woman. Her round face looked slightly sick at what she had just witnessed, but her kind brown eyes were also coloured with concern.

Locke straightened to acknowledge her with a smile, one that felt plastered on and that he was fairly certain looked completely unconvincing. "Fine, thanks," he said, a pool of sick still warm at his feet. "It must have been something I ate," he added, straightening his cloak. She forced a smile, as if she didn't believe him. He wished her a good day, and they parted as he continued home.

"Back so soon?" called Grace as he crashed through the doors of The Eagle. It was still early, and the tavern was quiet by normal standards, the same old suspects with their heads pressed flat to sticky, ale-drenched tables. In one corner, two grey-haired men exchanged money over a game of cards, and Rufus had his back turned behind the bar, polishing tankards as he always did, a seemingly never-ending task.

Locke wanted to speak to her, but what would he say? *Stay away from me, I'm a traitor, oh and sorry for the sick breath!* It wasn't the time. It was never the right time recently, and he wondered if it ever would be.

He never slowed his momentum, instead muttering, "I'm sorry, Grace, I can't," as he hastened past her toward his room, fumbling for the keys to let himself back into his very own cell.

The bed creaked as he crashed down upon it, curling up like a baby, and he was too upset to even feel ashamed at the pitiful sobs that wracked his body, the tears flowing freely. He was making such a racket, was so deep in his own guilt and grief, that he never even heard Grace enter until she perched down on the edge of the bed beside him.

"Whatever it is, it's all right," she said soothingly. She drew up closer and wrapped an arm around him tightly.

My father has Prince Leo, Locke thought to himself with a sense of dread, wishing more than anything that he could say it aloud, that he could share his burden with her, but he knew he never could. Instead, his sobs slowed as he tried to think of where Prince Leo could have been taken, and that's when it came to him…

Small hands banging on the underside of the door…

Locke knew exactly where to look.

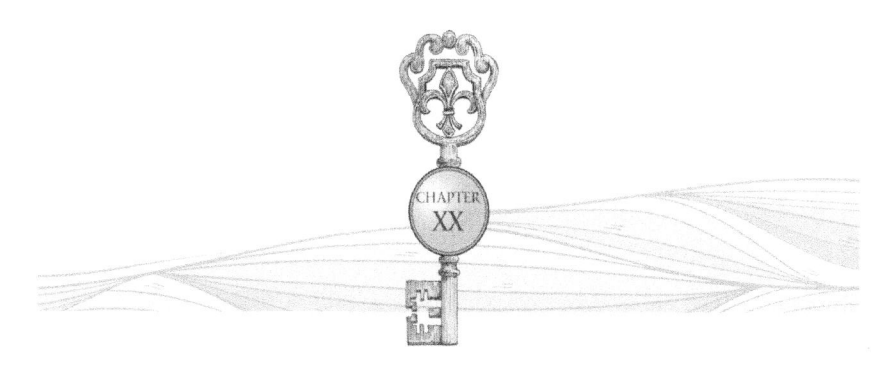

Francine

When they were clear of Sabina and her band of pirates, there was time for a small ceremony. The crew of the Silver Sword lined the deck in their reduced number. They were covered in scars, cuts, and bruises, and the ship looked scarcely better. As Fran gazed around, she noticed charred masts, woodwork chipped from arrowheads, and sections of the balustrade missing completely.

The ship and its crew were damaged but not broken, and perhaps for the first time, Fran felt that she was one of them. Tragedy has a wonderful way of bringing people together, she thought as she stared around at her comrades. Teeth had died helping to save her, and that was all that had mattered in the moment. Fran stood quietly and respectfully at Patch's side as final words were said and Teeth's body was sent crashing down into the water below.

"He wasn't all bad," said Patch quietly.

This final sentiment was somewhat more concise than Patch's eulogy had been, but Fran appreciated these simple words perhaps more than all the others. It reminded her of something that her brother had told her years ago, when discussing Wendell and his acts of treachery. "I've come to think that there is no such thing as a bad person," she recited from memory, her voice layering over Cyrus's in her head, "just people who do a mixture of good and bad things." She smiled and let her hand fall at her side, where it brushed against Patch's.

"Is that right?" he asked, smiling back at her.

Fran shrugged. "It's something to believe in. Take you for example—I never expected you to try and cook Sabina's crew in their sleep."

Patch recoiled at her words. "Cook them? I didn't, I wouldn't…"

Fran raised her eyebrows, enjoying Patch's discomfort.

After a moment, he caught her facial expression. "Still trying to even things up after I rescued you, are we?" Patch rolled his eyes and then smiled. "The fire was simply meant to…keep them busy, slow them down. It was no more than they attempted aboard the Silver Sword during your capture. I made sure to damage the main sail. I was rescuing a prince *and* a princess, don't you know? Couldn't bear the thought of any harm coming to either of them. Here, take this, you never know when you might need it…"

He handed her a small pouch, which she tucked into her pocket. She knew without asking that it was blast powder from its acrid smell.

"Well, don't you know how to treat a lady?" said Fran, her tone one of mock flattery. The crew of the Silver Sword broke away sullenly to return to their duties. "How is Taiwo, by the way? It's quiet without him."

"That's one way to put it," Patch chortled. "Seems the two of you really hit it off on Sabina's ship. Should I be worried?"

Fran's skin prickled with thoughts of the kiss, with the idea that Patch would be worried at all if she had affection for another…

Before Fran could cobble together a response, Patch smirked. "Let's call this one a draw, shall we? As for Taiwo, he's fine, I think his ego is hurt as much as anything, but he did take a beating. We'll reach Clerbonne by nightfall. Let him rest until then. He'll let us know when he's ready to talk."

"And Amare?" enquired Fran.

"Below deck, in his quarters as usual."

"I'm starting to think that this might not be the best job for him. Imagine seasickness like that with all the travel that's required of him."

"Yes, but you've seen him in action with King Othelu and Queen Mathilde. What else would you have him do?"

Fran nodded in agreement. "Fair point." She really couldn't imagine Amare doing anything different.

Patch turned away, and Fran followed him onto the upper deck, where he stopped suddenly. By the time Patch turned back to face her, Fran noticed that his eyes were lowered, and he seemed tense, but she couldn't say for sure.

"I've been meaning to ask you something," he began before pausing. He really did seem nervous; Fran noticed his hands fidgeting, his sudden loss of words. It reminded her suddenly and powerfully of Cyrus in the early days of his courtship with Marcia, and it was most unlike the confident captain she usually saw. "When all of this is done," he continued, "I mean, I know you will need to return to Nivelle…with Taiwo, I mean, but…"

Yes, what do you mean? She thought. She nodded, supportively. Impatiently. *Go on…*

"Well, what I'm trying to say is, I don't know what your plans are, but I don't want it to be another five or more years before I see you again, Fran. I like you. I like being around you." He scratched his head anxiously, and she felt her cheeks heating. She couldn't think of a response, but he continued, "I know we didn't get off to the best of starts, but the crew are really getting used to having you around…*I'm* getting used to having you around." He wrapped her hand in his. "I can't offer you castles or palaces, but there's a whole world out there to explore. I meant to tell you—I've had word from Roscoe."

"Roscoe? When?" she asked, temporarily distracted from Patch's display of emotions.

"When we were in Taboso," Patch answered. "He is to meet me in Clerbonne upon our arrival. He has need of me, fresh orders from the king apparently."

"Orders from my brother?"

"So, I'm told," Patch replied, turning to walk and rest on the balustrade. "The White Lands. The new frontier! The king is keen to build relations and discuss trade. He is a man of great ambition, your brother. We are to sail for the port of Manavik within ten days."

Fran's heart sunk. "Ten days? But that's so soon…"

"Such is the life of a pirate," said Patch, twisting to face her with a sad smile. "Always on the move, exploring new lands. I would escort you to Nivelle, but there is much to do provisioning for the trip. I need to find a new quartermaster, for one, and the crew will be keen to enjoy their time on land. You might wish to pray for the locals!"

Fran laughed, or did her best imitation at a laugh. The wind had thoroughly gone out of her sails with the idea that Patch would be gone in a mere ten days. And she hadn't even figured out a way to respond to his proclamation about his feelings for her, overshadowed as it had been by his news from Roscoe.

"I want you to come with me," Patch said firmly, redirecting the conversation back to the deeper talks about their feelings for each other. "I know you have a life in Nivelle and a family in Highcastle, but well...I'd kick myself if I let you slip through my fingers without at least asking. You don't need to answer now," he added, raising the palms of his hands as if to slow his own momentum, "but say you'll think on it, when you're back in Nivelle?"

Fran breathed deeply in an attempt to contain her excitement. A small smile escaped her against her best efforts. She nodded. "I will."

⚜ ⚜ ⚜

There was scarcely a moment in which she didn't consider his invitation.

From their parting in Clerbonne—where she, Amare, and Taiwo watched as their belongings were loaded onto the carriage before the port fell away behind them, and Patch and his crew with it—across every inch of stone, mud, turf, and road as they traversed

Cornesse toward the capital. She was both in the carriage with Amare and Taiwo and not there at all. Part of her was already back on the Silver Sword, at Patch's side as they set off on great adventures. And another part of her was already back with Mathilde, standing by her for what was to come. Yet another part of her was in Highcastle, with Cyrus and Marcia as they welcomed their new baby. Fran felt torn in so many different directions.

They should have been celebrating their arrival, their safe return to dry land. It looked to Fran as though Taiwo and Mathilde would indeed be married, with Amare's own brilliant foresight to thank. The thought of home should have thrilled Fran, but her mind was distracted, and it seemed that the prince was much the same. She and Taiwo had grown close during their ordeal aboard Sabina's ship, but things were somehow different with Amare around. Though curious to ask the cause of Taiwo's uncharacteristic quietness, there was never a right time with the envoy so close at hand.

"Not long now," Amare quipped, clearly trying to lighten the mood as he looked between the two of them as though questioning what was wrong with them.

Fran pressed her head to the window as the first signs of Nivelle emerged in the distance. *A little more than a week now to make my decision,* she thought. *Not nearly long enough.*

⚜ ⚜ ⚜

"How do you feel?" asked Amare, stepping back to gaze appraisingly at the prince.

Taiwo rolled his shoulders as though trying to stretch his discomfort away. For all his efforts to suggest otherwise, he was clearly unaccustomed to the fine cotton shirt and stiff, white jacket Amare had chosen for him. The bruises on his face had settled quickly, but a small pink scar added character to his cheek, and the cut on his arm clearly still caused some pain. "I'm fine," he said. "I'll be better when I get out of these clothes."

"Well now, don't get ahead of yourself, great prince. You haven't even met the girl yet!" Amare answered playfully. Fran rolled her eyes at Amare's crude joke but said nothing as the envoy, straightening the collar of Taiwo's shirt, continued, "Besides, you look wonderful. Very regal. I'm told this is the very latest fashion. It will help you to fit in. Tell him, Fran."

Fran watched on with no effort at hiding her amusement. Taiwo's brass buttons and gold tassels were quite something—an effect made even more humorous by how miserable he looked at being forced into such an ensemble—and she didn't doubt that Mathilde would get a good laugh out of his appearance if nothing else. There *was* some truth in Amare's words, Fran thought; though Taiwo's dark skin and exotic timbre would set him apart from the locals of Nivelle, he could very well have passed for a Cornessian nobleman, such was his impressive presence and stature. The gesture of the outfit would no doubt please Clement and the other council members, but Fran knew the queen well enough to know that this alone might put Taiwo at a disadvantage. Above all else, Mathilde valued someone who wasn't afraid to be himself.

"I think you look... *nice*," she said, looking him up and down. "It's not my opinion that matters though, is it? The person you need to impress is on the other side of those doors, and I can tell you one thing: she doesn't like to be kept waiting."

Taiwo rolled his eyes. "All right, all right. Let's get this over with!"

"Just as we discussed, my prince," said Amare. Fran had not been privy to that particular conversation, but she could guess that Amare would have made sure Taiwo was well-versed as to how this meeting would happen, such was his love of formality.

The prince flashed a broad smile, and Fran had to admit that he did look rather striking. "The two of you do worry!" he said with pure confidence.

Fran allowed herself to relax with quiet optimism. *It'll be fine*, she reassured herself, silently considering the outcomes. She'd never really seen Mathilde with a man, but the queen was strong, self-assured, and rarely short of words. If anything, she thought, it would probably be difficult for Taiwo to get a word in edgeways. She smiled as Taiwo spoke at Amare in rapid Kanthi.

"Come on then," she said, snatching at the next break in conversation. The guards parted, and the doors opened. Brass instruments sounded, and they walked toward the centre of the throne room, Taiwo's eyes wide with wonder as the low-hanging chandelier bathed them in prisms of multicoloured light.

"Welcoming, Prince Taiwo of the Kanthu Isles and the Kanthi envoy, Amare," announced Clement, addressing the room at large in his most pompous voice, though Fran hardly noticed him and gave even less thought to the fact that he had ignored her own presence.

It felt strange approaching the throne this way; usually, she would be standing at the queen's side. Instead, Lucien was there, a wide grin protruding through the thick mass of his dark beard. She didn't know if it was her time away or simply the foreign-feeling angle of her approach, but it all seemed so much more impressive than she remembered, from the gilded ceiling to the ornately embroidered carpet. It was undoubtedly spectacular. Taiwo's jaw hung loose with wonderment. Just when Fran was thinking that the prince could stand to show a little more decorum befitting his station, she realised that he was looking not at his surroundings, but at Mathilde. When Fran's eyes eventually fell upon the queen, she understood why poor Taiwo had found himself unable to look away. The queen's hair was plaited and tied into tightly coiled buns, one on either side of her head. Her dress consisted of a red bodice and long skirt lifted with ornate gold stitchwork, a matching ruby necklace resting on her chest. There was no denying it: Queen Mathilde looked magnificent, every bit the imposing, breathtaking monarch Fran had described back in Mutembu. A pang of guilt coursed through Fran, however, at the thought of her ill-chosen words with Sabina. This was the first time that Fran had seen Mathilde since, and she hoped that the feeling of betrayal was not obvious on her face. And that was without considering the decision that Patch left her to make, a predicament that still weighed heavily on her mind.

"My queen," said Fran, dropping to one knee in the centre of the throne room. The fanfare flourished before silence prevailed, and Amare followed her gesture, leaving Taiwo standing awkwardly beside them.

"Down," hissed Amare, and Taiwo startled as though coming out of a dream before joining them. Fran lifted her head a little, to find Mathilde smiling back at her.

Amare cleared his throat before rising to address the room. "It is an honour, great queen," he began, as only Amare could. "You, of course, know Francine already. But please allow me to introduce Prince Taiwo, secondborn son of the great king Othelu Bengatu of the Kanthu Isles. Prince Taiwo, join us?"

The prince remained on his knees, and Amare's smile soon gave way to a grimace.

"Introducing Prince Taiwo," the envoy repeated, offering a second chance. He cleared his throat once more, and Fran could sense Amare's frustration. "Come on, Taiwo," he said, more nervously this time and nearly in a whisper, leaning down to address the prince directly. "It's time to introduce yourself, as we discussed." He stood, flashing Mathilde a smile, as though this was all going exactly as he had intended.

Fran gave a reassuring look in the prince's direction. "It's okay," she mouthed quietly, and Taiwo finally rose to his feet, hands shaking, a nervous sheen glistening on his brow.

Not quite as confident as he would have us believe, Fran thought, almost smugly.

"Greetings, Queen Taiwo," he said, fidgeting with the sleeve of his jacket and refusing to make eye contact, instead staring at some point above the queen's head. "I am Prince Mathilde and—" He stopped and winced as the mistake caught up with him. Clement and his lackey Georges stifled laughter in the corner, and Fran's face twisted in sympathy as she silently urged him on. She knew Taiwo was overwhelmed with nerves after finding Mathilde to be every bit as impressive as Fran herself had promised. Taiwo was a perfectly good speaker but found himself struggling with the added pressure of conversing in the common tongue. For all her desire to call out words of comfort and support, Fran knew this was neither the time nor the place. Taiwo had to do this alone.

"No wait," the prince continued, correcting himself. "I'm…" He shook his head with frustration. "I mean, I'm—"

Amare stepped forward to spare the prince's blushes. "What the prince means to say is that our journey has been long and arduous. We are all delighted to be here with you, aren't we, Taiwo?"

"Yes, indeed, but—"

"As you see, the prince is tired. Perhaps we should—"

"What?" Mathilde asked curtly. She shifted to sit upright, her eyebrows raised as they had been when Amare had spoken before. "Perhaps we should let the prince speak for himself, Amare. What do you think of that?" A smile tugged at Lucien's lips with every word his queen spoke.

"Of course, great queen." Amare bowed and backed away.

"You were saying?" Mathilde persisted, her eyes shifting to fall on Taiwo once more. "An arduous journey, I don't doubt. I am yet to visit your beautiful islands, but I hope to make the journey someday soon." Fran knew Mathilde was allowing Taiwo to have his own agency, his own voice, and she was trying to coax him back into his confidence. A rush of respect flooded her, as it so often did, for Mathilde's grace.

At this, Taiwo's smile widened. His shoulders relaxed, and his nerves seemed to ease. "Thank you, Queen Mathilde," he said, his voice settling into its normal, sturdy rhythm. "I would be honoured to take you one day. The islands would only be more beautiful for your visit."

The queen was suddenly red-cheeked. "And my chosen shield?" she asked, seemingly keen to move the conversation along and take back control.

"Of all the hardships we faced during our journey, I fear that Francine was the most dangerous of them all."

"I hope she treated you well?" Mathilde glanced over at Fran, mischief twinkling in her eyes.

Taiwo paused. "No worse than we treat our animals," he said after a moment, and he smiled as Mathilde snorted unexpectedly. Clement and Georges turned to shake their heads with disapproval, but this exchange had the opposite effect on Amare, who nodded encouragingly at the quick and familiar rhythm of conversation Taiwo and Mathilde had fallen into.

"Very good," said Mathilde composing herself, and the room fell quiet as her laughter ceased. She silenced for a moment, as she looked the prince up and down. "Very good. That'll be all I think."

Clement stepped forward, "But, my queen—"

"That'll be all, thank you, Clement. I've heard enough from you."

"But—" said Clement again.

"Prince Taiwo," she said, turning her attention to cut Clement off. "I know this is very forward of me, but this is a rather, well, unusual situation after all. I wonder," she continued, and it was the queen's turn to seem a little uncertain, her face lowered as she picked at her nails. "Well, I wondered if you might join me for dinner this evening. I know you're tired, and you'll probably want to rest, and it's fine if you'd rather not, I am after all being a bit—"

"Yes."

"Sorry?"

"Yes," Taiwo repeated, and Fran couldn't have smiled wider if it was herself and not Mathilde that was to be married.

Mathilde pursed her lips, and her poise returned in an instant. "Well, good then, excellent," she said assertively as though remarking on the weather before a long journey. "Fran, as always, you've done everything I've asked of you. It occurs to me that you've been away from Nivelle for some time, but Highcastle longer still. You know me to be a woman of my word, and I would not see you miss the birth of another niece or nephew. I presume you are still keen to travel and be with your family?"

"Yes, my queen."

"Good," Mathilde responded with a nod. "Well, Lucien is a sorry replacement and not half so interesting to speak to..." She paused to smile at Lucien, who returned the act before rolling his eyes theatrically at Mathilde's jibe. "He has nevertheless kept me safe during your absence and has offered to remain at my side until your return. I cannot thank you enough, but you need not worry about me for now. I have a feeling things are going to work out just fine." She turned to Taiwo, whose eyes had never left her. "My final request is that you take the evening for yourself and prepare for home. I've asked much of you already, and I wouldn't see my priorities hinder yours."

"You're sure, my queen?"

"Quite sure," Mathilde smiled and glanced, once again, at Taiwo.

The room went silent, and Fran's eyes narrowed as though trying to figure out a difficult calculation. She watched Taiwo and Mathilde appraising each other wordlessly. *Love is finding someone who can steal your breath and leave you speechless,* the prince had said. Here were his words brought to life.

"Then...that all sounds just perfect. Thank you, my queen."

But as Francine took to her knee in thanks, she couldn't help but wonder if she knew where her own priorities lay anymore. She had some thinking to do, and fast.

⚜ ⚜ ⚜

Fran slumped down on her bed and sighed like a difficult child.

She'd completed the task she'd been set by her queen, and Mathilde had rewarded her with a most welcome leave of absence. It seemed Mathilde and Taiwo had a real chance, and that left Fran to return to her family, perhaps even in time for the birth of the new prince or princess. It had all worked out as intended. So why, she wondered, was she filled with such undeniable dismay?

She rolled over to find a bowl of steaming water on her side table. It had been prepared for her return and was intended as an opportunity to wash away the effects of life on the road, but her thoughts only turned to Patch once more—the thought he had put into her comfort onboard the ship—and she knew that such a thing was not possible. Nothing could wash away the marks this trip had left on her.

She had one week, give or take. One week before Patch was away, discovering new lands, with no indication as to when he would return. One week before he sailed off on a new adventure, and there was no telling what he might encounter along the way.

There would be danger, no doubt, but what about love? What if he found a home in the White Lands, perhaps a woman? Could Fran risk passing up this opportunity, passing up this chance with Patch? Could she settle back into city life like nothing had happened?

And what place existed for her here anyway? She owed her life to Cyrus, but they had spent little time together in recent years. The king had never denied her, but he had other responsibilities now: the hopes and dreams of a nation, for a start, and those of his growing family.

She thought of Marcia, a calm, considered wife whose every action supported and elevated her husband. Fran adored the queen, but she had none of Marcia's quiet planning and patience. Then there was Adaline, a woman of great composure and dignity, who had outlived her husband and spent her most recent years helping Cyrus fully understand what it meant to rule and put your country first.

Her thoughts shifted to Zimbeza in Taboso, a woman of great beauty and elegance, a family woman who steered her husband with her imposing presence. Then to the pirate queen, Sabina, a deceitful cut-throat to be sure, but one whose fearsome reputation had granted her captaincy over an entire crew and notoriety across borders and seas.

Fran was none of these women.

Finally, Fran's mind settled on Mathilde. The queen of Cornesse had captivated Fran's imagination since their very first meeting, but Taiwo's arrival signalled a new beginning for the queen. Mathilde had poise and control that demanded respect. She thought with her head, not her heart—though Fran thought there was a chance that her encounter with Taiwo might have shaken this particular conviction—and she was a woman to be admired. But Fran could shelter in her shadow no longer, nor her brother's. Cyrus had taken her hand all those years ago in the forests of Corhollow, and he had led her to safety and well beyond, into a life of privilege, elevating her first from a Low Country orphan to a treasured sister and then to the unthinkable: a princess. Without her brother, she would never have had the opportunity to join Mathilde in Nivelle, but the time for handholding was over; it was down to Fran now to find her own way out of the woods, to choose her own path forward.

She reached into her pocket and removed the necklace Zimbeza had given her in Mutembu. The chain was tangled after their long journey, but Fran unwound the silver links to hold it up to the light. It was a fine trinket. The metal was not without scratches and scrapes, but it was surprisingly strong, resilient, and it had a certain presence, as though it were more than a small, breakable thing but something with history, a story perhaps.

She smiled as she placed the chain around her neck, so that it rested lightly upon her collarbone. It was the sort of piece that could easily be overlooked or underestimated. It would have held little appeal for a discerning jewellery connoisseur, but to Fran, it was perfect. It made sense. She was no queen; she was hardly even a princess, really. Fran had no intention of emulating Sabina's bloodthirsty ambition, but perhaps there was another way, and maybe it didn't matter that she didn't know exactly what that was yet. Like Zimbeza's necklace, she knew what it was to be overlooked and underestimated, and this was her chance to write a new story, to create some history of her own in the White Lands, with Patch and the crew of the Silver Sword.

Cyrus would understand, surely, and there would be time for family reunions when she returned. It broke her heart to think of missing the birth of her new niece or nephew, but this opportunity was now or never, and despite everything it just felt…right. She'd need to speak to Mathilde, of course, but there would be time for that too, and the queen would surely send her with her best graces. This was, in many ways, the queen's own doing, after all.

Fran relaxed on the bed, and her eyes were suddenly heavy with contentment. *Clear thought and purpose,* wasn't that what Zimbeza had promised from the necklace? Fran had almost laughed at the time, but perhaps it was she who had underestimated the necklace all along.

⚜ ⚜ ⚜

Bright white moonlight met Fran's eyes. She was still so tired, but something had woken her. She reached to scratch an itch on her neck, but her skin felt unusually hot to the touch. *The necklace?* she wondered. She'd hardly worn any jewellery since she was a child, but she couldn't remember ever having an adverse reaction to any metal. Perhaps it really was just a cheap old ornament. And yet, the heat wasn't confined to her neck alone. She reached down to the top of her thigh, where the same heat radiated through the material of her breeches. Her hand hovered over the pocket, then after a moment, she reached in tentatively, her hand clasping around the source: the small mirror her brother had given her ten years ago. *The Mirror of Amabel,* she reminded herself, drawing the trinket from her pocket. She kept it with her always, as a reminder of her brother.

According to Cyrus, the mirror presented its owner with a sense of direction in times of need, but Fran had treated this idea with the same cynicism she had shown the necklace.

It was probably just a reaction. She *had* been travelling in different climates; perhaps the worry of her decision was affecting her in unusual ways, or perhaps it was the stress of the past couple of weeks. She wondered if the necklace had left a mark, and she sat up, raising the mirror to check. But to her surprise, the mirror's reflection provided little more than a dark, bewildering blur. The surface was marred with a few small cracks incurred during Cyrus's travels, and she thought it might be dusty from her own journey, so she wiped the screen with her sleeve, but the reflection offered no resemblance to her or the full moon radiating light behind her. This was odd, as Fran had looked into the mirror plenty of times before, always finding her reflection as usual. Fran brought the mirror closer, and her eyes widened as the blur began to swirl. She rubbed at her eyes, but the movement continued within the glass until the swirling slowed and a new image gradually began to settle. It was a dark room, but not her own, and as Fran squinted at the small surface, she began to discern various objects scattered around. There was a disorderly stack of hay in one corner, and as Fran turned the angle of the mirror, a jumble of wooden barrels came into view.

A cellar then, but whose? she wondered, her nose almost pressed to the glass as she continued to move around the room from her place in her bed. There was hardly any light, but Fran caught a flicker of movement in one corner of the mirror. She twitched it to one side, moving closer to distinguish a set of stairs, upon which she could just make out the silhouette of a small person sitting. The image offered no sound, but Fran could see the figure jerking, head in hands. Her heart wrenched; it was a child, based on the size of the stairs and the small legs braced upon them. A thin shard of light spilled down from above, and she detected curly hair, a boy most likely, though she couldn't be sure. Whoever it was, they were trapped. They were probably scared, and they were certainly alone. Then suddenly, the jerking stopped. The child moved their hands, and Fran's breath caught in her throat as one of her favourite faces in the world became clear. The sight knocked the air out of her.

Leo, her mind was practically wailing. *Leo.*

Where was her nephew? The mirror turned cold, or maybe it was her hand. A tear rolled down her face to match the young prince in the mirror. Her confusion turned to clarity, to a horrible sort of certainty: someone had taken Leo. It was the only way he would possibly find himself locked in this cold, dark place. He was adored, always looked after, at home. There was no way he could find himself trapped or lost for long in Highcastle, so Fran was forced to believe he had been taken against his will.

A thousand thoughts flooded her mind at once. How long had Leo been missing? Did Cyrus yet know that Leo was gone? Did he know who had taken him? Did he know *where* they had taken him?

Fran suddenly felt so useless, so far away. After everything Cyrus had done for her, had she really forsaken them, her only family, in pursuit of her own interests in Nivelle, in pursuit of glamour, travel, and glory? Worse still, she had intended to abandon the birth of the new prince or princess to set sail for the White Lands, and for what? Lust—for Patch, for adventure, perhaps both?

Her fingers left the handle of the mirror and moved to the glass. She wanted to comfort Leo, to stroke his cheek, but as she tried, the image faded. Whatever the answers to her questions, there was still time to make things right. She just needed to get to Highcastle, to Cyrus. She just needed to tell him what she'd seen and help him.

I should leave immediately. My bags are still packed, and I can still…

She shook her head, her eyes suddenly heavy.

I should leave but…no, too tired to leave now…tomorrow. I should sleep now…

The mirror slipped from her grasp as she succumbed to the irresistible lure of sleep.

⚜ ⚜ ⚜

Fran's eyes jerked open, and she was shocked to find sunlight streaming in, making her squint as panic immediately set in.

Morning already.

Leo! she thought, sitting upright, her heart racing. She reached for the necklace and found that it was still there upon her neck, though the chain felt entirely normal, with no hot discomfort on the skin beneath. Her mind darted to the mirror, and she climbed onto her knees, running her hand across the mattress in a frantic search. *It must be here somewhere*, she reasoned, but even in her fluster, she knew her efforts were in vain. She stopped and frowned as her thoughts began to clear. After a breath, she reached to her pocket, finding the mirror there as it always was. She raised it to her face but found no more than her own bewildered expression staring back at her from the pocked glass.

Had it all just been a dream? Or a hallucination? It had all seemed so real, too real to ignore.

If there was any chance that Leo was in danger, Fran knew she had to do something, or she would never forgive herself. In the end, there was only one way to find out.

She had to return to Highcastle. And fast.

Chapter XXI

Marcia

Marcia had never felt so helpless or so miserable. Leo had been taken. Her only son, her precious child, and Peacehaven's prince. He had been snatched from the castle, from right under her nose. She knew what it was to be a queen and had never fooled herself into thinking the role presented no dangers, but Leo was just a boy, an innocent.

She was left with two pressing questions. *Why?* And perhaps more importantly: *What next?*

She watched as Cyrus placed a letter down onto the highly polished table. Their group sat in silence in the Grand Hall of Eldred's Keep, as if waiting for Thaddeus to speak—but of course he wouldn't. Couldn't. Never again.

She'd never seen her husband like this before: an ungainly stubble left unshaven, his hair matted and unwashed. She suspected he might have been like this after the loss of his father, and maybe

Garrett all those years ago, if he had only had time to mourn, but he hadn't then. In truth, there wasn't time now. They also didn't know, yet, if they had anything to mourn.

"Is that a letter?" asked Broderick, his voice booming to fill the void, startling Marcia slightly.

Marcia sat up, wincing with discomfort. She could deal with her ever-growing size and weight in the late stages of pregnancy, as she had become accustomed to them during her time carrying Leo, but this child brought with it a heat in her chest that she had never experienced the first time around. "Yes, a letter," she said, speaking on Cyrus's behalf. She grimaced as a jolt of pain rushed through her back, steadying her expression when Adaline tilted her head as though asking if everything was okay. Marcia gave a subtle nod, thankful for all the help that her mother-in-law and Marcia's own handmaid, Lillian, had provided in recent times. She steadied herself once more and cleared her throat, the sound echoing around the Grand Hall. "An anonymous letter," she said, turning to face Seth and Broderick, who completed their assembly. "A young boy delivered it to the guards on the gate. Apparently, the letter was given to him by a man in a hood, or at least that's what he told us."

"And the contents?" Broderick asked hastily. "Is there anything about the prince?"

Marcia swallowed against the heat in her chest. "It says that they have him and that he is safe, for now at least." She paused to look at Cyrus. "It says that the prince will remain this way as long as we meet their demands."

"And what might those be?" said Seth, beating Broderick to it. "Are there any clues in the letter, any indication who Finnian might be working with? There has to be something, surely?" His words were frantic, desperate, and Marcia knew exactly how he felt: helpless to aid her son. She felt the same way. She also knew that Seth still harboured guilt for Augustus's death and was committed to protecting their family at all costs.

"The letter was sealed but bore no insignia," she answered. "The inscription is not familiar to me, but I doubt the culprit would be so careless in any case, and that's assuming we know this person."

"And the demands?" Broderick asked. "What do they want? Land, money, arms? I bet it's that Verderan dog, Alonso. I warned you not to trust him, my king, and..." He paused, remembering himself. "I'm sorry, my king. I spoke out of turn. I hope you know it comes only from a place of worry."

Marcia felt her mood darken further still, and it was all she could do to stop herself from screaming out. *You're worried?* she thought, silently considering Broderick. *Is it your son that is missing, High Commander? Is it your husband falling apart before your eyes? Is it you that must deal with all of this, while also trying to remain calm so as not to endanger the child still safe in your womb?*

But of course, she kept these thoughts to herself. "Your concern is appreciated," she answered flatly. "As for the demands, they ask only one thing." She stared at Cyrus, whose head rested in his hands, the picture of defeat. "An exchange. Prince Leo for the king. Two days from now in a small woodland to the west of a town called Edenbridge in the Northern Fells, not far from the Verderan border."

A prolonged silence followed before Broderick sat forward to slam his hand on the table and say, "Good, then we know what to aim for. I'll ready my men immediately, and we'll march..." But he trailed off as Cyrus raised a hand of his own, gesturing for silence.

The king breathed deeply, his eyes narrowed with intent. "You'll do no such thing, Broderick," he said assertively.

"But—"

"But nothing," Cyrus intoned, silencing the High Commander at once. The king steepled his fingers and sighed. His right eye was twitching ever so slightly, and Marcia's heart ached to see her husband so despondent. He was not a perfect man, but Marcia knew that she was not alone in her love for Cyrus. He had always striven for peace and the betterment of his people, none more so than their beloved Leo. Many were the occasions on which Cyrus had spoken of his own childhood in the Low Country and the perils he had faced with Francine, swearing that he would never see their son so endangered. She knew this entire situation was unexpected, and she knew it had hit Cyrus hard.

Cyrus emptied a large glass of red wine as the others watched on in silence. His lips were stained red, despite his efforts to wipe them with the back of his hand, and he swallowed a belch as he continued in a low voice, "There will be no army, Broderick. The letter is very clear that any such interference will endanger the deal, by which they mean the prince, and I simply cannot allow it. I can't risk it."

"But why?" asked Seth. "Who would do this, and why now?"

Broderick scoffed. "It can only be the Verderans! Look at the meeting point they've chosen!"

"But what if it isn't?" Marcia snapped, causing them all to glance at her quickly, surprised by her unusually sharp tone. "Peacehaven is a vast land of varied interests," she continued. "It would be foolish to overlook the possibility of treason within our own borders."

Adaline murmured her agreement. "Are we so quick to forget Wendell?" she asked. "Resentment and ambition are some of the most dangerous weapons."

"That they are," said Broderick immediately, "but you'll remember that Wendell did not act alone, and I don't believe Finnian is any different. I understand your position, my king." He presented his palms pleadingly. "But if resentment and ambition is what we seek, then one needs look no further than King Alonso. Do not forget that it was your own forces who repelled him from Highcastle, your own actions that forced him to kill his brother. Let me continue my search at least, my king. There is a captain, Ralph is his name. He is the son of Lord Ramsey and a man of great promise if ever I've seen one. His father is Warden of the Northern Fells, and Ralph himself was responsible for arresting Finnian in the first place."

"Lord Ramsey is known to me, of course, but what do you suggest?" asked Cyrus, pouring himself another drink. Marcia had to fight the urge to tell him to put the decanter of wine down, or at least to slow his momentum.

Broderick continued in earnest, "I suggest we scout the area, ask some questions in the towns and villages nearby. Perhaps someone has seen something."

"It's too risky," said Cyrus, shaking his head. "You saw what these people did to Thaddeus. And to what end? Whether Finnian is acting alone or with Alonso pulling his strings, this is my boy we're talking about, and I won't risk his life for…for this." He removed his crown, slamming it onto the table.

The sound reverberated around the room as Adaline placed a hand on Cyrus's shoulder. Marcia adjusted herself to try and find some measure of comfort, and as Broderick shifted uneasily, she imagined the commander was probably feeling much the same, albeit discomfort of a different type. It pained her to see Cyrus so utterly dejected—a feeling she herself shared—but it was her role to help the king find solutions, not problems. Her husband was a man who loved to be loved, but kingship is full of difficult decisions, and Marcia knew this sometimes meant upsetting individuals for the greater good. The formation of Peacehaven had not come without compromise: taxes had been raised, noble land had been claimed for farming, and the council had grown to accommodate new members and new voices from Auldhaven. Cyrus was not naïve to words of dissent that had sounded across the years, nor was Marcia. But she had never imagined that someone would be so angered by the way things were in their country these days that they would resort to the desperate act of kidnapping her son, her precious son.

"Cyrus," she said, gathering her thoughts, "you know I would do anything to see our son returned safely, but perhaps there is some truth in Broderick's words. I ask you, who would stand to gain from your absence?" She stopped to allow for any immediate answers, which were not forthcoming. "Let us assume that the exchange takes place. God forbid the very worst should happen to you—where does that leave us, both your family and your country? Leo is just a child. Our country has a turbulent past with young monarchs, and though we all know that Leo shares none of the infamous Boy King, Cecil's, bloodlust, the council is unlikely to take the chance. And where will that leave the leadership of this country that you worked so hard to build?"

"What are you saying?" Cyrus asked, his eyes looking beyond exhausted, nearly tortured.

"I'm saying," she said, choosing her words carefully, "I'm saying that there are people who might relish this opportunity to undermine our family, my king." She stopped to let the possibility sink in. "Leo is only five years old, Cyrus," she continued, her tone turned pleading. "The nobles are united by their ambition. They'd hound him out within the week, and what then? Instability, civil war?" Speaking of such matters when her son was missing was agony to Marcia. All she wanted, all her instincts were telling her to do, was to find Leo as soon as possible. But she knew that losing her head wouldn't help her son, or her husband, or her country.

"She's right, Cyrus," Adaline added softly. "I know you don't want to hear this, but you are King of Peacehaven, first and foremost. The crown is your birth-right, and you cannot be seen to negotiate with whoever is behind this terrible plot. I know Leo is your son—he's my only grandchild—but you cannot hand yourself over on their word alone. We must think of a different approach. There is no guarantee that the person who wrote this letter even *has* Leo, and if he does, there is no guarantee that Leo is—"

"What?" Cyrus demanded, standing to rest his hands on the table and stare down upon his mother, enraged. "Leo is what, Mother? Dead? Maybe he is, maybe this is all just a stupid idea, but what choice do I have? Some of us don't find it so easy to give up and walk away!"

Marcia could see that Cyrus's words cut Adaline like a knife. The dowager queen let her head lower to a wordless nod, refusing to meet Cyrus's eye again. It had been a low blow, Marcia thought, to bring up his own abandonment in his infancy, something she knew her mother-in-law struggled with every single day. Cyrus was never normally so spiteful, and Marcia knew this dark edge to his thoughts only came out of desperation. Seth and Broderick remained perfectly still, keen to avoid attention. Marcia glanced between Cyrus and Adaline and fidgeted uncomfortably.

The better part of ten years as queen, and it still hadn't sunk in. Her two sisters had married young, but Marcia's mother had always told her that she was too stubborn, too headstrong to make a good wife. They'd never had the best relationship, but it had still broken Marcia's heart to watch her mother fade with illness, a pain brought afresh by her absence on Marcia's wedding day. For her mother's many flaws, it was she who had taught Marcia to ride. It was the one passion they had shared, and after all those years, her mother's words still rang true in more ways than one: *You do not break a horse. You come to understand it.*

She looked to her husband and gave a small smile, trying fruitlessly to alleviate some of his worries. "There is no questioning your love for Leo, and we will support whatever decision you ultimately choose to take. You know all of this comes from a place of care," she said, letting the words hang in the air. "We do not wish to see any harm come to you, unless…well, unless there really is no other way. Perhaps we should allow Broderick his investigation. We have until sunset the day after tomorrow."

The king did not look up for a few seconds. When he finally did, he met her eyes and nodded.

"I can't see what value they'd find in harming Leo," Marcia continued, "whether it is Alonso or anyone else who has him. It is you they seek, my king. Let Broderick continue his enquiries and let us see if any loose ends might be uncovered."

Broderick's armour clattered as he stood abruptly. "My Seekers stand ready, my king," he said sternly. "I will summon the nobles and ensure that every one of them is questioned, that any roots of sedition are weeded out immediately."

"And I will remain at your side, my king," Seth added, standing with similar conviction. "These are trying times, but I will not see you harmed. I swear my life on it."

The king's face softened slightly. "Seems you have it worked out between you, as always. And you, my queen," he started, walking around the table to rest a hand on Marcia's shoulder, "where would I be without you? Always the voice of reason. All right, have it your way." He sighed. "Broderick, you have until noon tomorrow to unravel this mystery. Return empty-handed, and I will be forced to make the exchange—"

He stopped suddenly at the sound of approaching footsteps, and Marcia startled as the doors swung open to reveal a young squire. "What now?" the king asked, eyes narrowed with frustration. "There is a man, my king," the squire answered nervously. "A man in the castle who claims to have news of the prince."

Chapter XXII

Locke

Locke breathed deeply, fighting to compose himself. He admired the remarkable wrought iron detailing of the doors leading to the Grand Hall of Eldred's Keep, awed by it even in a moment as serious as this one.

It had been a long, lonely week, but that had only given him time to think. His first thoughts were, of course, to stay strong. This was what his father had asked of him, after all. He had steeled himself in his room at The Eagle, and though he rarely ventured into the tavern itself, he'd made a point of keeping his chin high whenever he saw Rufus or Grace.

"Everything okay, Locke?" Grace had asked.

"I'm fine," he had answered. "Better than fine actually!"

But surely she had seen through his false smile. Locke knew it had been a mistake to let Grace see him so emotional the day he had learned of the prince's kidnapping, Boyd's death, and Locke's own part in it all. He wondered if he had given her cause for suspicion. Grace had always been an open book, whereas Locke had offered very little in return, such was his father's instruction. Among all of Locke's mounting regrets, he hated the guilt of lying to Grace. The callous act of shutting her out. Whether he deserved it or not, she was perhaps the only one who truly wanted to help him. More than anything, he wanted to let her.

By the end of the week, Locke had been unable to face it anymore. He had hardly slept in days, and Grace's persistence only served to heighten his crippling guilt. He knew he needed to get out of The Eagle, so he had rushed into the streets of Highcastle, where yet more questioning faces waited to greet him. The day had been grey and wet, and Locke's hood had provided him with the anonymity he so keenly sought. He walked for hours in the drizzle and only stopped when his boots had filled with water. It was then, when perched atop a beer barrel, that he had seen them…

A father and son, that much was clear. The boy was small and close enough in age to prompt unwelcome thoughts of Prince Leo. Both man and boy shared the same chestnut brown hair, the father with the addition of a neatly trimmed beard framing his jawline.

"Are we nearly home?" Locke had heard the boy ask.

The two of them had walked past Locke without noticing him. The boy spoke at a relentless speed, with much of it lost to Locke's ears. He'd been holding his father's hand until he relinquished his grip and dashed a few strides away.

He turned back to his father. "Are you coming? I'll race you."

Just then, Locke had noticed a filthy puddle in the boy's path, but fortunately for the boy, Locke was not the only one.

"Wait," his father called, lunging forward to lift his son at the waist with both hands. He swung him round in the air and pulled him close; they laughed and hugged, and two sets of boots had remained dry.

"Thanks, Father. You saved me!" said the boy through his giggles.

His voice was so small, yet his words had sounded with enormous clarity in Locke's mind. He tried to think of a time when his father had held him so, but nothing surfaced. In that moment, his only memory was that of their last meeting: *News of the king will spread, but I'll protect you.*

But what good was his protection now, after everything Locke had been through? Years of pain and suffering had unfurled in Locke's mind as he watched the father and son walk away laughing. Locke finally saw the truth of it. A true parent would do anything in their power to keep their children from harm. It was too late for Locke's father to make things right; those boots were already dirty. Yet, Locke knew in his heart that King Cyrus deserved a chance to save his son.

His eyes focused on the doors of the Grand Hall once more. He knew what he had to do. It had brought him here, after all.

"Straight ahead," said the guard, and the thick, wooden doors opened, hinges creaking.

He'd heard this room referred to as the Grand Hall, and it occurred to Locke now that there couldn't have been a more appropriate description. He'd seen parts of the castle, of course, but never the most grandiose spaces reserved for the king. His eyes darted across the details: the elaborate candelabras, the enormous portraits of former kings, colourful crests hung to represent the noble families of Peacehaven. It felt a far cry from his first visit after the Battle of Highcastle, and the image of his father's broken body still lingered close in his memory. On that occasion, he had visited one of the lesser banquet halls, a makeshift hospital ward at the time. Locke would never forget the oppressive grey walls and the deathly cries that echoed upon them as the surgeon worked to piece his father back together.

He'd imagined this place that day. Sounds of celebration had set his wild, youthful curiosity racing as Cyrus's coronation had continued nearby. To be in the company of kings and queens, or at least in close proximity, had been almost intoxicating for young Locke. He had promised himself that he'd return one day. He realised with a jolt that he was keeping that promise to himself in some ways, but any happiness in this realisation was punctured by the grim circumstances under which he had returned.

The orange glow of a setting sun poured in through glass windows, and shards of red reflected from ruby gemstones in a golden crown resting upon a large table. Locke saw a small number of people gathered around the table, and though the Grand Hall itself was impressive, nothing could have prepared him for the illustrious assembly sitting ready to receive him. His stomach dropped, and his jaw threatened to follow suit. His eyes were, at first, drawn to the king, but only before noticing Queen. The queen was heavily pregnant, but no less radiant for it, her milk-white skin and wavy red hair stealing Locke's attention momentarily. He next noticed the Dowager Queen Adaline, resplendent in a red silk gown, and to her side, the king's chosen shield, Seth, his greying hair tied neatly atop his head. He noticed that Seth's eyes were narrowed appraisingly, but it was High Commander Broderick's stare that threatened to burn a hole in him.

"You," said the High Commander, his face twisting with confusion. His head shook and his eyes narrowed, and Locke wondered if he'd worked it out already. "You're the prison master, aren't you? Tell us your name, and make it quick. Think very carefully about your answers, boy. And remember your courtesy. You're stood before the king!"

Locke, flustered, dropped to his knee before his king.

"You know this man?" asked King Cyrus, staring down at Locke's bowed head.

High Commander Broderick gave a scoff of contempt. "One of the prison masters, my king. He was attacked by Finnian not too long ago, and his colleague, Boyd, was the man who died when…well, you know when…"

"And your name?" asked the king.

"Locke, Your Majesty," he said, rising to meet King Cyrus's gaze. "The High Commander is right. I am…or at least, I *was* one of your prison masters."

"A position you used to free a dangerous criminal?" King Cyrus asked shrewdly.

Locke's stomach plummeted. Though he had known such a question was inevitable when he had decided to come to Eldred's Keep, the idea of disappointing his king still ate away at Locke. "No," he said, his instincts telling him to protect himself. And then, accepting the truth, he acquiesced with a sigh. "Yes, my king."

King Cyrus nodded silently, and after a moment, he began to pace the room. Locke's heart thumped loudly in his chest, and his hands were shaking, but the faces that stared back at him were not angry or bloodthirsty, but rather a picture of concern. Queen Marcia's pale brow was furrowed, while High Commander Broderick's eyes followed King Cyrus as if magnetised.

"You have news, I presume. Demands maybe?" asked Dowager Queen Adaline. Locke noticed that frown lines had appeared around her lips.

"No demands," Locke answered, rising slowly to his feet. "I'm sorry," he pleaded. "I never meant for any of this to happen, I just..."

"There will be time for your reasons," said Queen Marcia, one hand on her swollen stomach. "Please put my mind at ease. Tell us he's all right. We've all been so worried."

Locke nodded. "I know where the prince is. I haven't seen him, but I know the king was the intended target. I know he'll keep the prince safe."

"And who is *he*?" asked the king's chosen shield, Seth, a gold tooth glinting as he spoke. "Is this your doing, or are you working for someone?" Seth's hand rested on the pommel of his sword, but he did not draw it.

"A Verderan, no doubt!" High Commander Broderick interjected loudly. A thick vein bulged on his forehead, and the rest of the group watched on in silence.

Locke wished he could confirm the High Commander's suspicions. A wave of doubt washed over him; a Verderan conspiracy made plenty of sense, and it wouldn't take a lot to convince them. The investigation alone would take time, time in which he could help his mother escape or try to talk sense into his father. Ralph was a brute, but he was not entirely without rational thought. Perhaps Locke *had* been wrong to come to the castle. Maybe there was still a way to work things out for the best…

Locke sighed again. His inner monologue was filled with a whole lot of ifs, buts, and maybes, and when had that approach ever served him well? Would he really send Peacehaven to war just to save his own family? He steadied himself as clouds of doubt passed over him. He'd come this far, and all that remained was to do the right thing.

"My father," he answered, his voice lost in the enormity of his surroundings. "I tried to stop him, but…I couldn't. You have to understand…" He trailed off, staring down at his boots, unable to meet their eyes.

Before High Commander Broderick or Seth could interject, likely to question Locke about his father's identity, he heard Queen Marcia's voice first. "Families can be most…challenging," she said, and Locke looked up to see her shaking her head. "What is it your father wants? The king is, of course, sympathetic to the needs of his people, and we are all eager to see the prince safe. Is it a question of money, or is there something more?"

"I don't know," said Locke. And it was the truth. "My father fought in the Battle of Highcastle—"

"So, a soldier?" asked Broderick, eyes narrowed to slits.

"Yes. Well, he once was. He's…a…a lord." Locke's nerve was on the brink of failing him. His mouth felt dry at the prospect of turning his father in.

"A lord?" the king repeated, his voice rising in derision. "What is the purpose of your Seekers, Broderick, if not to unearth such treasonous acts? You told me you could be relied upon to keep my family safe. Was I wrong to place faith in you? Perhaps it is time to bring Lambert back to the capital?"

The High Commander shrunk further into his chair with every word, but he seemed unwilling to defend himself against the king's harsh words.

Undeterred by Broderick's silence, King Cyrus continued, "My son, the prince, gone, and one of your own prison masters responsible. Did you even question this man? Do you even know who his father is?"

"Well, no, but—"

"But what, Broderick?" The king's lip curled into a disdainful sneer.

Locked noticed that the king's teeth were stained red, and his bloodshot eyes momentarily reminded Locke of his father. He hated that his mind was drawing this comparison because, in his mind, King Cyrus had always been a paradigm of good and righteousness, but in this moment, he seemed small and scared and a little drunk. Locke's father called wine "a remedy for any problem," but Locke had never seen any evidence to support this, and the remedy didn't seem to be working any better for the king.

"Did this line of enquiry not fit with your crusade against the Verderans?" the king spat at the High Commander, seething, "or are you really just that stupid?"

"Cyrus!" snapped Queen Marcia, her outburst bringing silence upon them. "This is not the time for blame. This man, Locke, is clearly here to help, thanks to what must have been quite a difficult change of heart. Perhaps we should hear what he has to say, or are you so desperate to martyr yourself as that letter intended?"

Locke's nerves fought their way to the surface. His hands were still shaking, and he clasped them behind his back in an effort to tamp down his growing fear. He didn't know a letter had been sent to the king, but he supposed he ought not to be surprised. How else would his father have named his terms?

The king's outburst had left the atmosphere tense and unpredictable, which had only heightened when his queen contradicted him in front of them all. The smell of wine hung in the air as King Cyrus returned to his place at the table, falling into his chair with a look of defeat.

Locke took a deep breath. "My father is Lord Ramsey," he started hesitantly. The High Commander's eyes widened. "The battle—I think it changed him. He says he wants money and recognition, but that's all just a cover. Power and change, I think that's what he fights for. He feels that he has been forgotten, that he is undervalued. His injuries still plague him, but there is no sense in him, not when the drinking starts." Locke felt slightly awkward adding the last bit, given the king's current state of inebriation, but he felt it had to be said in order to explain the situation with his own father.

"Ramsey?" the king repeated, eyes raised at Broderick. "The Warden of the Northern Fells, and the very family in which you intended to entrust your enquiries." He turned back to Locke. "You have a brother. Ralph, I believe? A captain?"

Locke nodded.

"And is he part of this plot? You have a mother as well, I presume?"

"Yes, my king," Locke answered meekly. "I believe my brother is involved one way or another, but my mother is one of the reasons I came here today." He paused to wince at how this sounded, and he stuttered, "And...and the prince, of course. But my mother, she is innocent in all this. My father is a dangerous man, but mother knew nothing of his plans."

"And where is the prince now?" asked Queen Marcia, sitting forward in her chair despite her obvious discomfort. Locke knew there was no turning back now, and his only option was to cooperate and see things to their conclusion. He thought of the prince, a small child, alone and scared in the darkness. Small hands beating on the cellar door. His own hands were larger now than they appeared in his memories of childhood, and as his fists clenched, he found that his secrets began to loosen, that years of being shut in the dark were now crying out to be let into the light. When had life ever given him choices anyway?

"Ardlyn Keep," he said, shoulders instantly relaxing as those heavy words fell from his lips. "My father doesn't know that I'm here, but he'll be keeping the prince at Ardlyn Keep."

Broderick cut him short. "Then we must leave immediately!"

"You can't!" Locke protested. "My father, he has supporters, the brigand Finnian among them. Ardlyn Keep will be full of their men. I know what this will mean for those who oppose you, but attacking now would put my mother—not to mention the prince—at risk. There must be a better way."

The king crossed his arms as he sat back in thought. "What is it that you suggest?"

Locke was taken aback that the king would even ask him, instead of turning to his own commander for advice. After a moment, Locke put on his best impression of confidence and said, "Something small, not a full-scale attack. There's a road that connects the town with my father's estate. There are trees...along the road, I mean, trees that could hide a small number of your men. My father will have prepared for an attack, but give me time in the castle, give me a chance to free the prince, and if I fail you..." He paused, wondering if the words were really his own, wondering how his pretence of confidence had caused a real surge of pride to fill his chest, bolstering his nerves. "If my plan fails," he finished sadly, "then perhaps my efforts will provide a diversion for the High Commander's men. Please, my king. My father's ambitions have already caused enough bloodshed. Let me do this. Let me make things right."

The room fell silent, and the king stared back at him appraisingly. Then he did what Locke had expected him to do first and turned toward his High Commander. "What do you think, Broderick?" he uttered eventually. "Perhaps you have some insight into the lay of the land? Ardlyn was, after all, your childhood home, if I'm not mistaken, before you moved to join my father's forces in the capital?"

Locke's mouth fell wide, but the commander nodded to confirm the king's revelation. "The boy's right," he said, in a tone more purposeful and professional than cavalier. "The road is exposed, but there is ample space to hide our men in the trees. Lord Ramsey was a very fine captain, perhaps one of my best, but the man was unpredictable even in his prime. You'll remember his efforts during the Battle of Highcastle, my king, heroics that earned him his title. Without Ramsey's charge on the Verderans...well, I'm not sure we'd be sat here today. But it was reckless to be sure. It cost very many lives, and I don't doubt that he would take the same risks to defend his position now. We don't know who stands with him, my king." Broderick's voice took a solemn turn. "But I believe Ramsey will be organised. If the boy thinks he can do this, then it has to be worth a chance to avoid bloodshed."

The king scratched at the rough stubble upon his chin. "Then that settles things," he said. "I want you to select thirty men, High Commander, and I expect you to choose wisely. Seth, prepare for our imminent departure. We will accompany Broderick and his men to ensure that the outcome is successful."

At this, Queen Marcia's eyes widened. "You cannot be serious! It's not enough that they have our boy, but now you want to put yourself in danger? Cyrus, please…" The queen inclined her head, looking down at her own swollen stomach to reinforce her point. "Not now."

"She's right, my king," Broderick added with newfound confidence. "There's no need to put yourself in danger. My men can take care of this."

The king rolled his eyes. "Take care of it? You suggest that I entrust the wellbeing of my son, the prince of Peacehaven, to a man who failed to detect even a hint of wrongdoing in a lord he claimed to know so well? Let's move beyond this for a moment, High Commander. Let us assume I am able to overlook your incompetence. I believe we've had similar conversations in the past. Perhaps you've forgotten the night I stole into King Simeon's camp, or my advance on Rafael in the conflict that followed? Yet more details that have slipped your mind, I suppose?"

Everyone in the room looked anywhere except at High Commander Broderick in that moment. Locke had to fight not to grimace, so furious was the king's tirade against the man.

King Cyrus paused to raise an eyebrow before turning to face his wife. "Your concern is appreciated, my queen, but this is our son, and I will be there to take him into my arms when he's returned to us safely."

Locke had just an instant to think he had seen tears glistening in the queen's eyes before the entire group was distracted by a clatter. They looked toward the doors to find a woman crashing into the Grand Hall, one Locke did not know, whose wild brown curls flew behind her as she ran toward them. Locke looked back at King Cyrus, who was smiling broadly all of a sudden.

"Prepare your very best men, Broderick," the king uttered after this pause, reiterating his point, "but make that twenty-nine."

Chapter XXIII

Francine

After hugging Cyrus frantically, Fran took a seat and listened as the others spoke, and her worst fears were quickly realised. Leo *had* been taken. It seemed the vision in the mirror was no dream nor hallucination, and as her hand hovered irresistibly over her pocket, Fran began to wonder how it worked and what other revelations the trinket might provide.

"So, that's the plan," said Cyrus. "You and me, just like old times."

Fran nodded. "You have my sword," she said, but she had seen too many good people die in "the old times," and her face remained serious as the evening sky turned pink and maids rushed to light candles about the hall. It was then that she noticed Thaddeus was missing.

"Wait," she snapped, lifting herself from the table to scour the room through narrowed eyes. It was ridiculous to think that this new perspective would change anything, but Fran was overcome with an immediate feeling of dread, already drawing the worst possible conclusion and hoping she was mistaken. "Thaddeus," she continued. "Where's Thaddeus?" There was only one possible explanation for the old man's absence at a time like this. Thaddeus was not just the king's mentor, but also his friend. A voice of reason and comfort. A constant. She had to ask, but she knew deep down that she didn't want to hear the answer.

"He's gone," Cyrus said solemnly, and his head lowered as it had when he'd confirmed that Prince Leo had been kidnapped. "I'm sorry, I should have said sooner. Thaddeus fought the brigand, Finnian, and tried to prevent his escape. The prison master…" he used his hand to gesture toward the only member of the group not known to Fran, a young man with messy, straw coloured hair and wide, nervous eyes, "His name is Locke, and the man that we seek is his father. It seems he ordered Finnian to kill me, but Thaddeus's bravery prevented him from doing so."

Fran forced down her sadness, glared at Locke and asked, "Is that true?" She wanted to hear it from his own voice. The pain of loss was heavy in her chest and only worsened by her guilt at failing to notice Thaddeus's absence sooner.

The room fell silent, and all in attendance watched on as the prison master, Locke, swallowed deeply. "It's true," he said flatly. "I never wanted any of this, but my father is dangerous and there is no talking sense to him. I know I should have come sooner, and this is too late for some, but I'm here to help the prince, I promise…" By now his voice was hurried, frantic with obvious nerves. "You must believe me. I just want to help. I wouldn't have come here if I didn't."

He seemed genuine, to Fran anyway. His hair was almost as dishevelled as Cyrus's, and his gaunt, dog-tired expression seemed to mirror the same worry in those around him. She'd wondered if it was all a ruse, a scheme to draw the king to Ramsey's estate where the lord's men might lie in waiting. It's what she would have done in Ramsey's position, sending Locke to bait them. And yet it was clear to her that Locke held no love for his father. There was an indisputable honesty about the prison master that made her trust him, despite his misguided actions. She trusted him, she thought, just as she'd trusted Sabina in Taboso, and Wendell all those years before. She couldn't help but wonder if she was mistaken once again or if this time would be different. She tried to push the worry out of her head and go with her gut.

For all the miles she'd travelled with scant rest, aching hunger, and chafing saddle sores, she had but one choice. "Okay," she said, before turning to face Cyrus. "Just like old times," she muttered with an air of reluctant inevitability.

⚜ ⚜ ⚜

Thaddeus's absence seemed to leave an unshakable darkness upon the room that mere candles could not light. It seemed like only yesterday that the wise old mentor had welcomed Fran to the castle. He had given her a sword and, with it, a sense of purpose, while others deigned to address her discomfort with pretty dresses and empty words. Between them, Thaddeus and Seth had not only trained Fran, but they had made her into the woman she was now. In that moment, it dawned on her. She might never be as beautiful as Zimbeza, as devoted as Marcia, or as ruthless as Sabina, but Fran was strong, and she would do anything to protect her family.

She knew she wouldn't be able to change Cyrus's mind even if she wanted to. She would be there, that was the main thing, not off chasing dreams in a foreign land. She owed this to Cyrus and to Leo. She could see the worry in Marcia's eyes and hoped that her own involvement would bring some comfort to the queen.

She gazed around the table and imagined how good it might have felt to be home under different circumstances. Marcia was glowing with the latter stages of pregnancy, while Adaline retained the easy elegance she had demonstrated since their very first meeting. In the end, the men surprised Fran the most. Behind Seth's gold-toothed grin, she found an unsettling eagerness, like a caged animal waiting to be set loose upon its prey. She had toiled with her brother's chosen shield for many years, and yet she had never seen him so restless, despite hours of infuriating and often fruitless repetition as she had honed her craft with a sword. High Commander Broderick, meanwhile, sat uncharacteristically quiet, lost in his own thoughts, perhaps planning another of his fabled strategies, or pondering the series of events that might have driven one of his own former captains to such treasonous acts.

"So that's that then," said Cyrus, "but before we go, tell me, how is Mathilde?" His question was unexpected. It seemed to Fran that her brother had been searching for answers in the bottom of a wine glass, but she supposed she couldn't blame him. He was a good man, one who deserved good things, but she knew from witnessing Mathilde's struggles that the crown was as much a curse as it was a blessing, and she was overcome by another pang of guilt at having ever left him.

"The queen is well," she answered, her guilt only worsening. Mathilde *was* well, and Fran had no intention of burdening her with worry while things were still developing with Taiwo. In the end, they had simply said their goodbyes, and Fran had left with her queen's best wishes for the new prince or princess of Peacehaven. Fran had masked her worry when she left, but her farewells to Taiwo and Amare had been similarly brief, while she hadn't even had time to write Patch a letter to explain. A sudden image formed in her mind: Patch stood alone upon the docks in Clerbonne, looking in the direction of Nivelle, waiting until the last possible moment to board the Silver Sword. Would he wonder why she never came? How long would he wait for her?

"Good," said Cyrus abruptly, and his chair scraped as it dragged across the flagstones. "You all know the plan," he said, and he stood to rest his hands on the table, glaring around at them all. "Broderick, prepare your men. We leave within the hour."

Chapter XXIV

Broderick

Broderick paced back and forth, inspecting his men. Twenty-nine of the very best the King's Guard had to offer. A selection of strong, brave warriors, their armour glistening in the moonlight, their weapons polished to a perfect shine and their faces lit by sheer determination.

He stopped and stared, and they snapped to attention accordingly. It was as impressive as any unit that he had ever assembled, he thought, but could they be trusted? The germ of doubt had wormed its way in at the revelation about Lord Ramsey. He was to place his trust, and the life of the king, in these select few hands, but did he really know them? He had thought he had known Wendell until the man's actions proved otherwise. King Cyrus had been justified in his criticism. The Truth Seekers had been established to combat such disloyalty, so how had Ramsey slipped through the net? In the end, Broderick found only one answer, one possible explanation: his own complacency. He sighed.

After a moment, he pursed his lips, and his eyes narrowed at the steely expressions before him. There were no nerves to be found among them, which Broderick attributed to a lack of prior experience—after all, these were soldiers trained and primed during peacetime. It had been ten years since his last serious battle, and Broderick turned to pace away, wondering how any man could simply march toward danger so willingly?

Renown. A reputation, that's what it was. He recognised it on their faces, as he'd seen it on his own once upon a time. Battle was where heroes were born. Where mere men were immortalised. Where acts of heroism could elevate a common soldier into the upper echelons of society.

It happened with Ramsey, Broderick thought with a shudder. He wondered if renown or reputation would still seem so important when these men had experienced even half of what he had seen…

He turned back to see King Cyrus marching into the courtyard. The king hadn't the presence of his father, but at least his body had developed to assume some of Anselm's imposing mass. There was no denying that he cut a rather impressive figure, clad in his quilted jacket and shining breastplate, the latter of which Broderick hoped was an unnecessary precaution. He was happy to see Seth and Francine following closely behind the king, as he knew them to be useful people in a tight spot, ones he would trust to protect the king if needed. Broderick had hoped he would have no further cause to call upon such deadly expertise, but he was glad to have them both there now.

He moved to stand at the king's side as Cyrus addressed the troops.

"Lord Ramsey was a soldier once, like all of you. He is experienced and dangerous, but he fights for all the wrong reasons. Tonight, we will fight together. We will fight for each other, and we will fight for Peacehaven. I know that together, we will prevail and see my son, your prince, returned safely!"

Calm, listening expressions gave way to the impassioned cry of battle. A roar of support sounded in the night sky, and clenched fists punched the air or crashed against armour to add to the din. Broderick smiled at the reminder that King Cyrus certainly had his father's voice, King Anselm's ability to inspire not just support but love among his people.

Yet, as King Cyrus continued, Broderick's smile wavered, and a nagging, ever-present thought tugged at the back of his mind. Broderick had been meaning to talk to the king for as long as he could remember, to share his true feelings. He knew it would come as some surprise to the king, but this was not the life Broderick had wanted. It never had been, and it never would be. He was ready to walk away…

There had never really been a choice for Broderick. His father had been a general, whose father had been a general. It was no great surprise, therefore, when he had joined the army as a young man. Good breeding kept him clear from the danger of the front lines, and his reputation had seemed to soar inexplicably until his father grew too old to continue his commission. Broderick had been destined to be another general for the family line; it hardly seemed to matter whether he'd wanted the job or not. The memory drew another sigh from his lips.

Broderick remembered being fascinated by troops of touring performers that had visited Ardlyn when he was a small boy. He would rush out from the castle to meet them as their carriages rolled into town, watching with rapt attention as the entertainers drew laughs and gasps from their crowds. In his quiet moments, Broderick had imagined stowing away on these carriages, escaping his family duty for a carefree life on the road. But his imagination was the only stage that these thoughts ever graced. Much to his father's pleasure, he joined the army as expected, and he had soon come to realise that life is less about actually wanting to do something than giving people the impression that you do. He had moved to Highcastle and promised to meet every duty required of him, but he had never ceased in his yearning to delight those around him with a joke, a song, or a story around a campfire.

"Time to grow up, son," his father had said. "Your behaviour is not befitting of a general. Do you want your men to laugh at you or respect you?"

There was no arguing with his father, so Broderick had accepted the role he'd been born to play: General Broderick, the blustering leader of King Anselm's army, ever ready to draw his sword and ride into the face of impossible odds. When his father died many years later, Broderick chose to remain in the capital rather than returning home. Ardlyn and its castle were no longer part of Broderick's life, only a memory of what had come before and what might have been. He felt he owed it to his father to fulfil the ambitions the old man had desired for him and devoted himself to steadfast service. Ardlyn Keep was returned to the crown at Broderick's request, and King Cyrus had awarded the castle to a new noble, though neither he nor Broderick could have envisaged that the keys would fall into such traitorous hands.

Broderick tensed as King Cyrus clasped a firm grip about his shoulder. The assembled men of the King's Guard had silenced, and their king turned back to face them before speaking once more.

"I'm told that you are the very best men this country has to offer," he said, eyes darting among them. "The only men for the job, or so I am led to believe. A fine endorsement, and from High Commander Broderick, no less!"

Their spirited response came in thundering unison. "High Commander! High Commander!" The very words caused hairs to raise on the back of Broderick's neck.

He smiled at the king and drew his sword to thrust it at the moon. In the end, Broderick *had* earned his title—one that outstripped both his father's and his grandfather's. Despite the king's earlier harsh words in the heat of the moment, Broderick found himself at the very pinnacle of King Cyrus's armed forces, and he had all the laurels to show for it. It was everything his father had wished for him, yet no amount of money or veneration would help him sleep at night. Would the vapid sycophants singing his praises ever understand what it meant to kill a man? To send men to be killed and ask them to be proud of it? The boy, Locke, spoke of changes in his father, and Broderick knew only too well the changes he had described.

Yet, for all Broderick's best intentions, life had simply gotten away from him. Here he was again, with Cyrus's rousing words readying the men as stable hands prepared the horses nearby. Maybe there had never been a right time to call it quits, or perhaps the money and veneration really were enough for a man like him, perhaps even too much? He'd been so busy playing the part that he scarcely recognised who he was anymore. He had no wife, no children, no one in whom he could leave a legacy behind when he departed this world. As the men broke apart to mount their horses, he realised that they were the closest thing he had to family, and yet he had failed them, those legions of men who had followed him. Look at the former captain, Lord Ramsey.

When he thought about it, he supposed Thaddeus had been the nearest thing Broderick had had to a close friend. He might have been stubborn, but Thaddeus had certainly been a good man, one with honest intentions, and Broderick had always felt a little better for having him around. The term "close friend" was perhaps a little strong. Maybe "colleague" or "acquaintance" would be more appropriate, as sad as it was to admit—if only to himself—that he'd never had any truly close friends. Either way, Thaddeus had given his life for his king, like Garrett had before him, and Broderick knew he wasn't alone in noticing the gaping void the old man had left behind.

He wondered, as grief for Thaddeus rushed in, who would mourn High Commander Broderick when he was dead and gone. Broderick's counterpart in the former Auldhaven, Lambert, was said to have established unquestionable peace in the west from his base in Ravensward. If Broderick were to die, he found it likely that the king would simply call Lambert back to the capital; perhaps King Cyrus should have done this many years ago, as he had suggested in the Grand Hall…

Broderick's stomach lurched with a sudden and intense dislike for himself. He needed to speak to the king and make his feelings known, but first, he had to make things right. He had to get the prince home safely, and with him, his men. Back into danger, and back to Ardlyn, where it had all begun.

"Everything all right, High Commander Broderick?" came King Cyrus's voice, breaking through the walls of memory that had enveloped Broderick.

"Never better, my king." He smiled as he climbed into the saddle, following King Cyrus's horse, Adagio, as they made for the castle gates in the darkening night.

CHAPTER XXV

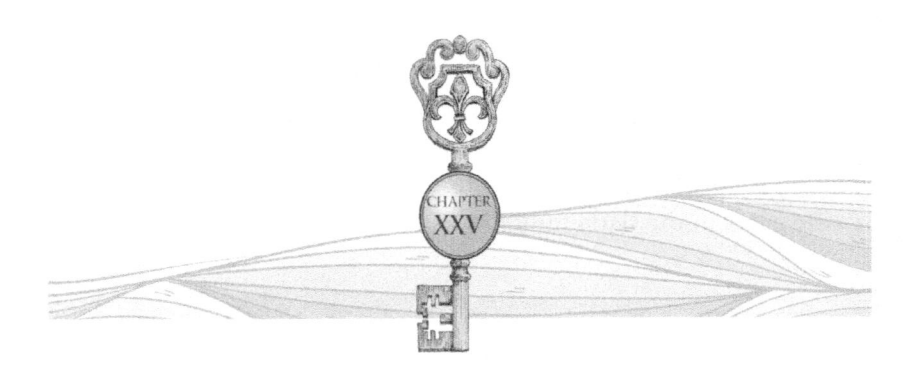

Locke & Francine

They arrived under the cover of darkness. King Cyrus sent riders ahead, and Locke followed as their retinue descended upon a small farm on the outskirts of Ardlyn. When they reached their destination, Locke followed the king's example, dismounting to encourage his horse into a paddock nearby. Locke knew the landowner, Garrick, and his two sons, and there was no mistaking the surprise on their hosts' faces when they answered the door to find Locke standing side by side with King Cyrus and High Commander Broderick in the moonlight.

"Everything all right, Locke?" asked Jerald, the eldest of Garrick's sons, in a low voice, glancing over at King Cyrus with worried eyes. This was the very same Jerald, albeit older now, that Locke had thought of only recently, thanks to his recollections of sparring unwillingly with his own father. Jerald had always seemed terribly strong and impressive in Locke's mind, though the tremble in Jerald's voice now reflected an air of tension, one to which Locke could easily relate.

In the end, Locke simply smiled and gave a quick nod in an attempt to reassure Jerald, not knowing what to say for the best. He noticed Broderick in hushed conversation with Garrick before the High Commander pressed coins into the unassuming farmer's hand and gave him a stiff slap on the back.

The king's sister, Princess Francine, gestured Locke out of the paddock with a wave, and their group reassembled, with the King's Guard standing in three disciplined rows. At Francine's request, Locke moved to stand awkwardly at her side. King Cyrus stood at her other shoulder, with High Commander Broderick beyond him. Locke couldn't help but feel a little out of place.

"Remain quiet but alert," said the king, his voice the only sound in the otherwise absolute silence. "Just as we discussed, remember? Locke here will guide us to our vantage point…" He paused, looking over at Locke, who gave a wordless nod in response. "They have my son, your prince, so nothing stupid. And let's ensure that we all make it out of here alive."

At this, King Cyrus turned and flashed a quick smile at his sister. Locke noticed that the king's hand was lowered toward the handle of his sword, and though his words hinted at a peaceful rescue, there was an unmistakable suggestion of vengeance in the king's expression that Locke was keen to quell.

"Lead on," said King Cyrus, and Locke murmured his quiet acceptance as he followed the earthy path leading toward town. He could hear the water wheel at the mill creaking gently and rhythmically in the distance as he walked, and his every step was matched by the dull thud of boots and clink of light armour of the men behind him.

This was a far cry from his previous arrival on market day, Locke thought, and he wondered if the townsfolk would greet him as kindly as they had on that occasion now that he was delivering an entourage of armed men into their quiet, untroubled existence. Occasional candles flickered in windows, but all was silent as Locke moved, quick-footed, through the main thoroughfare to where the road widened as they neared Ardlyn Keep. In a matter of moments, the silhouette of the castle appeared in the distance.

As planned, Locke darted into the trees lining the track on either side, slowing as the others joined him in the thicket. After Broderick arrived and ushered Locke forward, they proceeded slowly and silently. With his every step cautious and considered, Locke noticed after a few moments that his jaw ached from clenching it so tightly. He knew it would only take one mistake to cost lives, and too many had already been lost to his foolish mistakes. With each stride, their group moved closer to the castle. Silence gave way to the sudden sound of conversation, and Locke raised a finger to halt the others, stooping as he listened. He was fairly certain he recognised the voices of Tanner and Willard, his father's two longest-serving men. His suspicions were confirmed as he crept, alone, toward the treeline for a better view. Locke swallowed deeply as his roving eyes found two additional men upon the parapet of Ardlyn Keep, watching vigilantly with torches raised.

"What can you see?" whispered Broderick, appearing at Locke's flank unexpectedly.

Locke grimaced. "Four men, two more than usual. I had hoped to talk my way in, but it may not be so easy." He shook his head as he accepted the inevitable. "I'll have to try," he said defeatedly. "My father may not be expecting us, but he's prepared. Perhaps I can still get beyond the gate. It has to be worth a try."

Broderick shook his head. "We've little other option without storming the castle." He blew out his cheeks with impatience. "Fine, go and see if you can salvage this nightmare. I'll be watching you, though. Any hint of deceit or suggestion of failure, and my men will be waiting."

Locke nodded, accepting that he was equally unpopular with both of the two sides involved in this conflict. "Understood," he said, turning to make his way beyond through the trees to re-join the road, out of sight of his father's men. His heart was thumping in his chest as he approached, and he winced at the prospect of Tanner's scrutiny.

"Well, what have we here?" came Willard's voice as Locke drew to a halt in sight of Ardlyn Keep. Even despite his nerves, his heart leapt at the sight. Home.

Tanner stepped forward to peer over the rampart, and Locke raised a hand to spare his eyes from the glare of four torches now extended in his direction. "If it isn't young Lockey! Must say I'm surprised to see you," Tanner said confidently. "From what I hear, there's all sorts happening in the capital. What is it, missing your old mum and dad?"

Locke clasped his hands to conceal his increasing nervousness. "Something like that," he said, forcing a smile. "I've been travelling all evening to get here. I'm sure my parents will be pleased to see me. Now, will you open the gate?"

Even in the torchlight, Locke could see Tanner's head shaking. "No can do, I'm afraid, Lockey. Your father has given strict instructions to keep the gate closed no matter the circumstances."

"On what grounds?" asked Locke, face screwed up in his best impression of ignorance, trying to put as much indignation into his voice as possible.

"Who can say?" said Tanner with a shrug, and he broke out into a bout of laughter echoed by Willard. Tanner steadied himself. "Look, Lockey, you know your father, and I know better than to ignore his wishes. It's late. Why not try the inn and come back tomorrow?"

"Tomorrow?" Locke exclaimed, resisting every urge to scream out. "My father is a lord, the Warden of the Northern Fells, and you want me to go knocking at the inn? Perhaps even sleep in the dirt? This is my home. No, I will not—"

But at that moment, a twig snapped behind him.

Locke halted, eyes wide as all four of his father's men moved in unison to train their torches on someone unseen beyond him.

Tanner was the first to speak this time. "Who's there?" he called.

As Locke turned, he found a hooded figure drifting toward him.

"Play along," said a girl's voice, quiet enough that the men couldn't hear. Before he knew it, the hooded girl was at his side. Tanner cleared his throat, apparently about to repeat his question, but the girl removed her hood, and Locke's heart sank as Princess Francine revealed herself before him.

"Is there a problem, dear?" she asked, taking Locke by the arm, her voice as sweet as honey. "This is your home, isn't it? Only we've travelled so far, and I'm in need of rest."

Tanner laughed, his tone more playful than spiteful this time. "A girl, eh? Well, well, what about that, Will?" He turned to Willard, who played his part, recoiling with mock surprise. "Would you believe it, a few weeks in the city and you're a changed man! Wait until your father hears of this..." He sounded almost impressed.

"So, you'll let us in?" asked Locke.

Tanner's laughter ceased abruptly. "No," came his answer once again.

Francine's grip tightened around Locke's forearm. "It's all right," she said, projecting her voice for Tanner's benefit. "We'll try at the inn and take this up with your father tomorrow. He's a reasonable man from what I hear. I'm sure he'll understand..." She turned away, guiding Locke only a few steps before Willard called for them both to halt.

"Now wait, wait!" said Willard, flustered, and Locke turned as his father's men huddled to discuss the situation in hushed tones. After several moments of animated conversation, Tanner broke away to clear his throat and force his face into a reluctant smile.

"I suppose," he began hesitantly, with a shake of the head. "I suppose we can make an exception for young Lockey, especially since he has company, and a lady at that!" He paused, and his false smile widened. "Open the gate, but you two had better make it quick!"

An approving grunt sounded from beyond the walls. Unseen activity echoed in the darkness before the portcullis groaned, retracting to welcome Locke home.

"That wasn't so difficult, was it?" asked Francine, without ever moving her lips.

"No," said Locke, nodding at Tanner as they walked into the castle's courtyard. He tried not to feel nervous about having the king's sister with him, possibly putting her in grave danger, as they entered Ardlyn Keep. They'd overcome the first challenge, but Locke knew the hardest part was yet to come.

⚜ ⚜ ⚜

The courtyard was everything Fran had anticipated when she had worked through the possible scenarios in her mind on their way to Ardlyn. It had a small stable to one side, a stone staircase leading up onto the battlements, and towers facing back toward town at both corners of its front wall. When they entered, there were a handful of armed men propped against the stonework, either asleep or resting, and Fran felt eyes burning a hole in her back as she followed Locke toward the keep, keen to conceal the sword tucked beneath her hooded cloak. It was no easy task to survey their surroundings, but under the guise of seeming innocently curious, Fran managed a quick glance back as the portcullis lowered in their wake. The mechanism appeared to be housed within one of the small towers, which doubled as a gatehouse, and though the metal grille lowered with its own momentum, Fran knew to expect a winch and pulley with a heavy metal chain. This would not make their sure-to-be difficult escape any easier.

"It's just up ahead," said Locke, his voice shaking as they edged toward the door, Fran's arm still intwined with his to maintain their pretence. It was an odd feeling to be so physically close with this person she barely knew, but Fran reminded herself that it was all in aid of saving her nephew and pushed any awkwardness aside.

The castle's living quarters were accessed by an imposing set of thick, wooden doors, which creaked as Locke opened them, apprehension plain on his face. Though Fran grimaced at the noise, the hallway beyond was deathly silent, and the two of them stepped out of the night to continue the next stage of Locke's plan.

To Fran's surprise, the corridor was empty. Hunting prizes lined the walls, but those immobile, ever-open eyes were the only ones staring back at them. A soft orange glow flickered from wall-mounted candelabras, and as Locke guided them deeper into the castle, Fran noticed a series of closed doors lining their path, her attention snatched as what sounded like snoring grew louder, masking her own heavy breathing.

For a moment, Fran was forcefully reminded of her time aboard the Silver Sword and the discordant cacophony that had echoed throughout the ship as she returned to her cabin each evening after drinks with Patch. The very thought of Patch caused her heart to skip a beat, that image of him waiting in vain in Clerbonne once again wrenching her gut with sadness. This was no time for weakness, she knew, but she could not prevent her mind from wandering to the man she had left behind. If she ever saw him again, could she make him understand? She shook her head, watching as Locke crouched in a doorway and then gestured her forward with a silent wave. She knew her priority now was to ensure that Leo made it out of the castle alive, so she shook away the sad image of Patch and forced herself to focus.

⚜ ⚜ ⚜

Locke's heart was beating hard as the king's sister arrived to join him in the doorway. It had seemed a fine plan to attempt to take Prince Leo back on his own, a chance to ease his own guilt, but as Locke faced the reality of the room before him, he began to question the strength of his convictions.

In the middle of the room, as though looming up through his very nightmares, he saw the cellar door. The lingering smell of freshly baked cakes hung in the air, but there was nothing sweet about the task ahead, a prospect made more daunting as Locke realised that one of his father's men sat upright in a wooden chair next to the cellar door. He froze, and he felt Francine do the same next to him.

A loud snore suddenly pierced the silence, and Locke heard Francine breathe a nearly inaudible sigh of relief.

"Come on, he's asleep," she whispered, stooping as she proceeded into the kitchen.

A single candle provided the only light, and though the guard began to fidget in his sleep, there was no doubt that he was oblivious to their presence. It was a cardinal sin to fall asleep while looking after a prisoner, but as Locke arrived at the cellar door, his lips curled into a small smile. *Easily done*, he thought; of all people, Locke would know.

The room remained quiet as Locke knelt, finding the door exactly as he remembered it. He fought against the image of small hands welling up in his mind, trying his best to focus on the task ahead of him. There was no lock, but instead a simple, if heavy, iron bolt sealed the door from above. His hands were shaking, and he looked to Francine for reassurance, but his brow furrowed as he didn't immediately find her. Looking across the room, he felt a jolt in his stomach as he saw the king's sister silently choking a final breath from the sleeping guard. Locke's eyes widened as the man's legs stilled in the darkness. Locke had known Princess Francine must be dangerous—after all, she was Queen Mathilde's chosen shield—but he now saw her for what she was: a ruthless killer, one he was glad to have on his side.

A momentary silence prevailed, and Locke remained perfectly still until he was convinced no one in the house had heard a thing. Francine, meanwhile, turned and made for the doorway of the dining hall, her ear tilted as though listening hard for something. She paused to summon Locke with a wave. The look on her face suggested she was curious about something, her round eyes narrowed as she went. Her order drew Locke away from the cellar door, and as he stood at the entrance to the dining hall, he saw that the room had been rearranged to clear space for rows of sleeping men—sleeping warriors.

Though none of the men were immediately familiar to him in the meagre light, their weapons reflected in the moonlight, cutting through the darkness with streaks of white that left no doubt as to their deadly intentions. There were perhaps twenty of them, and the perilous nature of Locke's plight was suddenly crystal clear to him. His eyes caught his father's in the idealised portrait hanging above the fireplace, and he turned away with a gasp before hurrying back to the door that would see the prince free. He was desperate to get this over with.

It only took a moment to open the door, its heavy bolt swinging free. In his childhood, Locke had imagined the door to be impassable, impenetrable even, yet the bolt withdrew soundlessly in a way that spoke to its regular use. Though it was heavy, Locke was able to lift the door without assistance, but as he made to enter, his body turned cold. He knew the cellar only too well, and he had sworn to himself that he would never go back.

"Stay here and keep guard," said Francine, stepping beyond him to descend a set of stone steps leading into the darkness with a single candle to guide her. Locke nodded, wondering if she'd somehow sensed the fear upon him as he stared at this dreaded place, and though he was reluctant to be left alone with only his father's men for company, he accepted her command, relief swelling in his chest.

⚜ ⚜ ⚜

Fran had never known the meaning of dark until she entered that cellar, and she grimaced as she descended the steps, thinking about her poor nephew being stuck in such a grim place. The faint light from her candle was swallowed in the blackness, but Fran had seen the room in the mirror, so she was able to navigate it on instinct, the soft glow revealing little beyond the toe of her well-worn boots. Step by step, she pieced the space together in her mind. The mirror's reflection was as fresh as the day she had awoken to see it back in her quarters in Nivelle. She moved forward slowly until a suggestion of movement made her heart race.

"Leo," she whispered urgently, covering the final strides to find him in his makeshift bed of hay. It had only been a matter of weeks since she had seen her nephew in Nivelle, but even as Leo rolled to stretch out, he seemed noticeably taller to Fran, who smiled out of pure relief at finding him.

Leo rubbed his eyes, adjusting to the candlelight. "Aunt Fran," he murmured, his voice breaking as he spoke her name.

Fran's smile widened uncontrollably. "Yes, Leo, it's me. I've come to get you out of here. Your father is waiting for you, but you need to come with me," she finished urgently.

Leo sat up, his full attention focused on Fran. "But what about the bad men, Aunt Fran? What if they catch us?"

Fran placed a hand on his small shoulder. "They won't, Leo. I promise. I won't let them get you. We can get away from here without them noticing. We can escape like heroes, you understand?" Cyrus's similar words to her all those years ago, whispered in the forest where her parents had been killed, rushed back to her in that moment, but Fran pushed aside the emotion of this realisation to stare back at her nephew expectantly.

Leo nodded. "Okay, Aunt Fran. Like heroes."

"We will get out of here and get you home safely, but I need you to take my hand and come with me, all right?"

Leo stood and clenched her hand tightly, his head held high, shoulders back. The smallest picture of bravery.

"We're going to be heroes, Leo," Fran added, moving hastily toward the exit. "Don't you let go. We're going to be heroes…"

⚜ ⚜ ⚜

Locke startled as Fran emerged from the cellar, his heart settling to see Prince Leo apparently unharmed. "I need to save my mother," Locke said impulsively. They'd come this far, hadn't they? Perhaps there was still a chance to steal his mother away and bargain for a pardon from the king.

"We can't," said Francine with quiet urgency, effectively shattering Locke's hopes. "We came for Prince Leo, and we have to leave now."

"Aunt Fran?" came the boy's small voice.

"Shh, Leo, we need to be quiet, remember?"

The boy fell silent, his hand still clenched tightly within Francine's. Locke knew the king's sister to be ruthless, but did she seriously expect him to leave his mother?

"Wait," he called, as Francine made for the exit. "This isn't all about you and your family. My mother, she's a good person, she deserves—"

He stopped abruptly as movement sounded from the dining hall.

"Who's there?" came a man's voice.

Locke hardly dared to breathe, freezing in place. Francine remained similarly still, though her hand was now wrapped tightly about the prince's mouth.

"Everything okay, Shelton?" called the same voice. "You aren't sleeping again, are you? Tell me I don't need to come out there and check on you...rather me than Ramsey!" He chuckled lightly at his own joke.

By now, his wasn't the only voice. It seemed that the men were stirring, and Locke felt immediately sick at the sight of the dead man sprawled in his chair. He had a name now: Shelton.

Well, it seemed Shelton might well be the end of them.

⚜   ⚜   ⚜

"Come on," mouthed Fran, her words barely more than a breath as she released Leo, taking him by the hand once more. The young prince was shaking, but it was Locke's expression, like a startled deer, that worried her. Once more, she wondered if Locke had masterminded this entire situation, and with it her downfall. She considered if this could be the encounter with Sabina all over again. Would Leo be the one sacrificed this time, just as Teeth had been before? Maybe this had been Locke's plan all along? Perhaps he had intended to raise the alarm and see them trapped…

But no, she determined, glancing back at Locke. His wasn't a look of confidence or triumph, but fear. He was more afraid of his father's men than Fran was. In that moment, she resolved herself to keep a cool head. She'd promised Leo she would see him to safety, and though she didn't know how they were going to do it, she sensed she would need Locke's help, and he had not moved at her words.

"Let's go," she whispered to him, turning to race for the corridor, pulling Leo along behind her. She knew the courtyard would be full of men, and she desperately needed a moment to think, but then sounds of confusion began in their wake.

"Shelton, wake up!"

The clang of the cellar door, the sound of quick steps down the stairs and back up again. And then another voice shouting, "The boy's gone, sound the alarm!"

It seemed all of Ardlyn Keep was awake now and alive with movement. To exit through the front door would be tantamount to giving up their own lives. Their only hope, she thought, would be in alerting Cyrus's men, but how? Their options were running out.

A door stood ajar in the corridor from which they had arrived, and she rushed inside with Leo in tow, urging Locke to join them. The door closed just in time to hear boots trampling past toward the front entrance. They could hear the heavy doors crash open, and the hubbub subsided for the moment as the men made their way out into the courtyard.

Fran breathed heavily. They were safe. For now.

"Everything all right?" she asked, turning to Leo. She put on the closest thing to a smile she could muster, trying to reassure her nephew that all was well, and the boy nodded wordlessly in response.

Locke was silent and still, looking as though he had seen a ghost. He seemed too nervous to draw breath as Fran raised the candle to survey the room. It was little more than a small storeroom, yet a glint of metal caught her eye, and with it, Fran felt a sense of hope reignite in her chest.

"What is this place?" she asked, walking to find a large bow resting against the wall, accompanied by a quiver full of arrows.

"My father's hunting supplies," Locke answered quietly. "The nearest thing the house has to an armoury, at least as far as I know."

"Not bad," said Fran appreciatively, stepping back to flourish a sword she had removed from a rack on the wall. "The odds are against us, but there might yet be hope."

"You're not seriously suggesting—"

"Locke!" Fran snapped as loudly as was possible in her whispered tone. Leo startled, but it was Locke himself who seemed the most wounded at the sound of his name. "What did you think was going to happen here?" she asked, her eyes alight. "Did you think your father would simply hand the prince over and everything would be okay?"

"I didn't think…"

"No, you didn't think," snarled Fran, her eyes narrowed with contempt. She turned the sword and passed it to Locke at the handle. His hands were shaking, but this was no time for her only comrade to be unarmed, and a plan for escape was already forming in her mind. "Take the sword," she said, encouraging Locke to close his fingers tightly around the leather grip. "I need to alert my brother, but I can't do this alone. Do you hear me?"

He gripped the sword but let it fall to his side as he shook his head. "I want to help, but I can't…" he said, his voice impossibly small. "I came here to make things right, but I only ever wanted peace—for my mother, for the king. I can't, I'm sorry…"

"But you must, and you will," Fran answered with passion in her voice. "For your mother, for the king, and for him." She gestured at Leo. "It's not always easy to do the right thing, but you've seen what it means to do the wrong thing. We can make it out of here," she said, nervous excitement now pulsing through her veins. "We'll get your peace, but we're going to have to fight for it."

⚜ ⚜ ⚜

She was right. Locke balled his hands into fists. It was as though a lifetime of noise cleared in that moment, giving way to the only clarity he had ever known. That voice that had lived in his head on a loop for so long—the one telling him he wasn't good enough, wasn't enough at all—subsided, and Locke felt the sting of years spent walking away to avoid the fight, to avoid the truth, release him. He'd thought Francine to be ruthless and reckless when he saw her strangling the guard, Shelton, but now he saw her in a new light, one that allowed him to see the king's sister for what she really was: impulsive and brave, willing to do whatever it took to do the right thing.

His breathing levelled out, and his eyes took on a brand-new focus. "All right," he said with a nod, "what's the plan?"

Francine smiled. "We're going to need my brother's help," she said, handing the candle to Leo. She reached in her pocket to retrieve a small pouch, which she passed to Locke.

With the hallway still silent beyond the storeroom door, she tore a length of cloth from her sleeve, dividing it to create one long strip and one much smaller. It was intricate work deftly done, and Locke's brow furrowed, his own captivated expression reflected on the face of the young prince. Francine reclaimed the pouch before depositing a bit of its fine, dark contents—some kind of powder—into the smaller of the two pieces of material.

"Is that blast powder?" Locke asked, recognising the smell.

Francine ignored him, tying the end to create a smaller pouch of the explosive material, which she speared onto the arrowhead so that the tip emerged through the other side. She wrapped the longer piece of cloth tightly around the first, securing the small parcel onto the arrow more firmly and leaving a short length of the cloth hanging as a fuse to complete her craft. "That's the best I can do," she said with a half-smile.

Voices sounded in the corridor, and her expression dropped once more.

"They're still in the castle," one of the men called. "Aldous, man the door! The rest of you spread out! We will have to alert Lord Ramsey." The man did not sound excited at the prospect, and Locke did not blame him.

A unanimous, "Yes, sir!" echoed out as their unseen pursuers moved to search the castle. The candle flickered in Prince Leo's shaking hand, but Francine crouched down, whispering words of comfort to her nephew that Locke could not make out, before returning to her full height.

"Okay," she said, reaching to take another arrow, which she nocked as she moved toward the door. "It's now or never. Keep an eye on Prince Leo, and I'll let you know when the path is clear."

Locke nodded.

"Okay then." Francine pressed her ear to the door in a moment of total silence. The world seemed to slow, and Locke's breath caught in his throat as she edged the door open with her shoulder. The gap widened, slowly but surely, and the king's sister trained her bow on her intended target before a sudden hiss pierced the quiet, and a thudding sound drew Francine into the corridor. She moved with such speed that Locke only noticed she was gone as the door closed behind her. His heart was in his mouth, and he froze for a moment before lowering himself to hold the prince tightly.

"It's going to be okay," he said, not sure if his words were intended to reassure the little boy in his care or himself.

But just then, an unexpected grunt sounded from the direction of the front door. The unmistakeable sounds of a brief scuffle followed, and an agonising silence left Locke without words, wondering desperately as to Princess Francine's fate.

He gripped his sword tightly as footsteps began in their direction. The prince's safety was his priority—it had to be—and Locke stepped forward to shield the young boy from whatever new threat was heading their way.

The young prince whispered something then, words that sounded almost like an incantation, like a prayer. His voice was as quiet as possible, but Locke thought he heard Prince Leo say, "We're going to be heroes."

Some hero I am, Locke thought, his own hands shaking as the footsteps halted beyond the doorway. He put himself into the offensive stance his father had taught him years ago. The door swung open, and after one heart-stopping moment, his sword lowered with relief at the welcome sight of Francine.

"Someone found their fight!" she said mockingly, and her I-told-you-so smile only served to draw attention to a smear of fresh blood upon her cheek. "I've taken care of the guard at the door, but we need to move fast," she continued, gesturing Locke and Leo to the doorway. "Nearly there now, but stay with me, okay?"

The young prince answered, "Yes, Aunt Fran," in a tiny voice. He took Locke's hand and proceeded as instructed.

But whatever bravery Locke had tentatively built in his chest wavered dangerously at the horribly familiar sound that met them in the corridor.

"Well, where is she?" boomed Locke's father, his words carrying throughout the castle. It seemed the men had roused their master from his bedchambers above to inform him of Prince Leo's escape, and though his father's reaction was not unexpected to Locke, the hairs on his neck still stood on end as every word echoed from the walls despite the distance between them. Elsewhere, they heard the clamour of furniture being overturned as the frantic search for the young prince continued.

With a supreme effort, Locke shook his fear away to follow Francine to the front door where she waited. The prince's legs were small, but the boy moved quickly, the candle still grasped in the hand that was not holding Locke's in a vice grip. As they arrived to stand at Francine's side, she paused and breathed deeply.

"Okay, this is it. Stay back and wait for my call. If this doesn't work, run and hide. The king will storm the castle eventually, but you must deny me until then if you are captured. Say that I fooled you, do whatever you must to keep the prince safe."

"And what about you?" asked Locke, turning Leo to face away from the body of the man who'd been guarding the door.

Princess Francine gave a sad smile. "No need to worry about me."

She readied her bow with her makeshift arrowhead, the smell of the blast powder pervading even through its cloth pouch. Francine's lips curled, and her eyes narrowed purposefully, any hint of sadness instantly evaporating. She turned toward her nephew, who watched her every move.

"Leo, hand me that candle."

Chapter XXVI

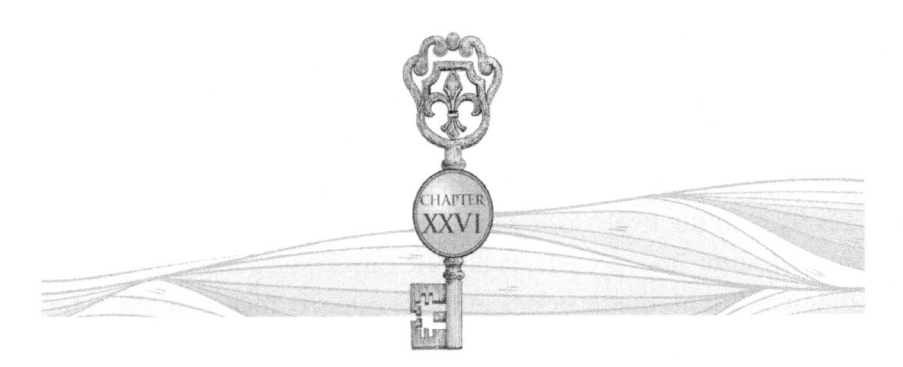

Francine & Locke

The dangling strip of cloth caught light, its flame producing a small plume of smoke as it climbed nearer to the arrowhead. Fran was keen to give the impression of confidence, but she had no idea if the arrow would even work, and her nerves surged as the arrowhead began to emit an orange glow, the flame licking its way up the length of cloth.

She looked at Leo a final time, noting that, even with his red hair, she saw a lot of her brother there in his face—the shape of his eyes, the set of his jaw. She couldn't fail Leo, and she wouldn't fail her brother. The flame had nearly reached the blast powder, a faint crackle drawing her back into the moment. It was time.

She slammed through the door and out into the courtyard. Her presence drew immediate attention from those on the ramparts, but nothing could steal her attention from the task at hand. She drew to a halt and steadied herself as a blur of commotion reached her ears. The flaming arrow, still held fast in her bow, was stark against the night sky. She took a final breath, aiming the bow up and over the battlement, before letting it fly.

Higher and higher the arrow soared, in a wide arc that seemed destined to clear the ramparts. Fran stepped back to appreciate her efforts, but her heart sank as the flame suddenly fizzled out and the shaft appeared to fall from the sky, shaking with wild imbalance before it was lost to the darkness.

She dropped the bow and reached for her sword as calls of, "Kill her!" sounded from the atop the walls. It was the voice of the man, Tanner, who had reluctantly allowed them entry into Ardlyn Keep, but Fran's more immediate concerns were directed toward two armed lackies running in her direction, swords raised with unquestionable purpose.

It should have been a moment of paralysing fear, but a smile crept across Fran's face, completely outside of her control. She'd failed to summon Cyrus and his men, but archery had never been her strong suit. Sword work, however, was a different story. This she knew well. This she could control. It wasn't going to be easy, she knew, but Leo was momentarily out of harm's way, and Fran prepared herself, her own words echoing in her mind.

We're going to be heroes.

Well, here was the moment to prove herself right.

She threw off her cloak and withdrew her sword from the scabbard concealed beneath. Her fists clenched. She braced herself, and then she let the red creep over her vision, let her body do the work it knew without her help.

The first kill was all too easy. The man's strike was heavy but slow, and Fran ducked instinctively, driving forward to run him through. Was it wrong that she was enjoying herself? She turned, and her sword met with the other assailant, metal ringing out to send a shower of red droplets to the ground, the remnants of her first strike. Fran pushed forward, hoping to stain her sword with yet more blood. This man was no different from many she had faced, another who underestimated her, and the mistake would be his last.

She crashed into the man with her shoulder, twisting as she skipped past him to drive her blade neatly between his shoulder blades. The contest was over already, and his lifeless body folded forward to hit the cobblestones with a sickening thud before blood pooled all around him.

Another worthless enemy. Would anyone ever challenge her?

"I said, kill her!" screamed Tanner from above, and then more men were circling. Perhaps there was one among them, Fran thought, and excitement bubbled to the surface at the thought of a worthy opponent. She found herself surrounded, and they'd know now that she was someone to be taken seriously, someone formidable. She flourished her sword and braced for them to come at her, and then another thud sounded. Fran's head wheeled around, searching for the source, and everything changed.

⚜ ⚜ ⚜

Locke's jaw fell open as Tanner plummeted from the parapet. His body was dashed on the stones just like the two Francine had disposed of, but Tanner had been long gone by the time he hit the ground. The arrow in his back had been the culprit, but Locke's father's men were in disarray with the volley that followed. Francine's attackers peeled away to man the walls, perhaps considering this the safer option. The king's sister wore a sadistic smile as she finished off the two that remained.

"Come on, we have to go!" said Locke, taking the prince's hand to dash forward into the courtyard where Francine stood stock-still, the bodies at her feet causing the ground to run red.

Prince Leo called for his aunt as they moved toward her, his voice sounding shocked and unsure. Locke wished he could have spared the little boy from seeing his aunt at work, but there was nothing he could have done. The pair of them approached Francine now as one might approach a frenzied animal, slowly, cautiously. Locke's father's men were engaged on the battlements by whatever was on the other side of the walls, and Locke felt his worry fade until Francine turned and raised her blade to stop them in their tracks.

Prince Leo gasped, and Locke stepped forward to yell, "Francine, what are you thinking?" The king's sister was snarling nonsensically. Her top half was red with the blood of the men she had cut down, while her eyes were full of madness. "It's just us," said Locke, edging forward slowly, palm raised, sword lowered to his side. "It's me, Locke, and the prince, Leo. You remember…?"

It seemed his words were breaking through. Though the mayhem continued upon the walls beyond them, Francine's sword dropped, her head shaking as if emerging from a trance.

"I'm sorry," came her eventual response, her words uncertain and choked. "I didn't mean to…" She trailed off, only to be silenced as Prince Leo took her hand.

"It's okay, Aunt Fran," the boy said without judgement. "We need to get out of here, remember? Away from the bad men."

At this, Francine's expression finally broke into a warm smile. She shook her head once more. "Quite right, our heroic escape!" she said, making it into a game for her nephew. "But first, we need to find a way out of here. I see you brought your sword, Locke?"

He nodded.

"Good," she said, that familiar look of mischief twinkling in her eyes. "Very good, I've a feeling you're going to need it."

⚜   ⚜   ⚜

Fran's smile fell as she ran for the gatehouse, her back to Leo and Locke, who were following her lead.

What had she been thinking, threatening Leo like that? She had sworn to see him safe, but perhaps she herself presented the greatest threat to his safety? Her stomach dropped. The prince of all people, her nephew. The heir to the throne, and Cyrus's son, Cyrus, who had saved Fran's own life many times over, including when she had been little older than Leo now and every bit as fragile.

She had to see him to safety, back into his father's arms. Away from harm, including—it seemed—herself.

Her arrow appeared to have done enough in that it had at least provided a signal, even if it wasn't as explosive as she'd have hoped. She could hear the sound of Cyrus's men as they attacked the walls. They were skilled and disciplined, but Ramsey's battlements offered the traitor an advantage. One that Fran planned to remove.

"To the gatehouse!" she called, cutting down another man who attempted to block their path. From the corner of her eye, through the bars of the portcullis, she saw some of the men of the

King's Guard firing arrows at Ramsey's defenders while others rushed the battlements. They seemed so close, but none had yet been able to scale the walls, and it would not be long before Ramsey himself arrived to aid his reinforcements, surely bringing more men with him from inside. She turned back to see panic etched in Leo's wide eyes. Time was running out, and she had to see the gate raised, lest they be trapped.

Within the gatehouse, a single guard stood waiting. He was young, sixteen if that, and his look of fear was scarcely different from Leo's. The young guard stepped back and raised his sword, crying out for help, but Fran knew reinforcements could not come soon enough. She saw the winch for the portcullis in the corner of her eye, and the guard, sensing her intent, struck out like a cornered animal. Another pitiful attempt, but Fran's haze had passed, and she had no desire to end the life of one so young, especially not in such close proximity to her nephew, who would be scarred enough from this entire experience if they made it out alive. She knew Locke had closed the gatehouse door behind them, and though the space was small, she dodged the guard's blade to twist and smash the boy, face-first, into the stone wall, attempting to send him into unconsciousness to spare his life.

A pitiful cry only served to emphasise the guard's fragility, and it ignited a small whisper of the red mist in her. Responding only with her body's intuition, she pressed him against the wall with her sword at his back, until a soft whimper from behind her drew her attention, and she paused to turn and face Leo, whose eyes were wide with terror.

His expression broke her heart all over again, and she knew he was remembering the carnage she had unleashed in the courtyard only a few minutes ago.

"It's okay," she said, imagining herself through his eyes. Her rising bloodlust began to fall. The guard was shaking as she held him in place, and Fran reminded herself that the boy was someone's son, perhaps a brother as Cyrus had been for her. She imagined some child at home who looked up to this boy as she had looked up to Cyrus, and she felt the last of the mist falter inside her. The sight of the winch gave clarity to her purpose, reminded her that all she wanted was to remove this boy out of her way and get her nephew to safety. He need not die. She raised her sword, ramming the hilt of it roughly into the back of the boy's head, sending him tumbling to the floor, unconscious at last. Enough blood had already been spilled, she thought. The young guard would live to see another day.

If only for a moment, the room was clear and silent. The gatehouse door was closed, but Fran noticed a thick, wooden bar on the floor and knew it would be useful as a barricade. "Here, help me," she said, summoning Locke to help lift the beam to secure it in place.

New voices could be heard shouting in the courtyard. It seemed Ramsey had arrived with the last of his men, and Fran knew her brother and his men were likely to be used as target practice for the archers if she couldn't open the gate and even the odds.

Once they'd secured the barricade in place as best as they could, she walked to the winch. The mechanism was stiff, but Fran used all her strength to begin the circular motion, and a heavy clang sounded from beyond the gatehouse walls as the portcullis began to lift.

Calls of, "The gatehouse!" echoed in the courtyard, and it was only a matter of moments before fists started beating on the doors, shaking the hinges. To Fran's right, Leo startled with terror. The prince had never seemed so small and vulnerable as he did in that moment, and Fran recalled the death and suffering that had marred her own youth.

And look how that turned out, she thought, considering recent events. She wasn't simply capable of killing—she enjoyed it. Pain was easy. No, it was love, she thought with a heady rush, that truly scared her. Unbidden, the image of Patch reappeared again in the forefront of her mind, even as she used all her might to keep the winch turning, to raise the portcullis.

Another huge effort, and the winch give a quarter turn. Locke was holding Leo tightly, and Fran gritted her teeth, lamenting her decision to ever leave Peacehaven. She could have prevented this if she had only stuck around, but she'd spent her entire life running, from the minute Cyrus had taken her hand in Coldwynne, and then in Corhollow thereafter. She'd left Highcastle to escape her brother's shadow, and she'd even had every intention of leaving Mathilde behind to follow Patch on his adventures across the seas.

Even as she cursed herself for abandoning her family, the thought occurred to her that if she had never left Peacehaven, she would never have been reunited with Patch. She put the thought out of her mind. Now was not the time.

It would take more than a difficult winch to stop Fran from making things right. She pulled on the metal handle with everything she had, and she was gaining traction when footsteps sounded on a small, winding staircase in the opposite corner of the room.

"The portcullis…we have to lower the portcullis!"

"The men from the battlements!" Locke said in a loud whisper. Leo tucked his head into Locke's neck, blocking his own view out of self-preservation.

Fran had no choice but to rush to meet the new arrivals. The stairwell was narrow and the stone stairs uneven. The two men stopped abruptly as Fran appeared before them. They were off-balance and presented little challenge for her superior technique. Fran hoped with all her heart that Leo still had his eyes averted, but she had a job to do, so she left both men slumped on the stairs before turning back to find Locke leveraging the winch in her absence, Leo now clinging to his leg.

The handle was turning slowly but surely, the noise drowned out by yet more boots clambering down the stairs.

⚜ ⚜ ⚜

Sweat poured from Locke's brow as the winch turned to lift the portcullis. Francine was fighting desperately at the stairs to protect their position, while Leo now crouched at Locke's side, hands covering his ears as Ramsey's men continued trying to break through the gatehouse door. Splintered wood seemed to be everywhere, and Locke wondered if he had yet done enough with the gate, or if he'd be able to do so before the door came down.

"There's no escape!" came the threatening voices of those trying to smash their way in.

Locke felt as though his head was going to explode. There was no way his father would allow him to survive this treason against his family, never mind the prince. Francine was doing her best, but more and more men continued to appear on the staircase. They were outnumbered, and things could hardly get worse.

Then a horrible splintering sound following by a monstrous thud caused Locke's heart to stutter as the door hit the stone floor. Locke stepped back out of instinct, fear rising as his father's man, Willard, appeared before them in the doorway. The man's face fell into an immediate smirk, his eyes narrowed with vengeance. Locke reached for his sword, but he knew the end was now inevitable. He braced himself as Willard strode forward.

"Good to see you again, Lockey. Didn't I tell you there was no escape?" Locke could tell Willard was enjoying himself, but his moment was to be short-lived. Locke gasped as a sword ripped through Willard's chest unexpectedly. The man's surprise seemed to match Locke's, and Willard wheezed a final breath before stumbling forward to fall at Locke's feet, lifeless, blood gushing out of the wound in his chest.

In Willard's place, High Commander Broderick stepped forward to snarl at his fallen enemy. It seemed Locke had done enough with the portcullis after all, and a wave of relief washed over him as sounds of battle echoed from the courtyard.

"Get the prince out of here!" Broderick boomed before rushing to join the Francine at the foot of the stairs. It was an order that Locke was only too happy to follow. He had begun to think the gatehouse might become their tomb, and it was with some relief that he retrieved his sword to encourage Leo back out into the courtyard.

But if Locke had hoped to escape the bloodshed, he was sorely mistaken. The courtyard was now an arena of battle, with King Cyrus leading a line of his men against those of Locke's father's. Each soldier seemed to find a partner effortlessly, as though the pairings were pre-arranged, before launching forward to begin a dance to the death.

Swords crashed together and cries of pain sounded on the walls of Ardlyn Keep, but the fighting was concentrated to the middle of the courtyard. The action was a frantic blur to Locke, who positioned himself in front of Prince Leo to obstruct the boy's view. He had already seen enough death for a lifetime, Locke thought. Keeping low to avoid notice, Locke rushed the prince to the stables, where he would be—at least temporarily—out of sight. From their hiding place behind a low wall, Locke saw his father and brother fighting fiercely with the king's men. His breath caught as his eyes fell upon Finnian, the brigand's face still fixed with the same savage smile. King Cyrus and his troops had passed through the main gate, but they'd arrived to find a fearsome welcome party. Things might have started out equally, with roughly thirty men to each side, but numbers were already thinning, and the cobblestones at their feet were littered with the bodies of their dead. His father was winning, and Locke had come too far to let that happen.

He turned to Leo, who seemed to know what was coming. "Stay down, my prince," he said sadly. "I'll be back for you, I promise."

⚜ ⚜ ⚜

The flow of enemies had stopped, giving Fran the smallest moment of relief to catch her breath. The gatehouse was clear once more.

"To the king!" yelled Broderick, turning for the courtyard. Though Fran followed, she felt herself halted by disbelief at the gatehouse door as she found Locke amongst Cyrus's men. She'd thought Locke a coward, if she was honest with herself, and yet there was nothing timid or spineless about the prison master's ferocious, though slightly ungainly, attack on his father's men. Over and again, Locke hacked into his enemies. The King's Guard was outnumbered, but the fight was not yet lost. Broderick had already returned to the melee, with Cyrus carrying their efforts from the front.

Fran shook her head. *Ever the hero…*

She dashed away from the gatehouse to lend her sword. Broderick attacked a man, shouting, "You'll pay for this, Finnian!" while Locke and her brother were surrounded, fighting back-to-back. Only a handful of Cyrus's men remained, and Fran grimaced as another crumpled under the blade of a warrior with blonde hair, who Fran decided to engage first.

She paused for a moment to observe her opponent. The man was broad and strong, and his features were somehow familiar, though she was sure that they had never met. He turned to face her before flourishing his sword nonchalantly. Whoever he was, she was sure she'd be the end of him. She lashed out with lightning speed. His grin was confident, but her own smile broadened as he parried her strike with an attack of his own.

This was the opponent she had been waiting for, the one who would finally challenge her, and Fran danced as the momentum swung back and forth. From the corner of her eye, she saw the man, Finnian, fall at Broderick's feet, and a wave of relief passed over her at the sight of Cyrus still standing, Locke at his side.

Her opponent had begun to sweat in earnest. He was good, but would he be good enough? Another of Ramsey's men rushed to join the fray, but Fran dispatched him with ease before pushing on to end the contest with the blonde warrior. With every jab, she felt him wilting. She had the measure of him and knew there was nothing he could do to stem the tide, nothing he could do to surprise her. Maybe he wasn't as challenging as she had first thought. The man's eyes were now wide with fear, and as he stared around them searching for help, his feeble expression recalled that of a small boy, frightened and desperately out of his depth. A small boy like…

Leo. Where was Leo? Her eyes wandered, scouring the courtyard, considering her nephew's whereabouts, and wondering if he was safe. She forced herself to turn her eyes back to her opponent, to focus on the matter at hand before getting ahead of herself. Escape was in sight now. The blonde man was spent, and victory was surely forthcoming. A sigh of relief escaped her lips as she prepared for the inevitable. But as her sword raised to claim yet another life, an unexpected punch landed in her side, knocking her legs out from under her and sending her crashing to the ground.

She was on her knees, face twisted with confusion. Who had hit her? The blonde man was grinning at her, and Fran grimaced as another sharp punch pummelled into her side, bringing with it fresh, excruciating pain that radiated out to her entire body. It took all her strength not to scream in agony.

She twisted in an attempt to figure out who had assaulted her, and her head dropped at the sight of two snarling men, their swords dripping with red. Her mind spun as she reached to inspect her side. The pain was already fading, but the world felt as though it was becoming distant. Her fingers were slick with blood as she raised them before her eyes. Her vision blurred, and her balance failed, leaving her sprawled on her back.

Sounds of battle grew more and more indistinct. Bodies were falling to the flagstones all around her, but Fran could do little more than gaze into the night sky at the twinkling stars. She was vaguely aware of a wetness on her own cheeks, and it took her a few breathless seconds to realise she was crying.

Once more, her mind flickered to Leo. She knew she could do no more for him, and she hoped with what little might she had left that he was safe. A face appeared above her, and she wondered if it was Leo himself, summoned here by her very thoughts, before shaking the notion away. Her vision cleared momentarily, and her expression relaxed into an easy smile as she recognised—who else?—her brother.

"It's going to be okay," said Cyrus gently, stooping down to her spot on the ground.

But her brother had never been any good at hiding his emotions, and the look of panic on his face told a different story. She smiled as Cyrus took her hand and held it tightly. Her breaths were shallow now, and her body felt numb, the pain a distant memory. A sense of calm prevailed around them, and if only for a moment, Fran dared to dream that the day was won. That they'd all walk out of here together, heads held high, Leo on his father's shoulders, Fran at his side. Where she belonged.

"I knew you'd come for me," she said hoarsely, trying her best to put on a brave face. Cyrus had always been a worrier, and she didn't want to scare him. It was one of the things she loved most about him: a desire to do better, to be better, and above all else, to care for those around him.

"You didn't make it easy. Couldn't have opened the gate any sooner?" Cyrus laughed, and then his voice turned serious. "You did it though. Leo is safe. I just need you to hold on, Fran, just stay with me. Don't you go anywhere…" He paused to squeeze her hand, his entire body shaking as tears welled in his eyes. "Stay with me, you hear me? I can't do this without you. We're going to get out of here, okay? We're going to…"

Fran closed her eyes, and her brother's words faded. She had expected darkness, but she could not have prepared for the sea of tall trees now towering above her. Fran realised she was in a forest, standing motionless on an earthy track. It all seemed so familiar, but from where, she couldn't place. Then desperate words interrupted her wonderment.

"Come on, Fran, I need you to stay with me!"

She knew that voice. It was her brother's voice. She looked around, and sure enough, Cyrus was suddenly running toward her. Fran's eyes narrowed in confusion. This wasn't King Cyrus of Peacehaven, but rather the boy she had met in the woods of Coldwynne a lifetime ago. This wasn't the man who had delivered peace to two kingdoms and fathered a prince, but scrawny Cyrus from the Low Country, whose only kingdom existed in his imagination.

The familiarity of their surrounding suddenly fell into place.

Then Cyrus's voice, "Stay with me, Fran. We're going to get you out of here!"

He took her hand, and she let him guide her. Together they ran, but Fran's legs were small and tired, and she didn't want to run anymore.

"I can't!" she wailed, weariness bearing down on her. His grip was tight, but Fran tried to wriggle free. She slowed, pulling back with all her weight, drawing Cyrus to a halt in the middle of the road. He was panting, looking at her with frenzied, frustrated eyes.

She heard voices behind them calling her name, and she whipped around to see who they belonged to. She saw a woman with blonde hair and a man who smelled like freshly baked bread and cakes, even at a distance. Their faces were blurry. She squinted, but nothing changed. There was something about them, though, something strangely familiar. Their silhouettes gave a soft, ethereal glow as they continued to call for her, and two names suddenly appeared in her mind…

Muriel and Virgil. But those were not the names she had called them.

She was making to close their distance when a painful breath escaped her. A sudden jerk caused her eyes to pop open, and Cyrus stared back at her, a king once more in the starry night.

"Please no," he said, his lower lip trembling.

But Fran let her hand fall. She smiled, and then she died.

⚜ ⚜ ⚜

Locke looked up to the tower of Ardlyn Keep. In the top window, he spotted his mother. Her expression was obscured by distance, but Locke suspected it was similar to his own: speechless with shock.

He'd seen it all unfold before him: Francine fighting with Ralph until the king's sister was blindsided, stabbed twice in the back by two of Locke's father's men. King Cyrus as he rushed forward to finish the job Francine had started, sending Ralph to the floor, defeated. Cries had echoed out as gold-toothed Seth sent a blade into Locke's father's shoulder, the latter left sprawled at the side of his oldest, most favoured son.

It had all happened in an instant, but it felt as though time had slowed down, as though the moment had been drawn out over weeks, maybe years. Locke felt the sting of loss as Ralph breathed his last. He didn't spare much thought for his father, lying next to him. It had been many years since Locke and his brother had been close, but you can't choose your family, and you certainly can't choose who you love.

He should have known what to expect. It was Locke, after all, who had brought the king's men to the castle. He wondered if he could have done more to prevent this violence, and he felt a burning shame at his own part in it all, from beginning to end, from the moment he had taken the lockpick from his father and passed it to Finnian.

The king's cries pulled his eyes away from Ralph's body and toward Francine's. The sound was cutting, going straight through Locke as he watched the king cradling his fallen sister. Locke, who had felt numb with shock until now, felt a lump rising in his throat.

Then, a sudden bout of laughter seized Locke's attention. He turned to find his father, bloodied at the shoulder but standing—

and he looked crazed, his eyes wide, his face contorted into a manic glee.

"I told you I'd make him suffer," said Locke's father, stumbling to his feet, smiling despite his wound. "He took my boy, but he will never get his sister back, and you..." His eyes narrowed with contempt as he stared at Locke. "He's welcome to you. I've told you before: you're no son of mine."

After all that had happened, his father's disdain still hurt him. "I never wanted this, Father," said Locke. "I never asked for any of this, but you went too far...you put us all in danger, and now Ralph..." He trailed off, the lump in his throat becoming too much to speak over.

With every moment, his father edged closer to him, bad leg dragging uselessly behind him. There was a sword in his hand and a horrible glint in his eye that told Locke all he needed to know about his father's intentions.

"Don't be stupid, Father!" Locke called. But he knew his words to be futile. Locke raised his blade and braced himself for the worst. In the other corner of the courtyard, the king's cries continued. He was too far gone into his own grief to consider helping Locke. High Commander Broderick watched on, standing his men down as they made to intervene, and Locke knew that—while they had been happy to accept his help in this matter—his life was not worth risking those of Broderick's remaining men.

"Looks like it's just you and me then, Lockey, eh? And after all I've done for you..." His father's face soured. He drew to a halt and steadied himself before striking with his sword in Locke's direction. "I only ever wanted what was best for this country and for my family," he said, breathing hard as Locke blocked his attack.

"We could have had it all, but you were too weak, too…incompetent. Just another coward with no ambition!"

Locke's jaw clenched with every word. There was no escaping the inevitable, and he stepped left to let a clumsy strike whistle past his side.

"Fight me!" said his father, and his words sounded like an echo from Locke's past. The man was beaten and broken, yet no less dangerous for it. If anything, he had lost it all so had nothing left to tether him to this life, giving way to reckless abandon. Locke wanted to turn and run, but he'd promised Francine he would fight, that he would get Prince Leo out alive. He'd promised *himself* that he would face his fears and overcome them. This time, he wouldn't walk away.

Locke jabbed sharply, testing his injured father's defence. A shrill clang filled the air, and Locke gasped as the returning blow left a thin but painful gash in his arm. His enthusiasm waned as the cut throbbed. It felt as though his arm had caught fire, such was the heat of the wound. His sword became heavy, and doubt crept in with the prospect of an experienced killer staring back at him. His own father.

But there was no turning back now, and everyone was watching. Locke breathed deeply, attempting to contain the voice in his head shouting that all was lost. For all his technique, Locke's father *was* injured, and he grimaced as he twisted, fending off Locke's full-blooded assault. Locke wondered if this could all be a ruse to bait him, but with every attack, his father seemed to parry lower and slower. His father's defence was spirited but sluggish, and Locke rallied his strength for a final burst that tore the sword from his father's hand, leaving the great Lord Ramsey, Warden of the Northern Fells, unarmed.

Locke stepped back, and after a completely silent moment, his father fell to his knees, defeated.

"Not bad, Locke," he said, smiling. "Not bad, but what now? You're a traitor to your family, and what use will the king have for you when all is said and done? No..." he said, shaking his head with another disdainful snigger. "Even if he chooses to forgive you, he'll soon see you for what you are: nothing more than a gutless, spineless worm. Finish it, you fool! Go on, finish it, I dare y—"

But Locke's blade turned his voice to a splutter.

Broderick gave an audible gasp from his position across the courtyard. The blade was lodged deep in Locke's father's chest, and Locke felt nothing more than pity and relief as his father's eye widened with surprise for the last time.

As his father breathed his final breath, the horrible, shouting voice in Locke's head finally quieted. The silence, the room to think, was astounding, like the first breath of fresh, spring air in the morning.

His father's body slumped to the ground, and in his mind's eye, Locke saw the cellar door of his nightmares fly open, leaving him free to walk out and begin his life.

Chapter XXVII

Locke

Ten days had passed since that night at Ardlyn Keep. In the end, little more than a handful of their retinue had survived, and Locke would never forget the sound of King Cyrus's cries, which had pierced the night as he held his sister in his arms. Worse still was the memory of Prince Leo running to console his father, staring with wide, uncomprehending eyes at the lifeless body that had belonged to his aunt. Guilt and helplessness had threatened to overwhelm Locke in those moments as he joined High Commander Broderick, Seth, and the two remaining members of the King's Guard to watch over their king in respectful silence as the sun emerged over the battlements.

It was a new dawn, at least for those who had lived to see it.

While King Cyrus arranged a carriage for his sister's body to be carried back to the capital, Locke had been granted time to bid farewell to his mother. He had wondered what he would say to her, whether she would be angry or disappointed in him, but he needn't have worried. The tight clench of her embrace spoke all the words left unsaid between them. She did not cry for the loss of her son and husband in front of Locke, and she had even forced a smile from Locke when, true to form, she refused to let him leave without a small, sweet-smelling parcel of bread and cakes that she had baked earlier in the day.

"I don't want you wasting away," she had joked, drawing him close to kiss his forehead.

Locke had savoured that moment, wondering when—or if—he would see her again, unsure as he was of his own fate. It was some relief to hear that his mother would be allowed to remain at Ardlyn Keep for the time being, but as Locke followed King Cyrus and the others away from the castle, he had glanced back to find her looking very small and alone in a place that held many painful memories for them all.

King Cyrus, meanwhile, portrayed a picture of regal composure, though Locke felt as though he could sense the king's ragged cries for his sister just below the surface. The townsfolk had already begun to wake as their group retraced their steps to reclaim the horses. People Locke had recognised but could not name due to sheer exhaustion stood wide-mouthed at the unexpected sight of their king. In response, the king had kept his chin high, his kind smile giving no suggestion of his suffering. He had even told Prince Leo to give the people a wave, and when he did, the people of Ardlyn had cooed in response, with no idea of the loss the royal family had so recently sustained.

And so it had remained throughout their journey. They rode hard and fast with only occasional breaks as they followed the River Aramere toward the capital. The two members of the King's Guard had ridden ahead to ensure safe passage, and Prince Leo had joined his father atop a majestic brown mare called Adagio, with Seth and Broderick at either flank. Locke had followed along in their wake, the odd man out again.

In their rare moments of rest, Locke was forcefully reminded of the king's anguish.

"So, Aunt Fran is never coming back?" Leo had asked as the horses drank from the river. Locke's face had twisted into a grimace, while the prince's brows were lowered in sadness, perhaps confusion, and his father's chest heaved with the emotion he sought to contain.

Locke had wondered how the king could even begin to answer such a question and had breathed a sigh of relief when Seth stepped forward to wrap an arm around the young prince.

"She's resting now," he had said, turning a sad smile upon the king before crouching to speak with Leo at eye level. "Your Aunt Fran was very brave, and she has worked hard all her life. She has earned her rest, don't you think?"

Prince Leo had nodded, as his father added, "She's not gone really." He ruffled his son's red curls. "She'll live on forever, for we will never stop telling her story."

They had arrived in the capital in the early afternoon, and Locke had remained in Eldred's Keep ever since, whether as a guest or prisoner, he wasn't sure. He hadn't been given any information in the ensuing days, and the only people he saw were the chambermaids who flitted in and out in their line of duty. Locke had many, many hours to relive the hellish time in Ardlyn Keep—his brother falling, Francine gasping her last breath, Locke's own sword running through his father's chest. The images haunted him, and he wished deeply for a summons, something to take him away from his comfortable, safe prison. But no one had called him. Until now, that is. The king had asked for him, so Locke guessed he would find out soon enough whether he was here as a punishment or reward.

He gazed upon the heavy-looking door leading to the Royal Chambers. High Commander Broderick escorted him, and the two armed guards who stood at the door stared back at them, with no expression that Locke could discern. Just as one of the guards made to speak, a baby's cry sounded out, cutting through the silence. The guard paused, lowered his halberd, smiled unexpectedly, and said, "The king is ready to see you now."

And with that, the doors opened.

Broderick's armour clinked as he strode into the room confidently, and Locke stepped forward with some hesitation, wondering how he had ever ended up in this position and what in the world would come next.

His heart was beating fast in his chest, and he fought to focus his eyes as he made his way inside the room.

"Prison Master Locke," the king said in welcome.

Locke nodded with a half-smile, following Broderick toward a roaring fire at one end of the room. The High Commander placed a hand on Locke's shoulder, bringing him to a halt. Locke pulled at his collar to loosen it as flames crackled in the hearth.

"Good to see you again, Prison Master Locke," said King Cyrus. He sat in a high-backed chair, Queen Marcia at his side with a cooing newborn baby pressed to her shoulder. Prince Leo was playing quietly in front of the fire with wooden soldiers. From the animated voices he was using to give life to his characters, it seemed that the events of their night at Ardlyn had done nothing to temper the young prince's enthusiasm.

For all that they had been through, Locke reminded himself that he still needed to observe the formalities. He dropped to one knee, "My king," he said, lowering his head.

King Cyrus laughed gently and called for Locke to return to his feet. "I trust your time in the castle has been comfortable?"

Locke thought of his spacious quarters, the silk shirts in the wardrobe, the sumptuous meals he'd been brought to enjoy on the small table by his window, which afforded him a staggering view over Highcastle. "More than comfortable, my king," he said graciously. "You have been most hospitable, especially after everything that…"

The king blanched, paling ever so slightly, and Locke trailed off into silence.

Queen Marcia reached across, placing a hand on her husband's shoulder. "It has been a trying time. We have all experienced great loss, but there is nothing to be gained by living in the past, isn't that right, my love?" As if to highlight the queen's point, the baby in her arms let out a sudden gurgle. Everyone in the room paused to give a quick smile, as though no one could resist bestowing a small token of happiness on this new child.

"Too true," said the king, turning his smile to rest upon his queen. "Sacrifices were made so we could be here, in this moment. The very least we can do is enjoy it. High Commander Broderick, can you excuse us?"

Broderick nodded and left without a word.

"As for you, Locke, I wonder if you'd take a seat and join us?" King Cyrus gestured to a third chair, which sat empty and inviting. The king reached to pour a glass of red wine, which he handed to Locke without standing. "To absent friends and family," he said, eyes lowered as their glasses clinked gently. "Gone but not forgotten."

Locke noticed Queen Marcia move her hand to steady her husband's. The king's love for his sister was almost tangible, as though Francine were still there in the room among them. Locke hadn't known her nearly long enough, but with a spirit like Francine's, he thought anything could be possible.

"My king..." he ventured, words of apology on the very tip of his tongue.

King Cyrus smiled. "I know what you're going to say, but there's no need. My sister always was the unpredictable one." He paused to laugh, and then his expression saddened. "She knew the risks, and I know she would have done anything for Leo...for me. As for you, Locke..." The king scratched the stubble on his chin as he considered his words. "I heard what happened with your father, and I know you lost your brother too. I can't imagine how difficult that must have been for you and your mother, what you both must feel now. What I do know is that without you, my son might not be here today, and for that, I thank you. We are all going to have to find a way to move on and rebuild, but life must go on. There is much still to live for—isn't that right, young lady?" The king reached across to the infant princess, whose curious little hands reached to meet her father's.

Locke let his head drop, his reaction somewhere between shame and relief. "You're too kind, my king," he said, taking a long sip of wine to settle his nerves. "I would have done anything to save the prince, but it doesn't change the fact that my family betrayed you, each in our own way. I don't know what plans you have for me, but my mother is innocent in this, and I would ask that you show her mercy."

The king recoiled with surprise, as though the thought of punishing Locke's mother had never even occurred to him. Locke realised in that moment that it clearly had not. "Oh, I see no need for that," King Cyrus said. "No, your mother will simply remain within her home at Ardlyn Keep. I expect the new lord will need her support and counsel."

Locke's eyes narrowed. "The new lord?" He couldn't help but wonder who his mother would be forced to share a home with, who would walk the halls he had grown up in, who would take Ardlyn Keep and attempt to scrub the memory of Lord Ramsey from it.

"Enough of your games, Cyrus. Just tell him!" said the queen, a smile tugging at the corners of her lips.

"Yes, of course," said the king, seeming to enjoy himself, if only for a moment. He pursed his lips thoughtfully before continuing, "I need people I can trust, Locke, now more than ever. It is no easy position, being Warden of the Northern Fells, but you know the land, the people. I don't doubt your reticence, but please consider my offer. It would bring peace and honour to your family name."

Locke was certain for a moment that he had misunderstood the king, and as his mind fought to catch up to the conversation, he shook his head in disbelief. "Me? Warden of the Northern Fells? I…I can't…I mean to say, thank you, my king, but I am not worthy of this privilege."

"Worthy?" King Cyrus answered sharply, leaving Locke wondering why he hadn't kept his mouth shut. "A wise man once told me that it's not who you are, but rather what you do. I see that you care for people. You want to do good, and more than anything, you are keen to learn from your mistakes. Are you familiar with the Pillars of Peace?" he asked, as he sat back in his chair, surveying Locke.

Locke chewed his lip in thought, surprised by the sudden question. His father had made him memorise them as a child, of course, but it had been some years since he had last been tested. "Respect," he began tentatively, extending a single finger to quantify his response.

He sought the king's assurance, which came in the form of a nod.

"Yes, respect," Locke continued, his voice rising as his confidence did. "Also, trust, participation, and—"

"Integrity," King Cyrus interjected to finish with a smile. At that, the king stood and paced toward a window. He stopped and turned, "Very good. My father wasn't perfect, but he was a smart man to set those pillars in place. I think we can all agree with those principles. Yet, with the benefit of experience, I wonder if he perhaps missed something. A fifth pillar…"

"A fifth?"

The king nodded. "Maybe the most important of all. Indeed, without this pillar, I believe there can be no peace at all…"

Locke waited, unwilling to interrupt his king.

"Forgiveness, Locke," the king said. "Forgiveness of ourselves and forgiveness of others. We all have our regrets, our grudges, but the past is unchangeable, and tomorrow is a blank page." He retraced his steps across the room, stopping to stand with the queen, his hands resting softly but supportively upon her shoulders. "No amount of anger will see my sister returned, nor your family restored, and it is my job as king to focus on where we are going, not where we have been."

Locke felt his skin prickle with the wisdom of his king's words. He knew what he had to do and nodded. "It would be an honour, my king. I will not let you down."

King Cyrus smiled. "I don't doubt it. And I had hoped you would say that because I have a task for you." He reached into his pocket to withdraw a piece of parchment. "It seems our dear friend Queen Mathilde is getting married, and to a Kanthi prince if you can believe that." He chuckled.

"The wedding is due to take place in the coming weeks," added the queen. "We would love to attend, of course, but…" She shrugged as much as was possible with the tiny princess still holding on tightly.

"I hoped you might travel in our stead and extend our apologies," the king continued. "Your land borders Cornesse to the north, and this might present an opportunity to introduce yourself and begin to build relations. You'll know that my sister was shield to the queen, so she will need to be informed of the news. All of the news…" He forced a smile and ruffled the princess's light crop of white-blonde hair.

The request was yet another surprise to Locke, who shook his head, still trying to catch up. It would be his first time travelling beyond the borders of Peacehaven, and as fear gave way to elation, he forced down his emotions to answer, "Yes, my king," as flatly as possible, before standing to bow, leaving the young family in peace.

On his exit, the door opened to reveal the same guards who had welcomed him. He made to leave, and then halted abruptly. The king's orders bounced around in his mind, and he realised there was one question that had been left unanswered.

He turned back to see Queen Marcia pass the princess into the king's arms. Prince Leo made to sit on his mother's lap, and it struck Locke that the four of them looked like a perfect family, the kind anyone would be lucky to grow up in.

Locke cleared his throat, stepping back inside the room. "I'm sorry, my king, but there was one last thing. The princess's name. I'm sure Queen Mathilde will want to know."

At this question, the king smiled deeply. He stood to raise the tiny baby so that Locke could see her face, and for the first time, Locke noticed a small bracelet of flowers decorating one of the princess's puffy little wrists. The king stopped, lowering his daughter, and smiled back in the queen's direction.

"Francine," he said, pausing to kiss the baby's head gently, "Tell Mathilde her name is Francine."

⚜ ⚜ ⚜

Locke left the royal chambers to find Broderick standing expectantly, a coin pouch jangling in his hand.

"For your journey," said the High Commander, as if there had never been any doubt as to the outcome of Locke's conversation with the king. Broderick offered his other hand before shaking Locke's with remarkable strength. "You did good, boy. There's a horse in the courtyard awaiting your departure. Now, if you'll please excuse me, I need to have words with the king." Broderick nodded, stepped beyond Locke, and said, "My king, there's something I wish to discuss with you..." before the doors closed, leaving Locke in silence.

From the corner of his eye, Locke noticed someone moving swiftly down the corridor. As he closed the gap between them, Locke saw that the man was far older than himself, but with a mischievous, childlike grin shadowed by a weather-beaten tricorn hat.

A pirate? Locke wondered, smiling courteously as the older man passed by. *Interesting company for the king to keep.*

But then the man stopped suddenly, and his grin seemed to widen. "Someone with the king?" he asked, removing his hat to reveal a hooped piercing through his eyebrow. When Locke nodded, the man continued, "Terrible business, isn't it? To steal a young boy away from his home like that, not to mention what happened to the king's sister. Have you seen the family, since—well—since it happened?"

Again, Locke nodded.

"And how is he?"

"He's fine, he was sitting on the queen's lap just a moment ago."

The pirate laughed loudly, causing Locke's skin to redden.

"Not Prince Leo," the pirate said, still chuckling. "I meant Cyrus! Leo's made of tougher stuff, but his father..." His face dropped, and he shook his head, his laughter already a ghost. "The king has been through so much. Times like this make me glad they have each other—Cyrus, and the queen, I mean. Anyway, where are my manners?" he said, clearing his throat to regain some composure. "My name's Roscoe, and I'm an old friend of the king's, despite his best efforts to burden me with a fancy title. You're a young man, son, but it won't always be that way. Learn from this. Never take life for granted, and never let it pass you by." The pirate paused to give Locke a heavy yet encouraging pat on the shoulder. In the corridor beyond them, Locke noticed the king's shield, Seth, laughing with a maid, their eyes fixed upon one another, hands touching gently at their sides.

"You're right," said Locke and his lips curled to form a purposeful smile. "It was a pleasure to meet you, Roscoe, but please excuse me. There's something I need to do."

⚜ ⚜ ⚜

"We're closed!" yelled Rufus without turning to see who had walked in.

Some things never change, thought Locke, and he smiled to see the landlord polishing tankards as Grace scrubbed away at the filthy surface of an empty table, intently focused on her task.

Locke raised an eyebrow. "Even to your tenants?"

There was a pause, and Locke figured Rufus was working out whose voice he had heard. After a moment, he said, "Even the tenants, especially those with money owing!" He turned to give a shrug that seemed to ask, "Where the hell have you been?" Grace seemed to have frozen in place, and Locke wondered if she was refusing to look up at him.

Where would he even begin?

"I'm sorry," he said, the words tumbling from his lips. "I've been busy. Something happened with my father, and I have to go…I have to leave here. I'm sorry." He noticed Grace finally look up from her work. His words lacked the composure they'd had in practise.

Rufus raised his hands to calm Locke's mood, and said, "It's okay," leaving Locke's eyes to shift toward Grace, who was looking back at him with concern of her own.

"I'm returning home to Ardlyn Keep," Locke continued, uncomfortable at the prospect of explaining all that had happened and the title he had gained in the process. This, he thought, could wait for another day. "I need to look after my mother, but I have an errand to run first for…" He paused and thought better of it. "For someone important. I have your money," he said, pulling a few coins from the pouch in his pocket. He walked to the bar and counted the money out for Rufus's benefit. "Thanks for letting me stay here, but it's time to go. I'll take my things now, if all is in order?"

"Sure," said the landlord, nonplussed. He gave another shrug.

But as Locke made for his room, he noticed Grace still watching on. It was now or never. His courage swelled.

"I've been meaning to ask you something," he said, turning to face her with as much conviction as he could muster. Grace paused in her work, her eyes upon him once more. He swallowed deeply and tried to forget that Rufus was within earshot, though the sound of clinking glasses told Locke that the old landlord was no longer listening anyway.

"I was wondering if you'd like to spend some time together," Locke ventured, his eyes now fixed firmly on the floor. "Perhaps come and visit my home in the country. I'm sure my mother would like to meet you, that is, if you'd like to…" he stuttered, trying to recover his train of thought, "And…and, I'll understand if not, it's probably a silly question anyway…"

He was all out of breath, and the room fell silent.

But contrary to his worst fears, Grace wasn't laughing. Locke's heartrate slowed as he raised his head and found that she was smiling. "I'd love that," she said, and Locke sighed with relief. The voice in his head that had once told him he couldn't, he wouldn't, he would never be good enough was silent, giving way instead to an inward roar of delight.

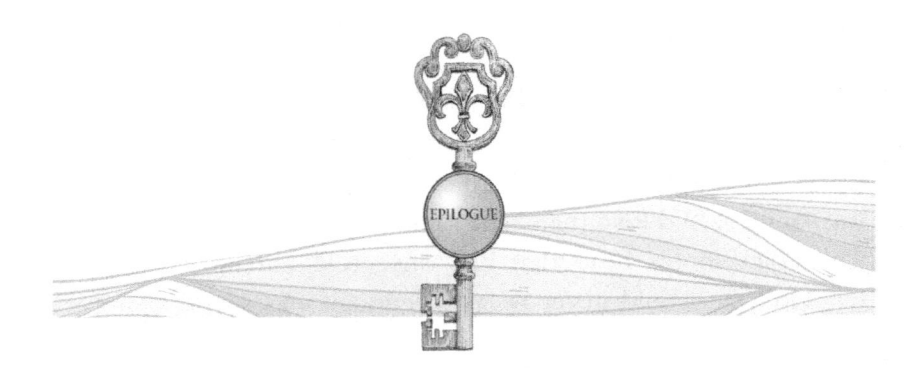

Adaline

Her footsteps made the only sound around as she wandered through the basilica. Her long gown whispered a kiss against the flagstones, but otherwise, all was quiet, and Adaline smiled at finding herself alone. She made for the apse and paused to rest against one of the wooden benches. On the ground before her was a section of dark, polished marble. The stone glistened in the candlelight, and Adaline observed the intricate lettering used to list their names.

Augustus.
Anselm.
Ailwin.
And all who had gone before them.

Her heart sank at the loss of life. Her son, her husband, taken too soon.

Adaline was one of the lucky ones, of course, at least by most standards. She still remembered the night the assassin had targeted her in her bed, all those years ago, the night he had almost succeeded, but for a little girl brave enough to stop him. She breathed deeply and closed her eyes in thanks that Fran had been there to save her.

But where had Adaline been when Fran was the one who had needed saving?

Her attention shifted instinctively to the basilica's newest addition, a small plaque engraved with Fran's name, along with the years of her birth and death. Numbers, that's all they were, no impression of the life that had passed in between, the vibrancy of the young woman Adaline had known, the sister her son had loved.

It was the long wooden bench below that told the full story. On its surface, a wreath of wildflowers complemented by an array of flickering candles, orange light dancing on the stone walls, bright and spirited—just as Adaline would always remember Fran. It was a tribute, not only from Cyrus, but from the people of Peacehaven. Fran had been beloved, and she would be dearly missed.

Adaline lowered her head. She had seen her world slowly dismantled, her walls of safety and security destroyed over the years, under siege from enemies fuelled by pride and ambition. But had she not known what to expect? Had she truly thought she would grow old sitting comfortably at Anselm's side?

Her father's words were still etched in her memory: *You must get his attention. He'll be king one day!*

She had been so young then. Truth be told, she had wanted to dance with all the boys. She had simply wanted to have fun. But then she had seen him, Prince Anselm—so charming, so funny, and handsome too.

He had her attention. And it was no time at all before she had his too.

She sighed as she thought of those early days. Anselm had been all she had imagined and so much more: loving, inspiring, and purposeful. It had not taken Adaline long to realise her new husband had the power to bring about change, and she knew their lives would never be the same once he did.

A fresh wave of sadness swelled within her as her eyes slid from Anselm's name etched in marble to her eldest son's. Augustus had been a difficult boy, but had his deficiencies been her fault? The question had plagued her every day since his death. Another question lingered with her, tortured her: who was the man Augustus might have grown to be? A king in his father's image, perhaps? Loving? Inspiring? Purposeful?

A king much like Cyrus, if so…

She shook her sorrow away, sitting down upon one of the wooden benches. She raised her hands and bowed her head in prayer.

This was why she was here, after all.

Nothing would change the past, much as she might wish it so, but in her prayers, Adaline hoped she might yet bring forth a peaceful future. Her thoughts returned to Cyrus. His eyes had been unable to produce further tears by the time he had returned to Highcastle and shared the news of his sister's passing with Adaline. She prayed for him now, and for Fran, that she might be rewarded with a restful sense of calm she had never found during her time amongst the living.

She prayed that Marcia would find the strength to support and protect Cyrus in a way that Adaline had failed with her own husband. And she prayed for her grandchildren, Leopold and Francine, hoping they would grow old in that "better world" their grandfather had designed and their father had seen brought to life.

Hopes and dreams, that's all that they were, that's all she had. But what more could Adaline do for them? She squeezed her eyes tightly, and a tear escaped her. She wondered if she might break down in that moment, but then the door of the basilica creaked open, and footsteps moved toward her.

Divine intervention? she thought before pushing such a notion away. Whoever it was, she was no longer alone. That was something.

A quick glimpse revealed a man obscured by the hood of a long brown cloak, spotted with rainwater. The door creaked to a slow close, and Adaline heard heavy rainfall beating on the cobblestones of the atrium beyond. As the man approached, she wiped her eyes for some composure, reminding herself that she was the dowager queen, after all. Whoever this man was, it would not do to have the people of Highcastle sensing weakness within the king's own family.

The man moved slowly, lowering his head in a courteous bow as he proceeded beyond Adaline to stand briefly at the apse, where he dropped to one knee in hushed prayer. Though Adaline could not hear his words, she sensed that the basilica was unfamiliar to the man, who eventually adjusted his cloak to return awkwardly to his feet. He sniffed, stifling apparent sadness, then turned toward Adaline, reaching into the folds of his robes in a moment that set Adaline on edge…

Who is this man? she wondered in a flash of panic. She tried to paint a picture of indifference upon her face, but her eyes were wide with nerves. She knew better than to assume her own safety, and she scolded herself for attending the basilica alone, however much she had needed space.

The man's face was still shrouded in the shadow of his hood, and Adaline's breath caught in her throat as his hand reappeared from his cloak, his fingers clenched tightly around whatever it was that he had sought to retrieve. She squinted...

It's just a candle, she realised with a quiet sigh of relief. Her heartrate slowed as he made his way toward Fran's memorial, and an aching sadness returned to Adaline as he lit his candle from the flame of another before placing it on the table. His face was turned away from her, but the silhouette of his shoulders shook as he sobbed quietly. She listened, almost guiltily for a few moments, then the man stopped, seeming to shake his emotion away. He reached with his hand and placed his fingers gently against Fran's plaque before turning to walk in Adaline's direction, where he sat at the end of the same long bench.

"You knew her?" she asked, the words falling instinctively from her lips. Perhaps she should have left him in silence, but she felt the need to comfort him. Perhaps it was her own need to share the weight of her grief.

The man turned to her, and a sad smile tugged at his cheek. Though his hood still covered the top half of his face, she could now see the glistening tracks of his tears. She knew she was safe, and she found the man to be somewhat familiar, though from where she could not place.

Finally, the man nodded. "I did, though not half as well as I would have liked." His voice was solemn and regretful.

"It's not fair, is it?" she answered, shaking her head. "What kind of world is this, that life can be so needlessly taken?" She stopped herself and took a moment. She missed them all: Fran, Augustus, Anselm, Thaddeus, and Garrett. And what fate awaited Cyrus? He had never asked for any of this—Cyrus, or his children, all born with targets on their backs.

"Life is rarely fair," the man answered, turning once again to face in the direction of Fran's memorial. "But it can be beautiful," he added, before removing his hood to reveal a head of thick, dark curls. A spark of recognition ignited within Adaline.

"I know you," she said, eyes narrowed as she considered him.

The man nodded. "We've met before, but not for many years. My name is Captain Goldhand these days," he said, brushing wet hair away from swollen eyes. "We have a mutual friend in Roscoe. You would probably remember me as Patch. Fran did." The last two words seemed to threaten to undo him.

Adaline smiled as she recalled the small boy who had first visited Eldred's Keep years before, close at Roscoe's side. How he knew Francine but for their few days in the same place over a decade ago, she had no idea. It hardly seemed to matter in that moment. Their unspoken sadness stretched out as they both turned to face the apse, and Adaline shuffled down the bench to close the distance between them.

She placed her hand on top of Patch's as they sat, their memories almost palpable in the silence between them. He was right: life wasn't fair, but it was full of beautiful moments. Adaline thought of all the beauty that remained around her—her son, her grandchildren, and the promising future built on the foundation her husband laid brick by brick—and her spirit lifted in hope that brighter days were yet to come.

Her walls of safety and security had been tested; maybe they'd even been knocked down. But who was to stop her rebuilding them, with her family by her side to help? Amidst all the pain and suffering they had endured, hope was the force that still fought within, the force that would propel them forward. Together.

THE END

Acknowledgements

So, here it is; we've arrived at the end. Unlike the first two books, *Where Heroes Were Born* did not come easily. As the world returns to something approaching normality, it is more difficult than before to make time for writing. Fortunately, the voices of these characters kept calling to me, asking for their story to be told. Though tinged with some sadness, I am delighted to bring the story to a close, something I could not have achieved without the following people:

Linda and Greg Dumbrell – for entertaining my new hobby and taking every opportunity to promote my work.

Steve Cooling-Smith at Chilligraphics – for absolutely smashing it with cover design for all three books, and perhaps saving the best for last! Steve took my words and gave these stories a real identity, for which I am truly grateful. You can find Steve at www.chilligraphics.com.

Breana Dumbrell at Bee, Your Editor – for patiently discussing this series over the course of two years, and for dragging me through my frustrations and limitations to make it the best it could be. Also, for contributing most of the best material! You can find Breana at www.beeyoureditor.wordpress.com.

Finally, thank you to everyone who has stuck with me throughout the *Pillars of Peace* series. Special acknowledgement for the Bookstagram and Twitter communities for providing an invaluable source of support throughout. I hope this book was worth the wait, and that you have enjoyed your journey with Cyrus and Francine as much as I have enjoyed writing it.

Note from the Author

Indulge me, if you will, as I build on my comments from the previous page...

I was very lucky to have started this series at a time when time was really all we had! It was this or get a puppy, and we already had three dogs, so that decision was a simple one.

Of all the struggles 2020 threw at us, I consider myself fortunate to have awoken in March of that year with an idea that would see me through the monotony of subsequent redundancy and two years of dedicated writing as the world has slowly returned to normal. Creative writing is not something that comes easy to me, that much is probably obvious, but this project has given me a wonderful sense of purpose and escapism, along with the opportunity to learn new skills. Which leads me nicely onto the primary purpose of this section: Breana...

Wife, editor, creative writing tutor, therapist.

For two years, Breana has forcibly moulded me into something that vaguely resembles an author. Truly, I could not have done this without her, and I wouldn't have wanted to. For all the words you see on the page, there are many more that have been written, discussed, changed, or disregarded. The end result is that these books are the very best they can be, and I have Breana to thank for that. It was easy to write Cyrus and Marcia's romance because I know what it is to be utterly captivated by someone from the moment you meet them. I can't wait to see what the first ten years of marriage hold for us and only hope they are a little smoother than those experienced by Peacehaven's young king and queen!

And so, finally to the readers. I hope that you have enjoyed this series and that it has left its mark. Ironically, *Pillars of Peace* wasn't built upon any particular ideal or message. Yet, as I reflect on the finished article, I see my thoughts of the past two years reflected within the pages. The world, whether ours or the Quadripartite, is often a hard and unpredictable place. Things won't always live up to our expectations, and life will throw challenges at us all when we least expect them. For all of that, though, life really does go on. As bruised and broken as we might emerge, hope and love keep us moving forward.

I have laughed, gasped, and shared all manner of emotions with these characters. Thank you to all who have come along and shared the journey.

Tom

May 2022

About the Author

Tom was born in 1987 in Chelmsford, Essex. As a boy, he fell in love with the fantasy worlds of video games, J.R.R Tolkien, and Philip Pullman.

Despite an early passion for storytelling, Tom obtained a BA in Tourism Management before a varied career in the travel industry, bringing to life another of his passions. When he is not working, Tom is an avid fan of his beloved Ipswich Town. He also writes and performs music and enjoys long walks with his wife and dogs.

Tom currently lives near Colchester, Essex, and *Where Heroes Were Born* is the final book in the Pillars of Peace trilogy. The first two, *The Look of a King* and *No Place for Peace,* were both written during the coronavirus pandemic with huge influence and editing support from his wife, Breana.

Contact Tom: tomdumbrell@aol.com
Instagram: @tom_dumbrell
Twitter: @tom_dumbrell

Suggested Reading
Joe Abercrombie – *Shattered Sea* & *First Law* Trilogies
Chris Wooding – *Tales of the Ketty Jay*
Scott Lynch – *The Gentleman Bastard Sequence*
V.E. Schwab – *The Invisible Life of Addie LaRue*

Printed in Great Britain
by Amazon